FIDELITY

THOMAS Perry

FIDELITY

An Otto Penzler Book

Quercus

First published in Great Britain in 2008 by

Quercus
21 Bloomsbury Square
London
WC1A 2NS

A CIP catalogue reference for this book is available
from the British Library

ISBN (HB) 978 1 84724 354 6
ISBN (TPB) 978 1 84724 355 3

This book is a work of fiction. Names, characters,
businesses, organizations, places and events are
either the product of the author's imagination
or are used fictitiously. Any resemblance to
actual persons, living or dead, events or
locales is entirely coincidental.

To Jo, Alix, and Isabel,
women who make me proud

Fidelity

1

Phil Kramer walked down the sidewalk under the big trees toward his car. It was quiet on this street, and the lights in the houses were almost all off. There was a strong, sweet scent of flowering vines that opened their blooms late on hot summer nights like this one—wisteria, he supposed, or some kind of jasmine. There was no way to limit it because there wasn't anything that wouldn't grow in Southern California. He supposed his senses were attuned to everything tonight. He had trained himself over the past twenty-five years to be intensely aware of his surroundings, particularly when he was alone at night. He knew there was a cat watching him from the safety of the porch railing to his right, and he knew there was a man walking along the sidewalk a half block behind him. He had seen him as he had turned the corner—not quite as tall as he was, but well built, and wearing a jacket on a night that was too warm for one. He could hear the footsteps just above the level of the cars swishing past on the boulevard.

He supposed the man could be the final attempt to make him feel uncomfortable—not a foolish attempt to scare him, but a way to remind him that he could be watched and followed and studied as easily as anyone else could. He could be fully known, and therefore vulnerable. The man might also be out walking for some reason that was completely unrelated to Phil Kramer's business.

Phil approached the spot where his car was parked—too near now to be stopped—and the man no longer mattered. He pressed the button on his key chain to unlock the locks, and the dome light came on. He swung the door open and sat in the driver's seat, then reached for the door to close it.

In the calm, warm night air he caught a sliding sound, with a faint squeak, and turned his head to find it. In one glance, he knew his mistake in all of its intricacies: He took in the van parked across the street from his car, the half-open window with the gun resting on it, and the bright muzzle-flash.

The bullet pounded into his skull, and the impact lit a thousand thoughts in an instant, burning and exploding them into nonbeing as synapses rapid-fired and went out. There was his brother Dan; a random instant in a baseball game, seeing the ground ball bounce up at his feet, feeling the sting in his palm as it smacked into his glove, even a flash of the white flannel of his uniform with tan dust; the pride and fear when he first saw his son; a composite, unbearably pleasant sensation of the women he had touched, amounting to a distilled impression of femaleness. Profound regret. Emily.

EMILY KRAMER AWOKE at five thirty, as she had for twenty-two years of mornings. The sun barely tinted the room a feeble blue, but Emily's chest already held a sense of alarm, and she couldn't expand her lungs in a full breath. She rolled to her left side to see, aware before she did it that the space was empty. It was a space that belonged to something, the big body of her husband, Phil. He was supposed to be there.

Fidelity

She sat up quickly, threw back the covers and swung her legs off the bed. She looked around the room noting other absences: his wallet and keys, his shoes, and the pants he always draped across the chair in the corner when he came to bed. He had not come to bed. That was why she had slept so soundly. She always woke up when he came in, but she had slept through the night.

Emily had the sense that she was already behind, already late. Something had happened, and in each second, events were galloping on ahead of her, maybe moving out of reach. She hurried out of the bedroom along the hall to the top of the stairs and listened. There was no human sound, no noise to reassure her.

Emily knew her house so well that she could hear its emptiness. Phil's presence would have brought sound, would have changed the volume of the space and dampened the bright, sharp echoes. She went down the stairs as quickly as she could, trusting her bare feet to grip the steps. She ran through the living room to the dining room to the kitchen, looking for a sign.

She pulled open the back door, stepped to the garage, and peered in the window. Her white Volvo station wagon was gleaming in the dim light, but Phil's car was gone. No, it wasn't gone. It had never come back at all.

Emily turned, went back into the kitchen, and picked up the telephone. She dialed Phil's cell phone. A cool, distant voice said, "The customer you have called is not in the service area at this time." That usually meant Phil had turned the phone off. She looked at the clock on the wall above the table.

It was too early to call anyone. Even as she was thinking that, she punched in the one number she knew by heart. It rang once, twice, three times, four times. His voice came on: "This is Ray Hall. Leave a message if you want." He must be sleeping, she thought. Of course he was sleeping. Every sane person on the planet was sleeping. She

3

hoped she hadn't awakened him. She stood with the phone in her hand, feeling relieved that he didn't know who had been stupid enough to call at five thirty in the morning.

But that feeling reversed itself instantly. She wasn't glad she hadn't awakened him. She wasn't in the mood to think about why she cared what Ray Hall thought. She knew only that she shouldn't care, so she punched his phone number again. She waited through his message, then said, "Ray, this is Emily Kramer. Phil didn't come home last night. It's five thirty. If you could give me a call, I'd appreciate it." She hesitated, waiting for him to pick up the telephone, then realized she had nothing else to say. "Thanks." She hung up.

While she had been speaking, several new thoughts had occurred to her. She set the phone down on the counter and walked through the house again. She had no reason to think Phil would kill himself, but no reason to imagine he was immune to depression and disappointment, either. And bad things happened to people without their talking about it—especially people like Phil.

Emily walked cautiously through the living room again. She looked at the polished cherry table near the front door under the mirror, where they sometimes left notes for each other. She forced herself to walk into the downstairs guest bathroom and look in the tub. There was no body. She reminded herself she shouldn't be looking for his body. A man who carried a gun would shoot himself, and she had heard nothing. If he *did* kill himself, she was sure he would have left a note. She kept moving, into the small office where Phil paid bills and Emily made lists or used the computer, into the den, where they sat and watched television.

There was no note. She knew she had not missed it because she knew what the note would look like. It would be propped up vertically with a book or something, with EM printed in big letters. For formal occasions like birthdays or anniversaries, he always used an envelope. Suicide would be one of the times for an envelope.

She walked back to the telephone and called the office. Phil's office line was an afterthought, but she knew she should have tried earlier. The telephone rang four times, and then clicked into voice mail. She recognized the soft, velvety voice of April Dougherty. It was an artificial phone voice, and Emily didn't like it. "You have reached the headquarters of Kramer Investigations. I'm sorry that there is no one able to take your call at the moment. For personal service, please call between the hours of nine A.M. and six P.M. weekdays. You may leave a message after the tone."

Emily had written that little speech and recorded it twenty-two years ago, and the moment came back to her sharply. She remembered thinking of calling the crummy walk-up on Reseda Boulevard the World Headquarters. Phil had hugged her and laughed aloud, and said even the word *headquarters* was stretching the truth enough.

Emily took the phone from her ear, punched in the voice-mail number and then the code to play back the messages. "We're sorry, but your code is invalid. Please try again." Emily stared at the phone and repeated the code. "We're sorry, but—" Emily disconnected. She considered calling back to leave a message telling Phil to call her, but she knew that idea was ridiculous. He could hardly *not* know that she was waiting to hear from him. She made a decision not to waste time thinking about the fact that Phil had changed the message-retrieval code. Maybe he hadn't even been the one to change the code. Maybe little April had put in a new code when she had recorded the new message. It would be just like Phil to not know that a new code would be something Emily would want to have, or that not telling her would hurt her feelings.

How could Ray Hall sleep through eight rings? Maybe he was with Phil. That was the first positive thought she'd had. Then she reminded herself that the ring sound was actually a signal, not a real sound. If Ray had turned off the ring, the phone company would still send that signal to Emily's phone.

She thought of Bill Przwalski. He was only about twenty-two years old—born about the time when she and Phil had gotten married and started the agency. He was trying to put in his two thousand hours a year for three years to get his private-investigator's license. Could he be out somewhere working with Phil? He got all the dull night-surveillance jobs and the assignments to follow somebody around town. She looked at the list in the drawer near the phone and tried his number, but got a message that sounded like a school kid reading aloud in class. "I am unable to come to the phone right now, but I will get back to you as soon as I can. Please wait for the beep, then leave me a message." She said, "Billy, this is Emily Kramer, Phil's wife. I'd like you to call us at home as soon as possible. Thank you." *Us?* She had said it without deciding to, getting caught by the reflex to protect herself from being so alone.

The next call was harder because she didn't know him as well as Ray, and he wasn't a trainee like Billy, but calling the others first had helped her to get past her shyness and reticence. She had already called Ray and Billy, so she had to call Dewey Burns. If she didn't call him, Dewey might feel strange, wondering if she had left him out just because he was black. She made the call, and there was only one ring.

"Yeah?"

"Dewey?"

"Yes."

"This is Emily Kramer. I'm sorry to call so early."

"It's all right. I'm up. What's happening?"

"I just woke up, and Phil isn't here. He never came home last night." She waited, but Dewey was waiting, too. Why didn't he say something? She prompted him: "I just started calling you guys to see if anybody knows where he is, and you're the first one who answered."

"I'm sorry, but I don't know where Phil is. He's had me working on a case by myself for a while, and he hasn't told me what he's doing. Have you called Ray yet?"

"Yes, and the office, and Billy. Nobody's up yet."

"It's early. But let me make a couple of calls and go to the office and look around. I'll call you from there."

"Thanks, Dewey."

"Talk to you in a little while." He hung up.

Emily stood holding the dead phone. His voice had sounded brusque, as though he were in a hurry to get rid of her. But maybe that terse manner had just been his time in the marines coming back to him—talk quickly and get going. He had been out for a couple of years, but he still stood so straight that he looked like he was guarding something, and still had a military haircut. Phil had told her he still did calisthenics and ran five miles a day, as if he were planning to go into battle. Still, he had sounded as though he wanted to get rid of her. And he had said he was going to make calls. Who was he going to call? Who else was there to call besides the men who worked for Phil?

She reminded herself that this was not the time to be jealous. Dewey might have numbers for Ray Hall and Bill Przwalski that she didn't—parents or girlfriends or someone. But what he had actually said was that he would make a couple of calls. What numbers would he have that he could call when Phil Kramer didn't come home one night? She hoped it meant Dewey had some idea of what was going on in Phil's latest investigation, or at least knew who the client was. But if he did, why had he said he didn't?

There was so much about Dewey that she didn't know, and she'd always had the feeling Phil must know more about him than he had said. Nobody seemed to know how Phil even knew Dewey. One day there was no Dewey Burns, and the next day there was. He and Phil always seemed to speak to each other in shorthand, in low tones, as though they had longer conversations when she wasn't around.

There was one more person to call. She looked at the sheet in the open drawer, dialed the number, and got a busy signal. She looked up at the clock on the wall. It said five forty. Had it stopped? Had all of this taken only ten minutes?

She hung up and redialed the number. This time the phone rang for an instant and was cut off. "What?" April Dougherty's voice was angry.

"April? This is Emily Kramer, Phil's wife. I'm sorry to call at this hour."

The voice turned small and meek. "That's okay."

"I'm calling everyone from the agency." Emily noticed that April didn't ask what was up. How could Emily not notice? She answered the question that April had not asked. "Phil didn't come home last night, and I'm trying to see if anybody knows where he is, or what he was working on, or if he's with someone."

"No," April said.

"No?"

"He didn't mention anything to me. I went home at six, and he was still at the office."

"Do you remember if Ray was there, or Billy?"

"Um, I think both of them were still there when I left. They were, in fact. But they were getting ready to leave, too."

"Do you remember what Phil was doing when you left? Did he have a case file, or was he packing a briefcase with surveillance gear or tape recorders, or anything?"

"I didn't notice. He could have. I mean, it's his office. He could have got anything he wanted after I left. I think he was sitting at his desk. Yes. He was."

"Was his computer turned on?"

"It's *always* on."

Emily was getting frustrated. "Look, April. I know it's early in the morning. I would never do this if I weren't worried sick. In twenty-two years, Phil has always managed to make it home, or at least call me and let me know where he is."

"I don't know why he didn't come home." April's voice was quiet and tense. "I'm sure there's a good reason."

Emily was shocked. She had not said anything critical of Phil, but here was this girl, defending him against her. Emily said, "If you hear from him, tell him to call home right away. I'm about to call the cops. If you know of any reason not to, I'd like to hear it."

"If I hear from him, I'll tell him."

"Thanks."

"'Bye." April hung up.

Emily dialed Phil's cell phone again, and listened to the message. "The customer you have called is not in the service area at this time." She put the phone back in its cradle. The chill on her feet reminded her that she was still barefoot, still wearing her nightgown. She picked up the telephone and hurried to the stairs to get dressed. On the way, she looked at the printed sticker on the phone and dialed the non-emergency number of the police.

2

Emily Kramer hurried from the elevator to the office door, staring at the hallway. She had not been in this space in at least five years, but it had not changed since the days when she and Phil had moved the agency here twenty years ago. There was a scuff mark on the right wall above the baseboard that she was sure she had seen before.

She reached the door with the raised gold letters that said KRAMER INVESTIGATIONS, tried to fit her key in the lock, and failed. Phil had not told her anything about changing locks. It was a simple, common sort of difficulty, but it had stopped her progress, and for the moment she couldn't think of a way to move forward. People like building managers tended to show up at ten or eleven, and it was barely six thirty. She felt dazed.

The door swung open, and Dewey Burns faced her. "Emily. What are you doing?"

"Same as you." She charged past him, as though he might shut the door on her. She took a few steps and stopped. Ray Hall and Bill Przwalski were standing together, leaning on one of the desks in the outer office.

"Ray? Billy?" she said. "I tried to call you."

Ray Hall returned her gaze. "Dewey got through to us." He was about forty years old, with gray, squinting eyes that seemed much older, as though he had been disappointed so many times that he was incapable of surprise. This morning he was wearing a black sport coat, a pale blue oxford shirt, and a pair of jeans.

"Phil didn't come home last night," she said.

"We heard," Hall said. "I'm sorry, Emily. But I think he'll turn up okay."

"But you've worked for him for at least ten years. You know he's never done this before. He would never just not show up."

Ray Hall sighed and looked at the floor for a second, then raised his eyes to her. "I think he's okay."

"What does that mean?"

"There are two ways people disappear—involuntarily, and voluntarily. When you have a healthy man who is six feet four, has been in a few fights, and carries a gun, it's hard to take him anyplace he doesn't want to go."

"You think he just took off, without saying anything to anybody?"

"That's one possibility, but I don't know yet."

"And what if you're wrong?"

"I can't be wrong, I haven't guessed yet," he said. "We've got to stay calm and find out what we can before we draw any conclusions."

Emily sat down at the receptionist's desk, because she felt her knees beginning to tremble. After a second, she realized the desk and chair were the same ones she'd used twenty years ago. She gained some strength from the familiarity. She tried to ignore the dwarf plants in cup-sized pots that April Dougherty had on the desk, and the little plush monkey with magnets on its hands that clung to the desk lamp. There was white blotter paper with doodle drawings of spindly-legged girls with long hair swept across big eyes, and the name April with a heart dotting the i. Emily noticed that Bill Przwalski was watching her and looking nervous, as though he were afraid she was about to search the desk.

She wanted to. Her hands itched to pull out the drawers and look, but she resisted. She said to Ray Hall, "I called the police."

"So did I," Dewey Burns said.

"You did?"

He frowned. "I told you I was going to."

"Not exactly. You said you were going to make some calls. What did they say?"

"They haven't arrested him or taken him to a hospital. They're checking now to see if they had any contact with him since yesterday afternoon—a traffic stop or something."

"That's what they told me, too." Emily glanced at Ray Hall, but he avoided her eyes.

She stood and walked to the door of Phil's glassed-in corner office. When she pushed open the door, she saw that the deadbolt was still extended and the woodwork was splintered. She spun around in alarm.

Ray Hall said, "That was me. He's the only one who has a key."

She nodded and went inside. Everything in Phil's office looked the same as it always had. She realized that she had been expecting something different. There should have been something that stood out, something that might not be instantly visible to other people, but that Emily Kramer would see. And that would tell her what was wrong. The desk was polished and smelling of lemons, with only a set of in and out boxes that held a phone directory and a hole punch. Phil was not really a neat person. His orderliness came from the military, where they had trained him to straighten and polish the surfaces that showed.

She opened the drawers and filing cabinets, looking for something that was not routine and ordinary. She found time cards and payroll documents that had been annotated in his handwriting as recently as yesterday. She found a copy of a letter he had signed requesting payment of a final bill for what looked like a divorce case. She took it out to Ray Hall. "See this letter? As of yesterday, he was still interested in having this woman pay him. If she gets the letter tomorrow and puts the check in the mail right away, he still wouldn't get it until two days later. He was expecting to be back."

"Marilyn Tynan," said Hall. The three men looked at each other and said nothing. Bill Przwalski began to empty the wastebaskets into a cardboard box.

"What?" she asked.

"That's not a new one. It's a divorce case we did three years ago. Phil just has April send a bill to her and a few others every month with all the current ones. She'll never pay. Did he even sign that?"

She turned it around and held it so Ray Hall could see it. "Yes."

Hall shrugged. "Sometimes he doesn't bother."

Bill Przwalski's cardboard box was full of trash. He lifted it.

"Put that down, Billy," she said. He lowered it to his desk. "Now, one of you tell me what you think is going on."

The others looked at Ray Hall. He took a breath, then let it out. "I don't feel happy about telling you this, Emily. On a hunch, when I went into Phil's office, I got the company bank-account numbers, and called them. The bank's computer says Kramer Investigations has a hundred and fifty in one account, and two hundred in the other."

"Dollars?" said Emily. "You're talking about a hundred and fifty *dollars?*"

"Yes."

Her eyes moved across the faces of the three men, who now

stared back at her openly. She reached into her purse, took out her checkbook, stepped to the front of April's desk, picked up the telephone, and dialed the number on her checks. The cheerful machine voice told her to give the account number and then the last four digits of her Social Security number. When she had punched in the numbers, the machine began to recite a list of choices. She pressed four for a balance. "Your account balance is . . . seventy-three dollars and . . . seventeen cents. To return to the main menu, press eight. To speak with a representative, press zero."

Emily muttered, "Oh, my God," then pressed the zero and waited. The voice said, "Please hold. All our representatives are busy right now, but your call is important to us."

She kept the telephone to her ear. "The money's gone from our account, too." The men didn't look surprised.

She heard the elevator doors open and close. She held the telephone and watched the office door with the others. When it swung open, she noticed that their eyes had all been focused at the level of Phil Kramer's face, but he was not the one who stepped in. Their eyes dropped about a foot to the face of April Dougherty. As she stepped inside, Emily and the three men stood still, watching her, but nobody greeted her. She glanced at the men without surprise, then faced Emily. "Good morning."

"Hi, April." Emily kept the phone to her ear.

"I'll just be a minute," April said. "I want to collect a few personal belongings, and then I'll be out of your way. Have the police been here yet?"

"Not yet."

April moved to her desk, and began opening the drawers and setting things on the white blotter. They were spare and pitiful: a coffee cup with a flower on it, a little male bee hovering over it and a little female bee hiding behind the stem. Beside it were a plastic dispenser for no-calorie chemical sweeteners, a little box with an emery board and six bottles of nail polish, and a couple of hairbrushes. The final item was a cheap makeup case.

"The cops aren't going to impound your hairbrush," Ray said. "If it embarrasses you to leave tampons lying around, then take them. But you don't want your desk so empty that the cops think you're hiding something."

"I'm not!" she snapped.

"Then act like it. Put your stuff back in your desk, sit in your chair, and see what you can bring yourself to do to help us find Phil."

April gaped at him, then sat down and pulled a file out of the deep lower right-hand drawer of her desk. "This is the log sheet. It's what everyone has been doing this week."

Emily's eyes widened. She spun it around on the desk to read it. "Christ, you didn't include him."

"Of course not. He's the boss," April said.

Emily knew that a part of her was grateful to April for not referring to Phil in the past tense. "Have you kept logs of incoming phone calls and appointments?"

"Sure." April showed Emily a notebook full of lined paper with two columns of names and numbers. Then she produced a bound calendar with a page for each day.

Emily could see that there were lots of calls, lots of people coming into the office. There were also whole days when Phil had been out of the office, and April had put a diagonal line through his square and written *No Appointments* on it in her neat, unhurried handwriting. Emily pointed to the most recent one. "What's this? Did he say in advance that he didn't want you to make any appointments, or just call from somewhere and say 'I'm not coming in today'?"

"Both," April said. "A lot of the time somebody will be here and then leave, so I have to cancel whatever else is up. Sometimes one of the men calls to say he's in Pomona or Irvine or someplace, and can't get back."

Emily held the three men in the corner of her eye while April spoke. She noted that none of them showed surprise at anything April said. Emily said, "You all know what I'm looking for. We need to know what Phil's working on, and where. He could be stuck somewhere and in trouble."

The recorded voice on the telephone said again, "Please hold. All our representatives are busy now, but your call is important to us." Emily hung up, then reached into her purse, found the slip of paper where she had written the number the police officer had given her when she had called before, and dialed it again.

She heard a voice say, "Officer Morris."

"Officer Morris, this is Emily Kramer. I spoke with you a little while ago about my husband. Well, now I've just learned that money has disappeared from his business accounts and our personal bank accounts. I'm afraid someone may have his identification or be holding him or—"

"Mrs. Kramer, wait. I've been trying to reach you. I just called your house, and I was about to try the office. I'm afraid we've found Mr. Kramer. I'm very sorry to say he's dead."

Emily felt thankful that he had not prolonged the revelation and made her listen for a long time, praying that he wasn't going to say what she had known he would say. "Thank you," she said.

Then she began to cry.

3

Jerry Hobart and Tim Whitley were stuck on the road to Las Vegas. Interstate 15 was always just the first part of the pleasure, the incredibly clear sky and the bright yellow morning sun striking the pavement ahead of the car and making the tiny diamond particles pressed into the asphalt glitter. It didn't matter that the diamonds were really bits of broken glass pressed into the hot asphalt by the weight of the cars passing at eighty or ninety. They were like the sequins on the little outfits of the waitresses and the girls in the shows. They weren't diamonds either, and the glitter in their makeup wasn't gold dust, and Tim Whitley didn't care. All that would have done was add to the price. The thought of the women made him eager to get there.

When they had started this morning, the cars on the road to Las Vegas had seemed to skim the pavement, barely touching it. The air was hot and dry and clean. Whitley had sat in the passenger seat and stared out at the high desert, looking at the rocky hills sprouting yuccas and small, paddle-shaped prickly pears, and the vast flatlands with

Joshua trees spread out like straggling migrations of men, the speed of the car making them appear to move.

But now it was after four o'clock, and they had been inching along at a walk, then stopping dead for a few minutes, then creeping forward a few feet for nearly seven hours. "Jesus," he said. "This is the worst."

Jerry Hobart's head turned slowly toward him like a tank turret. His eyes were slits. "The day isn't over yet."

"If it would just either speed up, or stop," Whitley complained. "Hell, if it would just stop. Then we could turn off the engine and save the gas for later, and take a decent piss by the side of the road."

Hobart said nothing. The jaw muscles on the side of his face kept tightening and going slack.

"We've been climbing for the past hour or two. Maybe I can find a station with news on it now." Whitley leaned close to the dashboard in spite of the fact that the speakers were in the door panels, and used a delicate touch to move the vertical line in minute increments from one band to the next. Once he managed to find the faint singing of Spanish voices that reminded him of a party inside a house far away. Once there was *banda* music, and he heard an announcer say something about *narcotraficantes*. "The whole fucking world is turning into Mexico."

Hobart said nothing, and the silence bothered Tim. Hobart was older and more experienced, and he was one of those men who had a solitary self-sufficiency, a strength that Tim knew he lacked. Each time Tim talked, he regretted it afterward. He knew that it was unseemly to complain, and there was no use whining to the man who had been at least moving the car forward when the cars ahead of it moved.

But Tim was frustrated. Four days ago they had rented a suite in the Venetian, and then yesterday they had driven to Los Angeles to do some work. They had done their job last night, collected their pay, packed up, and headed back toward Las Vegas in the morning. Hobart's establishment of an alibi was thoughtful: Check into a good hotel on the Las Vegas Strip, go out every day and every night, and then one night simply go out and drive to Los Angeles for the killing and drive back. Their suite was officially occupied while they were gone, and nobody was keeping track of anything else. Hobart had called the hotel a couple of times. Once he had complained that the water pressure in the shower wasn't strong enough and asked them to fix it while he was out gambling. Hobart had left their cell phones in the room and made calls to them so there would be a record that they had received calls from a signal repeater that was in Las Vegas within a few minutes of the killing.

But Tim Whitley was feeling increasingly agitated now. They had expected to be back in the hotel by ten or eleven. Now it was after four, and they had not gone a mile in the past hour. Who expected a traffic jam in the middle of the desert? It was the worst jam Whitley had ever seen, and they weren't even in a city. They were fifty miles from a real town, practically on the edge of Death Valley. The gas gauge looked from here as though the tank was barely above empty. He hoped it was just the angle making the gauge look that way. He wasn't facing it head-on like Hobart was in the driver's seat.

Of course, somebody would come along and help if they ran out of gas—there wasn't much solitude on Route 15 today—but that would make their beautiful alibi problematical: There would be somebody who had seen the two of them stalled on the road from Los Angeles to Las Vegas at the wrong time. If they stopped, they were vulnerable. And there was two hundred thousand dollars in cash in the trunk. It wasn't that people didn't drive into Las Vegas with two hundred thousand in cash every day, it was that a pair of shitheels in a six-year-old Hyundai didn't. If anything happened to separate them from the endless, anonymous current of traffic—if they had to get out to push the car to the shoulder and sit there with it while everybody stared at them in pity—then they would probably find themselves talking to a tow-truck driver or a cop. It wasn't fair. This should have been simple.

At first everything had been quick and easy. He and Hobart had been working together for about a year, and they were sure of each other. There was no indecision when they saw Philip Kramer come out of the house after the meeting. Hobart said, "We'll take him in his car so we don't have a body lying on the ground that we have to drag out of sight. Go find a place with a clear shot at the left side of his car."

That was not as easy as it sounded. A parked car has to be stopped with its right side to the curb and its left to the street. That didn't suggest a lot of hiding places. But Tim knew that Hobart never spoke idly, and not doing what he said was the same to Hobart as refusing to do it.

Tim Whitley ran down the street toward the place where Phil Kramer had left his Toyota sedan, and searched. The only hiding place he could find to the left of Kramer's car was inside the van parked across the street. Tim was a car thief, and he had his slim-jim with him. By the time Kramer came up the dark street, Tim Whitley was crouched down in the back of the van right behind the driver's seat. When Kramer's door opened, Tim heard it. He went to the window of the van and fired.

Tim felt good about it. It wasn't Hobart this time, with Tim only there to steal a car to use in the job and drive away afterward. This time Tim was the shooter. Hobart's only part in the job had been to walk up the street behind Kramer to keep him preoccupied and under the impression that he knew what to be afraid of.

Fidelity

Tim Whitley sensed a change in Hobart, who was shifting in his seat, trying to see around the car ahead. "What do you see?"

"Cars are getting off up there."

"That's probably good, isn't it?" Whitley said. "We've finally come to what's holding up the traffic. It's got to be an accident. Once we get past that, we'll be home-free." He kept watching Hobart for a reaction.

"I don't see an accident. They're just getting off. Like a detour."

Tim could see it now, too. There was an exit ramp far ahead, and cars were moving to the right to take it—not a huge stream of cars, but maybe one in ten. They climbed to a narrow road above, turned left to cross an overpass, and drove off somewhere to the left and away into the rocky hills.

He knew that Hobart was going to take that road, just from looking at his face. Nine out of ten drivers were staying on the interstate, but the one-tenth that were willing to veer off onto a road that was only two lanes at its widest would surely include Hobart. He had the peculiar, rare quality of absolute confidence in himself and depthless contempt for everybody else.

Hobart took the exit ramp and accelerated up the incline to the other road. He stopped only for an instant, not because he had to look to the right—nobody was coming from that direction, nor had there been since Whitley had first seen the exit—but just to look at the desert from up here.

"Jerry?"

"What?"

"Do you happen to know where this goes?"

"No. But you can get anywhere from anywhere else, if you're moving. Those people back there aren't."

Tim knew it wasn't a good idea to ask anything else for the moment. He knew that it wasn't manly to keep expressing uncertainty,

21

to keep demanding information that he had not earned by waiting and seeing. He did not want to squander the precious respect he had gained by taking Phil Kramer with one shot from the van. Doing that had shown he was calm and unafraid.

Still, Tim wanted to voice the concern he had that this might be a road that didn't go where Hobart imagined. He recalled hearing there was one road off Interstate 15 that people took to drive up and around to come out on the north side of the Grand Canyon, the side where there were practically no people. And he knew there was another exit that took you north into Death Valley.

Tim went back to fiddling idly with the radio tuner. It was a fake activity now, and he was just doing it to change the number on the digital indicator, to keep Hobart thinking he was doing a job, like the sonar man in a submarine movie where everybody stood around sweating while he listened for enemy ships. The radio should be picking up something intelligible, but it wasn't working right.

Hobart kept driving up the road between the dry, rocky hills. As the minutes passed and personalities reasserted themselves, the distances between the cars that had left the traffic jam lengthened. There were some drivers who just stomped on the gas pedal and tore through the desert as though the jam were chasing them. Others seemed to wonder if they had made the wrong decision to leave the only major highway in the desert and drive off hoping that the new road would magically take them to Vegas, where they wanted to be. They went slowly, looking back at the interstate as long as they could, hoping to see some improvement so they could go back.

Hobart flashed past a dozen of these cars and kept going for a half hour before Tim Whitley began to feel that he was going to have to speak. He considered various things he could say, but rejected each of them. Any reference to the time that had passed, the distance, or the traffic might sound like whining, and Hobart didn't respect whining. He had already foreclosed any talk about their destination. Hobart had said he didn't know where the road led, but seemed to think he could take it to Las Vegas even if it didn't go there.

Whitley let the miles slip past. As he looked out at the rock shapes and colors and the brightness, he conceded that the desert was beautiful. But it was beautiful in the same way the ocean was, in a hostile, treacherous way. If the boat were to spring a leak or the car to break down, the scenery would not be just a sight anymore, but a vast harshness. One was deadly cold and the other was deadly hot, and they were both too enormous for a person to slight in this thoughtless way. It was almost bad luck not to give the desert the fear it deserved.

He felt the car's engine stop racing. In the new silence, Hobart whispered, "Shit." Whitley could see his arm muscles straining as the car coasted. The power steering had cut off, and each adjustment Hobart made to the front wheels meant fighting the dead mechanism. He aimed the car at the shoulder of the road, brought it onto the gravel, and stopped. A second later, the cloud of dust they had kicked up drifted over the car and away.

Tim knew they were out of gas, but he had to say it anyway. "Out of gas?"

"Uh-huh." Hobart turned to look into Whitley's eyes.

"What are we going to do?"

"Walk to get some gas."

Tim Whitley turned and looked back at the long, empty road behind them, a thinning black surface that dissolved into shining pools of mirage water in the relentless sunshine. He tried to calculate. They had been driving for about a half hour. No, more. It was at least forty-five minutes. He didn't know how fast Hobart had been driving, but it had to be at least sixty miles an hour. That was a mile a minute. "We can't walk back that far. It's more than forty miles."

Hobart said, "No, we can't. We go in the other direction. There's a town up ahead."

"How do you know?"

"I happened to see it on a map. I think it was on the place mat in that diner in Baker. I know the road goes north this far. To the left is Death Valley, and the road swings off to the right to where the town is. We'll buy a three-gallon can of gas and pay somebody to drive us back here with it."

"Do you happen to know how far it is?"

"Well, if you walk on the road, it could be ten miles, but the road hooks to the right, so we can take a shortcut across country and meet it. I'd guess it would be four miles that way, maybe even two."

"Jesus, Jerry," said Tim. "Walk across the open desert like that?" The car's air conditioning had cut off with the engine, so the windows were heating the enclosed space like a greenhouse. "It must be over a hundred out there."

"Sure it's over a hundred. It's the fucking desert!" Hobart set the hand brake, wiggled the gearshift to be sure it had clicked into Park, and wrenched the steering wheel to lock it. He took the keys, got out and slammed the door.

The idea of waiting here alone in the car tried to form in Tim's mind, but he couldn't grasp and hold it. Being here was unthinkable. It wasn't that something terrible would happen if he were alone, being alone was terrible. He opened the door and got out. The air was so hot it hit the nerves of his skin like something sharp. He stood looking down at the black pavement with swirls of sand on it.

The road was only a layer of asphalt that some crew had dumped from a truck and rolled flat one day. It wasn't safety. It was only a sign that some men had been here once a few years ago.

Tim began to walk away from the pavement toward Hobart. After a few steps into the dirt, his tie to the road wasn't as strong, and he began to trot. When he caught up with Hobart, he was already sweating. They kept walking to the northeast between hills that were just piles of rocks. Tim knew that he needed to be smart and use the few advantages he had. There was the sun, and it was getting lower, so he could identify the west with his eyes closed. He knew that time was important.

He concentrated on keeping up with Hobart. It shouldn't have been difficult because he had longer legs and he was younger. But Hobart sometimes seemed to be something that wasn't quite human anymore. It wasn't that he hadn't started as human, but that he just wasn't as weak as a man anymore. He had burned the softness out of himself a while ago. Hobart kept going straight as though he were walking a surveyor's line. Tim supposed that was a kind of good news. If they went straighter, they'd go farther and meet the curve of the road sooner.

After walking until his shoes had gotten full of sand, Tim noticed that his face was dry. The air was so hot and parched that his sweat dried before it could form drops. He looked at his watch. "We've been walking for forty-five minutes. At this pace I make that three miles, give or take."

"That ought to be far enough," said Hobart. He took a gun out of his shirt and shot Tim through the chest, and then stood over him and shot him through the forehead.

He put the gun back into his belt under his shirt, grasped Tim's ankles, and dragged his body to the side of one of the innumerable piles of rocks. He dug down a few inches with his hands to make a depression, and rolled Tim into it. He covered the body with rocks and then walked the three miles back to the road.

When Hobart reached the car, he opened the trunk, took out the

4

Emily spent three hours with Detective Gruenthal, the police officer who was placed in charge of Phil's murder. He was a big man with a red face and thinning filaments of hair that were in the process of changing from blond to white. She told him about Phil's habits, and about the sudden departures: the missing money, not telling her where he was late at night. Gruenthal dutifully took notes, a constant illegible scribbling into a notebook that seemed smaller than his thick hand, then told her that the first avenue to pursue was the money.

Because one signatory was dead, Emily was not permitted to open the safe-deposit box that she and Phil rented. She had to meet Detective Gruenthal and a woman named Zia Mondani who represented the state of California at the bank, where the manager was waiting. Emily and the bank manager entered the vault to retrieve the box. Emily carried the box, and they went into a little room instead of the cubicle that Emily and Phil had always used before.

They all sat down at an empty table and she opened the long, narrow gray metal box. As she took things out she set them on the table in front of Detective Gruenthal. There was the deed to the house. There were Phil's, Emily's, and Pete's birth certificates and Social Security cards.

Gruenthal immediately picked up Pete's papers. "What's this?"

"They're our son Pete's. He died five years ago in a car crash. Neither of us ever thought to take them out, I guess." She noticed a copy of Pete's death certificate and set that in front of Gruenthal, too.

There was their marriage license, and she had to fight to keep from crying in front of these strangers at the sight of it. To distract herself, she quickly picked out the insurance policy for the house and the policy for the two cars, then the pink slips for the cars. There was Phil's Honorable Discharge from the Marine Corps, a few photographs of the house for insurance purposes, a copy of Phil's private-investigator's license in case something happened to the original that hung in the office. She came to the end.

Gruenthal said, "Is that it?"

"Yes," she said.

"Anything missing?"

"I don't think so. No."

Ms. Mondani, the woman from the state, stood up, said, "Thank you, Mrs. Kramer," and left the room.

Emily began to put the papers back in the box. She tried to remember the things that should have been here, but weren't. Phil had taken his mother's diamond pin, the necklace of real pearls that Emily's grandmother had given her, and the savings bonds. She wasn't even certain how much any of the items had been worth. The jewelry had never been appraised because Phil had said there was no point in insuring anything that was sitting in a bank. The bonds had been a gift from Phil's parents when Pete was born, the beginning of a fund for Pete's college tuition.

As she and the manager returned the box to its slot in the vault, she berated herself. She should have told Detective Gruenthal that things were missing, but she couldn't bring herself to do it. She had no idea why Phil had taken them. Was there some need that he had been hiding from her? He always hated to worry her. Maybe he had made some investment that she would have considered risky. She couldn't tell Detective Gruenthal something so private before she even knew the explanation. How could this stranger understand what she was telling him when she didn't yet understand it herself?

When the box had been locked away, she could see Gruenthal was feeling impatient. His time had been wasted. "Mrs. Kramer, I'd better be getting back to the station. If there's anything you remember later, or anything I can do, please call."

"Thank you," she said and watched him leave.

The bank manager saw his chance, too. "Anything else I can do?"

When she said, "Yes," he looked mildly surprised. "I'd like a printout of all the checks that were written against our account in the past year."

"Certainly. Why don't you come to my office where you can be comfortable while I get that information for you?"

When she had the copies in a neat file inside a big envelope, she took them home to study. The checking account was linked to the savings account, and both accounts had been gutted in a quiet, orderly way. Money had been deposited in the checking account from time to time, but the withdrawals were all bigger than the deposits, and the excess came out of the savings account. Phil had written one or two big checks a month for the whole year. All of them were made out to "Cash." As she looked at them, tears of frustration welled in her eyes so she had to keep wiping them away to see. She whispered over and over, "Jesus, Phil. What were you doing? What the hell were you *thinking*?"

She went to the computer and ordered credit checks from the three credit bureaus. What she was really trying to do was establish the extent of the financial disaster. Were there credit cards she had not seen, or had Phil borrowed money she didn't know about? The credit reports were transmitted, and she read them with a chill in her spine, but there seemed to be nothing in them that she had not already discovered. Nothing told her anything about Phil's state of mind, or what he had been doing the night he was killed.

Emily became more frantic. She began to search the house. She hunted through the office for credit-card slips or receipts, then through stacks of bills that had been paid and filed. She read the last two tax returns, which she had signed when Phil had asked her to, but never bothered to examine. The figures looked normal, but there was no way for her to tell whether they were accurate. At three A.M. she fell asleep on the couch in the den.

The garbage trucks grumbling up the street and lifting cans with their hydraulic claws woke her at six thirty. She put the papers away and assessed the damage. Phil had taken all of their money and either spent it or put it somewhere out of her reach. He didn't seem to have pushed them farther into debt than they already had been with the mortgage on the house and the payments on Phil's car. But why would he deplete their savings? Phil had never been a gambler.

It occurred to her that he might have been sick and not told her. That might explain his mysterious absences from work. He could have been seeing doctors. She called Dr. Kalamian, the family internist, told him what had happened, and asked if Phil had been sick.

Dr. Kalamian said, "I don't think so," then got his records. "I saw him April 27 for his physical. He was fine. His numbers were all normal, actually quite good for a man his age. There's very little chance anything was wrong, or it would have shown up in his tests. And if he'd had anything serious, he would have asked me to refer him to a specialist, and he didn't. Look, Emily, this is probably the most stressful time of your life. Would you like me to prescribe something to help you sleep? Maybe an antidepressant?"

"No, thanks."

"Don't convince yourself you're above it," Dr. Kalamian said. "Just keep in mind that I might be able to make some of this more bearable. When I'm not in, one of my group is always on call."

"I'm fine."

She wasn't fine. She wasn't able to sleep more than three hours at a time, and she was depressed and anxious. But the anxiety kept her moving, thinking, alert.

On the third day, Detective Gruenthal called her and said, "The autopsy is complete and the coroner has signed off. We're releasing Mr. Kramer's body."

Emily went to work on the funeral. She began by driving to Greenleaf Mortuary to make the arrangements. Phil had done a job for the owner once. There was a suspicion that one of the funeral directors or morticians was removing rings and bracelets from people just before their burials. Phil had found that they were all honest, a conclusion that he seldom reached in employee investigations. He had looked into every unappetizing aspect of their business, and said, "If I were dead, that's where I'd go." The owner recognized Phil's name and gave her a break on the price of the casket.

Emily felt a bit flustered by the thrown-together quality of Phil's funeral. She remembered having the same feeling of inadequacy when Pete had died. His funeral should have been huge and beautiful and solemn, but it had only been sad and lonely and heartbreaking. There had been plenty of people, and they had all fulfilled their roles, but she had found that they didn't matter. What had mattered was that a seventeen-year-old boy was put in the ground. Now it was Phil, and she was alone.

She needed to make arrangements for a plot near Pete's at Forest Lawn. She needed to call around to find a Presbyterian minister. It took her half a day to find the Reverend Dr. Massey of the Seventh Presbyterian Church in San Fernando. She spent the afternoon with him selecting scripture readings from a list she barely recognized from her childhood, and giving him a capsule account of who Phil had been. Many of the important things about Phil weren't things that could be said.

Phil Kramer was an ex-marine. He was six four and, in middle age, a bit scary-looking to strangers, a fact he often used to his advantage in his work. He was alert, a keen observer of people's quirks and tics that might reveal lies or vulnerabilities. Phil could tell a joke in a way that made Emily laugh. Even if it was one of those stupid adolescent jokes about sex, Phil always found it so funny that she couldn't help laughing, too. She couldn't tell the minister that Phil told dirty jokes, so she just said he had a sense of humor.

She couldn't tell him that Phil had been an acceptable lover, who paid a reasonable amount of attention to her while they worked up to having sex and during it, but fell asleep instantly afterward. She couldn't tell the minister she had come to know that was better for her than a sexual virtuoso would have been, or why she would miss those times with him.

When she had made the arrangements, she made a telephone call to her cousin Darlene, the one who had inherited the role of organizer from her mother, Aunt Rose, and asked her to spread the word to the people on her side of the family, and then asked Phil's sister Nancy to call Phil's relatives.

The funeral was three days later, seven days after Phil's murder. As Emily stood in the hallway of the chapel at Forest Lawn and spoke to the friends and relatives as they arrived, the biggest feeling was how alone she was. It made her remember that when Pete had died, she'd had Phil to stand beside her. Now she had nobody.

When four of Pete's high-school friends came in, she gaped at them because they looked so much older now. Two had wives with them, and showed her photographs of their kids. Seeing them didn't make her miss Pete, because every day of her life for five years had been partially devoted to missing him. It only reminded her that there were new stages of Pete's life that should have started by now, but never would.

Each person who came in would embrace her, a sensation that was mostly unpleasant, dominated by smells of perfume, hair treatment, or dry cleaning, and an awkward and uncertain placement of arms and necks, look at her with pity, and say one or more of the few available phrases of condolence: "I'm so sorry," "Please accept our sympathy," or "I'll miss him." It struck her as strange that after all of the centuries, nobody had invented anything to say that made any difference.

When she saw Sam Bowen walk in the door, she had to fight to keep from crying. Seeing that he had come down from Seattle for the funeral should have made her feel better, but it didn't. Seeing him just reminded her of the night of his retirement party, when she had thought that the next time she saw him it would be at his funeral. It had never occurred to her that she would see him at Phil's funeral only two years later.

In the end, Dr. Massey presided about as well as anyone could have. He gave a brief generic speech about how Phil had been her husband for twenty-two years, had plenty of friends present at the funeral, had been a private detective who had owned an agency. Dr. Massey was not able to resist guessing that Phil must have been a man of strong faith, who had believed deeply in the Lord. The hair on the back of Emily's neck stood up at the unintentional imposture. She hoped people knew that she had not told Massey to say that. She looked surreptitiously at the guests standing along the side and caught Billy Przwalski and one of the guys from Jailbreak Bail Bonds looking at each other skeptically.

Ray Hall and Dewey Burns both sat through the service in stone-faced silence, unmoved and unsurprised, like a pair of poker players. Both of them had brought women with them. Emily was glad that Dewey Burns was not the only dark face in this crowd. His date was somebody Emily had never seen before, but she was very thin and elegant in a black suit, and probably would have been nearly as tall as Dewey if she hadn't been too smart to wear heels to a cemetery. Ray Hall looked as though he were in the middle of some kind of binge. His eyes were bloodshot and his face tired. The woman he had brought was too young for him and not really as attractive as she had looked at first, once a person took the time to study her. She wasn't even slutty. She looked like a college girl who was getting straight A's in a dull subject.

At the graveside, while Dr. Massey droned through a prayer, Emily's eyes moved to April Dougherty and stayed there. April was sitting in the front row on the other side of the aisle between the two sets of folding chairs that the Greenleaf people had set out, and she was holding a handkerchief with a lace border to her face and weeping silently. Emily watched her for a few seconds, dry-eyed. Then she looked past the mourners and stared at each car within her field of vision and tried to detect one that had a person in it. She looked along the ridge at the upper end of the cemetery, and at the two other groups of people at other graves. One of them was another funeral, and the other was a family of four—mother, father, and two kids—putting flowers in the vase next to one of the flat grave markers. Nobody seemed to be carrying any object that had a lens.

Fidelity

It was frustrating because Emily was sure the killer must be watching, but she couldn't see him. If she had been the one who had killed Phil, she would have gone to his funeral and made sure she saw everyone who was there. Men like Phil had relatives and friends who might come after his killer. She hoped the police were up on the hill unseen but watching, and they would see someone she had missed.

The minister finished his remarks and then delivered the final prayer. The man from Greenleaf said solemnly, "This concludes our service. Well-wishers are invited to share a lunch at Mrs. Kramer's home immediately after we leave the graveside."

Emily quietly thanked the minister and the funeral director, and accepted a few hugs and mumbled words of comfort. Before even the first people to leave could make it to their cars, the cemetery's efficient gravediggers had lifted the wreaths of flowers off the casket and begun to lower Phil Kramer into the earth. Emily stopped and stared at the coffin as it sank. "Sorry it had to end like this, baby," she whispered. "The rest of it was okay."

When Emily arrived at her house, her cousins Darlene and Betty had already opened the door and laid out the buffet on the sideboard and the dining-room table. There were three natural divisions of people in the house balancing plates of food on their knees and trying to find socially acceptable places to put their drinks while they ate. There were the Kramers, all of them over six feet tall except Phil's sister Nancy, who was five feet ten inches in flat shoes. There were the McCalls, Emily's family, who were all about a foot shorter than the Kramers and blond or redheaded except Emily and Darlene. And there were the people who had known Phil from the detective agency, who were much more varied, but who all stood, seemed more interested in drinking than eating, and had a way of speaking to each other in very low voices while looking at some point across the room.

It occurred to Emily that this was probably the last time the Kramers and McCalls would be gathered together in one place. Now that Phil was gone, the relationship was going to weaken, then dissolve. The only connection had been the marriage of Phil and Emily, and that was over. People would forget. It made the hugs and the kind, solicitous words of the Kramers more poignant, because she knew that she might never see some of these people again.

Phil's sister Nancy wrapped her arms around Emily in a bear hug that left her breathless, then held her by the shoulders and stared into her eyes in a way that made her uncomfortable. "Who did this?"

"We don't know yet," Emily said. "The police are working on it, but they haven't found any leads yet."

Nancy shook her head, stared at Emily in despair for a few long seconds, and walked away.

Phil's aunt Toni cornered Emily and told her that she must force herself to come to the Kramer family picnic in September, but there was a distant look in her eyes when she said it that confirmed Emily's sense that things had already begun to change. Then Phil's uncle Bill intercepted her and said, "It's terrible. Just terrible. I told the big son of a bitch years ago that making a living snooping in other people's business was dangerous. He wouldn't listen."

"I know," Emily said. "It's the way he was. He loved the business."

"Well, I suppose if you want a lot of money, you've got to take some risks. I guess he left you pretty well off, didn't he?"

"Bill!" Aunt Toni said.

"What? He was practically a son to me."

"He always spoke well of you," Emily said, and moved on.

She tried to make the rounds of the relatives and friends, thanking people for coming and trying to feel grateful that they had. She made an effort to speak to the detectives, the bail-bond people, the lawyers and off-duty police officers. Many of them were people she didn't know, but she found she could cover it by speaking to them in little groups, which was the configuration they seemed to prefer, and then moving on.

At four o'clock, when her cousins Darlene and Betty were beginning to cover casserole dishes and hors d'oeuvres trays and collect cups and glasses from strange, precarious spots around the living room, Emily sensed that she had lost the last of her energy. She sat at the end of the couch under the front window, and then her cousin Dave's wife Sandy sat down beside her. Dave stood over them for a few seconds, then pulled a chair close so his knees almost touched Emily's. Sandy said, "We're all so sorry, Emily. You've really had more than your share of bad luck over the years."

"I don't know," Emily said. "It's hard to say what someone's share is."

"Well, Dave and I just wanted to let you know that we're always here for you. If there's anything we can ever do to help, or to make things easier for you, we really want to do it."

"That's right," Dave said.

"Well, thank you."

"No, we really mean it," Sandy said.

They seemed so sincere, and somehow so sane and strong as a couple, that Emily thought about their offer. It occurred to Emily that Dave was a successful lawyer—Aunt Lily had been bragging for fifteen years about their big house and their vacation home and how powerful Dave's firm was—and Sandy had some kind of important job in advertising. "Well, I don't know what to say. You're very kind."

"Come on." Sandy stroked Emily's back, petting her like a cat.

"Well, if you're really able to do it. With the funeral expenses and so on, I'm feeling a little pressed. I wonder if you could make me a small loan, just until I can straighten things out. I haven't been able to untangle our finances yet. Phil didn't tell me some things I probably should have known, and it's taking time."

At the word *loan*, she felt Sandy's hand stop on her back, then felt her withdraw it. "That's Dave's field," Sandy said. Emily could hear from her voice that she was glaring at her husband, ordering him to handle this.

"I'd love to, Emily," Dave said. "What we've got is kind of tied up right now, and locked in, but I might be able to help you out with a few ideas. I assume he had life insurance."

"We did at one time, term policies for both of us. But they were really for Pete, and when Pete died, I think Phil may have stopped paying the premiums."

Dave didn't pause. "You'll get his retirement, of course, and there's no tax for you because you were his wife." Dave looked very cheerful about that.

Emily didn't tell him that whatever retirement plan Phil had was gone. She just wanted this conversation to end.

"Then there's the house."

"I hadn't thought about moving."

"Well, think about it now. If you're alone, you don't need three bedrooms, a den, and an office." He looked around. "Even places like this have gone way, way up in the past few years. I think you'll be surprised."

"I guess so. I'll look into it. I'm sure everything will be fine." Emily wished fervently that she had not asked them for help.

"And then there's Phil's car."

"His car?"

"Well, one woman doesn't need two cars, and I assume his is the one you'll sell. Hey! You know, we've been looking for a good used car for Charlotte to take to school. I'll bet we can make a deal that's good for both of us."

Emily caught Sandy wincing and shaking her head. Emily said, "The police still have it. Phil was shot in his car."

"Oh!" Dave said.

Sandy rose. "Emily, we've just got to go. As I said, please call me if you need anything." She bent over, patted Emily's shoulder, and headed for the door, not looking to see whether Dave was following.

Once a few guests had left the house, the others seemed to feel that they had been released. They began to move toward the door in numbers. If they felt any obligation to Phil Kramer, they seemed to feel that they had now discharged it; and if they felt any sympathy toward his widow, they judged that the kindest thing they could do for her was to give her a chance to rest.

When she was alone, she lay on her bed, and closed her eyes.

Suddenly she sat up. She couldn't lie here like this. She had to do what she could to find out what had happened to Phil. She stepped out of her black dress, put on a pair of jeans and a pullover top, poured the contents of her small black purse into the one with the long shoulder strap that she used every day, and went down to the car. She could rest when it was her turn to be dead.

5

Emily was in the office sitting at Phil's desk and examining files. She remembered Phil's peculiar filing system from the old days when she'd worked with him. He kept the bottom drawer of each filing cabinet for guns and ammunition, on the theory that if he ever needed a firearm in a hurry he would already be ducking down low behind his steel desk. The top drawers were what he called "overhead" drawers: They contained bills and payment records for utilities, the building mortgage, the time sheets and payrolls. He kept them there just to give snoopers a sniff of something real, but useless. The next set of drawers were an odd assortment of ancient billing files interspersed with files that were fake—folders full of junk mail. By the time an interloper had gone this far, he would be too tired and exasperated to face the second row of drawers from the bottom, which looked just like all of the others, but which contained *real* case files, past and current.

Phil had been secretive.

Emily had examined the dozen most recent case files before she heard the sound of a key in the door of the outer office. She was terrified. The killer must have known today was the day of the funeral. What did he want? It was too late to turn off the lights, so she ducked behind Phil's desk, opened the bottom drawer of the filing cabinet behind her, and took out the gun Phil had left there. She heard the door rattle a little as she looked at the pistol frantically, found the safety, and switched it off. She put her eye to the side of the desk and watched as the door swung open.

Ray Hall walked into the office, looked around him, a puzzled expression on his face. He reached into his coat.

Emily called, "It's me, Ray. Emily." She got up from the floor, sat in Phil's chair, and hid the gun in a lower desk drawer so he wouldn't see it.

"Oh. You scared me. I was pretty sure we had left the lights off."

"You had," she said.

"Why aren't you home?" He walked to the door of Phil's office and stood there.

"Why aren't *you*?"

"I'm meeting the others here. We talked at the funeral, and we thought we'd come in." As he spoke, Dewey Burns and Billy Przwalski came in the door, stopped, and looked at Emily and Ray. A moment later, April Dougherty arrived.

They whispered to each other in the outer office, and then came to the door of Phil's glass cubicle. Ray Hall stepped inside with Emily and the others crowded in after him.

She lifted the dozen case files out of the file drawer, set them on Phil's desk, and said, "Thanks. I'm grateful to all of you for coming in."

"We talked after the funeral, and we thought we might come in and see what we could do about collecting Phil's things for you. We didn't expect you to be here. But since you are, maybe we can finish the job today and close up the office."

"Close up the office?" Emily said.

Ray shrugged. "Yes."

"Thanks for your offer. You've all been really kind, and I know things look bad right now. At the moment I don't have the money for this week's paychecks, but I do intend to make everything right as soon as I can."

"That's okay," Dewey Burns said. The others nodded, then stood where they were, looking uncomfortable.

"I can see you're all waiting politely to hear me say thanks for everything, and good luck in your next job. That's not why I came in today. I'm here to work."

"What?" Dewey Burns said.

"I said I'm here to work."

"Here?" Bill Przwalski said. "At the agency?"

"Phil's gone, Emily," Ray Hall said gently. "The agency is bankrupt."

"I'm afraid I can't just let it go at that, Ray. Phil not only cleaned out the agency's accounts, but he also emptied our savings, let his life insurance go, and—as far as I can tell—cleared out whatever money he had set aside for retirement. I don't know why he did. I don't know why he was killed. But I find that all I've got left is this business. I've got to try to run it."

Dewey Burns said, "You can't run a detective agency without a license."

"You and Ray both have licenses, and Billy's halfway there."

Ray Hall said, "Emily, this is probably not a great idea. It's true that technically, the agency still exists, and since you're Phil's heir, you own it. But running it is a different story. It's not an easy business, and with the bank accounts gone, the assets aren't much—a few last-generation computers, some steel filing cabinets, and a reputation that depended on Phil's credibility. You would probably be smarter to sell it."

"I'm not completely ignorant," she said. "I worked with Phil in the old days, when we started this agency. I'm not a detective, but I know how to run an office."

Dewey Burns said, "When was the last time you worked?"

"I quit when I was seven months pregnant."

The four attempted to conceal their skepticism. Ray Hall said, "That was what—twenty years ago?"

"I'm keeping the agency open. It's not because ever since I was a little girl I've wanted to hunt down deliverymen who file fake disability claims. It's because my husband's dead and I still have to pay the mortgage. I would like it if the four of you would stay."

April's lips moved as she counted the others: one, two, three. There didn't seem to be anybody else. "You mean me, too?"

The men watched Emily closely. "Of course I mean you, too," she said.

"Oh." April seemed unable to fathom how she got included. She was mired in thought.

Ray Hall said, "Emily, this isn't a good idea. We still have no idea why Phil was murdered. It's been a week, and the police don't seem to have a theory, either. There's no guarantee that whoever did it won't try to kill someone else who works here. This could be more than unprofitable. It's probably dangerous."

"I told you, Ray. I don't have any other choice. You're right that this could be some psychotic who has a grudge against the agency, or it could be someone who hates the world and wants to kill everybody in it. I won't blame anyone who doesn't want to keep working here, but I would love it if you would stay. Anybody who doesn't want to stay, please come back in a couple of weeks and we'll see what I can do to pay what I owe you. At the moment, I just don't have the money."

Ray Hall said, "I was just giving you my best advice. If you want to try to keep the place going, then of course I'll stay and try to help."

"Right," Dewey said. "Me, too."

"I still need another year of hours for my license," Bill said.

Emily moved past them to the outer office and set her stack of files on April's desk. "April, if you're staying, here's something to do. These are all cases that are closed, and the client owes money. I want you to call them all, and here's what I want you to say. Mr. Kramer has passed away and his heir is in negotiations to sell the agency. Since material produced in any investigation that hasn't been paid for remains the property of the agency, the files will be included in any sale. If you can't remember it exactly, write it down and read it to them."

"But what if they pay?" April asked.

"Then the files belong to them. When their checks clear, we'll FedEx them." Emily turned and walked back toward Phil's office.

April looked at the files doubtfully. "What are you going to do?"

"I'm going to look for more money we can collect. If I can scrape up enough, then you'll all get a paycheck this week." She stopped at the door to Phil's office. "If the rest of you are staying, see about completing the ongoing investigations, so we can bill for them."

Ray Hall hesitated, then sat at his desk and pulled a file out of his right-hand drawer.

"Not you, Ray. You just finished the Stevens case, right?"

"Almost. I just have to go show him what I've got and hand him the bill."

"Do it tomorrow morning, and then I want to put you on a new case right away."

"Who's the client?"

"Me. I want you to find out who murdered Phil."

6

Jerry Hobart had been in Las Vegas for five days now. He had told Tim Whitley to put the hotel bill on his credit card, and so, if Hobart wanted to, he could probably stay until Whitley's card got maxed out. But he sensed it was time to move out of the Venetian.

Having a sense of how long things were supposed to last was important. Parties ended, and the last one to leave might get stuck explaining the mess. He unlocked the safes in both closets, collected his two hundred thousand dollars, and packed the money in his suitcase. He filled out the express-checkout form as Tim Whitley and told them to leave the charges on the credit card, then dropped it in the box on his way out of the hotel at eleven in the morning.

He was feeling better today than he had felt for months. He had gotten sick of Tim Whitley's meaningless chatter and needed to put an end to it. Since he was a child in school, he had been amazed at the capacity some people had for being weak and annoying. If they weren't stopped, their needs would expand gradually to require everything their imaginations could encompass, and their talk would amplify to smother all silence and make real thought and feeling impossible.

Hobart was aware that he couldn't expect every person he met to be what he was. But he could expect them to carry their own weight and find ways to encourage and comfort themselves without making excessive demands on Jared Hobart. A man you were traveling with should be able to limit the amount of attention he needed to divert from the task at hand. He should be able to refrain from whining. He should be able to do what babies learned to do, which was to put themselves to sleep without talking long into the night to work their brains into exhaustion.

Leaving Tim Whitley under a pile of rocks in the desert had been the proper thing to do. Having two hundred thousand dollars was twice as good as having one hundred thousand, and Whitley's lack of self-discipline had made him a risky partner. A man who couldn't wait to tell stories about himself to impress a companion would never be able to resist telling somebody someday about killing Philip Kramer.

Hobart came out to the front of the hotel, gave the parking attendant his ticket, and went to stand in the waiting area across the driveway. He stood with his eyes closed and his muscles relaxed and savored the currents of hot desert air swirling in under the big canopy and touching his face and arms. He recognized the quiet engine of the Hyundai, opened his eyes, and watched the parking attendant setting his suitcase and Whitley's in the trunk. He handed the young man ten dollars, got into the car, and drove out onto the Strip.

Hobart didn't mind the traffic on the Strip. He was safe, well fed, rested, and he was in control of a vehicle with a full tank of gas. It was about the highest pinnacle that a creature on this planet could reach. The minor fillips and incentives that some people craved did not interest him. Once a man had been in prison, his mind became receptive to small improvements in his physical well-being, but he could recognize the emptiness of status and the illusory nature of security.

Hobart drove the Strip like the others, invisible because his car didn't excite envy and his driving didn't stimulate fear, and because it was difficult to be here without staring at the fantastic buildings and the lighted signs. In fifteen minutes, he was south of town heading out Route 15 in the stream of cars that ran toward Los Angeles. He took the exit to Route 95 and headed due south through the desert. Here he found relief from the congestion.

The world was getting too crowded. When he was growing up near Cabazon, the big attraction for outsiders was the giant concrete dinosaur that looked down over the freeway that led to Palm Springs. Now the Indians had built a big, fancy hotel and casino, and there were two huge outlet malls. People seldom got the point. One dinosaur or one outlet mall were kind of interesting. Two or three of them next to each other in the middle of the desert was just freakish.

He took the back way along 95 through Needles and Blythe, skirting the Arizona border down to Interstate 10, and west through Palm Springs, Indio, and Cabazon. It was night when Hobart drove up into the hills above the freeway exit and stopped at a driveway into an asphalt rectangle about the size of a football field. There were rows of trailers lined up along the sides of the square two deep, and in places three deep. There was a set of power lines strung up on a row of poles stepping up the hill, and smaller lines off the poles for hookups to the trailers, so there was light in many of the windows. The barbecues smoking in all ends of the place gave it the look of an encampment, a caravan of people who had just arrived at sundown and would be leaving in the morning, but it wasn't. Hobart's girlfriend Valerie had lived here for at least twenty years.

Her parents, Connie and Ralph, had come to the desert out of irritation. They seemed to have lost their tolerance for brushing against people, until their nerves were like old wiring with plastic insulation that had worn and cracked open. They spent their days behaving as though they still lived in Los Angeles, the mother taking Valerie to school and then coming home to water the flowers in the pots on the asphalt beside the trailer. Her husband drove fifty miles to Palm Springs every day to work fixing cars. He had been an engineer in Los Angeles, and the job was easy for him. He never had to talk to the customers directly. Valerie's parents could act that way, living in an imaginary place, but their daughter was in the world outside their heads. She went to school with the other desert kids, and spent her spare time walking the vast empty places with Jared Hobart.

He stepped up to the trailer, grasped the window frame, pulled himself up and looked in the window. He could see two clean dishes on the table, two glasses, and a vase of flowers, the kind that her mother used to grow in pots.

He walked around the side of the trailer to the back end. There was a dim light in the small window above the bed. Hobart looked around, found a big empty pot, turned it upside down and stood on it. He could only see a bit of the bed, but it seemed to be made, and he was sure it wasn't doing any moving. He heard a car coming, and then saw the headlights shining on the blacktop to his right. He stepped off the pot, spun it upright and set it on the pavement approximately where he had found it. He went around the left side of the trailer and waited near the door, one foot resting on the steps.

Valerie got out of her car, walked to the steps, put her arms around him and kissed him once quickly, then edged past him and unlocked the door. She pushed it open for him, said, "I'll be there in a second," and went into the dark.

After about a minute, she came back into the trailer and shut the door. "You feeling jealous, Hobart?"

"Why would you say that?"

"You moved my pot to look in my bedroom window."

"If you were asleep, I wouldn't want to wake you up."

"Sure you wouldn't."

He met her gaze for a moment. "Where were you?"

"I went to a movie with Maria."

Maria Sandoval was one of the people who had grown up with them in the desert. He looked out the window in the direction of the Sandoval trailer. When he looked back at Valerie, she was smiling. "There's the phone. If you feel like it, you can call her." She walked toward the back of the trailer.

"Where are you going?"

"To bed. I guess you don't want to come."

"Well, maybe I do. It's been a hell of a long drive, and I'm pretty tired."

"If you're tired, then maybe you ought to call Maria instead." She said it over her shoulder, but the head start she had wasn't enough, because Hobart was quick. Before she could reach the tiny bedroom he was scooping her up into his arms. He ducked to bring her through the door, flopped onto the bed with her, and in a moment they were wrestling each other out of their clothes.

Later he lay in Valerie's bed staring at the false ceiling. There was an inch-thin layer of old insulation above, but the roof was metal and he could hear when the desert wind blew the particles of sand and bits of dirt against the walls and made ticking sounds that usually soothed him and helped him sleep.

Tonight it wasn't working.

Hobart was aware that he had wasted his life, but he seldom spent time regretting it anymore. He could have married Valerie when they were young. She had always wanted to get married in those days, and had stopped wanting to only when he went to prison.

Probably they would have had a few kids and built a place outside Palm Springs, far up in the hills. That was where the really rich people had built winter homes since then, so it was too late now. It was too late anyway. After Hobart got out of prison, five years had passed, and Valerie was different. When he said anything about marrying her, she just laughed and shook her head and changed the subject. If he would let her, she would say, "Why buy the bull when I get the bullshit for free?" or "I'm saving myself for Jesus," or some other craziness to tell him the time had come and gone. His whole life was like that—burned up. He had no claim that anyone had done this to him. He had burned it up himself, for no particular reason except that he once thought he could get more of everything if he just took it.

Now, when he thought about the past, it was always the old days when he and Valerie had been kids. He would reach all the way back and try to get there and hold himself down, so the two of them would stay on the careful path. He would close his eyes and see her as a fifteen-year-old, walking with him in the desert after school. She was skinny and her long blond hair was sun-bleached, and her skin was always tanned like his. They would walk together but ten feet apart, because the land was empty and private for miles at a time.

The desert was almost silent because the wind needed something to blow against to make a noise, and there were no tree leaves or grass blades to swish and rustle. The only sound it could make was by blowing across the openings of their ears. Sometimes when Valerie talked, it was as though she were leaning her head against his shoulder—no, as though her thoughts found their way into his head. In those days children didn't talk to adults much, not even their parents. There was too much about their lives that their parents would have stomped on.

There was a group of kids who lived in the trailers and shotgun shacks north of the interstate who met in the desert after school: Maria Sandoval and her brother Augustin, Nancy DuVal, Bill Skinner, Mike Zellner, Hobart and Valerie. Now and then other kids would come into the group for a time because they had fallen into temporary disfavor with their regular cliques, or because they had heard something special was going on. Once Augustin picked up some cherry bombs and M-80s on a trip to Guadalajara, and there was a temporary swell in the gathering. On another occasion Hobart stole a case of beer from a truck idling near a diner in Indio. But most of the time there were only four or five of them who met in the desert to be together and smoke cigarettes.

The talk was sparse and weighted, the words chosen with great premeditation to convey and dispel anxieties, or designed like bait to elicit revealing admissions or concessions from the opposite sex. The answers were big, too, sometimes discussed in whispers by the members of one sex before they decided what answer was best to give. The speakers were representatives and exemplars of one-half of humanity. As the afternoon waned, they left in ones or twos, until most days, only Jerry and Valerie would remain.

There was no way for Hobart's mind to trace forward from that time to this, because the change, the damage, was so profound and the days in their thousands so full of other places and people that he forgot most of them. And during the intervening times he was often different kinds of men to different people, one no less real than any of the others. When he followed this thread—the boyfriend of Valerie Putnam—there were long gaps when that person had not existed. He had heard somebody say once that as long as a man's hopes outnumbered his regrets, he was still alive. But by that measure, he had been dead for years.

He just couldn't get himself to let go, close his eyes, and pull the trigger.

7

Ray Hall found a parking space near the courthouse complex on Van Nuys Boulevard, walked past the bail-bond shops and the stores playing Mexican music through their open doors, and down Delano Street to the police station. He went in to visit Al Campbell, the homicide cop. They talked about Campbell's wife, who grew up in Ray Hall's neighborhood, and about the strategy of the Dodgers, who were consistently beaten by players they had brought up, taught, and then traded to other teams. Then Hall asked him if he knew Gruenthal, the detective who had drawn the Kramer case, and Campbell took Hall to the next office to introduce him.

Gruenthal and Ray got coffee and sat down on opposite sides of Gruenthal's desk to talk. Gruenthal showed him the drawings and photographs of the crime scene and asked him the obvious questions: what case Phil had been working on, which old cases had left someone angry, what vices he'd had, what his relationships with women were like.

When they had each told each other what they knew, it was clear that they didn't know much. Hall said, "I'll let you know if I find out anything," but Gruenthal didn't make the same promise.

The conversation exhausted Ray Hall's will to talk. He was in the middle of a hangover, with a head that was pounding and light-sensitive eyes that had stopped producing moisture and stuck to his eyelids when he blinked. He had been expecting to show up at the office this morning only long enough to pick up his belongings and then go back home to bed, but now he was forced to think.

He decided to find a place to think where the sun wasn't in his eyes. It had to be one where people spoke English, because he had no idea how to say "shut up" in Spanish, and his head hurt. He stopped at a restaurant he knew called The Sea Grill on Van Nuys not far from the agency office and sat at the bar. The bartender was a middle-aged man who seemed to believe that the most important part of his job was cleaning the brass, wood, and glass for the evening, but he managed to pour Ray Hall a glass of scotch.

Hall drank half of it quickly, letting it burn down his throat, and almost immediately began to feel its anesthetic qualities. Then he took small sips and thought about Phil Kramer. Hall had known Phil for ten years, but nothing about his death made any sense to him.

Phil Kramer was big and aggressive, the kind of detective who would smile as he approached a man he wanted to talk to, and then stand too close to him when he asked questions. But he wasn't a bully, and he wasn't the sort of man who would forget that a bullet could kill him. Ray Hall had been with him on a number of investigations, and Phil had been careful. If he left his car in a dangerous neighborhood, he would return to it by a different route and see if he found anybody watching for him.

Despite his size, he was good at keeping a low profile. He dressed in drab colors, usually wore a nylon windbreaker, seldom a sport coat because cops and private detectives wore them. He could fade into a crowd of strangers, assess their posture and facial expressions, and imitate them. He would often start a conversation so he would appear to be one of the group instead of an outsider.

He was a credible liar. He never used a simple lie, always a story. When he pretended to be a deliveryman, he acted tired and irritated, a middle-aged guy forced to moonlight to pay off a debt. When he pretended to be a lawyer, he was an unethical overpaid one with the perfect amount of swagger and unfounded self-regard. That was his secret: an understanding of credulity. He let people assume the things he wanted them to believe. He didn't make some bogus claim and then stare into a person's eyes without blinking, like a bad poker player. Most people didn't want to stare into anyone's eyes like that. They wanted to be lazy and comfortable, and Phil Kramer let them.

Phil had always seemed too careful to be murdered in an ambush. And why would anyone want to kill him? Phil Kramer wasn't anybody's enemy. He was a mercenary. Nobody hired a private detective until he was pretty sure he knew what the detective would find. His clients were wives who already knew their husbands were getting laid somewhere else, lawyers who wanted to bolster the evidence in lawsuits that had already been filed, businessmen who already knew somebody was skimming the cash receipts. It wasn't as though killing Phil would end somebody's troubles. Phil Kramer had been in the business of proving what people already knew.

Hall had been withholding something from the investigators. He had been acting as though he believed the theory that Phil had been on a case when he was killed. That was what everybody on the outside assumed: Detective Gruenthal, Emily. But at the back of Ray Hall's mind there was a feeling that the idea wasn't quite right.

The thought brought Hall to a tangle of complications. After Phil got out of the marines over twenty years ago, he went to work as a trainee at Sam Bowen's agency until he got his license, then founded his own agency. At first he had worked cases alone. Emily would answer the phones, do the billing and filing, and probably write the reports for the clients.

When Sam Bowen closed his own detective agency, Phil had hired Sam to work for him. A couple of years later, he had hired Ray Hall. Ray had been inexperienced then, and he had tagged along with Phil or Sam at first and, in time, had learned to work on his own. As the business grew, Phil added people. He always hired young men who were physically rugged and had a reasonable level of untrained intelligence. He let them work their three years as trainees and tested them by giving them the worst jobs. They were the ones who sat watching an apartment building for seventy-two hours, or went through a neighborhood every day at three A.M. writing down the license numbers of the parked cars, and then spent the rest of the day at the DMV filling out forms to obtain the owners' names. When the trainees were ready, he would give them cases of their own and hire new trainees. Phil ran his agency like a pyramid scheme.

As the years went by, the young detectives got better and Phil Kramer got lazier and more careful about putting himself in dangerous places. First he stopped taking the hardest cases for himself. Eventually he stopped working cases with the young apprentices to teach them how things were done. Instead, he relied on Hall or Dewey Burns to take them on. Over the past year, he seemed to have lost all interest in the agency. He had let five of the other detectives go off on their own and had not replaced them. Bill Przwalski was now the only trainee, even though there were a dozen applicants a week calling April and asking for the chance to work for a license.

Phil still showed up at work every day, but he often left without telling anybody where he was going. The idea that what he was doing when he wasn't in the office was working cases had never occurred to

Ray Hall. When Ray had heard Phil Kramer had been shot, it had taken a minute or two before he could even concede that his death could possibly have anything to do with a case.

There were other complications to the task of investigating Phil Kramer's murder. As Hall sat in the bar sipping his second drink, he pictured Emily Kramer at the retirement party the night before Sam Bowen moved to Seattle. Everyone in the agency liked Sam Bowen, and everyone had benefited from Bowen's vast circle of snitches, cops, lawyers, bail bondsmen, and stringers. Emily Kramer had been grateful to Bowen because she still went over the books in the early years, and she knew what he had contributed to Phil's income and hers.

The party had been loud and jovial and chaotic at times, but it lapsed into periods of quiet, earnest talk about the past and the future. There had been an edge to these discussions because Sam Bowen said he was sixty-eight years old, but he was actually older. People at the party knew that once Sam Bowen was a thousand miles from L.A., they weren't likely to see him again.

Late in the evening, Ray happened to be out in a corridor with a group of people, and everyone seemed to go off to get a fresh drink at the same time except Ray and Emily Kramer. She was a woman who didn't wear much makeup or bother with hair and clothes during the day. For years she had been a housewife and the mother of a son who needed to be driven to practice for some sport every day. But that night she had worn a red dress with a low neckline and made of a fabric that clung to her a bit more than she probably knew. She placed her hand on Ray Hall's forearm. Her hand felt light, almost as though he were imagining her. But she blocked his way, stood close, and looked up into his eyes. "Tell me, Ray. I need the truth. Is Phil cheating on me?"

Hall's mind stalled. He had liked Emily Kramer since the day he first saw her. She always seemed so alert and quick, and it was fun to hear her talk. But it was her physical grace and the shape of her body that made it hard for him to look away from her, even when he knew he was taking a risk to look. And he knew that she thought about him, too. He couldn't be sure of the nature of her thoughts because there was always some wishful thinking in his mind, and friendships between men and women always incorporated some slight sexual attraction, but he was sure she felt something extra for him.

Asking him whether her husband was cheating told him so much that he couldn't examine all of the new information at once. She was revealing to Ray that things weren't going well between her and Phil, and that she trusted Ray not to betray her confidence to anyone. She trusted him not to think unflattering thoughts about her for her indiscretion in asking, or for her inability to keep a husband interested in her. She was implying that she was so close to Ray that he would tell her the truth just because she asked not to be spared. And he sensed without being able to analyze it, that if the answer was yes, then she would find a way to sleep with him tonight. But he knew it would be out of anger at Phil, not a desire for Ray Hall. In the years since then, he had thought about that moment a thousand times.

After a second, he gave her a wry, amused grin. "Jesus Christ, Emily. Look at you. How could he be cheating?"

But the hand she had placed on his arm tightened, so he was afraid he would spill his drink and draw attention to them. She said, "I really need to know, Ray. It matters."

"I don't know." It was the only answer that didn't need to be defended or shored up with evidence.

Emily stared at him. Maybe she already knew that regardless of what the truth was, he could never tell her Phil was cheating. She held his arm for a few more seconds, said, "Thanks, Ray," turned and joined the group in the main office. Ten minutes later, he went to find her, but found out that she and Phil had both left. Whether they left together or apart he never knew, because she had arrived in her own car after the office closed to bring some of the refreshments.

Now Phil was dead, and Ray Hall was the one Emily had asked to find out what had happened to him. He held up his glass and looked at the amber liquid inside, thought about the peculiar beauty of the whiskey with the light behind it, and then set the glass down on the bar. He took out a twenty-dollar bill, slipped it under the glass, and walked out of the restaurant into the sunshine.

He had left his car parked along the street. As he approached it, a woman got out of the car parked at the curb ahead of his: Emily Kramer. She leaned on the door of his car, her arms folded, until he was beside her. "Hi, Ray."

"You're right," he said. "I was in the bar. You caught me." He took out his car keys.

She didn't move. "You could tell me a soothing lie. You were interviewing somebody. I'd accept it even now."

"That's probably why I won't lie to you."

She looked up the block, then behind her. "Have you got anything at all yet?"

"I talked to Gruenthal, the lead homicide detective, a little while ago. He had the autopsy report and the crime-scene stuff."

"I don't want to stand around in the middle of the street while we do this. Why don't you take me for a ride?"

"Okay." He pressed the button on his key chain to unlock the doors, then hesitated. "I've been drinking."

"I'm aware of that. You want me to drive?"

"No. I just thought I should say it."

"Thank you." She slid into the passenger seat and closed the door.

He got in and drove north up Van Nuys Boulevard. "It pretty much agrees with what we heard before. It was after one A.M. Phil was walking up the sidewalk on Shoshone Street two blocks north of Victory. His car was parked on a dark, quiet stretch. He opened the door of his car, the dome light came on, and he got behind the wheel. There was a van parked across the street. Knowing Phil, I think he probably noticed the van parked in that spot when he arrived, and nothing about it looked different, so he figured it was harmless. But the shooter had broken into the van, hidden inside, and waited for him. The only shot hit Phil through the head, so he never felt it."

"You don't need to do that," she said.

"Do what?"

"Tell me things to make me feel better about how he died. I need to know what he was doing there when he was shot."

"Why?"

"A million reasons. I'm Phil's wife—his widow. I loved him. And I owe him that. Everybody has a right to have somebody care at least that much when he dies. He has a right to have somebody ask questions—who did this to him and why they would want to."

"What else?"

"What do you mean?"

"You said there were a million reasons."

"I didn't say I was going to tell you all of them."

Hall drove a block in silence. "He was up there north of Victory around one, but so far nobody knows what he was working on. It's a residential street, but there are big apartment buildings on Victory. There's also a golf course, a couple of good-sized schoolyards, and Balboa Park, all good places to meet somebody at night."

"You don't think he was out meeting an informant. You think it was a woman, don't you?"

He took a deep breath, then blew it out slowly. "I haven't said that. Is that what this is about?"

"Come on, Ray. How can it not be about that? My husband was shot to death in an ambush on a residential street at one A.M. I've looked at every case file I could find, and I don't see a current case that had anything to do with Shoshone Street. I don't see anything in anybody's Rolodex or on anybody's computer that would send him up there. Do you?"

"Not so far."

"Have you found anything that would tell you that he was working on a case at all?"

"Not yet. How about you? Have you searched your house?"

"Of course I have. Knowing Phil, I thought he would have left something where I would be sure to find it—maybe with the papers you have to look at when a person dies. I looked everywhere, but there's nothing so far—no addresses near where they found him, no mysterious phone numbers, nothing. Now I'm looking for hiding places."

"What about the cars?"

"I checked mine. The reason the police still have Phil's is that they're checking it."

"I still haven't figured out why Phil was keeping this a secret," Ray said.

"Because he had something big to hide. Now take me back to my car. We both have work to do."

8

Jerry Hobart climbed the slope toward the plateau above the trailer park with Valerie. He looked back down toward the freeway. From up here he could see the long sprawl of modern buildings that made up the outlet malls, and beside the freeway entrance, the small green-and-white box of the Hadley Date Farms store that had been here when Hobart was born. In the other direction was the high, narrow building of the Morongo Casino Resort that the Indians had built. Beyond the buildings was the gray line of freeway that stretched from the beach in Santa Monica across the whole country to the beach in Jacksonville, Florida. They reached the plateau and walked for a few minutes.

Valerie said, "What happened to that guy you were working with last time I saw you? That Whitley guy?"

Hobart walked on for a few steps, climbing higher. "He didn't work out, so we went our separate ways."

"When did you split up with him?"

"Not long ago. A week or two. Why?"

"I was just curious, I guess," she said. "I don't see you all that often, and I like to keep current. Sometimes I make predictions. I didn't like him much, and I was wondering how long it would take you to decide you didn't, either."

Hobart said, "He was a pretty good salesman because he was a talker, I'll give him that. People would start out thinking twenty bucks was a lot for a string of lightbulbs, but after a while they were thinking that twenty was damned cheap for getting him to stop talking and go away. The lightbulbs made a nice bonus."

Valerie gave the laugh she often gave as a comment, just "Huh!" once. When Hobart was away from her, even for a long time, he could always hear that laugh. When he closed his eyes at night and tried to picture her, he would see her begin to smile, then hear the laugh, the bright blue eyes wide and her mouth open just a little to show her perfect white top teeth. When they were young, Valerie's teeth weren't so good. He remembered them as small and oddly spaced. But in her twenties, while Hobart was in jail, she'd had them capped so they looked like a movie star's teeth.

He had assumed that she would probably get married to somebody else while he was in jail, and thinking about it every day in his cell was part of his punishment. Instead, she had spent a lot of effort making herself look better and a lot of time driving east to Phoenix or west to Los Angeles with a couple of girlfriends, or at least that was her story. Probably she'd had a lot of boyfriends, but there wasn't much he could do about it, then or now. She'd had the right to do whatever she pleased, and probably she had.

Sometimes she made vague remarks to hurt him. Once she said she was a whore with an expired "sell by" date on her. That was a couple of years ago. It was late in the evening when he was feeling sentimental about her, and he felt as though he had been stabbed. He hurt so

62

much that he became enraged, looked at his watch, made a transparent excuse about a plane he had to catch, and left. He had done that to make her think he was lying and had a date with someone else. They had loved each other for so long that they knew the best ways to wound each other. She was smart enough to know that she could make him crazy by reminding him that she'd had sex with other men—probably more than a few of them. But she also seemed to fear that if she mentioned a name, she would learn later that the man had died suddenly. It had happened once, about ten years ago. Afterward, he had not wanted her to hear that the man was dead and get a feeling of undeserved power—that she could just say a name and the man would die—so he had made sure he didn't come to see her for a long time. After six months, he had a postal service print up some cards that said he had a new cell-phone number, and sent one to her as though she were on a long mailing list. Since then, when she was in the mood to punish him for what happened to their lives when he went to jail, she would just imply that there had been other men. What she was implying was that the experiences had not been good—that they had ruined her—and that she considered every one of them his fault.

They walked for a half hour or more without talking, going up into the hills where other people seldom went, and they couldn't see Interstate 10 or the buildings that had been built beside it. They walked with the scorching stones under their feet, the sun blasting over their heads and the wind moving out of the east across the desert keeping them dry. The wind was constant out here, so there were big wind farms just down the interstate with huge white windmills with propellers that looked like airplane parts, spinning together, pivoting a little when the wind shifted.

The silence was part of the etiquette of walking together in the desert. They walked and thought about basic things. It wasn't a time to chatter about how the washing machine needed to get fixed or the damned government was getting worse or the car sounded funny. When they were together up here, they thought about each other and about themselves, and maybe a little about the other times up here over the years, and how it felt to be back.

Hobart's phone gave its irritating musical tone, and he looked at Valerie and frowned. She was watching him as she walked, waiting to see what he was going to do. He turned the phone off and put it back into his shirt pocket without looking at the number.

They walked on, but the feeling was not the same after that. He knew she was thinking that he had violated the rules by carrying a cell phone out there. She was thinking he had turned it off, not to preserve the open connection between them, but to hide a call from somebody he couldn't talk to in front of her. She was thinking it was a woman.

Hobart could see her shock hardening into resentment. This was deeper than the anger she felt when she tightened her jaw. When she was like this, the muscles around her mouth went slack again, so her face flattened. Turning off the phone had not restored the sanctity of their walk in the desert. Now all she was thinking about was that Hobart had a secret from her. He had another life away from here— away from her. Once the telephone had dragged her attention away from being with him, she could only think about the fact that he was away most of the time, and that when he was, there certainly were things he did that he never told her. He had to get rid of the telephone issue. He said, "Hold up a minute."

She stopped about ten feet away from him, half-turned and pretended to look toward something miles away, but held him in the corner of her eye.

He made sure she saw he wasn't punching in a new number, or using the navigation button to find a stored number. He just pushed the button for a missed call, so the phone would return it.

She didn't have to pretend she wasn't listening, and couldn't have, anyway. There were no other sounds she could pretend to be listening to. Even the wind was mild and steady.

"Hello," he said. "You called me." He listened for a few seconds, looking at the ground and moving small pieces of gravel around with his boot. "All right. Same price as last time." He listened again. "I don't bargain or give discounts. If you don't want to make that deal, it's up to you." He listened again. "Okay. Then I'll take care of it. Good-bye." He turned off the phone and put it away, and then began to walk toward Valerie.

He thought she looked less annoyed, a little softer. It made him remember a time when they were in high school and had come out on a walk like this. They had already had sex a few times, at night among the big rocks in the hills on a blanket laid out on the still-warm ground. On this afternoon they had been walking for two hours, so far into the desert that there was no chance that anyone would see them, even though they were in the open. They stopped in full sunlight on the flats and began to kiss. Neither of them ended the kiss, and things went further, and soon all of their clothes except their boots lay on the hot, sandy ground. At first they tried to lie together on their spread-out clothes. Nothing was thick enough except Hobart's jeans, but the sun found the tiny copper rivets and metal buttons and heated them enough to burn skin. Finally Valerie placed her elbows and knees on the fabric of his jeans so he could kneel and enter her from behind.

As he remembered, he could still see her in the bright sunlight, the most naked and exposed he had ever seen anyone up to then, and she was amazing and beautiful. Even then he was awed at the generosity and bravery she had. He loved her, and loved even the self he had been on that day, too, because of how young and clumsy and stupid and sincere they were then.

As Hobart approached Valerie, his hand reached out to her. She spun to turn away from him and said, "It's getting late. I need time to stop at the bank before work."

He stood there with his hand held out, feeling the wind blowing on his palm. Then he lowered his hand and followed. She stayed ahead of him, and she seemed to Hobart to be going faster now that they were on their way back, and it stung him.

When they reached the edge of the plateau and she started down the incline, he decided not to chase her, and she got still farther ahead. He watched her, letting her lengthen her lead until she was small and he no longer heard her feet on the stone and gravel.

He kept moving down the slope at his own steady pace. He watched her reach bottom, then raise her hand to shield her eyes and look up at him for a second or two. Then she turned and walked back to the trailer where she lived, went inside, and closed the door.

Hobart reached the bottom and walked at an unhurried pace along the path to the rectangle of asphalt. He passed her trailer without stopping and walked straight to where his car was parked. He got into the car, pulled his seat belt across his body, and saw the door of Valerie's trailer fly open. She was out and moving toward him. He started the engine, and he saw her walk faster. He pretended he didn't see her, turned his head, and backed the car up to turn around and head for the exit.

She appeared beside him and rapped on his window, hard, so he would press the button to lower it. "Where are you going?"

"You said you have to get ready for work, so I figured I might as well get on the road."

"Just like that?"

He stared at the dashboard, then raised his head and looked up at Valerie. "Don't you ever wonder what it would have been like if we could have kept from punishing each other?"

"I don't know what you're talking about," she lied. "I don't do that to you." She stared at him, the muscles in her neck taut. "I felt insecure when you got that call. I was trying to get over it. I would have. I am."

"Good." His voice was flat. "It was just business. Have a good evening at the restaurant. Get a lot of tips."

"I was over it, and now you're just being mean."

He hesitated and then said, "I think it's a shame that whenever I reach out, you hold me off, and then push me farther away. It's such a waste."

"It's because it's too late."

"We're here *now*. We're both alive and thirty-eight years old. I have enough money so you could call the restaurant and say you're not coming back. We could stay together and live, just the way we wanted to when we were kids."

"That was supposed to happen twenty years ago, Jerry. If you wanted it, you could have had it. Too much has happened since then. We know too much, we've done too much."

"You're doing it again. You're denying yourself a chance to be happy just to get back at me."

"What makes you think that just being with you is what would make me happy?"

"I'll be seeing you, Valerie." He turned in his seat, backed the car up the last few feet, and shifted to Drive.

She stayed beside him. "When? When will you be back?"

"Don't know," he said. "Don't know that it matters." He drove out of the trailer park onto the access road, went past Hadley's to the stop sign, and turned onto the interstate, headed west toward Los Angeles.

9

Emily sat beside April at the reception desk and patiently explained the process again. "The finance company lends money to people to buy things—say it's a TV set. The company offers this customer a period of twelve months with no payments. When the year is up, the customer has to start paying back the three thousand bucks he owes for the flat-screen high-definition TV. Only in the meantime, his wife ran off with a neighbor who wasn't sitting in front of a TV all day. The finance company wants the customer to start making payments, but he sold the house and moved away. The finance company puts together a list of these people and sends it to us. Here it is. We go down the list finding out where they live now."

Emily saw the expression of labored thought on April's face, but kept her own expression bland and calm. She had to keep the agency operating. She had to hold her emotions inside, so the others couldn't see her uncertainty, and maybe so they didn't sense the ferocious need she had for their help. She had to keep performing each of the small, irritating tasks, because if the agency died, so would her chance to know what had happened to Phil.

"It doesn't feel right to me."

"Very good." Emily smiled. "The glimmerings of a conscience in one so young."

"Are you making fun of me?"

"This is not fun. It's survival. I'm trying to make the payroll for this week, and skip-tracing is something I know how to do. The people who owe the finance company are mostly good people who don't intend to screw anybody. But they *do* owe the money."

"Okay," April said. "I just feel funny, chasing regular people for money."

"We're not getting into that end of it, and I hope we never have to. Let's do a couple of the traces on this list."

Emily turned the computer keyboard so she could reach it, and typed the name, Social Security number, and driver's-license number in the blank form on the screen, then clicked on "Search."

"You're such a good typist."

"Thanks. Typing used to be what paid the rent." It occurred to Emily that April probably thought of the boss's wife as a spoiled rich woman who spent her days getting facials and pedicures and going to the gym. After an instant she realized that she had not worked in the office since about the time when April was in kindergarten. April wasn't much older than her son Pete would have been.

The rest of the blank spaces on the skip-trace template on the screen began to fill themselves in rapidly: current address, current employer, vehicles registered. "Ah," she said. "This one has moved to Oregon. Save it, print it out, and go down the list to the next one. I'll be back in a bit to see how you're making out. I'll catch the phones." Emily went back to Phil's office and sat at his desk.

Emily had been married to a detective long enough to recognize that the police effort was essentially over. If the homicide detectives found nothing in the first week, they probably wouldn't find anything later. They had too many murders to spend all their time on an investigation that had stopped producing new information. For a year or two, the murder book they had compiled for Phil would stay within Detective Gruenthal's reach, and then it would be archived to make room for newer cases. Emily had to do what was necessary to keep the case alive, and the first thing she had to do was keep the detective agency going.

If she had to close the agency, there would no longer be detectives she could ask to follow leads in Phil's murder, and she could no longer search their memories for things they might have observed in the weeks before Phil was shot. There would be nobody to explain anomalies she found in the case files, payment receipts, and phone records. There would be no office, and the telephones would be disconnected. Anybody who had a tip about Phil's death that might get them in trouble would think there was nobody left to tell but the police.

She had Bill and Dewey out looking for two men who had jumped bail posted by the Open Bars Bail Bond Company. Neither suspect was violent, but both were out on crimes that were serious enough to rate bail over one hundred thousand dollars. The reward on either one would keep the agency open for another month or two.

Emily returned her attention to the filing cabinets behind Phil's desk. She had been going through the files for a week, ever since the day after Phil's death, starting with the ones that appeared to be the most recent, and moving backward to the older ones.

She had never heard any of the names she was now reading in the files, and there was nothing about the cases that seemed dangerous. Almost all of them were civil lawsuits, in which the agency had been hired by one side to investigate the other. No investigation seemed to have turned up anything especially damaging. There were no pieces of paper in any of the files that contained threats. There were no notations that said anybody was angry, or even dissatisfied.

At times the Kramer agency had taken on investigations that had to do with real crimes. Now and then Phil had been hired by a defense attorney to find exculpating evidence that the cops had missed or withheld. But she had not been able to find any cases from the past couple of years that had involved criminal charges, or even a file in which the police were mentioned prominently. She kept moving through the records, going back in time, not knowing precisely what she was looking for.

Then she sensed someone was in the doorway behind her. She looked up from the file she had taken out of a cabinet, composed her face in a motherly expression so she wouldn't scare April, and spun the desk chair around.

Ray Hall had been watching her.

"Hi," she said.

"You've got Dewey and Billy chasing bail jumpers?"

Emily nodded. "We're broke, Ray. I'm picking the low-hanging fruit so we can all pay our bills this month."

Hall closed the door. "What's April doing?"

"I'm teaching her skip-tracing. She can do it on her computer while she's answering the phones."

"She told me *you're* answering the phones."

"If she told you that, then she could have told you what she was doing."

"What's in the files?"

"I'm still trying to find cases we can collect fees on."

"Find any?"

"Not yet."

"That's what I thought."

"There's one other thing I haven't found, and it puzzles me," Emily said.

"What's that?"

"Phil's cases." She watched Ray. "I've been going through the files for the past year or two, and I can find pieces of paper with his handwriting on them, but they're just bills and correspondence. He's not the investigator in any of the cases. Do you have any idea of what he did with the cases he worked?"

Ray Hall stared at her, and she wondered if the complexity she read in the look was really there, or if she was just imposing it on him. After a few seconds, he answered, "It's something I still haven't figured out. In the past year or two I haven't known of any investigation he was doing on his own."

"Any? Not one?"

"None that I know of."

"Why not?"

Ray shrugged. "It's not unusual that the owner of an agency would decide that the best use of his knowledge and experience isn't taking telephoto shots of a workmen's-comp case playing basketball."

"So what did he consider the best use of his knowledge and experience?"

"I don't know."

"But you've been wondering about it, trying to figure out the answer?"

"Yes," he said.

"But you didn't mention it to me."

"I didn't notice that he was working cases, but he must have been. I haven't figured out a way to find out what any of the cases were. I searched that desk the morning after he died before you got here, but I found nothing. Whatever he was working on, he didn't write it down in any of the usual places."

"Do you know any reason why he wouldn't?"

"No. Not yet."

The telephone rang, and she could see April through the glass watching to see whether Emily really would answer it. Emily held up a finger to tell Ray Hall to stay for a minute, and said in her best receptionist voice, "Kramer Investigations." After a moment, she said, "Yes, Detective Gruenthal. It's me," and Ray Hall walked out.

Emily watched him through the glass wall. She thought she saw April's eyes meet his and stay there for a moment, but he didn't slow down on his way to the door. For an instant, Emily felt her chest constrict. Could Ray Hall be involved with little April? She wasn't sure why the idea mattered so much to her. She wanted to go after him and make him stay while she got rid of Detective Gruenthal, but it was too late to do it gracefully.

She closed her eyes and listened to Sergeant Gruenthal telling her the same things Ray Hall had already told her about the night of her husband's death. She was struck by the number of sentences he began with "We don't know if," or "We don't know who," or "We don't know what." When his pauses began to convey the message that he felt he had fulfilled his responsibility to her, she said, "Thank you. I'm glad you called. Please let me know if anything new comes up."

She hung up and went out to the front desk where April was working on the skip-tracing list. Emily noticed the sheets April had printed and said, "Very good, April. Why don't you go to lunch now?"

"All right." April got up, pulled her purse out of a desk drawer, and disappeared out the door.

Emily went to Phil's office and retrieved her purse, waited for a moment to give April time to ride the elevator down, then locked the office door and took the stairs. She knew the space in the basement garage where Ray Hall parked, and she thought there just might be a chance of catching him. When she arrived, she saw that Ray's space was empty. There was still April.

Emily went to her car, got in, and started the engine. She lowered her window, and heard another car coming up the ramp from the floor below. Emily ducked down until she heard the car go by, then sat up and looked. April's red Honda Civic was moving toward the exit.

Emily pulled out of her space and drove up the aisle to the exit, then turned right and found herself about a block behind April's red Honda. Emily felt guilty, but she had to do this. Everything for the past week had been mysterious to her, and anything she noticed might be important. If something was going on between April and Ray Hall, she couldn't ignore it.

Emily kept her distance. She gave April plenty of chances to get ahead and lose her, but whenever she thought she had, there would be the little red Honda. She followed April onto the freeway, and then to the exit for Forest Lawn Drive, the one that Emily took each time she came to the cemetery. April drove along the road beside the freeway for a distance, and Emily kept thinking she would take it all the way to Griffith Park. Emily hoped that April was going to have lunch in the park, not meet Ray Hall at one of the motels beyond it on Barham or Ventura.

April turned right at the big gateway into Forest Lawn Cemetery. Emily slowed down, gave April time, then turned in, too. She made a hard right and parked in the lot beside the chapel, where her car wouldn't be seen from the cemetery. She got out and walked to the end of the building, then stopped at the corner to see where April had gone. At first she assumed that April was going to drive to a different section, maybe to visit the grave of a relative, but she didn't. She stopped the Honda, got out, walked across the green lawn, and stood still.

It took Emily a minute to walk to the fresh grave. As Emily approached, she thought that April had not seen her coming, but then April turned around and said, "You followed me."

"I hadn't intended to. I've been here a lot. Usually I'm alone."

April said, "I thought *I* would be. I thought you were going after Ray Hall. It looked as though you were trying to say something to him when he left."

"I was, but I got a call. I guess Ray and I had pretty much finished our conversation, anyway."

"What did Ray tell you?"

"What do you mean?"

"About me."

"Nothing. If there were something I needed to know about you, I could have asked you." She looked at April sympathetically. "Is there something you want to tell me about you and Ray?"

"Me and *Ray*?" April glared at her. "Ray Hall and me? How could you think that?"

"I guess I just misunderstood what you were saying."

"I'm sure he'll tell you soon. He knows everything, and he pays attention to everything."

Emily looked closely at April, puzzled. "Tell me. Is this something Ray has talked to you about? Something he said to you?"

"No," April said in frustration. "I know if he hasn't told you yet, he's going to, because he's got to. So let's just say I quit, as of last Friday. Forget whatever work I've done since then. I know you can't pay me for it, anyway."

Emily said, "Honestly, I don't know what you think he'll tell me, but he hasn't said anything. I don't think that anything he could tell me would make me want you to leave. It's important to me that everybody who works at the agency stays. Once the four of you are gone, my chances of finding out what happened to Phil are gone, too. I need you."

"I'm sorry, Emily. The reason is that Phil and I were . . ." She stood there with her purse and began to cry. She sobbed, her shoulders shaking.

"Were what?"

"In love."

"Oh." Emily's voice was almost a whisper. "Oh. You're . . . Oh, God."

"Don't you believe me?"

"I wish I didn't." Emily's tears were starting, too. Instead of hating April, she felt concerned for her, the way she might have felt looking at a lost child. But even as she felt the urge to hold April and soothe her hurt, she wanted to hit her. She should not have had to watch this young woman weeping for Phil.

"I'm sorry, Emily. I'll leave now." April walked away from the grave.

Emily cried, "Wait!" April stopped, looking pained.

"I know that later on, we're both going to need to talk. When I'm up to it, I'll call you."

"Okay." April got into her car and drove down to the gate.

Emily stared down at Phil's grave. There was no marker yet, and it would be weeks before the earth settled to be even with the rest of the grass. She whispered, "I would have died before I ever did this to you. Fuck you, Phil."

She turned, then walked down the hill to her car, got in, and drove off.

10

Emily went into the office, carefully placed all the files she had been reading into the lower-right drawer of Phil Kramer's big steel desk and locked it, then dropped the silvery key into her purse. At the moment she didn't care what happened to the files. Putting them away was just a stray impulse in the part of her brain that disliked clutter. She locked the door of Phil's office, walked through the outer office, turned off the lights, and locked the door. She walked without having the sensation of her feet touching the floor, and for a moment she wondered if that meant she was fainting. Then she decided that she couldn't faint in the hall, so she wouldn't. She wanted to be away from this place. The thought of having people look at her right now brought a feeling like a burn to her face. As she walked toward the elevator, she began to move faster, trying to get out of this place where she was vulnerable. She passed the elevator because she didn't want to be trapped in there with someone looking at her, and stepped into the stairwell.

As she walked down the stairs, she tried to keep her steps quiet as though that would preserve her privacy. She tried to keep her mind off Phil. When she came to the foot of the stairwell, she opened the door a crack to see if anyone was in the foyer before she pulled it open the rest of the way. Then she was out of the building and in the parking structure.

She got into her car and started it, then began to pull forward when Bill Przwalski pulled into the structure in his dirty green Toyota Corolla. He waved and grinned as though passing each other in the lot were the greatest good luck, so she gave a little wave as she drove past him to the street. She wondered if he knew.

She drove out to the street in a detached, automatic way. Of course Billy knew. If April was so sure Ray Hall knew, then Billy knew, too. Billy must have been with Phil much more often than Ray was, because he was an apprentice, learning from Phil. And Billy was also young, practically a teenager. He would be very interested in everything about April. The thought triggered a wave of nausea so strong that Emily began to pull the car toward the curb. There was the blare of a horn, and she realized she had nearly cut off a young man in a tall white pickup truck lurking in her blind spot.

As he pulled forward on her right she glanced at him, cringed, and mouthed the word, "Sorry." He scowled, held his clenched fist toward her, raised the middle finger, then stomped on his gas pedal to accelerate past her.

When she reached the house, Emily drove all the way into the garage and sat still for a moment. While she had been approaching the house, she had been aware of the beautiful front lawn with the two towering trees, their wide canopies of leaves shading the house from the summer sun. It had always been a sight she stared at hungrily. Part of the sight was the improvements and replacements she and Phil had made: new roof, paint, the small addition. Now the sight of the house gave her no pleasure.

Fidelity

She noticed that she had not turned off the engine yet. All she would have to do was press the button on the garage-door opener, look in the rearview mirror to watch the door slide down behind her, and then sit here calmly for a little while. Phil had made sure the garage didn't have any leaks, so he could heat and air-condition it and do woodwork out here, but he had always been too tired or too busy. Most of the power tools in the world were probably sitting in suburban garages. She looked at the carefully fitted seams of the wallboard that covered the insulation. It wouldn't take very long to die in here.

As an experiment, Emily pressed the button and watched the door come down to close on the afternoon sky, like an eyelid shutting. She sat still for a few seconds, waiting to feel something, then opened the car window. She could smell the engine's exhaust, but she didn't feel any different. She got bored waiting for a feeling. She realized she could turn on the radio. The engine was running, after all, so it wouldn't drain the battery. Phil had always been afraid of exhausting the charge on a car battery.

The radio came on, and she recognized the voice of a familiar talk-radio host. Once again he was railing against the supposedly bad influence of college professors, reporters, lawyers, members of minorities, and laborers, who were mortgaging the country's future. She muttered, "Shut the fuck up!" and hit the power button. The words surprised her, but they expressed her feeling perfectly, so she was satisfied. She turned off the engine, opened the car door to get out, and realized she had forgotten about her suicide experiment. She went in the house and locked the door.

Emily sat at the kitchen table and stared through the window at the big tree in the side yard. There was a smudge on the window. She opened the cupboard under the sink, picked up the Windex and a paper towel, stepped to the window, keeping her eye on the spot so she wouldn't lose track of the smudge, and cleaned the pane. She didn't have the temperament for suicide. There was just too damned much to do.

She put the Windex away and went into the living room to sit on the couch. She began the thought, "How could he—" but then stopped. She *knew* how he could. Phil was a middle-aged man who was tall and trim and attractive, and he was the boss. April was pretty and sweet-natured, but brainless, and there she was, right in front of him all day long. How could he not? April must have been amazed by a man like Phil, may even have been naïve enough to think that there was a nice future in a relationship with a man old enough to be her father who was cheating on his wife.

Emily corrected herself. She was a fine one to be calling April stupid. April was twenty-five years old. Whether she wanted it to be or not, her unfortunate mistake with Phil Kramer was over. She had all those years ahead of her. She was sad right now, but she had lost nothing of any importance. Emily was forty-two. She had invested twenty-two years of her life—her attractive childbearing years—in loving Phil Kramer. As of today, there was no way to pretend that she had done the right thing, made the right choice. She had devoted her life to a man who hadn't really loved her but hadn't bothered to tell her, to bearing and raising the beautiful, strong son they named Pete after her father, and then having the child crash a car into the front of a tractor-trailer truck. It was a hard time to find out that Phil had been with other women.

Women. Plural. She had suspected it for years. April had certainly not been the first. The suspicions Emily had pushed to the back of her mind so many times were true. There had been a hundred moments over the years when the only reason she had to believe he was faithful was that she wanted to.

She realized she was crying, and hearing herself cry this way was the loneliest sound she had ever heard. Phil was dead, Pete was dead. It didn't matter if she cried loudly or softly. She was as alone as a person floating in the middle of the ocean.

She had been working frantically to learn the reason for Phil's murder and to find out who did it, because being engaged in the investigation let her stay close to Phil. The connection was thin and waning, constructed of memory and intellect and intention, but it was something. Now that the truth about April had been driven into her skull, the connection was painful and sour. She couldn't make herself think that Phil deserved her loyalty and devotion. She couldn't even say he would have done the same for her.

Emily couldn't sit still. She stood up and began to pace up and down the living room. She had to stop herself from formulating the idea that it was better for her to have learned about Phil's infidelity now because knowing would help her break the bond with him. It was a cowardly impulse to make excuses for circumstance. Things didn't happen for a reason, and people who thought they did were idiots. Knowing wasn't better, and it didn't make anything easier. She felt as bad about his cheating right now as she would have a year ago. She couldn't even talk to him now and ask him why, or tell him she was hurt and angry, or do anything else. It was simply a fact that could never be changed.

She heard the sound of a car engine, but no sound of the car passing. Then she heard the slam of a car door. She stepped to the front window just as the bell rang. The sound seemed incredibly loud and intrusive. She stood still for a few seconds, then moved the curtain aside a half inch.

Ray Hall stood on the porch, looking straight into her eye. She couldn't pretend she wasn't at home, or that she thought the person at the door was a salesman or a solicitor. She closed her eyes and sighed, then stepped to the door and opened it.

"I'm sorry, Ray. I'm just not feeling up to visitors right now. Can I call you tomorrow?"

"April told me."

"All right. Come in."

Ray stepped inside and Emily closed the door. He stood in the entry until Emily walked toward the kitchen, and then he followed her. She stood at the counter and started making coffee, and he sat down at the table.

Emily looked only at the coffeemaker as she spoke. "April said you knew, and that you were going to tell me. Is she right?"

"Not exactly. If I found out for sure, I would have told you."

"Why?"

"Because you asked me to find out who killed Phil and why. I've noticed that an extramarital relationship sometimes bears on those questions." He paused. "I wasn't ready to say anything because I could have been wrong."

"But you weren't wrong. When did you start to suspect it?"

There was nothing subtle about her questions. She wasn't imagining he had forgotten she'd asked him a couple of years ago. He chose to answer a narrower question than the one she had asked. "A few months ago, I noticed she would stay late with Phil after everyone else had left. There wasn't that much paperwork."

"Go on."

"Jesus, Emily. You really don't want to hear about that. April said she had confessed to you already. Take her word for it."

Emily shrugged. "I guess you're right. I probably know all of his moves already. I suppose I'm just reacting out of shock." She gave a single, unhappy laugh. "I don't know where the shock comes from. You remember we had a conversation about this a couple of years ago, before April came along."

"I remember," he said.

She folded her arms across her chest. He recognized that she was unconsciously protecting herself from what was coming. "Tell me, Ray. Were you lying then?"

"I don't know. I thought he might be seeing somebody. I wasn't sure, and I couldn't tell you he was cheating if I wasn't sure. I didn't think what I was saying was a lie."

"After I talked to you, did you try to find out?"

"No."

"Not an honorable thing to do to your friend?"

"No. Come on, Emily. I think it's time to go."

"Go where? What are you talking about?"

"I'm going to take you out to dinner."

"No. I'm not in the mood to get dressed up."

"You already *are* dressed up. You got dressed up to go to work."

"I can't go out. My husband just died, and I want to be alone."

"My friend just died, and I don't want to be alone." He took her hand and gently pulled her, picked up her purse, and conducted her to the door. "Nobody wants to be worthless on a bad day, Em. Not even me."

"I'm not going, Ray. I can't."

He studied her face, and realized that she meant it. He put the purse on the chair near the door. "I wish you would. If you change your mind, or just want to talk, call me."

"All right." She looked at the doorknob.

He saw where she was looking, opened the door, and stepped outside. He watched her shut the door, heard the lock, and then the faint sound of her going deeper into the house. He felt a twinge, an impulse to protect her. It was as though he were missing a chance, letting something happen that he shouldn't. He walked to his car. As he drove away up Emily's street he looked in his rearview mirror several times, but he couldn't find an excuse to stop or go back.

11

Jerry Hobart looked in the telephone book, then drove the blue Hyundai to the Disabled American Veterans storefront a few miles north of Los Angeles in Sun Valley. There he arranged to donate the car in exchange for a tax deduction. The pink slip carried the name David Finlay, so the tax deduction wasn't much use to Jerry Hobart, who had not paid taxes since before his incarceration nearly twenty years ago. There was no immediate need to get rid of the car, but he liked to get rid of anything that might be connected to a shooting. He accepted a ride in the Hyundai from the man in charge of the office, a volunteer named Don who hit the pedals with his left foot because his right leg was made of glossy plastic. The part that Hobart could see above the sock looked like the leg of a doll.

Hobart didn't talk much to Don because he didn't like to be memorable. He did manage to plant in Don's mind the idea that he was from Texas and was divorced. Before Hobart said anything while he was working, he always contemplated it to be sure nothing about it was true. Don let Hobart off in front of the apartment complex he had given as his address.

When Don had driven the donated car away, Hobart walked a few blocks and took a bus to the subway station at Universal City. He walked across the street past the big electronic marquee and up the hill to the Hilton Hotel where he was staying. He kicked off his shoes, put the Do Not Disturb sign on the door and took a long nap. When he woke, he knew he'd had a dream about Valerie, but he couldn't quite bring it back. He remembered that they had been married in the dream, and she'd had some children with her who had the same blond hair that she had. He supposed they must have been his children, too.

As he showered and dressed, he felt Valerie's presence in the room, and he continued his argument with her in his mind. It was late afternoon when he went out to pick up the equipment he would need. He had ordered a Kimber version of the .45 ACP 1911 over the telephone when he was in Las Vegas. The store was a small one in Burbank where he had bought several other guns under the name Harold Keynes, and he had been glad to learn that once again Mr. Keynes had stood up to the background checks. Since Keynes had been dead for six years, he could not have gotten himself into any trouble, but it was good to learn that Harold Keynes's body still had not been found and identified.

Hobart had also ordered a gun-cleaning kit and a Remington Model 700 .308 rifle with a scope. He didn't know whether this job would require any distance work, but having the rifle for it made him feel good. For a few hundred dollars, he had bought enough range and accuracy to place a bullet through a teacup at six hundred yards.

Hobart had learned to be an expert marksman when he was a boy. He had become accustomed early to the mil-dot reticle that had been invented for military snipers. Reading the dots on the crosshairs had become automatic for him before he was thirteen. At 600 yards, the space between two dots on the crosshairs of a 10X scope was 21.6

inches. He could estimate the range of a shot by comparing the sizes of objects to that, so he memorized the sizes of things. A license plate was 12 inches long. A standard table was about 30 inches high. Most exterior doors were 36 inches wide and 80 high. At that range, a woman who was 5'3" was three dots tall.

He would spend days alone in the desert, pacing the distances and shooting until he could do it all reflexively. In those days he had very little money and a box of ammunition was expensive, so he needed to do much more measuring, aiming, and thinking than shooting.

Hobart loaded his new rifle into the trunk of his rental car, but kept the new pistol in its box on the floor beside him, then drove to the hotel and parked in the parking structure. He left the rifle in the trunk, but he took the pistol, cleaning kit, and ammunition with him because in the shopping bag they didn't look like anything in particular. In his room he put on a pair of thin surgical gloves, opened the box, took out the gun, broke it down, cleaned it thoroughly, and left a thin layer of gun oil on the working parts.

There were people who liked hollow point ammunition with a .45 because the bullet mushroomed a bit when it hit, and supposedly did a lot of damage to the target without going through and piercing walls and doors. But Hobart had found that regular ball ammo had never failed to stop anybody, and he didn't consider a bullet going through a wall or a door to be a disadvantage. He had bought a couple of twenty-round boxes of ball ammunition, so he opened one and, keeping his gloves on, he began to pick the bullets out of their little plastic tray and insert them into one of the two magazines that had come with the gun.

Whenever he touched the internal parts of a gun or loaded a magazine, he wore gloves. Jerry Hobart had survived a long time in a dangerous world by maintaining the view that if he wasn't stupid, a great many other people probably weren't, either. Some cop might be enterprising enough to check a surface other than the obvious ones.

He hid the gun in his inner jacket pocket, collected his boxes and bags, and went out to the car. As he opened the trunk and tossed the bag inside, he glanced at the rifle again. He would leave it in its box, and the scope too, until he needed them. He liked the Model 700. It was about as accurate and reliable as it needed to be, and many thousands had been sold. The kind of shooting he was doing these days didn't require anything it couldn't give him. In a city, there were very few shots that were longer than two hundred yards. Buildings got in the way.

Hobart drove down the steep hill from the Universal City complex, past the Red Line subway lots, and onto Ventura Boulevard. He was going to take a look at a house. He had been given this address once before, but he had not seen any advantage in going there and risking being noticed. Whenever anyone died from any kind of incident, the people who had been in proximity all searched their memories to convince themselves they'd seen some sign that it was going to happen. While they were searching their memories for signs and portents, he hadn't wanted any of them to stumble across the image of Jerry Hobart. But this time things were different. He would probably need to visit this address.

He drove west about three miles to Van Nuys Boulevard, then north another mile to a neighborhood called Valley Glen. He drove up and down a few major east-west streets—Vanowen, Victory, Sherman Way, and Burbank Boulevard, Oxnard—to see which ones had road crews working on them, which were clogged by traffic. In this part of town over the past year, there had been a lot of streets torn up so concrete storm drainpipes five feet in diameter could be laid in deep trenches. A man who planned to do something but didn't pay attention to how he was going to get out afterward didn't deserve to get out.

Hobart drove past the house and studied it from the street. There were signs stuck on the lawn that said HAMMER SECURITY and a smaller ARMED RESPONSE. That meant he would have to examine the doors and windows for the lapses. The electronics in these systems were all the same. The devices were reliable and difficult to defeat, but what Hobart needed to defeat wasn't devices, it was people: the installer who left some point of access to the house unwired because it was too difficult, and the homeowner who didn't bother to turn on the system. From here Hobart could see two rectangular cement boxes at the sides of the house that gave workmen access to the crawl space under it, and a vent on the roof that he could unscrew to gain access to the attic. He was sure those wouldn't be wired. On some houses even the second-floor windows weren't.

There was no sign of a dog, which was good news to Hobart. Befriending or killing a dog before it barked was a chore he would prefer to avoid. The structure of the house made it easy for him, too. The bedrooms would be on the second floor in the back, and on the floor below would be the living room. The living room was usually the easiest place to enter these houses in the San Fernando Valley, because there were often double French doors or big sliding windows to open onto the patio and the swimming pool. The living room was always worth a visit anyway, because those windows transformed the room into a museum diorama—the inhabitants like game animals stuffed and posed behind glass for his inspection.

Hobart liked the way the garage was placed at the rear of the property behind the house. He would be able to stand at the back corner and look into the house unseen. He sped up, pleased. There was nothing about the house that posed an obstacle to Jared Hobart. He could practically walk in through the walls.

The one thing he wondered about was why a man like Forrest would hire him to do this. Hobart had simply accepted the notion that a private detective knew or was about to learn something unpleasant about Forrest, so Forrest had wanted him dead.

But Hobart had to wonder what Forrest had to fear from the detective's widow. Maybe—before he killed her—it would be worthwhile to find out.

12

It was late at night, and the traffic near the detective's office was thin. Jerry Hobart wore a black baseball cap with the brim pulled low above his eyes as he walked along the side of the office building. Security cameras were always mounted high, partly to give them an unobstructed view, and partly to keep them out of reach. He didn't have any confidence in his ability to find them all, so he kept his face averted and shielded from view by the brim. He saw the underground parking entrance and exit had been closed with iron grates, so he kept going.

It took him a few seconds to see a way in. He could see that the windows on the first and second floors were all bordered by thin silver alarm tape, but there was no tape on the ones farther up the side. Landlords always tried to save money, and paying to wire every window on the third floor and above must have seemed like a needless expense. Hobart knew there would be other ways in, so he continued to look for the easiest.

He walked to the back of the building where he was shielded from view by the backs of other, taller structures, and looked up at the fire escape. There was a ladder about ten feet from the ground, weighted so a person coming down would cause the ladder to descend. Hobart took off his belt, jumped and swung the buckle over the bottom step of the ladder, and lodged the buckle in the corner where the step met the frame. As soon as the buckle caught, Hobart's weight brought the ladder down.

Hobart climbed the ladder to the top floor of the building. As he ascended, he looked in the windows, and saw the hallway on each floor, so he began to have a sense of the building's structure. It was built on an old-fashioned pattern, each floor a single hallway with a stairwell on each end, offices on both sides and the elevator shafts running up the center. When he reached the top, he pulled himself up so he could get his elbows over the edge of the roof and look. The top was a flat tar covering with a cluster of pipes, a big box for the air conditioning, and louvered vents. There was also a right triangular structure jutting upward with a door in it. That was what he had hoped he would find.

Hobart climbed up and walked to the door. He tried the knob, but it was locked. He took out his lock-blade knife, flipped it open and slid it between the door and the jamb to get the feel of the locking mechanism. After a second or two, he realized the lock wasn't a serious one. It was just enough to keep tenants off the roof. He withdrew the knife, then pushed the blade into the space at the right spot, eased the spring-loaded plunger aside, and opened the door. He waited and listened for an alarm, but there was no sound. He wasn't in a hurry, so he disengaged the lock, pushed the door shut so nobody who passed in the hall below would notice an open door, and sat down beside it.

Jerry Hobart had found in the past that his enterprises were most successful when he took the time to think, to listen, and to observe. That method also provided time for things to happen around him.

Tonight, if he had miscalculated and set off a silent alarm, he would be able to hear and see the police cars pulling up to the building below him. While he waited for them, he considered what he needed to do and what he should search for.

Forrest was a man with standing. If he'd had a problem with Phil Kramer the private detective, it probably was about money—getting or keeping it—or his reputation. There probably was no social connection, no business relationship that would have been public. That meant that what Jerry Hobart needed to find was secret information that either had Forrest's name on it or the makings of a business deal that was so big that Forrest would be drawn to it.

Hobart looked at his watch. It was only eight twenty-five. He had begun his preliminary reconnaissance trip in the late afternoon, so he could see the way people and houses looked, what the traffic was like on a randomly chosen day, what the points of entry to important buildings were. Now that he was inside the security perimeter of the detective agency's building, he wanted to be sure he was alone. He had given the cops fifteen minutes to arrive, and he had seen no office with its business-hours lights on while he was climbing up.

He went to the other side of the roof and looked over the edge at the street. There were cars parked at the curb, and while he watched, another pulled up and parked. The two front doors opened, and a young man with dark hair got out of the driver's seat while a girl with very long black hair got out of the passenger seat. They waited while a couple of cars flashed past, then ran across the street, holding hands. Hobart watched them walk quickly a half block farther and go to the ticket window outside a movie theater.

Hobart turned and went inside the building. He stepped cautiously down the stairs and waited a few seconds, then looked into the hallway. It was empty. He walked to the stairwell and descended quietly to the fourth floor. He listened and opened the door a crack to verify that the hallway was clear, then stepped into it.

He moved up the corridor, reading the doors until he came to the one that said KRAMER INVESTIGATIONS in gold letters. He tried his knife again, but this time the lock was serious. Hobart was a patient man, so he went to work on the wood beside the lock with the lock-blade knife. He carved his way to the two screws that held the strike plate, cut away the wood around them, then pushed the door open. He picked up the inch-square piece of wood he had cut from the jamb, pushed it back into the woodwork, gathered the shavings, and then stepped inside and closed the door.

Hobart turned on the lights and examined the office. It looked to him as though four people besides the boss worked here. Phil Kramer's desk must have been the one in the private office with the big windows, and the one with the big telephone near the office door had to be for a secretary or receptionist. The remaining three desks must belong to the detectives. He could see there were filing cabinets in the inner office. He assumed the room would be locked, but he could break the glass without making much noise. When he reached the door, he saw that it would not be necessary: The door had already been kicked inward, splintering the frame that held it.

Hobart sat at the desk and looked around. It was always a good idea to determine what the other person could see when he was in his habitual position because that was probably where he'd been when he'd chosen the hiding place. Hobart could see the walls—mostly glass—of the inner office. There were a couple of visitors' chairs along the wall, a computer and printer on a table, and the filing cabinets. The place was sparsely furnished. There wasn't even a couch in here. It reminded him of the various offices in the state prison. He had been assigned to clean offices a few times near the end of his sentence, when he had served five years and had lost interest in pocketing things.

Hobart slowly rotated the desk chair around, making a full circle. There was the chance it was hidden in one of the desks of the detectives, or taped under a drawer. After a moment, he decided that would be one of the last places he would look because Kramer would have known that trusting another person with anything valuable was a bad idea.

Hobart assumed that there were at least two hiding places. No matter what form the information took—pieces of paper, a computer disk, an audio or video tape, or photographs—there would be one copy to show, talk about, and trade, and one to keep hidden as insurance. One—and only one—hiding place would be in this building. If Phil Kramer had information that Forrest wanted, Kramer would have made sure Forrest couldn't simply take the only copy.

Hobart looked up, stood on the desk, and lifted one of the acoustic ceiling tiles out of its suspended metal frame. He stuck his head into the recess above the frame so he could see whether anything was hidden on one of the other tiles. He took out his Maglite to illuminate the dark space, and found it was clear.

He climbed down from the desk instead of jumping, so the sound wouldn't reach the ears of anyone downstairs. Then he went on with his search. He looked inside and under each of the desks, the drawers, the tables and chairs for anything that showed signs of being hidden rather than stored. He moved heavy furniture and checked the floors for tiles that had been lifted. He went into the storeroom and examined the supply cabinets. He knew that a good way to hide a few pieces of paper was to open the wrapping on a new ream, put the paper in the middle and then glue the wrapper back together, so he opened all the packages of copier paper he could find.

After three hours he had narrowed the search to the inner-office filing cabinets. It took him a few seconds to recognize that Phil Kramer had an idiosyncratic filing system. The obvious file drawers, the ones that an average-sized man could reach without kneeling, were full of old time sheets and phone bills and rent receipts. The bottom drawers were devoted to guns and ammunition. This year's files were in the rear of the middle drawers, behind what looked like junk mail, opened, flattened, and put into file folders.

The sight intrigued Jerry Hobart. It proved to him that Phil Kramer had been suspicious and secretive, and had routinely hidden even things that few intruders would care about. If Phil Kramer had wanted to hide a few sheets of paper in these cabinets, he could have slipped them in with the junk mail, or stapled them into the middle of one of the innumerable contracts and reports stored in the back of each drawer. It made him wonder how anyone as suspicious and secretive as Phil Kramer could have put himself alone in front of a gun on a dark street. Hobart glanced at his watch. It was after midnight, and he judged that he would have to be out of the building by five A.M. He had a bit under five hours left for the filing cabinets. He began the process of leafing through each file, finding nothing that seemed important, then putting the contents back and pulling the next file. After two hours of this, he heard a faint noise from the hallway.

Hobart heard it again. It sounded distant, but he closed the cabinet carefully, stepped quickly across the room and turned off the light switch. He stood just inside the door and listened. He heard the sound again, this time louder. It was the squawk of a radio. He felt a chill in his spine. This wasn't a time when he could talk his way past a couple of cops. He was a convicted felon carrying a .45 automatic in an office that belonged to a detective who had been shot in the head just over a week ago.

Hobart pulled out the gun, disengaged the safety, and waited for the man coming along the hall to notice the damaged doorjamb. He heard footsteps coming closer, and the radio hiss, and the voice of a woman who sounded like a dispatcher. It stopped suddenly. The door swung inward toward Hobart. He held his pistol at chest height and watched the uniformed man step in to search for the light switch.

Hobart was surprised. This wasn't a cop. It was a young Hispanic man about twenty years old wearing a baggy navy-blue uniform with a patch on the shoulder that said something about Ready Security. Hobart's thumb reengaged the safety catch on his gun, and he set it in the potted plant by the door.

The boy's ear caught the sound of movement, and he reached toward the revolver in his holster, but Hobart was already in motion. Hobart's left hand gripped the boy's wrist while his right plucked the gun out of the holster and tossed it behind him. His left arm curled around the boy's neck and tightened.

The boy tried the predictable moves he had been taught: stamping his heel on what he thought would be Hobart's instep, trying to throw his head back into Hobart's face, jabbing his elbows at Hobart's midsection, trying to deliver a hammer punch to Hobart's groin. His flailing was quick and wild, but he simply wasn't strong enough. Hobart's stranglehold tightened, the struggling became urgent, and stopped, the boy's hands now simply trying to grip Hobart's thick forearm to wrench it away from his throat so he could prolong his consciousness for a few more breaths. Finally, the hands went limp, and Hobart was holding the unconscious boy upright.

Hobart loosened his grip tentatively to see if the boy was faking, but there was no swift move, no wriggle. The boy had been choked out. Hobart lowered the boy gently to the floor. He picked up his gun and the boy's and stuck them in his jacket pockets. Then he unplugged the receptionist's telephone at the wall and the receiver and used the cord to hog-tie the unconscious boy. He took the boy's radio and keys, closed the office door, walked down the hall to the elevator, and rode it to the ground floor. He let himself out the back door with the keys. As Hobart trotted down the street to his rental car, he accepted the fact that he would have to make one more stop tonight.

13

Hobart drove back along the Ventura Freeway. Even though the drive was short, it was always safest late at night to be on the freeway instead of a residential street, or even a major boulevard. Late at night was when the ratio of police to civilians was highest, and the police were convinced that only cops and robbers were out.

He pulled off the freeway at Reseda, wishing he didn't have to do this. But now that he had broken into the detective agency, everybody involved with the agency would know within a few hours that someone was searching for something. He had to try to finish this tonight. By this time tomorrow night, she would be scared, and it might be very difficult to find her.

If his visit to the office made the newspapers, it was almost certain that Forrest or someone who worked for him would figure out what had happened and why. The more he thought about it, the better he felt about his decision to leave the young security guard alive. Killing him would have put the small-time office break-in on the television news and in the *L.A. Times*. As it was, there wasn't much to report, and the detective agency, the security company, and the landlord would all have an interest in keeping it quiet.

Hobart went up Reseda Boulevard and then east along Vanowen to the street where he had studied the house in the early evening. He drove around the block and parked on the next street. He sat in his car for a few minutes, considering what he was about to do. He had brought a knit pullover ski mask with holes for the eyes and mouth, just in case he needed it to get out of the detective agency, but he had left it in the car when he had seen that it was best to go in during the early evening. This time he put it under his coat. It was after four in the morning—not a bad hour to go visiting—but he wished he had more time. There were only about two hours before sunrise, when there would be lots of cars out and people on their way to work. At least some of the people in this neighborhood would be up cooking breakfast before then.

Hobart got out of his car and walked quickly up the street and around both corners, then stopped at the Kramer house. He walked beside the house to the back yard and all the way to the far corner. He looked over the back fence to find his car and verify that he had parked where he thought he had. Then he stared at the back of the house.

He looked in the big set of sliding doors that he had seen earlier. A lamp had been left on in the living room, so he could see the layout clearly: two couches and two armchairs arranged to face each other across a big knee-high oval-shaped coffee table, and outward from there, a few chairs and tables with lamps along the wall between the windows. On the second floor above the living room he could see a light on in one of the bedrooms in the back, and the wavering, changing glow of a television screen illuminating the ceiling. She must be having trouble sleeping.

The lights gave him a small hope. Hobart stepped closer to the back windows and looked inside for the alarm-system keypad. It was beside the front door. He shaded his eyes and studied the electronic glow on the liquid-crystal display. There were three red letters: RDY. Ready. The alarm had not been turned on. She must have planned to activate it when she was going to sleep, and never gotten around to it.

Hobart opened his pocketknife, and put on his thin rubber gloves and his ski mask. He tugged the sliding glass door to the side until the hook-shaped lock mechanism caught on its bar, then slid his knife under the strip of aluminum frame that protected the lock and made it waterproof, bent it outward, inserted the blade to lift the hook from its bar, and folded the knife and put it away.

He knew that he would have to be very quiet on the stairs, or she would hear him. He took the gun out of his pocket and held it as he climbed. He reached the upper floor and listened. He heard what seemed to be the soundtrack of an old movie. He followed it to the lighted room at the end of the hall, and peered in.

She was lying on the bed wearing a business suit with a skirt and a little jacket. She had obviously fallen asleep fully dressed with the television on. On the screen was a black-and-white movie from the thirties, with men wearing tuxedos and women in evening gowns shouting dialogue at each other in a room that had a set of huge double doors flanked by pillars and pedestals.

Hobart kicked the bed to shake her, and watched her wake up. She blinked her eyes, raised her head a few inches, and squinted at the television. Hobart could see she was a very pretty woman, with dark shoulder-length hair and a smooth, light complexion and big hazel eyes. She looked childlike this way, in the process of remembering why she was lying on top of the bedspread in a suit. Whatever she was remembering, it didn't seem to please her.

She sat up, turned toward the nightstand to reach for the remote control, and saw him. She gasped, and Hobart saw her change the direction of her movement to reach lower than the remote control.

"If you reach for a gun, you're dead," he said.

Her hand stopped moving and her body stiffened with alarm. "I—no." Her voice was scratchy from sleep. She was terrified, looking up at him with disbelief. After a couple of seconds, she added, "It's the phone."

Hobart stepped into the room and stood beside the bed. He could see that what she had been reaching for wasn't a drawer. It was just a shelf, and it *did* have a telephone on it. He was relieved because he hadn't wanted to kill her. "I see," he said. "That's not a good idea, either."

"What . . . what do you want? My purse is on the dresser."

"I'm here to talk. If you cooperate, I'll leave and you'll be alive. If you don't, I can kill you in a second. Do you understand?" He was ready for her to begin screaming. He had to remember not to kill her when he silenced her.

"I understand," she said calmly. "I want to be alive."

His right hand shot out and slapped her across the face. Her head bounced to the side and hit the headboard, and a line of bright blood began to run from the corner of her lip. He had needed to hit her. She had begun to manipulate him by being agreeable, and it had made her feel less frightened. He needed her fear. It had to be complete, a fear of his unpredictability and craziness. He said, "You're living from second to second. Don't plan, don't think you know what I want until I say it." Her cheek was already reddened where he had hit her, and she held her hand over it as she stared at him with wide, teary eyes. Hobart decided that was sufficient for now.

"I want to know what got your husband killed."

"I don't know."

Hobart raised his gun with his left hand and aimed it at her head. "Your husband had something, some piece of information that a powerful man thought he shouldn't have. The man wanted it. Your husband may have handed over a copy and thought that ended things. If he did, I'm positive that he didn't give up the only copy."

"I never heard anything like that. He never said anything."

"And you didn't look for it? Your husband gets shot, and you don't even look for what got him killed?"

"No."

"Take off your clothes."

"Oh, no. Please." She looked sick, horrified.

He gave her a quick backhand, then aimed the gun at her again. This time he cocked the hammer with his thumb.

She swung her legs off the bed, stood and undressed quickly, like a woman in a hurry to get into the shower. Then she stood perfectly still, not looking at him, but at the floor.

Hobart stayed on the other side of the bed, waiting for a sign that her feelings of humiliation and vulnerability and fear had become unbearable. As he watched, her knees began to lose their stiffness. One of them began to tremble. She began to cry, and her hands moved to cover herself.

He said quietly, "Can't you see the difference between us? If you could keep the information away from me, what would you even do with it? Nothing. The man who wants the information your husband had is powerful. You're not strong enough to talk to him and make him leave you alive. I can use it. I can make the man who had your husband killed pay a price. You can't do anything."

"I don't have anything."

"Don't say that. I can do anything I want to you—make you hurt, destroy your face, kill you—whatever occurs to me. If you don't have anything, you have nothing to trade that will make me leave you alone."

She mumbled something, too low to understand.

"What?"

"My husband was cheating on me."

Hobart was surprised that he understood. "You mean he wouldn't tell you if he had something going because you were breaking up?"

"I mean he was fooling me, keeping things from me—big things, lots of them—and what you want might have been one of them. I only found out about the cheating today. No, that was yesterday, now. I don't know if we were breaking up or not. All I know is he kept secrets."

Hobart stared at her. He had thought that by this point she would have given him the paper that would make him rich. He had certainly done enough to scare her, to make her feel frightened and helpless. Now he felt lost, off balance. He needed to go away and think before he did anything irreversible. Above all, he had to regain control. "What the fuck are you thinking? Do you think I care about this? I can tell you that having me come for a visit is about the worst thing that can happen to a woman like you." He took a step toward the end of the bed.

She half-crouched, shocked and afraid. "Please," she said. "Don't. Don't do this."

"If you'd given me what I came for, I'd be gone now."

"It didn't occur to me that there was any such thing until you asked for it. I haven't had time to think."

"I'll give you lots of time to think about what it is and where it might be. Turn around, very slowly and carefully. You're going to make very slow, deliberate moves. You're going to describe to me what you're doing. If you make a mistake, or move too quickly, I'm going to have to assume you're reaching for a gun. I know your husband had lots of them around. If I think for even a second that you're doing that, I'll shoot you dead. Do you hear?"

"Yes."

"Then I want you to get dressed, right now."

She was wary. "What do you want me to wear?"

He could hear in her voice a kind of surprise, mixed with the terror he had been trying to instill in her.

She desperately wanted to be dressed, hated the vulnerability and humiliation of being naked in front of a stranger, and hoped that getting dressed meant the danger of rape was passing. But she also had wildly contradictory theories—that this was the worst sign possible, because it meant he was going to kill her, or that he merely had some fantasy about taking a partially dressed woman, or that he was a sadist who got his victims to hope, and took pleasure in taking away the hope.

"A pair of jeans, a pullover shirt of some kind, a pair of sandals."

She bent to the floor and picked up the underwear and bra she had just taken off, and put them on. "I'm going to the closet for the jeans." She stepped to the closet, took a pair of jeans from a hanger, set the hanger on the bed, and stepped into the jeans. "I'm going to the dresser for a top."

Hobart knew she must be thinking about the places where the guns were kept, trying to judge the angles to tell whether she could pick up a gun, turn, and fire before he could pull a trigger. She had to be thinking about that. He stepped to the side quickly to change his view and test her, and she simply stopped. She stood perfectly still with both hands held out in front of her with the fingers spread so he could see she wasn't holding anything. She remained there, her eyes staring at the dresser in front of her.

"All right," he said. "Keep going."

She reached into the drawer and took out a thin red pullover top with long sleeves. She slipped it on over her head. "I'm going back to the closet for the sandals." She walked to the closet, stepped into a pair of sandals, and waited.

"Okay," he said. "Come with me."

"With you? You're taking me away?" She looked shocked.

"I could kill you right now, or I can give you time to remember something that will help me find what I want. For the moment, that sounds better than killing you."

She was terrified. He could tell that until now she had been keeping herself from collapsing by reminding herself that she was in her house. No matter what he did, at some point it would be over, and he would leave. She would still be here, alive in this house. "You're kidnapping me?"

He glared at her, and she stepped around the bed toward him meekly, her shoulders hunched a little to ward off the blow that she expected to feel when she passed near him. He stepped aside and she walked out of the room to the upstairs hallway.

Hobart was still in the room. He pulled up the blinds to look out the window, and the sight confirmed his feeling that too much time had passed. Light was beginning to illuminate the sky in the east, and every second the outlines of objects outside were becoming almost imperceptibly clearer and sharper. If he waited any longer, he would find himself trying to abduct a woman at the start of the morning rush, stuck in traffic with commuters all around him.

He stepped quickly to the staircase and took her arm. "Hurry."

The silence was broken by a sound outside the house. It was a car engine, and Hobart could tell it was slowing down for a turn. Then he saw headlights sweep across the front windows near the bottom of the stairs, brighten, and then go out.

Hobart dragged her back up the stairs, then along the hall to the bedroom at the front of the house. It was a guest bedroom, furnished with a bed, dresser, nightstand and lamp, a comfortable chair. Hobart held her wrist as he went to the front window. He peered between the blinds to look down at the front steps, then jerked her arm, grasped the back of her neck, and forced her to look. "Who is that?"

"It's just one of the guys from the agency."

"What's his name?"

"Dewey Burns."

"What's he doing here at this hour?"

"I don't know. I know he gets up early every day, and he knows I do, too."

Hobart said, "All right." He took out a big lock-blade knife, opened it, and cut the ropes from the blinds. He pushed her down on the bed, dragged her wrists behind her and tied them, then tied the wrists to her ankles. It felt terribly tight, but she didn't dare speak. He slashed two strips of cloth from a pillowcase, stuffed one in her mouth and tied the other behind her head for a gag to keep it there. He put his face right behind her ear and said, "If he comes after me, I'll kill him. If he comes in before I'm gone, I'll kill you both."

She lay still on the bed, and heard his footsteps receding, then the door to the hallway closing.

14

The man was gone. Emily lay on the bed with the cords from the blinds cutting into her wrists and ankles. She bent her knees to bring her ankles closer to relieve the pressure, but the effort quickly tired her legs.

She heard the doorbell again, so loud in the empty house. She tried wriggling her wrists out of the cord, but the man had tied them too tightly. She fought against the cord, but it seemed to tighten the knots. She knew that the next part was not going to feel good, but she began to rock. She rocked until she was sitting on one haunch with her knees bent and her feet beside her.

In this awkward position, the weight of her body kept her knees bent as far as they could be, and let some of the rope go slack. She could reach the knot around her ankles with her fingertips.

The doorbell chimed a third time, and she tried to shout, but the gag was tight, and the scream she had intended was muted to a small squeal through her nose. She worked harder on the knot.

And then she had it. Her legs straightened, the cord lashing out from around the ankles quickly as she pulled.

Emily swung her legs off the bed, ran to the door, then side-stepped quickly down the stairs to the front door. She kicked it to let Dewey know she was in here. She turned away from the door and tried to turn the knob. She was barely able to reach it with her hands tied behind her. She strained to turn it and, after a couple of tries, succeeded.

Dewey pushed the door inward.

"Emily!" He pulled the gag down so it was like a scarf around her neck, and she leaned to spit the cloth out on the floor. He was behind her, untying her wrists. "What happened? Who did this?"

"A man. I didn't know him. I woke up and he was there in my bedroom. He had a gun, and a ski mask. He was trying to kidnap me, but you got here." As she spoke, she felt as though she were conjuring the man, and her words might bring him back. She pushed herself away from Dewey and stepped cautiously to the entrance to the living room, looking for a place where the man might still be hiding.

Dewey had his cell phone out, and he was dialing. "My name is Dewey Burns. I'm going to put Mrs. Emily Kramer on. She's been assaulted by a man with a gun and ski mask at 9553 Sunnyland Avenue in Van Nuys. The man just left. I'll let her describe him." He put the phone in Emily's hand, pulled a gun out of a holster under his coat, and slipped past her to the big sliding door in the living room. He slid it open and moved outside, the gun held ready in his hand.

Emily said, "Hello?"

"Yes, ma'am." The woman's voice was distant, as though she were talking into a speakerphone. "Officers are on their way, but right now you need to give me a description."

"He was about six feet tall, maybe one eighty or so. He was muscular, but not really big. He wore a ski mask, but I could see he was white, with blue eyes."

"Hair color?"

"I couldn't see it."

"What else was he wearing?"

"A jacket that was blue, like a windbreaker, nylon. It made a sound like a whisper when he moved fast. Black jeans. Not blue, black. And a dark blue shirt."

"Did he wear glasses?"

"No."

"Did you notice his shoes?"

"They were black leather, with rubber soles."

"Was there anything else that was distinctive about him?"

"He had a gun. It was big, an automatic. Kind of a dull gray color."

"Did he hurt you?"

"He hit me a couple of times with his hand, but I think I'm okay."

"Was there a sexual assault?"

"Not exactly." Emily looked for Dewey Burns, feeling embarrassed to talk in front of him, then realizing she was being ridiculous. "He made me take my clothes off, but he didn't do anything to me. I think he was just trying to make me scared and keep me from making trouble. He didn't—you know—touch me that way."

She saw Dewey Burns slip in through the sliding door again. Something began to work in her mind; an idea began to form. Dewey Burns met her gaze, shrugged, and shook his head to tell her that the man was gone.

The woman said, "Can you give me your full name, please?"

"Emily Jean Kramer, with a K."

"That's K-R-A-M-E-R."

"Yes."

"And the address is 9553 Sunnyland Avenue in Van Nuys."

"Yes."

"Your phone number?"

She gave the woman the information she asked for and stood waiting in the foyer while Dewey went from room to room with his gun in his hand checking doors and windows. He went into the kitchen, turned toward her with the dim predawn glow behind him, and the idea that had been forming in Emily's mind suddenly became clear. She said, "Miss, please tell the officers the man seems to be gone, and my friend is here with me. I've got to go now." She disconnected the call and walked into the kitchen. She watched Dewey Burns as she walked, never moving her eyes from him as he tested the back door, then went to the door of the laundry room to turn on the light, then came back.

He saw that there was something odd about the way she was staring at him. "What?"

"I see it now."

"What do you mean? Who?"

"You. Just now when I was on the phone and I was so scared and confused that I must have been half crazy, I saw you come in from outside, and I thought I was having a hallucination. When you pushed that sliding door open and kind of leaned to the side to close it after you were in, it was just like seeing Phil do it. It was exactly like him. You move just like him."

Dewey avoided her stare, and appeared to ignore what she was saying. He stepped past her into the dining room, but she followed. "Maybe it was because you held me when you came in and untied me, and it felt familiar. At first I thought it was just that you were both big and tall, but it wasn't just that, was it? You're his son."

He showed no reaction, no surprise or denial. He kept moving, checking the French doors that led from the dining room into the garden.

110

She said, "I don't know why I never noticed, it's so obvious to me now. Maybe even letting myself notice a slight resemblance would have been too dangerous. It would have made me think of the possibility that he was with other women."

He stood still. "Are you expecting me to say whether you're right or wrong?"

"I'm sorry, Dewey. No, I'm not. I just realized the truth, and I blurted it out because—I don't know. I've just been through something horrible, and I wasn't thinking at all, and then looked at you and I knew, and I said it. I honestly never knew until yesterday afternoon that Phil hadn't been faithful."

She sat down at the kitchen table. After a moment she realized that she was shivering. Dewey sat down across from her and put his hand on hers. "Can you tell me what happened to you?"

"He scared me. He hit me a couple of times, and I thought he was going to rape me. But what he wants is some kind of information. He thinks Phil had some information—maybe papers or something—that some powerful man wants. He thought I would know about it and he could scare me or hurt me enough so I would give it to him. And all this time, I've been trying every day to find something like that—anything that would explain why Phil isn't here with me." She paused, then looked into Dewey's eyes.

"I don't know what it is," he said. "He didn't confide in me. All we had was that one secret."

They could both hear the sound of the police cars moving fast up the street, then stopping. There were a couple of door slams, then the noise of the police radios.

15

Ted Forrest stood at the eighteenth tee and adjusted the brim of his cap to shade his eyes as he stared at the long strip of deep green fairway. He had played this course as a child. He knew the five hundred and sixty yards, the dogleg to the right that began about two hundred and fifty yards out, and the stand of tall eucalyptus trees that made a straight drive to the right across the curve an illusion. He knew he must try to place the ball in the center of the fairway as far out as possible so he would be able to see the green for his second shot. All day he had noticed the fact that there wasn't much roll on the fairway because the liberal watering had caused a lush growth of grass.

Forrest planted his feet, riveted his eyes on the ball, and began his backswing. At the top of it, his left arm was straight and his hands in a firm, comfortable grip. Then he swung. There was his fluid hip motion, and he caught a glimpse of the perfect silver whip-flash of the shaft coming around. The clean clop when the head hit made the ball whistle off straight into the distance like something fired from a launcher.

Forrest didn't really have to look because he could tell from the feel and the sound that the ball was on its way to the spot he had chosen, but he watched because he loved the sight. The trajectory was low, straight and accurate, the ball retaining its momentum for second after second, the air finally slowing it enough to make it drop. He had been right about the roll. The ball bounced once, then dribbled and rolled a short distance. But he could tell it had cleared the eucalyptus woods.

"Perfect," Cameron Powers said. "We might as well pay you now."

Forrest held out his hand. "I'm perfectly willing to save you the trouble of paying me in front of the club, if you'd prefer to give me this hole."

"Very kind," Dave Collier said. "But paying gambling losses in public builds a reputation as a good sport and a gentleman. So go fuck yourself."

"Said like a true sport and gentleman. Good luck with that reputation." Forrest turned to the others in the foursome. "Anyone else want to take advantage of my thoughtful offer? You won't even have to humiliate yourselves by teeing off."

Owen Rowland said, "Thank you, but no."

Cameron Powers merely shook his head without speaking because Collier was taking a practice swing. They all watched in silence as he smacked the ball and it flew with perverse intelligence straight to the woods, caromed off a tall tree to the ground, and caused a small explosion of dry eucalyptus leaves and shredded bark. His companions guffawed, but he said, "What? That was the tree I was aiming at."

The others took their turns. No drive was as good as Forrest's or as bad as Collier's. This was as it had been all morning, and as it had been for most of the past forty years. It was always Ted Forrest who hit the best drive, or, when they were in high school together, threw

113

the pass for the touchdown, or won the race. It was the natural order of things. The others competed hard, but when one of them won, there was always the same agreement among them that it was an oddity, that the story of the game wasn't what had worked for the winner, but what had kept Ted Forrest from winning.

The four friends were nearly the same age—all in the last few seasons of their prime. They had already turned fifty, but still looked like hard-worn forty, and each of them felt the poignancy of these games they played together, but expressed it only in jibes and self-deprecating humor. They had all been born to the class who found open sincerity between men to be in poor taste except on the battlefield or in a hospital, but somehow jokes about age had come up more than once in this game, and had dampened some of the group's exuberance.

Forrest walked with Cameron Powers for their second shot. The Los Ochos Club was one of the old-style private courses where golf carts where not permitted. The members whose physical infirmities or moral laxity kept them from carrying their clubs could hire caddies at the pro shop, but the four friends never did. It was partly because they were all vain about fitness, but partly because the presence of another person would have violated the exclusivity of the foursome, and inhibited conversation. They carried their own clubs, just as they sailed their own boats in the summer and carried their own skis in the winter.

They all worked hard, although none of the four had ever performed services for money. When they spoke of work, it was understood that they meant some form of regular practice to improve their skills or their fitness. Cameron Powers said, "You've been working on your drive."

"That's right," said Forrest. "I've been working with Dolan, the new pro. I figure we've reached the top of the mountain. We joke about age, but it's going to start being a factor. Strength and flexibility decline. Eventually even stamina becomes a problem. So from here on, it's all going to be about technique. Whoever goes into middle age with the best technique is going to be the one to beat."

"Goes into middle age? Aren't we middle-aged now?"

Forrest looked at Powers with an expression of exaggerated concern, moving his eyes from Powers's golf shoes up his pressed pants, lingering for a second at the way his knitted golf shirt stretched at his belt line, and up to his forehead. "I guess you are. Sorry, buddy."

"Come on. I mean we're over fifty. If I remember, you turned fifty-two last month. In fact, didn't fifty used to be the end of middle age?"

"Yep. We're practically dead."

"I'm not tying to depress you, but hell, Ted. Those of us who don't have technique by now are just going to have to accept the news that we missed it."

"Suit yourself," Forrest said. "I'm fighting it."

"No, I meant I already have the perfect technique," Powers said. "I was just feeling bad for you."

"We'll have to see whether that's justified, or it's just stray voltage in your ancient brain." They arrived at the part of the fairway where their balls lay. Forrest's drive had been at least fifty yards farther. They selected their clubs for their second shots and stood patiently while the other players went first.

When it was his turn, Forrest made the green in two. Powers hit a sand trap to the left of the green, topped the ball with his wedge shot and sailed it over the green into the rough beyond. Rowland's cautious play got him on the green in four and a short putt put him in second place to Forrest's birdie four.

Afterward, the four men walked to the clubhouse and had lunch together. A membership in Los Ochos was now officially two hundred and fifty thousand dollars, but it was whispered that the going price had recently gone to a million, because the bylaws required that a new member be nominated by one member and seconded by two. There were rumored to be some unfortunates who had begun to make a business out of the nominations so they could remain solvent until some business embarrassment reversed itself. The foursome didn't especially care about the scandal because they didn't associate often with any of the newer members, and they didn't care about price because they had all been enrolled at birth. The club had been constructed on land donated by the great-grandfathers of Owen Rowland and Ted Forrest, and the older fake-adobe part of the club-house had been built by a consortium of founding members, including a few named Powers and Collier.

When the lunch was finished, the three losers made a show of giving Ted Forrest their long-standing hundred-dollar bets. As always, the winner signed the lunch bill to celebrate, so with the bar charges and tips, the four went to the parking lot about even. Forrest loaded his clubs into his BMW, waved at the others, and drove toward home.

In the ten miles from the club to his house, he passed through several stretches of land that his family cooperative still owned. The land was mostly fallow fields now, with only a couple of the larger properties occupied by caretakers, and used for horse pasture or shooting. Now only the quail and deer came to harvest the wild descendant plants that had once been crops. When Forrest was a teenager, he used to cultivate small plots of high-quality marijuana on remote parts of the parcels.

He would have had a difficult time saying what was growing on any of the Forrest properties now; before his marijuana crops, it had been at least forty years since anything had been planted on any of them.

Fidelity

Two generations ago, the family's farmland had been permanently allotted thousands of acre-feet of federal water per year from the Colorado River projects. Over the decades, the water had become much too valuable to pipe in and pour over rice, hops, and barley that nobody could sell for a profit anymore. The Forrest family business was selling federal water, and each year business had gotten better. The coast of California from Mexico to Oregon was populated, the Los Angeles basin was full, and the houses just kept going up, farther and farther inland toward Las Vegas. All the water for those extra people had to be bought on the open market.

He reached the gate at the end of his long driveway, pressed the button on the opener in his car to make the gate slide out of the way, and then pressed it again to close it when he had driven through. The house was built on what used to be a ranch bought from a family called Hardin. That had given Forrest's wife Caroline an excuse to call the place Hardinfield. Seeing the artificially aged bronze sign on the gate's ornamental pillar always made his stomach tighten.

Forrest had been forced to tolerate Caroline and her pretensions for so many years that most of the time he could barely remember how things had been when he had met her. She had been seventeen and he had been thirty. He could just bring together the sight and feeling by conscious effort now because his memory had been dimmed by years of attempts to keep from looking at her, even when he was talking to her.

He remembered the moment. It was a party in the afternoon at the Sheffield family's winery. The sun had the peculiar golden quality it took on in the late afternoon sometimes in Napa. She had been a classmate of one of the Sheffields at the Moorhead School—was it Mary Ellen or Jennifer? There had been about five or six of them that afternoon, all in light summer dresses that made them look like girls in a French Impressionist painting. He had not scouted Caroline. She had simply held the center of the group, and he couldn't look at any of them without following their eyes to her. She had been beautiful that summer. Now he knew that it was because beauty was one of the attributes of the young, only imputed to older people retroactively by an act of the imagination. After about ten minutes, during part of which he had gone to get a fresh glass of wine from one of the roving waiters, and listened to Collier tell a joke badly, he had decided he would meet Caroline Pacquette.

Hundreds of times since then he had strained to reproduce the logic of that moment: *First I saw her looks and liveliness, then I listened to her voice and found the sound of it pleasant, and then I thought—But what did I think?* There was no way to reclaim it now. He was not thirty and she was not seventeen, and so the eye and what it saw were both gone beyond retrieval.

She had changed. He'd had some suspicion at the time that she was desirable partly because she was so young. At her age she was sure to be sweet-tempered and sincere, and if she was at the Moorhead School she was certainly smart enough to learn: She and Mary Ellen Sheffield had been admitted, but Don Sheffield and Ted Forrest had been turned down many years earlier. She was unspoiled. That was the word he had been searching for—she had not been ruined by cynicism and selfishness, like most of the women his age. By claiming her now, he could shield her from the rejection and disappointment that ruined college-age women, and allow her naturally to become the perfect wife.

He watched surreptitiously until she and Mary Ellen Sheffield were on their way across the lawn, made sure his path intersected with theirs, and forced Mary Ellen to introduce him. Now it seemed only moments until they had married, but it had taken about four years for her to reach the socially acceptable age. By then she was nearly finished with college.

It was the most egregious case of marrying under false pretenses that he had ever heard of. Everyone had assumed, because she was a Pacquette, that she would bring significant assets to the merger. The appearance was deceiving, and that deception, he was sure now, was the root of the problem. The Pacquettes had managed to decline very slowly, without letting the change be visible. Instead of selling the plots of land along the Sacramento River or the big old house in San Francisco, which would have caused talk, they had mortgaged their properties one at a time, so that year by year, the big holdings that had been owned outright a hundred years ago were hollowed out by debt. The only reason Caroline could attend the Moorhead School and Princeton was that the house where she had grown up was gradually converted to a series of tuition payments.

Even at the age of seventeen, Caroline was acutely aware of the financial disaster she lived in. For at least a generation, the Pacquettes had been living in a kind of desperation, essentially burning the furniture to keep people from knowing they couldn't afford firewood. Caroline's parents had taught her to understand the gamble. They were impoverishing themselves at an ever-increasing rate to maintain her access to the most exclusive strata of Central California society. They were decimating their fortune to give her the education, the clothes, and the spending money to maintain a presence among the children of the honestly wealthy. But it was a race, a struggle to make the funds and the credit last until she was settled. The public extravagance required a brutal frugality in private. Later, Ted Forrest had calculated that if Caroline Pacquette had not married a rich man by the age of twenty-three, there would not have been enough assets left to keep up the pretense. She and her family would have had to move out of their ancestral home and slink off to some suburb to look for jobs. As it was, within a few days of returning from their honeymoon in Europe, Ted Forrest learned that a number of bills for their opulent wedding had been re-charged to his accounts by the signature of his new bride.

Caroline won. She detected the vulnerability in Ted Forrest, his sensitivity to her delicate beauty and the air of innocent grace that she had been cultivating under her mother's coaching since she could first walk and talk. Her father had retained Dun & Bradstreet to do a work-up on Ted's financial health only a few months after they met, and did some investigating of his own, and so did his wife. They spoke quietly to people who were close to the Forrests and would know of any scandals in the family or any vices of Ted's that would make him a poor prospect for future support.

As soon as the inquiries were completed, Caroline began her campaign. Forrest supposed that her decision to choose him, when she must have met hundreds of single men between her seventeenth year and her twenty-first, was a kind of love at first sight. She clearly had marriage in mind from the outset, and she accomplished it in the simplest and most businesslike way.

She told a couple of friends—including Don Sheffield's sister, after placing them under vows of secrecy—that she had a crush on Ted Forrest that made her feel weak when he came near. Then she contrived to be where he was. As soon as they'd had a proper date or two, she made sure that the next date culminated in sex. This she did in a particularly opportunistic way. He had asked her to dinner at a restaurant in Sonoma. When he picked her up, she made it clear to him that she was planning to spend the night at a friend's house— Owen Rowland's cousin Emma, if he remembered right—and wasn't expected home. At dinner she had asked, "Wouldn't it be fun if this date didn't have to end at all?" He rented a hotel room and then suggested she tell Emma by phone that she couldn't make it.

Caroline handled him expertly. She managed to give the impression that even mild intimacy was not an event that had occurred often in her life. She had to convey that in sharing a room with him she was sacrificing her own scruples and risking her own reputation and interests out of extreme devotion to his. Then, during and after the event, she had to flatter him into believing that he had changed her view of the practice, and that she was eager to have the event repeated frequently for the rest of her life, thus qualifying herself as the ideal wife. That was more than she could communicate in a single night. It took a few similar evenings for her to persuade him, but she did.

Almost immediately after the wedding, Caroline became less attentive to Forrest, and spent more of her time being Mrs. Forrest, the beneficiary of Forrest's money and position. She spent her early mornings in pajamas at the computer e-mailing friends in the East and looking for advertisements for items that she would later go out to buy in person. Then she exercised. Her lunch times and afternoons were for her friends—the same six or seven who had been with her the day he met her at Sheffield's and a couple of others—and her evenings were for him to escort her to dinners, plays, and parties. Increasingly, her nights were spent going to sleep early and alone to keep up her strength for the next day's repetition of her routines. By the end of the third year, the admiration and desire for him that she had expressed so recently was already gone.

When he tried to be affectionate, her indifference made his attempts painful. When he tried asking about her lack of interest in him, she turned defensive. To bring up the deterioration of their relations was unspeakably indelicate and insensitive to her feelings. To imply that *she* was responsible was unfair and cruel. She hadn't said she had changed her feelings about him, so how could he say it was her fault? His questioning was what was causing their problems—his implied criticisms had made her feel under scrutiny, and made sex unbearable.

He still had a naïve belief that she was sincere, and so he kept trying for a long time. He managed to get her to relent and sleep with him once every month or two, and kept himself going by assuring himself that their relationship was improving and the marriage was preserved. But the truth was that it was mummified, retained in a desiccated state with its guts removed. He was sure it probably looked about the same from the outside: Caroline was an expert in conveying to the rest of the world that all was well. She had been doing it all her life.

Forrest never found any indication that Caroline was engaged in relationships with other men, and he looked hard for one. Like many women who were incapable of conducting marriages, she was excessively warm in greeting male friends, but he could not detect any indication that she did worse than that. She was very demonstrative with her female friends, too, but she had never seemed to be sexually interested in women. And she always had lots of pets, and spoke to every one of them with more affection than she showed when she spoke to him. She would turn away from him so he wouldn't spoil her makeup, and then kneel to kiss a dog or cat on the mouth.

He had no choice but to pursue other women, and she never seemed to notice. Sometimes he thought she was simply retaliating: What greater proof of his insignificance than that she didn't even notice that he had moved on? At other times he thought she was operating according to obscure plans of her own—perhaps a relationship that was carried on in safety at times when he was out trying to avoid her attention.

Fidelity

They held each other this way. It was to his advantage and to hers that they never let any of the truth become overt and undeniable. For her a divorce would be a demotion, either a reversion to the status of her genteel but déclassé family, or the half-life of an aging woman who had some money that wasn't really hers, a person who could still use the Forrest name, but who was no longer welcome at any of the Forrest estates, and whom the family's relatives and friends would consider an embarrassment, someone to be forgotten. For Ted Forrest, a divorce would be financially crippling, and would give the same relatives who would ostracize Caroline an excuse to patronize him. For years any woman he cared to date would be scrutinized as *the one*—the woman whom Caroline must have caught fornicating with Ted Forrest.

He and Caroline lived in Hardinfield but avoided each other as much as possible. They gave the servants nothing tangible to repeat. They gave their friends no hint that when they went home together after a party, they might not speak again until a day or two had passed, and there was some practical reason to talk.

Ted Forrest had made a big mistake once, but he had managed to salvage things and keep Caroline from knowing about it. That was eight years ago, and he had survived. He had held his head high and behaved as though nothing was bothering him, and nobody had ever suspected he was in agony. He had been the same old Ted Forrest day after day, a man who would listen to a friend's troubles as though he had none of his own, or laugh at a joke about himself.

But there was one part of the mistake that he had not been able to overcome with a simple reassertion of self-control, and that was the private detective, Philip Kramer. Forrest had made a point of doing everything in the most cautious and premeditated way, so that none of his trouble would stick to him or come back later. Hiring the detective had been the first example of his caution. Normally he would never have considered hiring such a person without a recommendation from someone whose judgment he trusted. Usually, he would have had one of his attorneys make inquiries and then act as his go-between in dealing with the detective. Not this time. He had driven down to Los Angeles, chosen a private investigator out of the phone directory, and called him. He had decided in advance to choose one who had his own agency, whose ad said he had been in business for over ten years, and gave a license number. That had led him to Philip Kramer. He met Kramer in his office, told him the story he had constructed, and gave him an advance payment in cash. That day had set off such a monstrous set of surprises that it was sometimes difficult to remember that it was all done for love. All Ted Forrest had ever suffered had been for love.

Now he stopped his car at the top of the driveway where it became a circle, then pulled ahead so he wouldn't block the front entrance. He didn't mind. The extra walk would give him another half minute before he had to face the wall of resentment that Caroline kept between them.

Forrest opened his trunk, took out his golf bag, slung it over his shoulder and walked under the high portico, through the courtyard to the big front doors. Caroline hated it when he came in the front way after golf. She was convinced that he would bring pieces of grass and leaves and burrs into the formal foyer, even though he wasn't wearing his golf shoes, and hadn't been on the course for three hours.

He opened the door and walked in. The marble floor shone so the reflection brought a blinding replica of the chandelier into his eyes at this angle. He heard a loud sigh.

She was standing ahead and to his left in the entrance to the library. "Ted! How many times have I asked you to come in the other way?"

"Not sure. It's my house and I can drive cattle through it if I want to, so I don't pay much attention."

"No, you sure don't. I just had that floor polished."

"Then have somebody polish it again, or don't. I haven't brought anything alive in."

"I'm having a dinner party in two hours, remember?"

"No, actually, I didn't. Remind me who this one is for?"

"It's the party for the donors to the chamber orchestra," she said. "Is it coming back, sounding familiar?"

"Vaguely," he said. "I'm sure you have lots to do, so I'll head up to the shower." He climbed the stairs, and she had the sense to stay down there and do whatever it was that a woman with a half dozen servants and another half dozen caterers needed to do.

He reached the top of the stairs and one of his moments—attacks, really—took him. He felt slightly dizzy and weak, looked down at the floor to steady himself, and realized he had been disoriented because there were tears in his eyes. He went into the master suite, locked the door, and set his clubs in the closet. He took a cell phone out of his golf bag, went into the bathroom, locked that door, too, and turned on the shower.

He dialed a number that wasn't in the telephone's memory. "Baby? It's me. I just had to hear your voice. I just got back from the club, and the horror of this place got to me. God, it's hard to be here without you. I'm about love. I've never been about anything but love."

16

Emily Kramer spent the whole morning repeating the story of her night to the first police officers to arrive, then to others. From nine o'clock on, there were cops all over the house spreading black dust on walls, woodwork, doorknobs, and glass. They gave special attention to the windows because glass held fingerprints better than any other surface.

She spent most of the time with a policewoman about her own age. Emily could tell that she was the one who always had to do the sexual-assault interviews, because she had developed a practiced motherly manner. The policewoman asked Emily "Did he—" questions that didn't apply to the events of the night, but which reminded Emily that there were a great many things that could have happened and might have if the man had managed to get her to some lonely spot outside town.

During the early afternoon, Dewey Burns left and Ray Hall took his place. The cops didn't see Ray Hall as a family friend coming to lend support, so much as another source to interview. Two of them took him into the den just off the living room and asked him a lot of questions. Now and then when she was looking in that direction, she would see him. Their eyes would meet and stay locked for a moment, but then one of them would turn away. She knew that was best because if one of the cops thought they were behaving oddly, then dealing with the police would become difficult. She was still a woman whose husband had been shot to death in the middle of the night in a place where he had no known business. Emily knew that any male friend of the widow was always a convenient suspect.

In the afternoon, the cops all packed up and left Emily and Ray alone. She said, "Thanks for coming over. It was good to see one friendly face."

"I'm sorry I just left you here last night, and didn't stay around to be sure you were safe. I've been feeling terrible since I heard."

"Don't be silly. For one thing, I told you to leave me. For another, the man didn't arrive until something like four in the morning. You would have had to sit outside all night."

"At least Dewey showed up."

"He probably saved my life. What am I being uncertain about? Not probably—*did* save my life. It was just a lucky accident, too. He had gone to the office early and found—"

"He told me," Hall said. "I went over there after he called me. The guy who broke in doesn't seem to have messed anything up but the doors, but he definitely searched the place. We're going to have to invest in some steel fire doors and steel frames. Maybe we can get the landlord to chip in."

"Were the police there?"

"Yeah. They found out first. A couple of them were the same ones you saw here. They're trying to confirm it was the same guy. I don't think anybody doubts it."

"He didn't say he had broken into the office, but he's looking for something Phil had, and I suppose now he's been to the two most obvious places to find it," she said.

Ray said carefully, "I don't want to scare you, Emily, but since he didn't find it, we've—"

"I know. He'll come back for me."

"Maybe just to search the house, but . . ." He shrugged.

"What do you think I should do?"

"We've been trying to work that out while you were with the cops. You and I can go through the house now and collect anything that you care much about—jewelry, papers, and so on. Then you sleep somewhere else—a different place each night. Tonight it can be my place, and Dewey and Billy will stay here and take turns keeping watch. Then you go to Dewey's, and Billy and I stay here."

"You're trying to ambush the man?"

"I don't have very high hopes that the cops will chase him down if they haven't already. Maybe he left a print, and it will be one they've seen before. But the only thing we can do is sit where we know he'll be and wait for him to show up."

"I don't know, Ray. He's dangerous, probably crazy. He got off on making me feel helpless and powerless. That's not a good sign. He's not exactly logical, either. He thinks there's something Phil had that would be worth a lot of money to him, but he made it clear he doesn't know what it is. I don't think you guys should do this."

"What are you worried about?"

"What else? That he'll kill one of you."

"And *we're* worried that he'll kill *you.*"

Emily shook her head. "Let's think about this clearly."

"Meaning what?"

"All I've wanted since Phil died was just to find out why this happened to him. Now I know most of it. Phil had this item—this piece

128

of information—about some powerful man. Maybe Phil knew what he had, or maybe he didn't, but the man thought he did. The man paid someone to lie in wait for Phil and kill him on the street."

"You're satisfied with that?"

"Of course not. But it's a lot more than I knew yesterday. It might be all we're ever going to know."

"It's an opportunity," Ray said. "It gives us a lead—something to look for—and a couple of places to look. It's our first breakthrough."

"It's the opposite. It gives us a way out of this. We have scary people out looking for this information, and we even know roughly what it is. It's something this man thinks he can use to get money, either from the powerful man or from the man's enemies. Don't you see? It's just incriminating stuff about somebody we don't care about. If he paid to have Phil murdered, he's no friend of mine. What we know for sure is that it's not worth risking our lives to protect him."

"You're suggesting we do nothing?"

"What if we did? What if I just take what I want from this house and walk away from it? Then the man who was here last night could sneak in and look for the information until he finds it. Then he can do whatever he wants with it. Is this powerful man who killed Phil worth dying for?"

"No, but *you* are."

"But I just told you—"

"You were the one who wanted to think about this clearly, so think. What if we *do* walk away?"

"Then everybody goes away happy but the man who had Phil murdered."

"The other man—the intruder in the ski mask—has already searched the agency office. He didn't find anything, so he came here to your house. Suppose we abandon the house and let him tear it apart searching for whatever Phil hid. And the office, too. What if he looks everywhere and doesn't find it?"

"I think he *will* find it," Emily said.

"You and I have both been searching for over a week, looking for anything that might explain what happened. I didn't find anything incriminating about a powerful man. Did you?"

"I didn't know what to look for. *He* knows the name of the man."

"We knew Phil, and we had access to every hiding place."

"All right," she said. "Say he searches everywhere, and doesn't find any more than we did. Then what? He realizes it's a lost cause and goes away."

"But that isn't what he did. He didn't come during the day, when you would be gone, and search the house. He came here at night, when he knew you would be here alone, and put a gun to your head. And he wasn't planning to tie you up and leave you in the guest room when he left. He did that only because Dewey showed up unexpectedly. He was planning to take you with him."

"But—"

"And if we let him search your house for whatever it is and go away without it, we've lost our best chance. Where will he show up next? Wherever you are, as soon as you're alone again."

Emily stared at him for a few seconds. Finally she said, "All right. I'll get a suitcase."

Emily went upstairs to the bedroom. It was hard for her to look at the room. It wasn't a sanctuary now because it was the place where she had been in the greatest danger of her life. It wasn't even a private place anymore, after about ten cops had trooped through, looking at the clothes she had left on the floor when the man had made her take them off, dusting the furniture for prints, crawling around looking for anything that might later prove some suspect had been the intruder.

Fidelity

Emily had an overpowering urge to get out, to never be alone in this house again. But first she needed to collect the things that she couldn't afford to leave behind. She pulled two big suitcases from the bedroom down the hall, opened one on the floor of her bedroom, and began to pack. She filled the first one with clothes, then opened the other one and began to fill it. There were tax returns and credit-card bills and bank statements that he could use to rob her. There were address books and letters that he could use to find her. And when she had brought all of the practical things she could think of, she put in the photo album with pictures of her dead husband and son. And there was still the problem of the locked box bolted to the closet wall behind Phil's clothes. She had thought about the box a hundred times while the man had her cornered in this room.

Emily stepped into the walk-in closet and stumbled over one of the cartons she had left on Phil's side. It was full of shoes that she had been planning to drive to the Goodwill thrift store. Beyond it was the gun safe. She used the combination Phil had told her. It was the house number of his parents' house when she had first met him. The fact that they were gone now—and so was he—made pushing the four numbers feel strange, but the metal door swung open.

Inside was the big Springfield Armory .45 ACP pistol. It looked to her a lot like the gun that the man in the ski mask had pointed at her a few hours ago. She took it out of the box, feeling anxious. She found the catch that released the magazine into her hand, and held the magazine for a few seconds. It was light, just a hollow shell of metal with a spring inside. There were no bullets in it. She replaced the magazine and took the other gun out of the box. This one was a Glock Sub-Compact 9mm pistol. She found the magazine release on that one, too, held her breath, and pushed it. She held the magazine

in her hand. She felt the light emptiness of it, looked down, and realized that tears had formed in her eyes.

If she had managed to get to the back of the closet, opened the
box, and pulled out one of the guns, it would have been empty, and
she would be dead. Every time she had sensed that the man's attention was flagging, every time his eyes strayed from her, she had urged
herself to take the chance. She had accused herself of cowardice. All
along, she had known that as soon as she was alone, she would come,
open the box, and look.

Emily stood in the closet, then realized that something was different. She had not come in here only to find out whether she had
guessed wrong. She had opened the gun safe because the man who
had come into her bedroom in the middle of the night wearing a ski
mask had caused a profound change in her. Before he had appeared,
she had lots of doubts about prudence and paranoia, what was self-
defense and what was murder. She had no doubts at all now.

She reached farther into the gun safe and found a box of 9mm
bullets. She put the Glock pistol and the ammunition into her purse
and slipped the big .45 into her suitcase. Then she stepped to the railing above the staircase and called, "Can you give me a hand with the
suitcases? I'm all set."

17

Ted Forrest had been raised well. His parents had instilled in him the values of the old California upper class. Although he seldom went to chamber concerts, he was one of the orchestra's most generous patrons. He had been to the art gallery in Golden Gate Park in San Francisco exactly twice—once when he was in elementary school and once for a charitable party held there—but there were plaques in the entrance wall and in one of the galleries acknowledging the support of the Theodore and Caroline Forrest Foundation. He also signed checks each year to museums in San Jose, Santa Cruz, and Napa, and two zoos. He helped sponsor annual pageants celebrating the founding of four towns in the central valley that were near family holdings. He occasionally went to those celebrations, partly because he liked the unjustified gaiety. There was always good food, a liberal pouring of local wines, and some kind of fiesta that involved the crowning of a queen. He liked getting a look at the young lady and her court, who were always the most impressive examples of the local livestock, raised on sunshine, exercise, clean air, and fresh vegetables.

Tonight he was forced to spend his charm on the chamber-music lovers. A few of them were bony retired female professors, librarians, and others completely alien to him, but there were also a number of people who were like Ted Forrest. They were men and women of his class who cared little about spending evenings listening to violinists, but felt that not to have an orchestra would leave their reputations for gentility diminished. Collier and Rowland were here with their nearly identical blond wives, who were cousins. Powers and his wife weren't going to make it this time, supposedly because they had a prior engagement. Ted Forrest suspected that it was because Janice Powers couldn't bear the thought of spending an evening so utterly in the power of Caroline Forrest. He had noticed years ago that Jan was usually willing to go places were she and Caroline were on an equal footing and there were enough people so they could avoid each other, but these evenings of Caroline's required Jan to spend too many hours with her face set in a fixed, muscle-cramping smile.

Ted Forrest felt the same way about Caroline's events. He also felt a certain relief that Caroline took such an interest in civic and philanthropic causes, because he knew it reflected well on him and preserved the Forrest family's visibility in the region. Since the family's livelihood depended entirely on the continued favor—or at least tacit approval—of politicians, it was essential to keep projecting the impression of money, influence, and conditional benevolence.

He stood at the head of the giant table in the grand dining room, looked down it at the forty-two faces, and held up his wineglass. "As always, I drink first to our superb musicians, gathered to us from all over the world, to our brilliant and renowned music director, Aaron Mills, and to our tireless, dedicated staff." He sipped the wine to a smattering of applause, but he did not sit down. "No, you're applauding between movements, because I'm not finished. Tonight I also offer a toast to our many volunteers, led by our able president Dr. David Feiniger, and to the generous donors who have supported the orchestra throughout the year. May your enthusiasm never wane." He drank again and the clapping was much louder and more prolonged, as he had known it would be, because they were applauding themselves.

As usual, Ted Forrest had brought glory to himself, with little effort. It was like giving a shake to a tree exploding with blossoms. The petals simply fell around him. The orchestra crowd was easy because they were self-trained never to allow critical thoughts about any praise connected with the institution. They were satisfied with the chamber orchestra because it was an expensive entertainment that gave its patrons the reputation for being high-minded, intelligent, and public-spirited.

White-coated waiters from the catering company that Caroline had selected scuttled around behind the guests at the long table, serving and pouring and then deftly shooting a hand in to withdraw an empty plate here and there. Ted Forrest had an elderly lady from Germany on his left. For the first part of the dinner he addressed to her a great many pleasant observations, but because he hadn't attended any concerts this year, they were vague. He commented mainly about the new chamber-concert facility made by a remodeling of an historic stone mansion a few miles from here, and his approval of music in general. He repeated a couple of comments about the season that he had overheard Caroline make to friends and that for no known reason had stuck in his memory.

It was far too late to ask the lady's name, and he couldn't manage to get her to volunteer it, what her reason for being here could be, or how she felt about anything other than the food, which she ate with enthusiasm. Forrest judged that she was probably an appendage of somebody high in the organization, just as he was, and that she preferred to keep still.

For the second half of the dinner, he turned to his right to speak with the first violinist, Maria Chun. She was very pretty, with long straight black hair that swung when she moved, as though it were heavy. It might have been Forrest's imagination, but he felt sure that she had read his mind, realized what he was thinking, and begun to despise him within the first few seconds of her arrival. Women did tend to make irrevocable judgments of that sort without letting much time elapse or wasting much thought reconsidering. He supposed it was possible that she had spent an entire life dividing her time between playing the violin and evading men over fifty. But Ted Forrest was the host, and he didn't have the luxury of rejecting anyone or refusing to speak with them.

He said, "I've often wondered what you do in the off-season, when there are no concerts."

"Oh, different things," Maria Chun said. "Francisco, the other first violin, serves as a guest concertmaster for the symphony orchestra in Buenos Aires. Some of the others teach master classes in universities. Some go on tour."

"I meant you, specifically. What do you do—give the Stradivarius a rest?"

"It's a Guarnerius." She didn't take him seriously enough to be offended or surprised. "Rest isn't good for it, or for me. I study, practice, and spend time with my husband and kids."

"Oh?' he said. "Tell me about them. How old are your children?"

"Ten and thirteen."

"Are they musicians?"

"Sort of."

"Sort of? You mean we can't expect a next generation of virtuosos?"

"My daughter Simone plays the cello. My son Anthony plays the electric guitar."

"But you're not satisfied. Parents can be pretty tough." Ted Forrest was mystified by his own transgression, as he often was. She had mentioned the husband and kids to keep him from pursuing her. Why did these attempts to fend him off titillate him? He kept trying to learn more, to make his way into her personal life like a voyeur. He had a wife, and he had a girlfriend. He had no time for Maria Chun. What was he after?

"They're great kids," she said. "But neither of them really wants to be a professional musician. And it's getting late to start. Most people who do this are pretty well launched into it by thirteen."

"And what does your husband feel about this? I assume he's a musician, too."

"No." She smiled with an unexpected amusement at the idea, and her smile made Ted Forrest jealous. "My husband is a professional hockey player."

"Really?" Ted Forrest feigned amusement, mixed with a tiny bit of contempt. "What's his name?"

"Gus Kopcynski. He plays for the Los Angeles Kings."

Forrest was stung. He had heard of her husband, and it rankled. "I've heard of him." Her husband was a star, a veteran who scored now and then, but was more famous for his assists and for the sort of body check that sent an opponent into the boards with bone-shaking impact. He was about thirty. He had the body of a fighter and a smile that was no less engaging when the gaps in his front teeth were showing. He was a man whom other men respected, a special man with toughness and world-class skill.

And suddenly Ted Forrest became nothing. He had, at times, attracted women with the very qualities Maria's husband had, but he had never been the equal of her husband, and now he was well past his prime. He sometimes half-admitted to himself that to some women the compelling attraction was his money. Gus Kopcynski might not have the kind of money Ted Forrest had, but he had plenty by now, enough so Forrest's had no attraction for this woman.

The next thing Forrest felt was a grip on his arm—hard, like a pinch. He kept himself from jumping, because he didn't want Maria to see he was startled. Caroline's face was no more than six inches from his ear, between him and Maria Chun. "I'm sorry, Maria, but I've got to borrow Ted for a moment. When I get back, I'd like to introduce you. Will that be okay?"

"Sure. Give me time to tune up, and I'll be set." She was up and walking before Ted could stand.

He smiled and said to the elderly lady on his left, "Excuse me, please," but she didn't seem to hear him.

He followed Caroline through the swinging door into the busy kitchen, past cooks and waiters and busboys and out the back door to the delivery entrance off the driveway. Caroline got a few yards from the house, where there were boxes of supplies piled, but no caterers were visible. She whirled and said, "You've been ignoring Monika Zellin, and she's practically the guest of honor."

"You mean the old lady?"

"Yes, Ted. I mean the old lady. I put her next to you on purpose because I thought I could count on you to be gracious."

"I talked to her for an hour. Half the time she didn't seem to hear me, and the other half she didn't seem to understand English. Who is she, anyway?"

"She's a famous composer, one of the few living women composers of the thirties. She was also a hero in the war."

"Which side?"

"Very funny. When I put you there, I didn't think you'd spend your time chatting with the help."

"You mean Maria Chun?"

"You know I do. Maybe I'm underestimating her. You seemed positively dazzled. Don't embarrass me, Ted. Just don't." She spun and hurried back through the kitchen, and was lost behind a sudden convergence of taller figures in white coats.

Ted Forrest took a step toward the kitchen door, then stopped. It was a perfect opportunity. He walked down the back lawn into the darkness, took out his cell phone, and dialed. He waited through five rings, then heard Hobart's voice. "Yes."

At the sound, Forrest felt an onset of dry-mouthed fear. He wished he hadn't called, but now that the connection had been made, Hobart would see his number on the bill. "Hi," he said as casually as he could. "It's me. Can you talk?"

"It's not a good idea to call me."

"I know, but I wanted to know if it's done. Is it? Do I need to get you the rest of the money?"

"No. I'll tell you when it's done."

"All right. I just didn't want to keep you waiting if it was." It was such a blatant, childish lie that he began to sweat. He could hear Hobart breathing, but Hobart didn't deign to respond.

After a few seconds, Hobart said, "There's nothing about this that needs your attention. No more calls unless you have something urgent and important to tell me. It's an unnecessary risk."

"Since I've already called, can you tell me anything?"

"I've found her. I've seen her. I looked around the office, and I could tell she's trying to keep the agency open. That means she's got people around her most of the time, so it will take longer. I'm working on it. Satisfied?"

"You're taking care of it, though? I don't have to worry?"

"Not as long as you don't draw attention to yourself."

"Okay, then. I'll just wait until I hear from you."

"Do that."

The telephone went dead. Forrest looked at his watch, holding it close to his face so he could decipher the glowing radium dots and lines. It was nine thirty. As he walked back toward the house, he heard distant applause. When it subsided, he heard the high, clear tone of a violin.

He went in through the kitchen to the dining room. The waiters had closed the big oak doors on the far side so they could clear dishes without fear of making noise. Ted Forrest made his way past them toward the door to the foyer, slipped through and quickly closed the door behind him. He walked to the high portal that led to the immense formal living room, stepped in, and stopped with his back to the wall.

The only other person standing was Maria Chun, who was playing a strikingly complicated passage with lots of rapid fingering and the bow bouncing up and down the strings. Her eyes passed across him, but he could tell that they were not seeing him. They were looking inward at some memory of the music she was playing.

Caroline's eyes found him. She was sitting in her usual chair near the back of the room, where she could oversee the proceedings. She had given the seat beside her—his seat—to a woman from the chamber-series patrons' group. He could tell Caroline's eyes had been on the door, waiting for him. They narrowed and she turned away, staring at Maria Chun.

Ted Forrest backed out of the room, and in a moment he was through the foyer and in the library. He went out the French doors to the rose garden. He could see that even the circular part of the drive at the front of the house had cars parked along the edge of it. There were a couple of chauffeurs down near the end of the driveway standing between their big dark-colored cars smoking cigarettes.

Forrest walked up the two-hundred-foot paved path that led to the garage. He decided he liked the sound of Maria Chun's violin wailing and chirping in the distance. Maybe next year he would try to make it to a concert or two. That, of course, would depend to some extent on the state of his truce with Caroline. He wasn't going to want to sit next to her for hours if she was in the avenging-bitch mode she was in tonight.

He kept walking, beginning to enjoy the night air. The garage was far from the house because it had originally been the stable and carriage house, and the Forrests of the time had not wanted odors and horseflies too close. He went in through the side door and the motion detector switched on the light. The high ceiling and painted rough-hewn rafters were all that remained from the carriage-house days, but the garage felt like a link with his family because Caroline had not brought decorators and architects in to embellish or disguise it. He got into his BMW, pressed the remote control to open the garage door, and started the engine. He went out slowly, the engine just above an idle so the sound of it didn't interfere with Maria Chun's recital, and then coasted, letting the natural slope of the driveway build his momentum.

As he passed the two chauffeurs, he gave a friendly wave. He didn't know who either of them worked for, but he approved of servants who knew what they were doing. They had let off their passengers at the front entrance, then parked far down the drive to leave the most desirable spaces for people who had driven themselves. Now they were on their feet watching the house for signs of their employers, and not smoking inside their cars.

He reached the open gate and pulled onto the road, giving his car some gas. The sensation of speed raised his spirits, and he found himself thinking of Powers's wife Jan. At the time of their fling twenty years ago, he had anticipated that he would feel remorse. Powers had been his friend since early childhood, and Janice was practically still a bride at the time. She had barely turned twenty. It was true that he did occasionally feel he owed Powers some guilt. But the surprise was that the strongest and most sincere feeling he had was joy at having Powers's wife. It was a victory over Powers, better than any other kind of victory there was, and he still felt it strongly every time he saw them together.

He had also anticipated the probability that there would be awkwardness between him and Jan after they had been in bed together. Since he and Powers would be friends forever, the awkwardness might be a problem. It didn't turn out to be the sort of problem he had expected. He had been younger then, and not known himself very well yet. The awkwardness was real and it had lasted for two decades so far, but it wasn't exactly unpleasant. Jan had trouble meeting his eyes, and if he touched her hands they would sweat, and she always tried to avoid being alone with him, even for a minute. He found her discomfort interesting, even flattering.

The part he didn't anticipate showed how little imagination he'd had when he was young. It had never occurred to him that being close friends with her husband meant that through the years he would be forced to watch her age. Already she wasn't the beautiful, tempting young bride he had seduced. She was forty and beginning to show a broadening of the hips, a few wrinkles ruining her forehead and upper lip, and a slackening of the skin of her neck.

The girl he remembered was better. Powers had been in New York on some kind of business. Ted Forrest recalled that there was some meeting connected with property that Powers had inherited, some legal papers to sign. In the morning, Forrest watched Caroline drive off toward San Francisco to shop, then made a telephone call to Powers's hotel in New York. Powers was out doing whatever he was there for, but the hotel clerk made it clear he was still registered. Then Forrest drove to Powers's house for a surprise visit to the little woman.

He had a new Corvette. When he pulled up to the house he stopped directly in front of the door so when she opened it she saw the car, a waxed and shining image of speed and freedom. He told her that her husband had asked him to be sure Janice got out of the house while he was away and had some fun. Forrest talked about Powers as he drove her to a restaurant above the ocean at Half Moon Bay. They had a bottle of wine with lunch, and he kept filling her glass as he told funny stories. By then none of the stories included a mention of Powers.

They drove a few miles to another spot he knew that had the best view of the ocean. When they arrived, he extravagantly rented a room on an upper floor with a balcony, so she could see it. And the view really was spectacular. The horizon line of the deep blue Pacific seemed so high it appeared to be over their heads. As they were on the balcony sipping drinks he had made from the minibar, he put his arm around her waist. She gave a slight jump with an almost-silent intake of breath and stiffened a bit. He kept his hand there and waited. He could tell she was thinking, trying to decide what to do, what to say. He gave her ten seconds, then kissed her.

As he thought about that day, the rest of it came back to him. He remembered her saying no a couple of times, feebly. And he remembered rolling over in bed and reaching into the pocket of the pants he'd left on the floor to get the condom, then seeing the shocked, almost-angry expression on her face. "You brought that?" she said. "You knew?"

He said, "I hoped."

After that, she was different—better, really, because she'd had to stop pretending she didn't know that this wasn't an accident. The sex was certainly better—spiteful, selfish, greedy. They stayed as late as they dared. On the ride home she told him that she hated him, and that she would do everything possible to be sure she and her husband never saw him again. But it was a long, long ride home, and by the time he turned to go up the driveway to her house, they were agreeing when they should meet again. It lasted a couple of years, and then it ended, by another agreement, when she was pregnant with her first child.

Ted looked at his watch. He could be sure that Caroline's ordeal would last at least another couple of hours, and probably three. He took out his cell phone and dialed. This time it rang only once.

"Hi," he said. "I escaped."

He could hear the sweet young voice say, "I'm so happy. How long can you stay?"

It was good to hear somebody say things like that again.

18

Jerry Hobart lay on the bed in his hotel room. The lights in the valley below Universal City had come on, and the sky above looked black. He wanted to get back to sleep, but now that Forrest had called him, he couldn't. It wasn't the call, but the wave of deep hatred he had allowed himself to feel for Theodore Forrest that had made him alert and restless, and kept him thinking. Why had Forrest even called—to get Hobart's assurance that he wasn't goofing off? He must know that if Hobart had already killed Mrs. Kramer, he would have let Forrest know he was ready to get paid. Forrest was just calling because he was impatient, and he imagined that his voice would speed things up.

Rich people thought that telling someone to do something was the same as doing it. And Forrest was a member of the class that wasn't used to waiting for things. They didn't wait for anything they wanted to go on sale; they didn't save up for anything; they didn't wait in lines. Rich people had a bizarre, unshakable belief in the magical power of their own neediness.

Hobart had been awake all night rummaging through the detective-agency office, tying up the night watchman, and then scaring the shit out of Mrs. Kramer, and he had not yet caught up on his sleep. He resented the fact that Forrest had cut his rest short.

He had wondered why Forrest would worry so much about this detective in Los Angeles that he wanted him killed. Two hundred thousand for having somebody popped was probably not a problem for a man like Forrest. Very rich people had complicated finances, so it was easy for them to pay out money without having anybody else notice it was missing and wonder where it went. But what would induce a man like Forrest to take the risk? Paying a shooter was a risky way to solve a problem. If Hobart was caught or killed, then police would spend the next few months examining every phone call he had made or received, attempting to figure out the source of every dollar he had. They would look at every credit-card transaction to piece together all of his movements for the past year. They would do their best to make a list of everyone Hobart had seen or talked to in that period. Why would a man who didn't have to take risks accept that one? The only answer Hobart could think of was that Phil Kramer had known something ugly and dangerous about Forrest that he might decide to reveal.

Hobart had assumed that whatever the dirt on Forrest was, it was only in Phil Kramer's head, not hidden in his house or office or something. Otherwise, killing him would be pointless. But now that it was done, suddenly Forrest wanted Phil Kramer's widow killed, too. That changed everything. The information Forrest was worried about couldn't have been destroyed with Phil Kramer. It was still out there. And if it was, then there was no reason why Jerry Hobart couldn't use it for himself.

Hobart's impatience was growing. He needed to find out what the secret was. He already regretted that he had committed himself to finding out, but he had. If Hobart had simply stepped into Mrs. Kramer's bedroom and shot her dead last night, then Hobart would never have a problem. But instead of killing her, he had committed himself to finding out what the hell Theodore Forrest was so anxious to keep secret.

Hobart sat up in bed. When he had broken the lock on the door of the detective agency, he had started a clock. He didn't find the secret there, so he had to go straight to the Kramer house. He had cut the process short by trying to scare Emily Kramer into telling him, and now he was no longer certain that Emily Kramer even knew what it was.

Hobart had not done well with Mrs. Kramer. Wearing a ski mask wasn't the same as being unseen. She knew his height and weight, had heard his voice, had seen his eyes and hands. Going to see the widow had seemed necessary to him last night, but it was a misstep. He had learned nothing about Forrest's secret.

Hobart tried out various plans. He could walk away from the job and leave Emily Kramer alive. What she had already told the police by now was all she would ever tell. What was it? She would have told the police what he had asked her for: a piece of information, printed or recorded in some way, that was embarrassing or incriminating to a powerful man. Tonight, telling her even that much struck him as another mistake. She, possibly with their help, would already be searching the house and the office for anything Hobart had missed.

But maybe she was too smart to have told the police about that part of it. If she knew that the information was valuable and illegal, and that her husband had been hiding it, she would have lots of reasons to keep that knowledge to herself. And maybe she had known about it all along. Maybe her husband had let her in on his plans at the beginning. No, he decided. She really had not known what Hobart was talking about when he had demanded she give it to him.

Hobart had created a terrible problem for himself. He had set Emily Kramer—and possibly the police—to looking for the information. If Emily Kramer or the police found it before he did, then they would know that Theodore Forrest was the one who'd had Phil Kramer killed. The police would arrest him, or at least watch him closely and talk to him. At some point, Forrest would learn what had set off the search that led to him. When he did, what were the chances that he would not turn in Jerry Hobart?

Hobart could simply kill Emily Kramer now and collect his fee from Theodore Forrest. That would keep both Emily Kramer and Forrest quiet. But it would still leave Hobart open to an unknown risk. The police and Mrs. Kramer's detective friends would search even harder for the piece of information.

If only he had walked into Emily Kramer's room and blown a hole in her head while she slept. She would not have had a chance to describe him or tell anyone he was looking for something. He would have had a couple of hours, at least, to search the house and find the information. He might even have been able to stay in the Kramer house all day searching, then left sometime tonight.

Hobart stood up and dressed quickly. He had set off the search for the secret, and now he had to be the one to find it.

19

Ted Forrest looked at his watch. It was still early. The night was dark, out here away from the city lights, and stars were visible—bright, glowing blue-white dots on a sky that looked black. At one time, probably even after his great-grandfather had moved the family out to occupy the land along the San Joaquin River, there had been eight thousand stars visible on a clear night. He had read that somewhere, and it had stuck with him. Now that there was light and air pollution in the valley he supposed there were only a few hundred, but they must be the biggest, brightest ones, and they made an incredible sight on a night like this.

He opened the window of his car an inch. The air felt wonderful to him, and he pressed the button again to open the window farther and let the wind blow through his hair as he drove. At home he had felt as though he had a belt tightening around his chest, so he could barely inhale, and every time he exhaled, it tightened another notch. But now he felt free, and each breath made him feel stronger, younger.

Caroline had no feeling about the outdoors. The land was just a vast flatness that had no special shape or character or meaning for her. For their whole marriage she had spent as much time in cities as possible—San Francisco at least once a week, New York maybe four times a year, London and Paris and Rome whenever she could get any of her friends to go with her. He had never been able to understand how a woman who was so devoted to enjoying beauty could ignore what was in front of her nose, above her head and under her feet. She didn't dislike nature or find it frightening. It didn't exist for her. Color was the shade of a paint or a fabric.

The land that had come into his stewardship was mainly in the Central Valley south of the San Joaquin between Merced and Fresno, some of it in farms as small as a couple of hundred acres, and some of it bought up in contiguous plots. Lots of chances came up in the Depression or during World War II, or in recent years when farming stopped being something families could do themselves. Some of those pieced-together places were like reassembled Spanish land grants.

It was special land. Three-quarters of the vegetables produced in the whole country were grown in these valleys. The state was a big long animal in repose, the raised spine of the Sierras running down the middle of it. The west wind pushed the clouds from the ocean right into that wall of mountains so it rained, and the water ran back down in a set of rivers arranged at regular intervals like the ribs of the animal: the Yuba, Bear, American, Cosumnes, Calaveras, Mokelumne, Stanislaus, Tuolumne, Merced, Chowchilla, Fresno, San Joaquin, Kings, Kaweah rivers, one after another. The water made the enormous lowland between the coast and the mountains the most valuable farmland on earth. His family had been part of that for five generations.

He might not be raising crops, but he was part of the tradition, and leaving the land fallow, giving it a rest for a couple of generations, was almost an act of patriotism. He was protecting and preserving it. He was also keeping the level of air pollution in the Central Valley down, not contributing to the chemical runoff into the rivers, and even keeping the prices up for other agricultural corporations. And of course, the water the Forrests didn't use had been going to cities while they had grown, and without it they wouldn't survive. The southern half of the state was all arid savanna and desert.

He drove into the downtown area of Merced, along a block of small shops. It was after nine, so the stores that sold china and women's clothes and the hairstylists were closed, but the restaurants were just filling up. Forrest let his BMW coast into the turn at the corner beside Marlene's Coffee and Sympathy, and found a parking space at the curb down the street just past a tall sycamore. He was far from a streetlamp, and the tree's broad canopy threw the car into deeper shadow. As he got out he looked up into the night sky anxiously. In hot weather old trees sometimes dropped limbs, but he didn't plan to be here long.

He took a couple of steps and saw the back door of Marlene's open, and a small, thin creature appear. She stood under the light near the door for a couple of seconds, looking for him. He could see the shining honey-blond hair as she shaded her eyes and looked up the street. She began to walk toward him, but as soon as she was well away from the building, allowed herself to break into a run.

When she came into the deep shadows away from the glow of the commercial street, he heard her voice, a half-suppressed, delighted laugh. She took a little hop and threw her arms around his neck. She spoke into his ear. "What a treat! Come on and get me out of here."

Forrest turned his head as he opened the car door for her, trying to be sure nobody was watching. There were still people walking on the commercial street, but none of them seemed to be able to pay any attention to one more couple getting into a black car on the side street past Marlene's. Forrest started the engine and then pulled out.

Kylie said, "God, Ted. You are so sweet to sneak out of a dinner just to rescue me from barista servitude." He felt her soft, wet lips on his cheek, then her left hand playing with the hair at the back of his neck.

He moved his head slightly to get rid of the tickle. "Put your seat belt on."

She turned to face forward and slid back into the seat, then pulled the belt across her chest and clicked the buckle. "Don't worry. There aren't any cops to give us a ticket. Terry and Dan just came into Marlene's for their coffee ten minutes ago. From here they go out to prowl those new streets up by the freeway entrance."

"You know that?"

"Of course. They come in the same time every night."

"If you know there are no cops, then the speeders and drunk drivers probably know it, too. You're even more likely to need a seat belt."

She laughed, untroubled, but Ted Forrest felt slightly uncomfortable. His voice sounded old to him, like a father or even a grandfather. The similarity wasn't a coincidence. Her father was six years younger than Forrest, and her mother at least fifteen years younger. He glanced at Kylie as they passed under a streetlamp, and saw a remnant of a smile on her lips. Kylie. Even the name reminded him. When he had been young, there were no names like that. Girls had familiar names, like their mothers. Most had names from the Bible, like their grandmothers.

As long as he thought about Kylie instead of himself, he would preserve his good mood. Even in the scarce light pulled from the glow of the dashboard and the reflected lights from windows her hair shone, long and thick and alive, and her skin was milky-smooth. This generation of girls seemed to be different, physically. They had more muscle and bone, and no fat at all except rounded breasts and buttocks—shapes that made fourteen-year-olds look like designers' drawings of idealized women. Just looking at girls on the street gave him hope for the future of the species, and Kylie was a prize, a grand champion, without even knowing it. That ingenuousness, the apparent unawareness of her beauty was one of the things about her that he loved. He knew that teenaged girls were not unconscious of themselves. Their most arduous study was given over to their own waists-eyes-chins-cheeks-necks-hair-fingers-toes-legs-feet. But Kylie had already outgrown part of that and learned to take her looks as she took everything else, as a gift that she'd received years ago and never thought about anymore.

He drove back out onto the highway. "How was work?"

"Boring as usual, and it's not over. I'm still on until eleven, and then we have to clean up."

"Why do you do it?"

"A lot of reasons. I like having money that's mine and nobody gave me. If I want to waste it, then I don't have to feel guilty or pretend I'm sorry."

"I suppose not."

"And besides, it gives me freedom to do what I want."

"Really? What do you want?"

She looked at him slyly. "You. Would you come to my house to pick me up? You know—wait downstairs with my daddy while I put on my makeup?"

"You're pretty smart."

"I'm *very* smart," she agreed. "Where are we going to do it?"

"What?"

"You didn't sneak away in the middle of Caroline's big party just so I wouldn't have to wash the cappuccino machine. You want to get me out of my clothes, as usual."

"Well, since you suggested it, maybe you have something in mind."

"Me suggest it? Shut up. I just know how you are." Her sly look returned. "My parents are out tonight. They probably won't be back until midnight, at least."

Forrest shook his head. "I've got a better idea. I think I'll show you a place you've never been to."

"You just don't want to get caught. It's because I'm jailbait."

"Charming term," said Forrest. "But yes, I think it's fair to say I don't want to get caught. Do you? Then we could have a trial. You could get dragged in to testify in public about everything we ever did together in great detail. Maybe we'd get to be on television. Your mother could cry for the jury, and your father, too, probably. I suppose it might prompt Caroline to finally get around to killing herself. God knows, nothing else has."

"*There's* a thought. Maybe I'll turn you in myself."

"I'd get twenty-five years." He looked at her sadly. "That's the risk I'm taking to be with you."

"I know." She gripped his right hand so he had to take it off the wheel. "I love you so much."

"Me, too." As soon as he had his hand back he grasped the wheel with his right hand and raised his left to look at his watch. He was on schedule. She had been waiting, so they had not wasted any time. He was pleased. He drove faster now, but he was careful never to go higher than the speed limit when Kylie was with him. He made full stops at stop signs, signaled for lane changes, and watched his mirrors. Even a simple fender-bender with the girl in the car could bring police to write down his name and the name of his passenger, and then there would be trouble.

He drove the ten miles out of town toward Espinoza Ranch. His family had always kept the original name, even though they'd had it for over a hundred years, and had bought it from a man named Parker. Family folklore said Espinoza Ranch was a spectacularly fertile piece of farmland because it was the floodplain of an ancient meandering creek that came from a spring in the foothills. A couple of days after any big winter rainstorm, and two weeks after the melting of the mountain snowpack each year, the water rushed down and inundated the loops and curves of the creek and choked the plain with fresh mud. At some point the creek had been diverted somewhere upstream, so the floods didn't happen anymore, but nothing had been planted on the Espinoza Ranch for fifty years. Someday, Forrest was sure, it was probably going to be covered with houses. For the moment there was only the house his grandfather had built on the foundation of the old main house about two hundred yards from the highway at the end of a gravel road. It took vigilance to spot the unmarked road on the right, but he had been here many times. He turned at the entrance to the ranch and stopped in front of the big steel gate.

"What's this?" Kylie asked.

"I own it. I thought I'd show it to you." He got out, opened the combination lock on the gate and walked with it to swing it open, then came back and moved his car forward, got out again and locked the gate behind him.

He drove up the packed-gravel road to the house and stopped, the dust swirling ahead of him in the headlights. He inched forward and Kylie could see the two-story clapboard house with a covered porch that skirted around the three sides that were visible. There was no landscaping or gardens, but someone had recently driven a tractor mower around the house in circles to keep it clear of brush and cut down the tall grass, so it seemed to have a lush green lawn.

Kylie said, "It's pretty. Does somebody live here?"

"No, not at the moment. I have a couple who live on another place come by and keep it nice."

"What's it for?"

Forrest turned off the engine and got out, then walked with Kylie toward the steps. "There's a stream, a creek about a quarter mile back from here just before the land rises. See? Over there. I guess you can't really make it out in the dark. My grandfather stocked it with trout, and this was supposed to be a fishing lodge. He, and later my father, used to bring friends from town here for a few days at a time. They'd fish and play cards and so on."

As they stepped up onto the porch, she said, "What happened?"

"A lot of things. I got the impression that some of the friends weren't men. I think that occurred to my mother sometime in the fifties."

"I'll bet she was pissed."

"I never really knew. I heard that much from an old guy my father kept on here as a caretaker when I was a kid. My father stopped coming here, anyway. I think by now the trout have died off." He took a key from a nail above one of the rafters of the roof over the porch, unlocked the door, and turned on the lights.

Kylie stepped in slowly and looked around her. "This was a fishing lodge?" She stared at the big stone fireplace, the stained-glass light fixtures on the walls, the mission-style antique furniture. She peered into the big doorway that led to the billiard room. "This is nicer than our house."

"I guess he wanted to impress the girls," he said. He put his arm around her waist. "So do I, of course."

"Girls? Plural?"

"Girl."

"That's better." She set her purse on the floor, put her arms around Forrest's neck and kissed him. The kiss started gently and tentatively, then became more passionate. It was clear that she intended it not to be a single touch of the lips, but the beginning of a much longer, deeper experience.

Ted Forrest reciprocated, and the affection began to build into arousal, his hands moving over her clothes and then inside them.

She broke off the kiss. "I suppose the bedrooms upstairs are dirty and yucky?"

"No. I have them keep some rooms furnished in case I want to spend some time by myself."

"Show me." She took his hand and tugged him toward the staircase.

He climbed the stairs with her, then pushed open the door to the old master bedroom and switched on the light. The room was all heavy wood furniture that matched the woodwork and cabinets. Half of the room was a sitting area. There was a stone fireplace here, too, and a small bar. He took a step toward it, but Kylie tugged his arm again, and he went with her to the bed.

They said nothing about the time that was passing, but it was in the room like a third presence. They had no time, no leisure to be gradual or linger over anything. They undressed quickly, impatiently, dropping their clothes on the floor and resuming the interrupted kiss.

They made love feverishly, and then, when it was over, they rolled apart on the bed and lay still. Ted Forrest closed his eyes. He could feel his heart still beating hard as his breathing slowed gradually.

After only a few seconds Kylie rolled back to him, grasped his wrist in both hands and turned it.

"Hmm?" He opened one eye.

"You didn't even take off your watch."

"Sorry. I guess my mind was elsewhere."

"I know what it was on." She kissed the back of his hand and then dropped it. "It's after ten. We'd better go."

He raised himself on one elbow. "I suppose." He was still winded, and he didn't want her to notice that it was taking him longer to recover. He pushed himself up and took the long way around the bed.

She hopped off and began to dress quickly. By the time Forrest reached the pile of clothes, she was already fastening her bra. She stopped and hugged him. "That was so nice."

"Yes, it was." He edged away and began to dress, thinking about the time. It might still be possible to get her back to the coffee shop before it closed at eleven, but getting home before the music lovers left was going to be more difficult.

"Have you ever brought Caroline here?"

"You mean this way? To sleep here?" He wasn't sure which answer was the one she wanted. She might like it if she was usurping some of Caroline's territory.

"You know I do."

He took a guess. "Never. She wouldn't come to any of these places. To her, 'rustic' means the concierge doesn't bow."

"Then it can be our place. Our special place."

"Our special place. What a nice idea." He had been considering bringing her here for weeks, but he had been afraid it would scare her, maybe depress her. There was no way of predicting what women were going to think, even when they were young.

She was nearly dressed now, just tying the sneakers she wore because of the hours she spent on her feet working the coffee machines at Marlene's. "Yep, our place. When Caroline catches us and throws you out, maybe we can even live here."

He joined her laugh, but his voice was hollow and weak. "It had better not happen for a few years. The police around here probably wouldn't let me reach the station alive."

"Don't," she said. "That's not funny to me."

"Me either."

She went to the bed and started to make it, but he held her arm. "You don't want to make any beds."

"Won't somebody know?"

"No. The caretakers will come tomorrow. It's their job to put fresh sheets on if the bed has been used, not to figure out what happened in them."

He tucked in his shirt and buttoned the last two buttons on the way to the door, turned off the light, and ushered Kylie downstairs. Her purse was lying in the middle of the floor where she had left it. She scooped it up and they went outside. He locked the door and placed the key up on the rafter where he had found it.

The efficiency of their movements was exhilarating to him. They got into the car and he drove to the highway. This time Kylie said, "What's the combination?"

"It's 8—14—32."

She got out, ran and opened the gate, watched him drive through, and then closed and locked it to the ringbolt on the steel stanchion and got back into the car. The car began to move while she was fastening her seat belt.

On the way back to town, he looked at Kylie's expression. She seemed happy, relaxed, and confident. She rested her hand on his thigh in a proprietary way and looked out the window as though she were memorizing every sight.

"What are you thinking?"

"That I love you. That I never met anyone who was like you in any way. That I wish I were older, or that you were younger."

"I'll vote for the second one," he said.

"I won't. If you were younger, you wouldn't love just me. You would have, like, forty or fifty girlfriends."

"I would not."

"Yes, you would," Kylie insisted. "You forget that I know all about you."

"Well, the vote is one to one then. I guess it doesn't matter. We have to live with the ages we are, and do our best." He was feeling uneasy, and at first he wasn't sure why, but then he realized that there was something about Kylie that was bothering him. She seemed too relaxed, too confident. He added, "And please, don't forget what I said earlier tonight. You're an underage girl, and I'm somebody who is more vulnerable than other men would be."

"What do you mean?"

"My family name is known all over this part of the state, and I have a social position in the Valley. When everything is going fine, it's an advantage. It gets me a good table in a restaurant. But if I get caught with you, the whole world will get turned upside down. If that happens, *you* will be a big news story, and *I'll* probably be as good as dead."

"Come on. They give you the death penalty for sleeping with somebody?"

"A man like me is in the same position as a girl like you. Other girls hear about your good grades, see your beautiful eyes and hair and figure, and they get jealous. They're going to be compared to you, and they're going to be second best. They'll be nice to you to be associated with you. But they all secretly envy you, and some of them hate you."

"You're flattering me. I don't understand."

"It's the same for me. Cops and people like that look at me and think my life has been easy compared to theirs. I have more, I do more, I don't have to punch a time clock or defer to anyone. A cop who hears about me might secretly wish I would get knocked down a bit, but he would never harm me. But the second I get in trouble with the law, it will be different. You know what he'll do then?"

"What?"

"Try to make sure I don't get off—use my name or my money or my friendships to save myself. He'll cook up whatever he can to make me look as bad as possible. And he'll try to be sure I don't get special treatment. He'll put me in a cell with a bunch of career criminals who hate people like me. If they kill me, the cop will get praised because he didn't give me special privileges."

Kylie moved closer to him, leaning her head on his shoulder. "I'm sorry, Ted. I'll never let them put you in danger."

He drove on, trying to keep his speed just under the limit. He began to feel safer now that he had reminded her of the stakes. He couldn't have her getting into a gossipy mood and confiding to some little friend of hers that she's having an affair with a married man. He couldn't let her get sloppy and careless about hiding their meetings. He had noticed many times that the generation of women now in their thirties had no reluctance to chatter about their sex lives to anyone who would listen. How much worse Kylie's generation was going to be nobody knew, but a return to tasteful silence was too much to hope for. He had to keep her scared.

He drove into town and made his way along dimly lighted back streets to the block behind Marlene's where she had been waiting for him. He stopped by the curb under the same old sycamore tree.

Kylie said, "Don't worry anymore. I love you. Call me when you can."

"I will."

She got out, closed the car door, and trotted toward the back door of Marlene's. When she reached the building, Forrest saw her half-turn in the small semicircle of light. She stood still for a second, staring into the shadows on the street. It looked as though she were staring straight at him, although he knew she probably couldn't see him in the dim light. Then she hurried inside.

He let out an audible breath in relief, then drew in another. She was a vulnerable little creature, and he had just seen her return to safety once more. Her safety made him safer, and that was what mattered.

Ted Forrest turned the car around and drove back the way he had come, made two turns, and emerged on the highway five blocks from Marlene's. As soon as he was beyond the town limits, he accelerated as much as he dared. He was alone now, so he could afford to push the speed limit a bit. He opened his window to let the cool air blow on his face. He supposed he might have picked up a lingering scent of her perfume, and the wind would help get rid of it.

As he approached his house, his heart began to pound. He could still see cars parked along the length of his driveway. He had made it back in time. Guests were still inside. He drove up the driveway and around the house into the garage, slipped out to the path, and walked quickly. He cut through the rose garden to the French doors into the library. He reached out to touch the handle, and felt relief once again. Nobody had noticed the doors were unlocked and relocked them. He slipped inside and set the locks.

He moved into the foyer just as people began to stream out of the living room. He smiled and joined the fringe of the group, as though he were already in the middle of a conversation. He saw Collier and his wife Susanne, and said, "Suzy. Nice that the old boy brought you over here for once."

"It's part of my training program," she said. "I'm trying to link music and good food in his subconscious so when I mention a concert, he'll begin to salivate and take me."

"Well, good luck with that. He's smart enough to get the concept, but too loyal to let his old friends like me look dumb."

"He's a great guy, isn't he?" She kissed Collier's cheek.

Forrest felt a twinge of jealousy. When had Caroline ever said he was a great guy, let alone kissed him in public? He patted Collier's arm in a way that gave the Colliers his permission to move on, and let the next set of guests take their place. One by one, they returned his smile, and he said something to acknowledge that he knew them and remembered the last time he had seen them. He let them know that for a few seconds, at least, he was paying attention to them exclusively.

His interest bordered on affection because each of them was bolstering his credibility as a host. But he was also aware that as each couple passed him, they were moving toward the front door and heading off into the night. Each time the door behind him swung open, it brought closer the time when he would have to be alone in this house with Caroline. As the time approached, he spoke with the stragglers in a kind of desperation, giving them the impression that he truly did not like to see them go.

The last one in the foyer was Dr. Feiniger, the president of the group. He was an old, wiry-looking professor who was almost a head shorter than Caroline. Feiniger thanked her for the special evening. Forrest was aware of his bristly little beard, the hair on the rims of his ears, and the springy wild hairs sprouting from his eyebrows. Dr. Feiniger kept talking, and Forrest used the opportunity to step out of the foyer into the hallway that ran along the center of the house to the back stairs.

"Ted!"

He considered pretending he had not heard her, but there was the sound of her footsteps coming after him. She had freed herself of the professor. Forrest stopped, took a deep breath, and turned to face her.

She stood six feet from him in the narrow hallway. It was her customary distance, just far enough away so he could not touch her unexpectedly, but near enough so he could not walk away from her. "Where the hell were you? Where did you go?"

He had to make an effort to unclench his jaw. He spoke carefully and quietly. "Caroline. I did my best to be gracious and help host your event. After dinner you made it clear that I was not wanted. I came back in time to say good night to your guests. Now I'm going to bed."

"Oh. So now this is my fault?"

"It can be *my* fault, if you like. Good night." He turned and stepped toward the back stairs.

"Ted." There was an unexpected tone—softer, perhaps conciliatory. He was curious. He looked back at her. "What?"

"Jesus, Ted. You should see yourself. That look of hatred on your face." She held out both hands to him, her eyes beginning to fill with tears. "Can't we just talk?"

"Not tonight." He went up the back stairs, entered his closet, found some pajamas, and carried them to the nearest guest suite. After he got out of the shower, he heard Caroline slamming doors in the master suite, so he moved to another guest room farther down the hall.

20

Jerry Hobart got into his car, took out his pistol, checked the load and the safety, then slipped it into his jacket pocket. It was after midnight again, and he could go back to searching for the missing information. He was impatient to find it, but he knew he had to use this opportunity to spring the traps first and see who was watching them.

He drove to Van Nuys and turned toward the building where Kramer Investigations had its office. He knew it would be foolish to go inside right now, but he wanted to see who was waiting for him to try. At night he could make it difficult for anyone to see him well enough to remember him, but he might be able to identify some of the people who wanted to cause him trouble.

He drove to the neighborhood, parked on a street three blocks away, and walked toward the office building. He approached from the side where he had seen the movie theater from the roof of the building. As soon as he was on the street outside the theater, he pretended to be waiting for someone while he studied the office building. He saw no lighted windows in the Kramer Investigations office, or in any of the windows near it. He surveyed the parking lots and the curbs nearby. There were no cars of the models that the police used as unmarked vehicles, and no windowless vans. He saw no men loitering in the area, and no signs that anyone was watching the office from a building in the vicinity. He abandoned the safety of the theater entrance and walked closer to the office building.

He was trying to make himself a bit more obvious, to see if he could draw any watchers to move out of position to new spots where they could control him. He walked purposefully in the general direction of the building, but he could detect no movement. He walked past the front entrance, kept going to the end of the block, and turned left, away from the office building. As he walked along the side street, he looked behind him occasionally to see if anyone had followed.

Hobart saw nothing. As he walked the next two blocks, he kept up his vigilance, but still could not see any indication that the area was under surveillance. He tried to evaluate his visit to the building. It could be good news. If the police didn't see any reason to watch the office, then maybe they were not taking his break-in seriously.

Of course, the police didn't have to be sitting in the office all night with their feet on the desks to watch it. They could have a webcam set up on one of the computers in there and watch it from a computer in the nearest station. As he walked away from the building, he decided that the problem was complicated enough so he could never eliminate the possibility that the office was a trap. Even though he could see nothing out of place, he had an instinctive feeling that something was wrong.

Hobart got into his car and drove toward the Kramer house. When he reached the right street, he repeated the steps he always followed to avoid an ambush. First he drove past the house to see if it appeared inhabited, then drove on, looking for occupants in every vehicle parked within view. Then he widened his search for three blocks in every direction to find a small truck or a van that could contain surveillance equipment. All along his route he looked at the windows of buildings that had an unobstructed view of the Kramer house.

Hobart spent a half hour at his search. If there were people watching the Kramer house tonight, then they were very good at it, and very patient. He could detect nothing on his second time past the house that indicated it might be occupied or under surveillance. If there were cops nearby, then they had done a spectacular job of hiding. Cops always brought chase cars in a situation like this. It did them little good to see some guy in the dark trying to commit a crime if they let him drive off afterward. They always had a couple of big plain cars nearby. They couldn't bear to go without them.

Then it occurred to Hobart that the chase car could be very close without being visible. The garage door at the Kramer house was shut. If the cops were in the house, the car could be in the garage, all ready to go after him if he ran, or to transport him in handcuffs if he couldn't.

This time Hobart parked his car on a dark street three blocks from the Kramer house. He didn't want to have anyone look out a window and notice that the car parked there the night when he had been in the Kramer house was here again. But in Los Angeles, people didn't know what went on three blocks away. As he got out of his car, he caught a glimpse of a low shadow moving up a driveway to the back of a house: A foraging coyote had waited to be sure of his intentions.

Hobart respected coyotes. When he was young, he used to see them in the desert if he stayed out alone after full darkness set in. They were always aware of him before they showed themselves, always sure of the limits of his capabilities. They stayed just far enough away so he couldn't harm them if he wanted to. He would see one walking beside the road, a skinny canine with pointy ears and muzzle, then trotting across the pavement to get from wherever it had spent the day to a different area that didn't carry the scent of coyote.

Now Hobart's business involved prowling the city late at night trying to find a way into a building to get at somebody inside. While he was out, he often came across coyotes. They were in the city doing what Hobart was doing: foraging for a way to stay alive. They had thrived in the city. They traveled from one place to another by trotting along the empty concrete riverbeds that ran from the Santa Monica Mountains along the north rim of the valley all the way to the ocean. They slipped between the iron bars of fences to drink from swimming pools. He often met them as they scavenged in alleys among open Dumpsters and garbage cans. Now and then he would see one trotting along a suburban sidewalk with a dead cat in its mouth.

They always detected danger, and always appraised it accurately. They didn't run from a man on foot until he was less than forty feet away. If one of them was going up a street at his characteristic tireless trot and a car appeared suddenly with its size and noise and blinding headlights and speed, the coyote would merely divert his course up over the curb and onto a lawn, where he would wait for the car to pass. The coyote knew that no matter how nightmarish the car was, it wasn't able to jump off the pavement and chase him up the lawn and around the house.

People had been poisoning and trapping coyotes for two hundred years, but there were more coyotes than ever. A coyote would approach the bait and sniff around it, and it would know. A coyote seemed to smell not just the food, but the small quantity of extra chemical that didn't belong, and something else, too. Maybe it was only that the smell of human beings was stronger than it ought to be near a day-old chunk of meat. But maybe what the coyote smelled was the malice, some ingredient in the mixture of smells that revealed the excitement of the trapper. It could be the minuscule shot of adrenaline that made it into the sweat on the trapper's hands while he was thinking about how clever he was and imagining the death of the coyote. Even though the coyote was hungry, his ribs visible through the mangy fur along his sides, he would nose the bait and move on. He didn't let his optimism tell him that everything must be safe just because he couldn't see anyone watching him.

Hobart approached the Kramer house through the neighbor's back yard. He moved to the back wall and sat down quietly on a plastic lawn chair near the pool. He remained there for a time, listening to the sounds of the neighborhood. Entering a neighborhood meant crossing invisible lines of force, stepping on the territories of various dogs, cats, and other animals, making tiny noises that disturbed people's sleep and violated the tranquillity of the place. It was necessary to remain still and let any ripples he had stirred up settle and leave the surface smooth again.

People and animals had a sense of duration, a feeling for how long things took. When he had waited much longer than any intruder would, he stood and quietly climbed the cinder-block wall into the Kramer yard. He crouched at the corner of the yard, with the thick foliage at his back so he didn't stand out, and stared in the windows of the house, looking for signs that it was occupied. There were no windows that were open, no lights that he could see in any room.

It was past one o'clock, but anyone who was waiting in the house would still be fairly alert. There might be a radio on to keep them awake, or they might be walking from place to place to look out various doors and windows to spot him. Hobart saw no signs, but he waited ten more minutes in his corner before he put on his ski mask and gloves and approached the back of the house.

He moved along the windows, peering in at different angles to try to pick out a light, and then searching for objects that had not been in the living room on his last visit—a coat or a magazine or a coffee cup—but he saw none of those things. He moved from the big windows to the garage, and looked in the window. Emily Kramer's car was still inside, but that meant nothing except that she had not driven herself when she had left. No cop would use it as a chase car. He moved back along the wall to the living room again, trying to decide.

Emily Kramer was not here, and that was as he had expected. He had intended to terrify her on his first visit, and he had never doubted that he would succeed. But he wasn't sure how to interpret the apparent absence of other people. Could the police have listened to Emily Kramer's story and not known that Hobart would come back? He had told her what he had come for, and she had seen him leave without it. The cops should be in this house waiting for him. He thought of electronic surveillance again. They could be keeping watch on both the office and the house from somewhere else.

Hobart moved to the side of the house and looked up, traced the power line from the pole at the street to the corner of the house, and moved toward it until he found the meter and the circuit box beside it. He moved his face close to the meter and saw the wheel inside turning. Power was being used, but the wheel was turning very slowly. It was the sort of power that ran the refrigerator and a few electric clocks.

Hobart looked around and chose a spot in the back corner of the yard where there were two trees with thick trunks that appeared to rise from a single spot. He flipped the main switch to turn off the electricity. The click was loud in the silence, and the sound made him move more quickly to the hiding place he had chosen. He stood behind the forked trunks, rested his pistol arm on the nub of a pruned branch, and waited. From here he could see through the rear windows into the living room, and he could see the circuit box. If someone was here, Hobart would probably see him either coming to find out which of the circuit breakers was flipped, or sweeping the back yard with a flashlight.

He waited fifteen minutes. Then he moved to the sliding door where he had entered the house the previous night. He could see the residue of the police technicians' fingerprint dust all over the area near the lock. Nobody had made any attempt to clean it, or their wipes and smudges would have shown up, too. Hobart used his knife to push up the door latch, then closed the blade and put it away while he watched to see if any of the shadows in the house changed shape. He slid the door open a few inches and listened. There were no footsteps, no creaking floorboards. He entered.

Hobart sidestepped away from the sliding door so his back was to a solid wall and his silhouette would not stand out. There were still no sounds, no lights. He slid the door shut.

If there were surveillance cameras or similar devices in the house, they would be run off the house current, so he was confident he had killed them. He was in, and he was alone. Now he could begin his search. He had already formed a mental map of the house on his first visit. People usually hid things like papers and tapes in places where they would be out of sight, but where they could still reach them in a hurry. They didn't want them in spots where a routine cleanup would uncover them, or a burglar would know something valuable was hidden—like a wall safe.

Phil Kramer had been devious. He had not been the sort of man who would put papers in a bank safe-deposit box and have to wait for business hours to retrieve them. He was the sort of man who would put papers in with other papers, or put tapes with other tapes, and Hobart already had a theory about where that might be. There was a hall that ran between the living room and the kitchen and then picked up past the kitchen, and led to a room. It must have been a maid's room at one time, but now it was a den or office. He stepped to the hallway.

"Hold it!"

Hobart spun, dropped to a squat and fired in the general direction of the deep male voice. He didn't pause, but sprang, launching himself in the direction of the sliding windows in the living room. He knew he couldn't make it to the one he had unlocked, so he dashed for the other one. As he ran, he held his pistol in front of him and fired through the glass as quickly as he could, spreading his shots over the large pane and shattering it. He managed to get off six shots, crossed his forearms in front of his face and hurled himself through the curtain of still-falling shards.

In that instant, he was aware of shots behind him, but he knew that his best chance was to keep moving. He sprinted to the back of the yard, hauled himself to the top of the wall, and rolled over it just as somebody found the circuit box and a bright light came on, transforming the back yard of the Kramer house into a white glare.

Hobart dashed for the next street, ran across it and up the driveway of the house on the far side. He saw a wooden gate between the two houses, reached over the top to feel for a latch and release it, and ran between the two houses to the next yard. This time there was a chain-link fence with thick shrubbery growing on both sides of it, but he clambered over it to the sound of ringing clinks and breaking branches, and kept running.

Fidelity

He made it to the street where his rental car was parked. He was winded now, but he sprinted up the sidewalk to the car. As he got into the driver's seat, he heard the growl of an engine. A car was accelerating somewhere nearby, as though it were driving up and down the streets he had just crossed.

Jerry Hobart had been hunted before. He knew he couldn't stay here in his parked car and hope he wouldn't be found, and he couldn't hide in the shrubbery somewhere in the neighborhood. His only chance was to go. He started the engine and accelerated, trying to get out of this small grid of streets and onto one of the big boulevards that would take him to a freeway entrance. He built up speed as he reached the first intersection, then let his foot hover over the brake pedal while he glanced to his left to be sure nothing was coming toward him on the side street, then hit the accelerator again. He ejected the magazine from his gun and clicked the spare into place.

As he reached the second intersection, he looked to his left and saw another car flash across the side street one block to his left. There was somebody driving a parallel course to his. He turned to the left. If the driver was a cop, he would assert his innocence by following him out of the neighborhood. If the cop didn't buy it, he would have the inevitable confrontation facing the cop instead of looking over his shoulder. When he reached the next street, he turned to the right to follow the speeding car.

What he saw wasn't what he had expected. The other driver had seen him, too, and the car was swinging into a driveway on the left. He could see it was a dark green Toyota, not a model that cops used. Now it was backing into the street to come back toward him. Hobart pushed the button to lower his side window, gripped his gun in his left hand, and drove toward it. The other car backed quickly across the road to block him.

Hobart opened fire at the driver. He saw the driver's side window shatter and saw one shot hit the edge of the car's roof and throw sparks as it glanced off into the night. After that he couldn't see the driver anymore, but he fired three rounds at the driver's door, and then he was past the car. As he coasted into a turn at the next block to get away from the small residential streets, he looked into his mirrors, but he couldn't tell whether he had hit the man or not. The car hadn't moved yet. Then he turned left onto Vanowen, moving fast toward the east. He tore off his ski mask and put it in his pocket, and felt the cool air on his sweating face.

He turned right on Van Nuys Boulevard to avoid waiting at a red light, then left onto Riverside. At this time of night, he could go forty-five along unobstructed streets and not look as though he was running from something. In ten minutes he reached Lankershim, and that took him to the entrance of the complex at Universal City. In three more minutes, he was driving up to his hotel on the hill overlooking Universal Studios and the eastern end of the San Fernando Valley.

He gave his car to the parking attendant and watched him drive it away to store it with the hundreds of others in the parking structure. As Hobart walked toward the hotel lobby, he stopped and looked to the northwest, toward Emily Kramer's house. Far off, he could see a couple of helicopters in the air, weaving back and forth over the flat grid of unidentifiable streets. Now and then one of them would circle, and the strong beam of a floodlight would emanate from its belly and illuminate something below for a few seconds, and then move on.

21

For an instant, Emily was in her own bed in her house, with Phil beside her. The warm, comfortable sensation collapsed, and she remembered: Phil was dead. He had been doing something that had brought her into the world of that horrible man in the ski mask. Her eyes opened and she saw that there was a man standing above her in the dark. She jumped and pulled back, pressing herself into the wall.

"Emily," said the man. She knew it was familiar, then remembered what she was doing here. "It's me—Ray."

"Oh," she said. "You startled me. I must have been sound asleep." Her voice was hoarse. She cleared her throat. "What's wrong?" She sat up, holding the blanket to her chest.

"The guy came back to your house a little while ago. Apparently, he got away. I just got the call."

"Is everybody okay?"

"Yeah. There was some shooting, but he didn't hit anybody. The cops are looking for him, but I don't think they're having much luck." He paused. "I'm sorry to wake you up, but I think we ought to go over there and have a look."

"Of course." Emily couldn't see his face, just the shape of his body. She could tell he was standing awkwardly, his muscles tense. He still had the phone receiver in his hand. "Just give me a minute to get dressed."

"Sure." He turned and moved down the hall toward his room.

Emily sat on the edge of the bed and looked around to get her bearings before she stood up. She stepped carefully to the doorway, closed her eyes, and switched on the light. She squinted so she could move around in the glare. She found the pair of jeans she had worn that day and pulled a shirt from the top layer in the suitcase. She took her sneakers to the bed to put them on.

At first it didn't seem like Ray Hall to wake her up and make her go. Then she realized he must not feel comfortable leaving her alone.

She stood and snatched the hairbrush off Ray Hall's dresser and brushed her hair with rapid, hard, painful strokes. She picked up her jacket and purse and hurried out of the room.

Ray was already standing at the foot of the stairs, tapping his keys against his thigh and looking up at her expectantly. As she descended the stairs, she caught herself thinking how good he looked for someone who had just dragged himself out of bed, and how horrible she must look with no makeup and her hair just raked straight.

She ducked past him out the door and hurried to his car. The air was cool now, and she was fully awake. As he started the car and pulled out of the driveway, she said, "You *did* say everybody was okay?"

"That's what Dewey said on the phone." He drove up the street and turned toward Vanowen Street, driving faster now that he was on bigger, wider streets. "Apparently, Billy got carried away and tried to cut the guy off in his car, and the guy opened up on him. Not too surprisingly, he hit the car, but missed Billy. He's a much smaller target."

"Jesus," she muttered. "He could be dead. And for what?"

"I don't know what he's after," Hall said. "If we could just figure out what Phil had that this guy thinks is so important, we could—"

"I didn't mean *him*, I meant *us*. I don't think we're going to accomplish anything that's worth getting anybody killed. And Billy's only twenty-two years old, barely old enough to drink."

As they moved up the streets toward Emily's house, there was the deep, gut-shaking throb of helicopters. Emily could see lights turned on in most of the houses in her neighborhood. She craned her neck to look at the clock on Ray Hall's dashboard. It was two A.M.

Hall pulled up in front of her house, and they both walked up to the front door. When Hall turned the knob and pushed the door open, Emily could see Dewey Burns in the living room move his right hand toward his back, where she knew his gun was. Ray Hall said loudly, "Hi, guys." He stepped inside and held the door so Dewey and Bill could see Emily step in. "I brought Emily with me."

As she moved past Ray, she could see the big window at the back of the room had been blown out. "What a mess." She turned to look directly at Dewey and then at Bill. "But you're both okay?"

"Yeah," Dewey said. "When he came in, we tried to get him to put up his hands. He turned and ran for that window. I lost him a block from here and called the cops. Meanwhile, Billy hopped in his car and tried to head him off that way. He fired a few rounds into the car. Billy's lucky to still be with us."

Emily stepped to Bill and hugged him. "I'm so glad you're not hurt, Billy." Then she hugged Dewey and released him. "You both could have died, and I feel terrible about this."

"I'm sorry we didn't get him, Emily," Bill said.

Dewey frowned. "You knew he had a gun, and you had nothing. Going after him alone was stupid."

177

"I didn't expect to get shot. I was only trying to get a look at his license plate or his face, but he was moving too fast, and then he was shooting." Bill looked at the empty frame of the living-room window and the spray of broken glass that extended out onto the patio. "He really is one crazy son of a bitch, though. Look at that."

Emily didn't know what to say. "The police have seen that?"

"Yes," Dewey said. "A couple of them stopped by to radio the details to the others that were out looking for him."

"I suppose I should get that boarded up, or I'm going to have rats in here."

Ray said, "I can call in a couple of hours and have the glass replaced. There are services that replace glass for businesses. They can probably have it looking normal by noon."

"I suppose." Emily looked around the room, and felt the contrast between the way it used to be and the way it was now. This was her house—hers and Phil's. They had moved in as a young couple, when Phil had just gotten out of the marines, the possibilities were still unlimited, and this typical L.A. bungalow had seemed like a palace to her. They had raised their son here, and after they had lost him, the house had become a retreat.

Now the house seemed to have been revealed as a fraud. The big window that had blown out let the breeze blow through, and reminded her that the house wasn't even closed to the elements anymore, let alone safe. During any instant in all of the years while she had lived here, anything could have happened—how could glass keep it out?—but she had felt safe. She had been stupid. Now the house had made her a target and an easy victim.

"Are the police finished in here?" she asked.

Dewey said, "Yeah, they're done. They dusted a couple of test spots by the door, but he was wearing gloves. They were hoping maybe he had cut himself going out through that window, but they couldn't find any blood."

Ray said, "We'd better figure out what to do next."

Emily said, "I already have. I'm going to search this house completely. I'd like you to help me, if you're willing." She looked at the others. "I would like both of you to go and talk to April and ask her to help you search the office."

Dewey and Bill looked at each other uneasily. Emily said, "I know about it. She told me. I don't think she'll feel comfortable if I talk to her right now, but I can't let that get in the way because we need her help. She'll want to find out who killed Phil, so please ask her."

"Say we *do* get her to help," Bill said. "What are we doing? What are we looking for?"

"You're looking at everything. You and April and Dewey go to the office and check each piece of paper and then set it aside. When you have a pile, put it in a cardboard file box. I'm going to rent a self-storage bay, and at the end of each day, we'll take the boxes you've filled and move them there."

He frowned. "But how do we know which things to put in which boxes?"

She tried to be patient with Bill because he was young and brave and had just had a hard night. "April knows the filing system, so she'll help. But we'll keep it simple, and use the three categories we already have. There are current cases, alphabetized by the last name of the client. That's the smallest group. There are old cases arranged the same way, and internal business files, like phone bills and payrolls and leases."

"Are you closing down Kramer Investigations?"

Emily looked at Dewey Burns. His expression was attentive, but she couldn't tell whether he cared what the answer was. She said, "I'm just making the next move to fight off this guy. I'm trying to beat him to this piece of evidence he wants. I don't know what happens when we have it. I suppose it depends on what it is."

Dewey nodded. "Okay. But tell us again. What, as close as you can figure, is it going to look like?"

"I'm sorry, but I just don't know. It's something Phil had. I thought I knew him better than I did, so I can't tell what form it's in. It's a piece of paper, a photograph, an audiotape, a videotape, a computer disk, or maybe a piece of film, or the memory card from a digital camera. All I know is that it would make some powerful man uncomfortable. That's what the man who broke in said. He implied that it was what got Phil murdered, but that it's still around, and he wants it."

"Did the guy say it's something Phil made, or something he just happened to get his hands on?" Bill asked.

"It could be either. It could be he got it in one form and put it into a different form, or even more than one form. Anything is possible. You knew Phil. He was clever, secretive."

Dewey Burns was staring into Emily's eyes with a fresh intensity, reminding her of Phil. She realized it had stopped being their secret now: Phil's and Dewey's. Now it was Dewey's and hers, and it felt as though she had known it for a long time. He said, "We should go over there and get started, and get as far as we can right away."

The two men began to move toward the door, and Emily followed them. "Thank you, guys. But you know, you could get some sleep first. The security company has men watching the office tonight, so you could start tomorrow."

"No," Dewey said. "The sooner we find it, the sooner this will be over."

He and Bill went out, and Ray closed the door.

Emily said, "You can get some sleep. I'm going to get started here."

"No. I'm up, so I might as well help. How do you want to search the house?"

"The same way I told them to search the office. We'll start by moving everything out of the bedroom upstairs, and search the bare room. We'll search each piece of furniture, too, and then move it down here. When we're done with that room, we'll go to the next-most-likely place, which is that little den off the hallway over there."

"All the furniture is going to end up in the living room?"

"For a while. It will be going into storage, too."

"You're selling the house."

"When this is over."

"You didn't tell me."

"I didn't know it until a few minutes ago. I just realized I'm never going to live here again." She moved to the staircase and climbed to the second floor. After a moment, he heard a drawer slide shut with a bang, and another one slide open.

He climbed after her.

22

Jerry Hobart showered and changed his clothes to be sure there were no glass fragments sticking to him and to remove the gunpowder residue from his hands, but he knew he wouldn't sleep. He sat on the bed in his hotel room and looked out over the lights in the San Fernando Valley. It was a clear night, and from his window on the tenth floor he could see the long rows of street lamps stretching off to the west, where they seemed to lose their definition and fade to become only an impression that the valley was lighter than the ridge of mountains to the north or the sky above.

Hobart was frustrated and angry that he could not go back out and find Emily Kramer right away. Now that he had gone to her house a second time, she would be hiding, staying with someone probably, and maybe with an armed guard. Phil Kramer's office was out of reach now, too. Hobart was not going to be able to go back there.

But he had planted a suggestion in Emily Kramer's skull, and now he had to hope that the suggestion had stuck with her and started to irritate and intrigue her until she couldn't keep from acting on it. He still wasn't sure whether she had known all along everything her husband knew about Theodore Forrest, or had known nothing. If Hobart had to take a guess, he would now bet that Phil Kramer hadn't told her anything. She had seemed genuinely hurt and disappointed when he'd told her that her husband had been holding valuable secret information about a rich man. Hobart had also noticed that she did not doubt it was true.

Hobart brought back the sight of her standing there beside her bed saying she had just learned that her husband was cheating on her. The way she had blurted it out had surprised her as much as it surprised Hobart. It was as though the interrogation he was conducting was, to her, only a part of a much larger, unpleasant conversation she was having with herself. Saying he was cheating on her had made sense to her for an instant. It had seemed to her to be proof that her husband was in the habit of lying to her. Hobart supposed a detective who blackmailed people might also be somebody who wouldn't tell his wife what he was doing. That wasn't a stretch of the imagination. He wondered what Phil had planned to tell Emily when he had his million dollars, or whatever price he had set.

Suddenly Hobart realized he had made a false assumption. Phil Kramer had been cheating on her, and he had not told her where he was going the night Whitley had shot him. Kramer had not been planning to walk in the house with a sack of money and say, "Honey, I'm home. Look what I've got." He had been planning to divorce her without letting her know the money existed, or maybe not come home that night at all. What she had learned about her marriage was why she had looked so defeated. Her hurt had been a bigger feeling than her fear of Hobart. She had known—maybe really just learned that day—that when Kramer died, her marriage had already been

over for a while. She had already figured out that if Phil Kramer had been paid off that night, he would have been on his way to the airport.

Hobart couldn't help including in his memory the fact that she had been naked. He had made her strip because it was a quick way to make progress in an interrogation. A person who was naked among enemies started to feel scared and vulnerable and powerless. For a woman it was worse, because it conformed exactly to a nightmare she'd been having since she was a child. When he met her, he had judged her to be someone who would fall apart and hand over everything Phil Kramer had on Forrest. Now he wasn't sure she wouldn't have held out, but he was almost sure she didn't have what he wanted, at least that night.

But now she had to be searching as hard as she could to find the information he had asked her about. It was almost impossible that she wouldn't. No woman could find out that her husband had been killed over a secret and not ache to know what the secret was. Certainly nobody could be stripped and threatened and humiliated and not want to frustrate and outsmart the man who had done those things to her.

Hobart could only step back now and wait until Emily Kramer found what he wanted. Even if she found the information right away, he knew he could do nothing more tonight because the police would be out searching for him until daylight. He was eager to have the prize quickly, but he could not afford to be impatient and put himself into more situations like the one at the house. He felt restless and dissatisfied. All he could do was let Emily Kramer search, and wait for the moment when the cops ran out of patience and left her alone again.

23

Ted Forrest awoke knowing it was late. He could see that the level of the sun was high, that it must be at least ten. He also knew that something had come to him during the night while he was asleep, some idea, some decision. He got up and went into the bathroom. He had not brought any of his toiletries into the guest suite, but the guest bathrooms were always stocked with toothbrushes and razors and combs. He showered and wore the bathrobe from the suite to walk down the hall to the master suite.

When he entered the bedroom, he saw that the maids had already been here. They had made the bed, emptied the clothes hampers, opened the curtains and replaced the flowers on the table. He was aware of these things, and he liked reliability and efficiency in service people. He detested their opposite.

Forrest took a moment to look in the mirror on the way to his closet. If someone had asked him why, he would have had to say it was to be sure he looked the same. It was not that he would have changed, but that he had so many things on his mind that he wondered if they showed. He went into the dressing area of the big closet and dressed in a pair of gray, unpleated pants that had a simple, informal look, a plain blue oxford shirt, and a black cashmere sport coat. He packed a single small suitcase with the things he might need over a period of a couple of days.

He finished his packing, went to the little wall safe where he kept a few good watches and some cash, and took out a thousand dollars for pocket money. He heard footsteps in the bedroom and stood still, preparing himself. He had been trained since he was a small child to exert control over his feelings. This moment was no different from that second when he stood ready with his tennis racket in his hand and his knees flexed and waited to read the green flash of ball coming off his opponent's racket to streak over the net. Until he knew which way to move, any move was wrong.

She came in and stood six feet away, as always. "You're packing."

"Yes."

"Are you leaving me?"

"I'm going away for a day or two."

"To get away from me?" She was physically rigid, as though her sense of outrage had tightened her into paralysis.

"To get away."

"Is that all you're planning to say to me?" she asked. He could see that her eyes were tearing, and it intrigued him. She must be crying for herself because she felt insulted. Her brain was filled with impressions of undeserved injuries inflicted on her by an uncaring world. She never seemed to be aware that she had done things to precipitate them, and she was always certain she knew what other people were thinking. She was never right.

He exerted self-control. "I hadn't been planning to say anything to you. I delayed my trip so I would be available for your event last night. It's over, and now I've got things to do. Good-bye."

He picked up his suitcase, but she held her position, blocking the door to the bedroom. He turned and walked through the bathroom door into the hall. He moved along the hall and down the stairs quickly, hoping to deny her the time to deliver some angry comment, or at least to be far enough away not to hear it distinctly.

Ted Forrest got to the foot of the staircase, across the foyer, and out the door. He shut it behind him quietly so she would not be certain which way he had gone, then walked down the gravel path to the garage. He put his small suitcase in the trunk of the BMW and left the trunk open.

He went through the door to the back room of the garage. When the building had been the stable, that side had been the front of the building, where the carriages and tack had been kept, and the horses had been led around to be hitched. Now it was the workshop, where the gardeners stored their mowers and blowers, the pool man put spare filters and chemicals, and the caretakers stored tools and supplies. Along the back wall there were three workbenches, and above them was a shelf with a row of paint cans in shades matching each room in the house for touch-ups. Forrest took two unopened half-gallon cans of mineral spirits, placed a strip of duct tape over the cap of each to prevent subtle leakage, and set them in his trunk in a plastic leaf bag. Then he took a battery-charged electric drill and a set of bits and put those in, too.

He started his engine, pulled down the long driveway, and out onto the road. He turned off his cell phone and put it into his pocket. He didn't want to receive calls and create a record of which repeater towers had relayed the signals to him. After a moment he took the phone out again. It would be wise to make one call before he left the area. He dialed the number with his thumb. "Hi. I'm afraid I had to go out of town unexpectedly. I won't be anyplace where I can be reached by phone, so don't call. I'll get in touch the second I get back. Erase this. 'Bye."

He turned off the phone again and put it into the glove compartment, so he wouldn't be tempted to use it on the daylong drive. Maybe he would buy Kylie a present while he was gone. It would have to be small enough to be paid for plausibly by her paycheck from Marlene's. Of course, the present would depend upon whether she followed his instructions about the message he had just left. He had the four-digit code she used to replay her messages, and he sometimes used it to listen to them. Usually what he heard was vapid voices of fourteen- and fifteen-year-old girls asking whether she was going to this or that, and what she was going to wear. In the past sometimes she had saved a message of his so she could replay it and listen to his voice on her cell phone after she had gone to bed. Later tonight he would check to be sure she had erased his message.

He drove to the Golden State Freeway, pulled onto the southbound entrance ramp, and accelerated into the stream of traffic. He drove steadily for two hours before he stopped outside Bakersfield at a large complex where rows of trucks sat idling at the back of the lot, went into the restaurant and ate steak and eggs, then pulled into the gas station and refilled his tank. Down the road in the suburbs, he stopped at a Rite Aid drugstore and bought a box of wooden kitchen matches and two cans of charcoal starter.

The drive from Bakersfield seemed longer than he had anticipated, because from here on the traffic grew gradually thicker and slower. There were long-haul trucks in the right lane, then recreational vehicles as big as buses beside them, and then the left lanes full of SUVs and pickup trucks fighting for inches, passing each other for illusory advantages or for spite. It was dangerous and tiring, and Ted Forrest didn't want to get into an accident or be pulled over by a highway-patrol officer, so he tolerated a spot in the middle lanes.

Fidelity

He came down Tejon Pass out of the hills into Castaic and the Santa Clarita Valley, places that had barely existed twenty years ago, but now were so choked with houses and strip malls and chain restaurants that they were beginning to seem dirty and worn out and unbearable. Then he was past the Cascade, the long, open sluice at the end of the aqueduct that in the 1900s had turned the San Fernando Valley into a garden and the backers and their friends into millionaires. A few minutes later, Forrest was in the northern part of the valley, fighting the real traffic toward the city of Los Angeles.

He was getting closer to his destination a few feet at a time, and the impatience and frustration invited him to think about why he was working so hard to get to a place where he didn't want to be. He had made a small mistake in Los Angeles eight years ago, and now, in order to fix things, he had to come back to complete a missing step. But the underlying problem was the nature of women. He struggled to obtain them, only to find that what he got had changed into something he had never wanted.

The human species had evolved so that the females matured earlier than the males. They seemed to grow and ripen steadily until they reached near perfection at about the age of fourteen. They were not exactly at their physical zenith at that moment, but they were on the verge of it, still getting better every day, and still not showing any deterioration of any kind. Their skin was luminous, their hair thick and shiny, the whites of their eyes really white. Their waists seemed impossibly thin, and their breasts and buttocks were round and firm.

When they got older, all of that began to change. Having a physical relationship with a woman over thirty was a compromise. It was like eating fruit that was just a bit too soft. It might not be bad enough to throw away just yet, but it was past its peak, and a man tended to catch himself letting it lie untouched in the bowl and reaching for newer fruit. Their skin lost some of its elasticity and began to crease

189

around the eyes and mouth. Their hair turned dull. They put on weight. If they stopped eating and did hard, punishing exercise each day, they began to look like skinny men. If they chose surgery and injections, they became nightmare creatures, with smooth, fishlike faces that had bloated mouths and wide, staring eyes.

They started out sweet-tempered and curious and pliable at thirteen, but within a decade they became spoiled and wised up, cynical and stupid simultaneously. A woman who had been told she was beautiful from the time she was fourteen became a monster of overconfidence and self-congratulation by the time she was twenty-four. She was psychotically suspicious of others and lenient with herself. She allowed herself to dignify whatever selfish nonsense she felt as though it were a philosophy, but she turned what he felt into a crime.

He had kept his feelings from causing trouble until the annual harvest festival in Mendota nine years ago. It was the first day of the festival, when they introduced the Harvest Queen and her court. The Harvest Queen was a pug-nosed girl with vacant eyes and a smile that had grown stale because it had been on her face sunrise to sunset since she was three and learned she would be rewarded for it. The one to look at was one of the princesses named Allison Straight.

She had dark brown hair with reddish highlights and huge green eyes. Her petite, curved body was the sort that drew the eyes away from the tall, greyhound-thin princesses around her, and her mouth had full Cupid's-bow lips. Even in her princess gown, what she evoked was not cold, empty elegance, but fecundity. A stranger to the small towns of the Central Valley might have marveled that she was not the one who had been chosen Harvest Queen. She had the magnetic quality that some actresses had: a singularity that served to remind the eye that beautiful women didn't all look like sisters. The best looked as though they had arrived from an undiscovered country on the other side of the earth.

Fidelity

Allison Straight wasn't queen because she didn't come from a well-established local family, didn't have a father who owned the Chevrolet agency or served on the town council. Ted Forrest had been born in the vegetable country. He had seen so many of these contests that he always looked at the whole court with little interest in which child of the local merchants had been chosen queen.

He had stood around for a time being important while the notables had found their way to him. These events were organized and operated by boosters' groups, and these people always wanted to ensure that Ted Forrest continued to sponsor their civic improvements. On this occasion, the one who took charge of him was a woman named Gail Hargrove. She was the former president of the chamber of commerce, a four-time councilwoman, and before that, a member of the board of education. She was a tall blond woman with a helmet of stiff hair and a lot of makeup who was as sexless as a civic-renovation project.

She conducted him to a big table where the local wines were being sampled in tiny plastic cups, and got him a real glass of the special cabernet that had reached its peak this year. She took him to see bins of exotic strains of white asparagus, broccoli rabe, radicchio, Japanese eggplant. She took him to see the architects' model of the new municipal-refurbishment plans, and compared them to the concept drawings that had been done in elementary-school classes under the title "City of the Future." Just when Gail Hargrove began to run out of other sights to show him, a bright flash distracted them. She took him toward the flashes, where she showed him the Harvest Queen and her court, who were on display across the room. They were on fake Louis XV armchairs from Zinsser's Furniture, posing for group portraits.

Allison Straight caught his attention instantly. He felt the same sort of certainty he had felt when he had seen Caroline at about the same age twenty years earlier. She was simply the most attractive human being he had seen in years, a natural miracle.

Gail Hargrove seemed to notice the effect that Allison had on him, but maybe she was simply acting on some protective instinct around young girls by spelling out how young they were. She said, "Our queen and her court are particularly lovely this year, aren't they? Whatever they're giving them in the school cafeteria seems to be having wondrous effects."

"Very pretty," he said without much enthusiasm. He had to be careful around women like Gail Hargrove.

Part of her status in the town depended upon her reputation as a graceful and skilled ambassador to the powerful. Despite his tepid response, she seemed to believe she had figured out what interested him, so she offered him a closer look. The photographer had exposed enough film, and he was folding his tripod and putting equipment in padded cases, so she took Ted Forrest by the arm and led him to the girls.

They had little notion of who Ted was. One or two probably knew the name Forrest because they had seen it engraved on plaques on public buildings and parks; the others were ignorant. But they knew who Gail Hargrove was, and they saw her defer to Forrest and treat him like a visiting potentate. They all perked up as they had been trained to do, looked him in the eye, and gave him nearly identical good-student smiles—all but one, whose smile was distinctly different.

He surprised everyone by going down on one knee, bowing his head, and saying, "Your majesty, I'm deeply honored to be admitted to the presence of such a gracious queen and her beautiful princesses." Gail Hargrove and the rest of the civic boosters laughed and applauded, and when the noise died down a bit, she introduced the girls.

Fidelity

The queen was Rebecca Sanders, the daughter of the plant manager for the packing and canning plant owned by a supermarket chain. Forrest said to her, "Say hello to your dad for me." He was not surprised when he heard the names of three of the six princesses were Milton, Keller, and Cole, all names he knew. He said something friendly to each. Two of the others were Martinez and Garcia, and he said merely, "Very pleased to meet you," as though it were true. Gail Hargrove, with a small-town politician's delight in showmanship, saved Allison to the very end.

When Ted Forrest heard the name, at first he felt cheated. If she had been from a family he knew, he might have been able to contrive a way to visit her at home. If she had been from a family with business ties to his holding company or his water interests, he might at least have had some excuse to run into her. But he had never heard of anyone named Straight. He said, "Straight. That's such a familiar name. Do I know your family?"

She gave him the mischievous look he thought he had detected earlier. "It's only familiar because everybody you meet says they're straight, even if they're not."

Ted Forrest laughed, the other girls joined him, and a half second later, the adults laughed nervously, too. But Gail Hargrove was not amused, and she didn't pretend to be. After a moment, enough people noticed it and the irreverence was strangled. Gail Hargrove restored her frozen smile, took Ted Forrest away, and showed him the Japanese cucumbers and Chinese eggplants. After a minute or two, she had recovered enough to launch into her pitch for his support in the municipal-redevelopment effort.

Ted Forrest listened attentively, but did not say exactly how much money he was likely to give, or for which portions of the project. He had learned over time that his status diminished when agreement was reached. He also wanted an excuse to stay longer. He had at first planned to drive home at four o'clock, but he decided to stay for the evening's fiesta. Ted Forrest had noticed that in order to obtain what he wanted, usually all that was required was patience and alertness.

Between the day's events and the fiesta that began at seven, there was a lull, and he used the time to call for a room reservation, not in Mendota, but along Route 180 outside Fresno. He also drove to a liquor store and bought a quart of vodka, then stopped at a pharmacy for a flat white plastic bottle designed for a woman's travel kit. He filled the plastic bottle with vodka, put the bottle in his coat pocket and locked the rest of the vodka in his car trunk, then went to the party.

The fiesta was held in the same few blocks downtown that the police had cordoned off for the earlier events. Mariachi bands strolled the sidewalks playing. There was a stage at the far end of the main street where two Mexican dance troupes performed folk dances in alternation. There was a beer tent run by a local bar, a wine-tasting tent run by a confederation of wineries, with the profits split in some unnamed formula with charities. If a person could make it past the crowds around those two tents, there was a long row of open booths where hot food was for sale.

Ted Forrest endured a couple of hours of the chatter of the town politicians and businesspeople. He knew that their patience and stamina weren't as prodigious as his, and they drank more than he did. As they each expressed their bid for his support of some specific part of the renewal project, then ran out of words, fell silent, and finally wandered off, he waited. The time came when he was free.

He sauntered along the edges of the fiesta, scanning the crowd. He found the queen and her court, surrounded loosely by a swirl of people their age, slipped into the group, and asked the queen to dance with him.

They danced something like a Mexican polka to the music from the stage for a minute or two, and he handed her off to a boy she had been talking to. The boy seemed to have mixed feelings about dancing, but had no time to think of an excuse not to. Ted Forrest took the hand of the princess who was standing nearest, danced with her, and then handed her off to another boy. He had started a trend. Either the other boys were less afraid to dance, or the girls were more insistent, but he noted that most of the other princesses were dancing by now, so he moved to Allison Straight. As they began to dance, he guided her into the center of the court so it was clear he was simply showing the shy kids how to have fun. But he said to her, "You're the most beautiful girl in the county."

"You know that, huh?"

"Yes."

"Then thanks."

He tried again. "You seem much more sophisticated than the others. Have you traveled, or are you some kind of prodigy?"

"Kind of what?"

"Prodigy. You know, like a genius."

She laughed hard, collapsing against his chest. "Oh, my God," she said.

"You didn't hear me wrong, did you?"

"So much for being a genius. But it's not just me, it's this band. It's so loud." She leaned against his chest again, then pulled back and patted his sport coat. "What's this?"

He leaned close and said into her ear, "I brought a little vodka to get me through this."

She looked up at him, her eyes excited. "Can I have some?"

"How old are you?"

She looked disappointed. "Busted. I'm sixteen."

"If you think that's old enough, then so do I. When this dance is over, go get some juice or a soft drink. It goes best with fruity ones, like orange." He looked around. "Meet me by that row of trees at the edge of the park."

"That's no good. Couples go in there to fool around."

"Where, then?"

"Don't you have a car?" she asked.

"Sure."

"Then we can go there. Where did you park?"

"Up the street and around the corner behind the hardware store."

Her eyes ignited with excitement. "Perfect. I'll meet you there in, like, five minutes."

She was there in three. They sat in the car and he poured some vodka into her orange juice, and they talked. Within a half hour, he had heard about how her father had left when she was four, and about her mother's inept attempt to raise her, which she saw as comical rather than tragic. Her mother was working tonight. She was a secretary at a dentist's office during the day and a waitress in a bar at night. The more Ted Forrest heard, the better he liked Allison. After an hour of talking, he kissed her. She stared at him for a few seconds as though she were trying to be sure she had not imagined it, then a few more to decide how she ought to feel about it, and then kissed him back.

It seemed to Ted Forrest that it was only a few minutes after that when he began to see small groups of people walking along the street, getting into cars to go home. He said, "I think we ought to get out of here."

She slouched low, held her hand beside her face and said, "I can't let those people see me with you like this."

"Get down and stay low while I drive past them."

She crouched on the floor in front of the passenger seat, and he drove out of the lot and past a steady stream of pedestrians. "This is so great," she said.

"Uh-oh," Forrest said. "There are police cars ahead. Stay low."

She stayed where she was as he drove past the policemen who were standing beside their cars and watching for people who appeared to be driving under the influence. He drove out onto Route 180 and increased his speed warily. When he was outside of town and had spotted the sheriff's-department car waiting for speeders beyond the second overpass, he said, "You can sit up now."

She got up and looked out the window at the dark farmland around her. "Where are we going?"

"Want to go home?" he asked.

"Not really."

"Well, if you'd like to talk some more, the only place I can think of where it's safe would be my hotel."

"Fine."

They stayed at his hotel until just after one, and then he drove her to the small one-story house on the edge of Mendota between the carpet warehouse and the Greek restaurant. She was inside and in bed before her mother came home from work.

After that, Allison Straight was his. At times he wondered if she was the girl he was supposed to have met instead of Caroline. He and Allison each lived two lives. She continued from day to day as one of the poorer girls in the high school, whose mother couldn't afford to buy her clothes as nice as the ones her classmates wore. But when she was with Ted Forrest, she had a wardrobe that was like an actress's. She would look in fashion magazines, and he would take her to buy the clothes in Los Angeles and San Francisco. They had to be kept in the closet in the apartment he had rented in San Francisco:

There was no place to wear them in Mendota, and no way to explain them if there were.

He also rented a place nearby in Fresno where they could go together without worrying too much about being seen. He told the managers of both of his apartment complexes that he had a teenaged daughter who lived most of the time with her mother, and that he was out of town much of the time. If anyone saw Ted Forrest and Allison at the apartment and wondered, the landlord could satisfy his curiosity. Forrest did everything right. He took her to San Francisco for wonderful weekends. They went to plays and concerts and ate in restaurants, always as an indulgent father and his daughter.

That summer he hired her for an imaginary job in public relations at Forrest Enterprises. She told her mother that she was working during the long, unhurried summer days they spent together. He added her name to the payroll so she received a regular paycheck in the mail that her mother could open and deposit in the bank.

Ted Forrest was in love with Allison Straight, and he built a separate reality that he and she could visit for limited periods of time. He made sure their time together was always exciting and new, and that it included a taste of luxuries she could never have experienced in any way other than being with a rich man. It was a terrible thing—the tragedy of both their lives, really—when the whole affair ended. It had left him changed, he was sure—sadder forever, more guarded and less trusting.

That was nine years ago, and here he was, still trying to recover from it. He drove slowly, moving ahead one yard at a time, then stopping again to wait as he made his way into Los Angeles. He was tired and he had time to kill, but he didn't want to rent a room and leave a record that he had been here. He parked in the lot of a shopping center and went to a twelve-screen movie theater.

He watched two films. By the time the second was over, he was hungry. Forrest chose to eat dinner at a small Chinese restaurant in a strip mall. He had a theory that Chinese people had trouble distinguishing one average-looking Caucasian from another, but they had always been too polite to admit it in public. He paid for his dinner in cash, then drove around the San Fernando Valley for an hour making sure that he could find the exact addresses that he would need later.

He stopped at a supermarket, bought a box of thumbtacks, a set of writing pads with cardboard covers, and a box of candles. Then he went to another theater and watched his third movie of the day.

When he walked out into the warm night air, it was after midnight at last. He drove to Philip Kramer's house in Van Nuys. He looked and found there was no car in the garage. He wondered whether Jerry Hobart had succeeded in taking Emily Kramer out to kill her, and simply had not reached him yet because his telephone had been turned off. He thought for a moment and realized it didn't matter. He still had to do what he had come here to do.

He walked around the house and found a big window in the back that had a glazier's sticker on it, and a lot of white streaks and dirt that had not been cleaned off it. He felt the edge of the glass and confirmed his theory: The putty was still wet. He had a penknife on his key chain, so he opened it and scraped away as much of the putty as he could reach, then slipped the blade in beside the glass and pried it out carefully. He removed the big pane from the frame and leaned it against the side of the house, then stepped inside.

He was surprised to see that so much furniture had been piled in the living room. The room looked like a warehouse. He set down his bags and went through the house with his flashlight. The upstairs had been stripped, and all of the furniture removed except three beds that had been dismantled and left lying on the floor in one room. He judged that Mrs. Kramer must be in the process of moving away.

Ted Forrest set about assembling his primitive devices. First he would put a thumbtack through a piece of cardboard and into the bottom of a candle so the candle would stand up. Then he placed candles in the corners of all of the rooms. The candles would provide delay. Then he went through the house adding fuel. In most places, he soaked the floors and walls with fire starter, then placed stick matches and crumpled writing paper at strategic places where a candle flame would eventually reach them. In the living room, he poured kerosene on all of the wooden furniture, the walls, and the floor, and then set six of his candles around the room. Next he picked up his bags of equipment and set them outside, took a box of stick matches, and went through the house lighting the candles, one by one. The last ones he lit were in the living room near the piles of furniture. Finally he stepped out of the empty window frame. He leaned the big sheet of glass against the frame so it would keep any breeze from blowing in and extinguishing his candles.

Then Ted Forrest drove to the office building where he had gone to meet Philip Kramer eight years ago. There were only two places he could think of where Kramer might have hidden the file, and in a few hours both would be in ashes.

24

Emily and Ray had spent the whole day doing hard physical labor, lifting and packing and loading, moving boxes of small things and large pieces of furniture out of upstairs bedrooms and down the staircase to the living room. Working beside Ray made her feel close to him. There was the physical proximity, and the very specific choreography—the "I've got this end and you take that end" that built familiarity.

They had also trusted each other enough to let themselves be seen in a sweaty shirt and with tousled hair stuck to a damp forehead, to be unconcerned about appearance for a time because they had to concentrate on the job of clearing the rooms.

And they had talked.

Emily's private life had stopped being private the moment Phil had been murdered. Even before, the privacy had been an illusion. Ray Hall had already known more about some parts of her life than she did.

In those days, Phil would tell her his version of things and she would listen and wonder fleetingly whether he was telling the truth, and then remind herself that part of what was required of her was that she believe him when he spoke. She didn't want to be the enemy waiting for him in his own house, the person who was trying to catch him at something.

Today she had moved another step away from those days, and as she did, she realized that Ray had been as deluded as she had. He might not have been fooled about Phil's cheating, but he was still living by the same rules of conduct that she was. Neither of them could acknowledge the truth without irrefutable evidence. Neither had really known the truth until Phil was dead.

Today she and Ray spent the whole day talking about things that weren't big or momentous, and so were more intimate than the big things that they had been forced to talk about since the night when Phil had not come home.

Emily talked about the items she was putting into boxes. Almost all of the clothes she kept were outfits that she had bought for special occasions. There were books she had bought but never read. There was a painting of the Santa Monica Mountains that she had never really liked, but had kept on a wall in the hall where it wouldn't do much damage, like an old pet that was ugly but sweet-tempered.

Ray talked to her about the job he'd had when he was in college, working on a moving van. He found that for the first whole summer the money almost didn't matter because of his intense curiosity about the hoards of things that people owned. He specialized in the seemingly tedious task of packing delicate or valuable items in boxes, just so he could see them and learn what he could about their owners' lives and histories. He had pretended that he hated the chore, partly so the other moving men didn't think he was odd, and shouldn't keep doing it. But by the second summer he had learned the contents of homes so thoroughly that there were no more surprises. Everybody's house was full of the same things, with the variations so minor that they revealed little except differences in income. Emily loved the way he laughed at his own curiosity.

They talked for long periods, and then were silent for stretches, and the silence built a kind of intimacy, too, because as they worked together, they were thinking about each other, each of them thinking about what the other had said.

There were times when one of them would stop in the act of moving some item—once, an old suitcase left in the guest-bedroom closet—and they would realize simultaneously that this could be it— the hiding place—and search it together.

When either of them took a book from a shelf, the next move would be to shake it, turn it over and riffle the pages. Each time something fluttered from between the pages to the floor they would both stop, feeling the same excitement at the same instant, then release the held breath in disappointment.

The things in her house—nearly all of them by now—were hers, not Phil's. When Phil had been dead a few days, she had gone through his clothes. She had decided it was the right thing to do because good clothes should not go to waste. But she had known she could not simply take clothes off hangers and give them away. Phil was perfectly capable of sewing something inside a piece of clothing. When he was in the marines, he had sometimes gone on leave with money sewn into a jacket. So Emily had gone through all of the clothes, felt the seams of the garments, folded them carefully, and taken them to Goodwill.

At ten thirty at night, after they had been working together for fourteen hours, they loaded what Ray referred to as Emily's "valuables" into the truck Billy had rented. She found that there were things of hers that she had kept for years simply because she expected always to live in this house, but which she didn't feel as though she wanted to move or pay to store. They ended up taking surprisingly little—her good clothes, a dozen photo albums, a few paintings and prints, and a few things she kept only because she couldn't give them away—Phil's guns and ammunition, a collection of gold coins he'd had for years, a small lacquer box of inexpensive jewelry, a couple of clocks, two radios, and two television sets. Ray filled the rest of the bay of the truck with a few favorite pieces of furniture. They drove the truck to the storage building and unloaded it, then drove to Ray's house.

It was late now, after three, and she was lying in Ray Hall's bed—one of his beds, anyway. It was her second night in his guest bedroom, and she noted that she had begun to have a new relationship with the room. On the first night it felt alien and empty and cold, as guest rooms often did. There wasn't much furniture. The sheets and bedspread had a subtle smell of detergent that wasn't the same as hers, and she could tell that nobody had ever slept on the mattress.

On the first night, she had kept her suitcase on a chair, opened it to take out things that she needed, and then closed it again. That changed tonight. Now she had clothes hanging in the closet so the wrinkles would hang out, and the bathroom counter was crowded with bottles of her shampoo and makeup containers and toothbrush and hairbrushes.

When she and Ray had come in this evening, she had been exhausted and dirty. They ate at a diner on the boulevard near Ray's neighborhood, where the waitress knew Ray's name and looked at him with a bit too much interest while she leaned close to him to get his order exactly right.

Emily had taken a hot bath and gone to bed, then slept deeply. But now she was awake. Since Phil's death, she had been unable to

sleep past the first few hours, the sort of sleep that was simple col-
lapse. Once she had used up that sleep, insistent problems came back
into her mind. She thought for hours about the single simple problem
of where Phil could have hidden the evidence about the nameless
powerful man. So far the theories and guesses that had kept tumbling
out of Emily's brain were all clever, all just like Phil, and all wrong.

Before long she found herself thinking once again about Dewey
Burns. There was a great deal to think about, and she had been putting the topic off for a whole day and most of the night. Dewey was
Phil's son. Dewey had a mother. How and when had Phil Kramer
met her? How could Phil have gotten a young black woman pregnant
when he had just married Emily?

She tried to remember what must have been happening between
her and Phil twenty-two years ago, or twenty-one years ago, but she
was having a terrible time bringing back the feeling. She remembered, intellectually, that they had fought sometimes when they were
very young. In later years, she had learned that it was better not to
point out every single thing that wasn't as she wanted it to be. Could
that have been the problem? Could they have had a fight, and Phil
had gone out and decided to get quiet revenge, or maybe gone to another woman for solace? That thought hurt too much. Maybe he had
been out celebrating some case that he had solved. He had gotten
drunk in some nightspot and met a pretty girl. Emily could tell by
looking at Dewey that his mother must have been pretty. Those big
light-brown eyes and high cheekbones had not come from Phil.

What bothered Emily the most was that something should have
been happening at that time between her and Phil. She should have
noticed that something was wrong, but nothing had made an impression on her. It should have, but it hadn't.

She thought at first that the sound of footsteps in the hallway was
part of a dream and that she had slipped into a nightmare repetition

of the way she had been awakened only one night ago. Then she recognized that the sounds were real. She sat up and watched the door open. "Emily?"

"What, Ray?"

"More trouble."

"What is it?"

"It's your house again. Apparently there's a fire."

"I'll be out in a minute." She threw the covers aside, slid off the bed, and walked toward the bathroom, then realized that she had stood up wearing only a T-shirt, and that she had already walked too far to retreat. She told herself it didn't matter. It was dark in the room; he was probably already turning away before she had moved; they were both adults; it was an emergency. Then she hit on the truth: She didn't care if Ray saw her that way.

Her house. She tugged on some clean clothes, then sat on the bed to tie her running shoes. Her house. That man must have been back, trying to find exactly the same thing she had spent the day looking for. She felt afraid, but at the same time she felt urgency. She wanted to get there and see.

She met Ray at the upstairs landing. This time she took her purse because it had Phil's gun in it. She knew it was illegal for her to carry a gun, but she didn't care. She followed Ray down the stairs and saw that he had his gun tonight. He must be thinking what she was thinking: Anything could be a ploy, a trick to get her out in the open. She got into Ray's car and he drove toward her neighborhood, but neither of them spoke at first.

When they were near Emily's street, it was hardly necessary to say anything. The sky had an orange glow, and pieces of black ash floated upward against it, swirling in the hot updraft. Emily could see a big sycamore silhouetted against the orange luminescence. Beyond it the sky seemed to brighten as rolling sheets of flame came up off the siding on the second floor, flickering around the fireproof shingles of the roof. The windows were all shattered and black smoke streamed out, but the rooms inside were bright with fire. There was a hot wall of fire beyond every window frame, as though everything had gone up at once.

Ray pulled the car to the curb. Ahead was a jam of parked fire trucks and, on the pavement, a complicated slither of hoses leading from the hydrants toward her house. Firefighters in yellow turnout coats with stripes of tape that reflected their headlights dragged more hoses, so she realized that the trucks must have arrived only a few minutes ahead of them.

She looked at Ray. "Do you think he's here?"

"I don't know. The firemen will be taking videos of the crowd, and probably the cars parked close enough to see. They always do that when there's a chance of arson. I doubt that they'll have much question about this one."

Emily and Ray got out of the car. She stayed close to him, but she began looking in every direction except the direction of the fire. A small crowd had gathered, and she recognized a few of her neighbors standing on the sidewalk near their own houses, their faces illuminated by the fire. A few were still in bathrobes, and others dressed in what must have been the clothes they took off a few hours ago.

She scanned the crowd for a stranger who might be the man who had come into her bedroom in a ski mask, but she didn't see anyone who frightened her. She saw the O'Connors, all seven of them lined up on their front lawn, staring up at the sparks rising on the heated air above the flames on Emily's house. Denny had the garden hose connected to the spigot at the corner of their house. She hoped that the flying sparks didn't ignite anybody else's roof.

There were the Weilers on the other side, all the kids on their front steps as though they were bleachers. The parents must be on the other side or in the back yard. After a moment, she saw the Weilers' car back out of the garage slowly and stop just above the sidewalk. It was probably a wise precaution. The fire could easily catch their garage, and this would save their car. If they planned to move anything out of their house, this might be the time.

She saw a couple of firefighters walking along the line of people on the sidewalk, and it looked to her as though one of them had a camera on a strap around his neck. This could be the one Ray had mentioned: the fireman who would take a long, careful look at who was there to watch the spectacle of her house burning down.

A woman came out of the line and spoke to the fireman for a few seconds. She pointed at Emily, and the firefighter looked over his shoulder at her. The woman hurried across the street, and Emily saw she was Margaret Santora. "Oh, my God, Emily!" she said. "We were all so afraid you didn't get out. We were so scared. How did it happen?"

"I . . . was out," said Emily. "I have no idea."

Emily didn't miss the way Margaret's eyes flicked to the side to take in Ray Hall, then back to Emily's face.

"Margaret, this is Ray Hall, one of the detectives from the agency."

"Pleased to meet you," Margaret said. She didn't seem to be, and her left hand rose to the neck of her robe to pinch the sides together in an unconscious gesture. She said to Emily, "Well, I'm just glad you're okay, that's all. The rest of it is the insurance company's problem." She waited for a moment to see Emily's reaction.

Emily had not thought about financial loss, or about insurance. She was thinking about destructive power, the heat of the flames, the malice of the man who had tried to burn her to death in her sleep.

She was distracted by the firefighter she had noticed with her neighbors. He had appeared only a few feet off. "Mrs. Kramer?"

"Yes?"

"I'm Captain Rossman. I need to talk with you for a few minutes."

Emily was alarmed by his manner, which seemed more insistent than she would have expected. But she noticed that Ray had moved to the man's side and a step behind, and he was nodding. "Sure," she said. "Here?"

"Let's go to my car."

He half-turned and nearly bumped into Ray. "This is Ray Hall," she said. "He's a . . . colleague of mine."

"Hello," said Captain Rossman. He gave Ray's hand a perfunctory shake, barely looking at him. He took Emily to a Ford Crown Victoria that looked like a police car that had been painted red, opened the door for her and got in behind the wheel.

She said, "Are you the arson investigator?"

"I'm one of them."

"Do you know yet if it was?"

"Yes. There were accelerants in the corners of all the rooms. The first people in said it looked and smelled like the whole place was soaked."

"I was afraid of that."

"Oh?" he said. "You expected this? Why?"

"It's complicated. My husband owned a detective agency. He was murdered nine days ago—shot on the street. Two days ago, I had a visit here in the middle of the night from a man with a gun and a ski mask. He wanted some information that my husband supposedly had about someone."

"What was it?"

"I have no idea."

"Who was the person the information was about?"

"I don't know that, either. But the man in the ski mask said he'd kill me if I didn't give it to him. I think he would have, but he got interrupted when another of our detectives showed up and scared him off. He was back last night, but the guys couldn't catch him."

Rossman sat scribbling in his notebook, but she was sure he had a recorder. He had reached into his coat as they had sat in the car, and his hand had come back empty. Finally he said, "You called the police?"

"Yes. They were here for hours two days ago, then again last night."

"So there's a police report?"

"I assume there is, or will be." She stared at him. "Are you having trouble believing me?"

He turned in his seat to face her. "I'm sorry to give that impression. At this stage, I'm just collecting all the facts I can while they're still fresh. The firefighters told me that the house wasn't arranged in the usual way. The living room had furniture piled up in it, and the rest of the house was empty. Why was that?"

"I had just had a horrible experience in that house. When the man broke in the second night, I knew that whatever else happened, I didn't intend to live there again. But I knew that it was also the most likely place to find whatever it was that my husband had hidden and that the man in the ski mask wanted. Mr. Hall and I were searching the furniture—mostly drawers and cabinets—and then moving everything to storage so that when it was gone we could search the house itself. We had already taken a couple of loads out. The furniture in the living room was going tomorrow."

"Did anybody besides Mr. Hall know you were doing that?"

"Yes. The other people from the detective agency." Various thoughts raced through her mind. She couldn't mention that April had loved Phil; she couldn't tell this man that Dewey was Phil's son. "They were my husband's friends, and my friends. They were working all day doing the same to the agency office."

Rossman looked at her for a moment, but this time it was different, less distrustful. "I guess I should be the one to tell you, Mrs. Kramer. Your office had a fire tonight, too."

25

Jerry Hobart walked along the street, looking over the low rooftops of smaller buildings at the office fire. Smoke from the office building looked black against the sky, but inside the blackness there were flames, appearing at first like small lightning flashes inside a dark cloud. But as he walked toward the building, the flames seemed to gain rapidly, now coming out of the roof of the building and flickering above the smoke.

The firefighters swarmed around the foot of the building, but the fire seemed to Jerry Hobart to be all above the fourth floor, where Kramer Investigations had its office. The firefighters had gone up on long ladders and broken widows to spray hoses inside, but they were mainly soaking the levels below the fire because that was all they could reach.

There seemed to be yellow raincoats moving past upper windows now and then, but Hobart supposed they were just searching for people trapped inside, and before long those firefighters were going to have to come out, too. Hobart stopped almost two blocks from the building and watched for a minute. He heard more sirens, coming fast from somewhere behind him. The sirens weren't police sirens, but Hobart decided it was time to go. There was no reason to see more. He walked across the street and around the corner where he had left his car, then heard the sirens grow louder. He looked over his shoulder and saw an ambulance flash by.

Hobart got into this car and drove away from the fire, and away from the direction where the fire trucks had come from. He thought about the ambulance. It was hard to guess what that meant. Old buildings were bad places to be in a fire. They were trimmed with lots of wood that had been cut, shaped, and varnished fifty or sixty years ago, and had been drying in the parched air ever since. The firemen he had seen scrambling around in the building on the upper floors had a lot of wooden beams and staircases between them and the ground. Maybe one of them had gotten hurt. Of course, the person most in danger at an arson fire was usually the arsonist. He was the one splashing gasoline around and lighting matches.

As Hobart drove away from the office building, he tried to get past his shock. It was hard for him to imagine Emily Kramer burning her husband's detective agency. He had not anticipated it. He had intended to terrify her, to make her angry, to force her to find the evidence her husband had hidden from Theodore Forrest. But maybe Hobart had overdone it. Maybe he had induced her to kick over all of the game pieces. She might have realized that having evidence to use against a man like Theodore Forrest was worth nothing to her. All she really wanted was to be left alone, so it was possible she had taken away Jerry Hobart's incentive to bother her. If so, she hadn't thought it through to the next step: Hobart's killing her for throwing away his chance.

He had to know. He drove the rented car to Winnetka, then took the 101 Freeway east toward the city. He left the freeway at Van Nuys Boulevard and drove north toward Emily Kramer's house.

It occurred to him that the fire might not be such bad news. Maybe she had found the evidence, and now she was trying to throw him off by making him believe the evidence was burned. Then she could make whatever deal she wanted with Theodore Forrest and not worry about Jerry Hobart.

Forrest would make her rich, and she would move away. What else could she do if her husband's business was burned up? And any deal with Forrest would mean giving him the evidence. She wouldn't ever be bothered again, and neither would Forrest. Whatever Forrest had done would be forgotten forever.

Hobart drove toward Emily Kramer's house. When he was still several blocks away, he realized that was burning, too. The sky was bright with fire, and the flashing of lights from fire trucks and emergency vehicles. He parked on Vanowen past the intersection with the street that crossed hers. He looked up and down the street, then trotted across it to the sidewalk and walked toward the glow. As he approached on foot, he felt the odd breeze that came up around fires. A big, hot fire seemed to create its own weather, pulling in air and blowing it out in hot swirls.

When he reached Emily Kramer's block, there was already a growing crowd of people standing around watching the firemen dragging hoses to the sides and back of the house. The roof and the upper floor where he had cornered her a couple of nights ago had burned through and collapsed into the big empty space of the living room, and now the flames were devouring splintered woodwork and broken two-by-fours and beams. The fire was burning now with such ferocity that he knew their biggest worry was that the hot sparks were being carried to the neighboring houses and yards.

Hobart paid no further attention to the fire. Instead he walked the street searching for Emily Kramer. He made his way among the gawkers, shouldering carefully past people in bathrobes and pajamas and sweatpants, making sure he gave none of them a reason to look directly at him. He kept himself between them and the glare of the fire, so their faces were illuminated and his was a dark shape that passed quickly across their vision.

Then he saw her. He kept walking as he stared at her. She was sitting in an official red car a half block from the house. She opened the passenger door and got out, then took a few steps and looked in the direction of her house. She stopped, as though she were a machine that had suddenly lost power and stalled. The sight she was staring at no longer looked much like a house, and she seemed to be trying to remember what it had looked like an hour ago.

The driver of the red car got out. He was wearing a fireman's yellow turnout coat and carrying a clipboard. He saw Emily Kramer standing there and followed her eyes to the fire, and then stood there looking, too. It seemed to Hobart that the two of them must have been in the car doing an interview and neither of them had seen the house lately. The progress of the fire seemed to surprise them. The fireman reached into his car to retrieve his helmet, and then shut the door.

Another man got out of a car parked nearby, walked up to Emily Kramer, and put his arm around her shoulders, as though he were comforting her. Her reaction was revealing. She did not look up at the man or speak to him, and she didn't express surprise. She simply let the man's arm be around her, and stayed where she was, her eyes on the fire. She seemed to lean into him slightly, like a woman who was cold or tired might lean into a man she considered to be hers.

The fire had reached a kind of peak now that the big pieces of wood were bared and had fallen into a pile. The house was like a gigantic bonfire. Hobart kept moving. He kept his back to the flames as he moved along the street, then turned at the first corner to go to where he had left his rental car.

Hobart swung the car around to face the intersection with the side street so he would be able to see any vehicle driving away from the Kramer house onto the boulevard. He still wasn't sure whether Emily Kramer had burned her house and her husband's agency or not. If she had, she was a hell of an actress. But the fire certainly had been set, and what could that fireman talking to her in the car have been but an arson investigator? She might not know it yet, but she was under suspicion.

Hobart opened the side window of his car, lit a cigarette, and listened. Now and then, above the constant thrum of the big truck engines and the pumps, there would be shouts. The smoke coming up from the fire was still a swirl of black. The white clouds of steam had not replaced the black even now, and Jerry Hobart could tell that by the time the fire was out it wouldn't much matter. The Kramer house was going to be a pile of charcoal.

He inhaled smoke from the cigarette and blew it slowly out into the night air. No matter what the reason for the fires, they were a problem for him, and so was the sudden appearance of this new man. Hobart had hoped that Emily Kramer was not interested in competing with him for Theodore Forrest's money. Maybe that man she was with tonight had talked her into doing this. Trying to go eyeball-to-eyeball with Hobart didn't seem to be something she would have thought of on her own.

He put out his cigarette and found himself thinking about Valerie. He could always see Valerie's face in his memory, even bring it back from different times of their lives. He could see her at fifteen or at twenty or at thirty, but she always seemed best to him as he had seen her last. As she broadened, her shape had the look of a woman, and the age on her face made her look smarter and softer. He hated it when she made fun of herself, saying she was old and losing her looks. It felt as though she was reminding him of his own age—the same as hers—and saying he was ugly, and at the same time telling him he was foolish and pitiful for hanging around a woman like her, instead of a newer model. He pictured her now, leaning into his car window as he prepared to drive off and leave her a few days ago.

He saw the cone-shaped beams of a pair of headlights appear from the direction of the Kramer house, and realized that the smoke must be lower now, spreading like a hazy smog on the boulevard. He closed his window. The car appeared at the intersection ahead of him and stopped, and he could see the driver. It was the tall man who had put his arm around Emily Kramer.

Hobart waited until the man had made the right turn onto Vanowen, then started his engine. He waited, watching the car move off. He could see there was a second, smaller person in the passenger seat. Hobart kept his eyes on the car, letting it get farther and farther away. A pair of cars passed him in the same direction. When the car was almost too far ahead to see, he turned on his headlights and followed.

He gained on it until he was about a quarter mile behind. When a truck came up behind him, he let the truck pass him, and then moved into the space behind it so the man with Emily Kramer would look in his rearview mirror and see the truck's headlights and not Hobart's.

Hobart followed the truck up the street for about two miles, keeping his eyes ahead on the car carrying Emily Kramer. When the truck in front of him turned off to the right, he sped up a bit and fell in with a pickup truck and an SUV, hiding by being part of the traffic instead of a single car for a time. The SUV peeled off to the left-turn lane, and a few blocks later the pickup coasted up the driveway and between the pumps of a gas station.

Hobart lay back in the right lane and kept his distance until the man made a right turn onto a side street. Hobart decreased his speed. He didn't believe there was any chance the driver had noticed his set of headlights more than any of the others, but on a residential street this late at night, his car would be the only one. He made the turn after the man, pulled to the curb, turned off his headlights, and watched the man's taillights until he turned again.

Hobart crept forward until he reached the corner where the other car had turned. He stopped at the stop sign and saw the car going into a driveway beside a house. He waited for fifteen minutes, drove around the block to go past the driveway where the car had gone, and noted the house number. The garage door was closed now. There was a dim light visible on the second floor of the house, but then it went out.

Jerry Hobart made the left turn at the corner, switched on his lights, and drove back out to Vanowen. He was tired, ready to go to his hotel and get into bed, but this had been a good night for him. Emily Kramer must have found the evidence her husband had hidden. Torching her own house and office could only be an attempt to make Hobart believe that the evidence was destroyed. He knew that she was spending time with a man, but he knew exactly where they were living. He could take her anytime he wanted to.

26

Ted Forrest reached Route 33 and passed west of Mendota just as the night was showing signs of giving way to the dim gray light before the sunrise. As he drove through the Central Valley, now and then his car would dip into a low, shallow pocket of fog. It was what the old people used to call the bean fog. In the days before heavy, efficient irrigation, the fog was a big source of free water for the vegetable crops.

He knew this highway so well that he descended into the basins of fog without slowing. He believed he would detect any obstacle blocking his lane in plenty of time, and if he couldn't, he could veer off the road and let the car exhaust its momentum in the level rows of artichokes and radishes he had been passing for the last couple of miles.

When he reached a rise and recognized the long flat road ahead, he took his cell phone out of the glove compartment and turned it on. As it awoke, he heard the familiar musical tone, and then almost instantly, the one that said he had a message. He glanced at the screen: thirteen messages, twenty-one missed calls.

Forrest had already felt tired and anxious from his night's work, and listening to the messages seemed like an insurmountable task. He decided not to listen to them. He would be home in a little while anyway. Then he changed his mind. He had to know if Kylie had called, and it wasn't safe to leave her calls in his voice mail. He dialed the message number and the code, then listened.

"Ted." It was Caroline's voice, not Kylie's. "I think you should come home right now. You know that we need to talk, and putting it off isn't helping."

He pressed the three key to erase it, and left his finger on the key while he listened to the next message. "It's now seven o'clock. I'm going out for dinner with some friends. I assume that you heard my earlier message and decided to ignore it. Or maybe you left your phone off all day, which amounts to the same thing. I won't be home before ten, but you can call my cell number."

He listened to the next call. At first there was near silence, but he could hear a woman breathing, and sounds that could be traffic. Then she said, "Sorry I missed your call during business hours, Mr. Forrest." It was Kylie. "I was still at violin practice and then I went to work, and didn't get a chance to check messages. I'll be available and waiting for your call from now until tomorrow." She didn't seem to know how to end her message. "This is Kylie Miller. My number is—" He hit the three and erased it.

Next there were eight more calls from Caroline, each one just a second or two. "Call me," or "It's Caroline," "Me again," and once, "Shit!" Her final call was at three in the morning—he looked at his watch—about forty-five minutes ago. That was good. She had probably given up and gone to sleep. He could go in, take another of the spare bedrooms, and get some sleep, too.

He remembered that when he had left he had resolved to check Kylie's voice mail to be sure she had erased his call from yesterday. He took his eyes off the road long enough to dial her mailbox number, then her phone number. On the first call, a young girl's voice said, "Hey, Kyl. This is Tina. Get back to me on the party tonight." The time on the call was six fifteen. Why had Kylie's phone not been on at six fifteen? Oh, yes. He remembered. Violin lesson. His own message had been left in the morning, so if she had neglected to erase it, he would already have heard it.

He still didn't hang up.

The next message was the same voice: "Kylie? Do you still want a ride tonight? Call me." Ted Forrest felt his breathing become shallow, and noticed a hollow feeling in his stomach. He told himself it was all right. He had called her early and left his message that he would be gone. She had erased it, tried to call him back, and then decided to go to a party with her girlfriend Tina. He had heard of Tina, he thought. Kylie talked constantly, but it was like a cat purring, just a steady sound that come out because she was comfortable and contented. He had not listened to her anecdotes closely enough to know all the names with confidence.

He knew that he should be delighted. It wasn't good for a young girl to be isolated from friends her own age. It might even make her feel restless and tired of him, her young mind reacting to get what it needed, the way a growing body did when it was missing some nutrient. Going to a party was good in a dozen ways. Kylie was gregarious and had lots of friends. If a few of them started to notice that she was hardly ever available in the evening, they might begin to talk. That was probably the danger he had to worry about most because it was out of his control. If they talked, the gossip would eventually reach one of her friends' mothers.

But he couldn't keep from feeling a blind, galloping sort of jealousy. He knew that there was no realistic hope of keeping Kylie away from boys her age, and absolutely no chance that any of them wouldn't be interested in her.

He kept listening. "Kylie, this is Mark. I was wondering if you were doing anything on Friday. My number is—" Forrest erased the call.

Forrest erased two more calls from boys, and one from a girl who sounded too giggly to be a safe, sensible companion, and who invited Kylie to "hang out" because Hunter and Shane were going to be there.

When he had heard all of the messages he put his phone in his pocket and began to feel a manic energy. He knew it was only the shallow, nervous agitation that came from too many hours at the wheel. He had driven all the way to Los Angeles, spent a night awake there, and driven all the way back, all in changing states of worry or fear or excitement.

But he had done it. He had managed to burn both the Kramer house and the office in one night. He had destroyed the evidence that Phil Kramer had wanted to use to blackmail him, and probably any secret copies that Kramer had never intended to hand over. If Philip Kramer had been devious enough to hide the evidence in a third place, then Kramer had defeated himself. If it hadn't turned up by now, then he had not left word where it was hidden. It would stay hidden forever.

This was a masterstroke, the sort of big thinking and bold, decisive action that won wars. The realization that he actually had accomplished the coup and made it home without discovery began to make him giddy. He was free, he was safe, he was invulnerable. He still had Jerry Hobart out preparing to kill Emily Kramer, and that was good, but now that he had burned the evidence, it wasn't essential. As soon as he paid Hobart, he would forget all of this unpleasantness.

As he drove along the ever-more-familiar stretch of highway toward his house, he knew he was going to beat the sun by a long mar-

gin. As soon as it was light enough to work, there were always work-
ers in the fields who might see a car out at dawn and maybe remember it. But by then Forrest would be asleep. In a few more minutes,
Forrest saw his home ahead, standing on its rise at the end of its long
drive.

The gate was closed. He reached for the remote control in the
door's well, pressed the first button, and watched the gate slide aside
to admit him, then pressed the button again to close it behind him.
It felt good to be inside that iron gate again.

Forrest kept his car slow all the way up the long driveway and
around the big house to the old carriage-house garage. He felt a moment of suspense as he reached for the remote control again to open
the garage door. What if the garage was empty except for the pickup
truck and the riding lawn mower the gardeners used? What if Caroline had gotten into her Jaguar and simply driven off toward whatever
vision of a future her self-absorbed mind had been constructing since
he had left? The fact that his thought had come from nowhere
seemed to give it divine provenance and make it prophetic. The current of the universe had been running his way for the past twenty-
four hours. Would there be a last gift?

He pressed the second button.

As soon as the door began to rise, he recognized the tires of the
Jaguar in its parking space, then the gleaming metal. His premonition
was only a fantasy. He moved his car into its space beside the Jaguar,
pressed the second button on the remote control again to close the
door, then turned off the car's engine.

He sat still for a moment, staring at the back wall of the garage.
There was the door to the old tack room, and it reminded him of the
things he had taken when he had left. He pushed the button to pop
his trunk, then got out, picked up his small suitcase, and looked into

the space behind it. His car was clean. He closed the trunk, then walked out the side door of the garage onto the stone walkway to the house. It was still dark, but he could hear a few chirps from birds beginning to move around in anticipation of the sun.

He was careful to grip his keys in his palm so they wouldn't jingle when he unlocked the front door. He prepared to punch in the code to turn off the alarm before it sounded, then pushed the door inward. The alarm was off, and he let out a breath in relief. Caroline had undoubtedly decided she didn't want to be awakened.

He stepped into the broad foyer of his house and felt the hard, slippery surface of the marble tiles, the black-and-white pattern just visible in the dim star-glow from the skylight. The substantial, weighty presence of the architecture made him feel even more protected and invulnerable than before. The house was not just big interior spaces and thick walls. Hardinfield was several generations of importance and unassailable position. He was aware that there were mobs of people living on the coast to the south and the north of him—movie-studio people and computer billionaires—who each had the money to build several houses like his. But it would not have been appropriate, and even they seemed to sense it. When they opened their windows they didn't see vistas of open land running all the way to barely visible foothills. They saw the houses of the rest of the rich rabble, all shouldered up to each other along streets in Beverly Hills or San Francisco, and actually touching each other in Malibu.

"I see you're back."

His head spun toward Caroline's voice. A love seat that belonged beyond the vaulted arch in the living room had been pushed across the marble floor into the foyer. As his eyes adjusted to the deeper shadows along the far wall, he could see that she was wearing a pair of jeans and a sweatshirt, and there was a quilt pushed into a lump beside her. "What are you doing here? Did you sleep here?"

"I didn't want to miss you."

"Very interesting. You can tell me about it another time. I'm going up to bed." He started toward the staircase.

"I want to talk now, Ted. There are no servants in the house. I told Maria to give them the rest of the week off, so we can settle this. We're going to start right now."

He had almost made it to the stairway, but he heard something in her voice that made him stop. "Oh? Something's urgent?"

"You bet. It's very urgent. I would like you to put your suitcase down and come with me to the library where we can see each other and talk."

"And what will happen if we wait until I've had some sleep and a shower and maybe even some breakfast?"

"Are you trying to goad me into saying something that will give you an excuse to stomp off? I don't want to threaten you."

"That's good. I don't think there's much you could threaten me with at this point, is there? That there will be *less* than no sex? That you'll be *more* extravagant and demanding? When would you find time?"

"You just wanted to hurt me, and it always works, I guess, because your wanting to do it is what hurts. In spite of that, in spite of everything that's gone on in the past few years, I find that you're still more important to me than anyone else. Whenever I do something, or even think something, part of me is already looking around for you, to be sure you noticed. I know it's just a reflex now because you haven't been there watching or listening in years. What hurts most is the unfairness."

"What's unfair?"

"We don't have a better relationship because *you* haven't wanted one. When I went off to find ways of keeping busy, I wasn't choosing them instead of you. I was filling a vacancy." She looked down and

225

shook her head, as though to push away a distraction. "It doesn't matter. I don't want to fight, I want to save you."

His jaw was tight, but he spoke quietly. "What the hell are you talking about?"

"I listened to your phone messages."

"You what?"

"You heard me. You're having a—I don't even know what to call it— Is it called an affair if it's with a child?"

His heart seemed to him to have stopped, but then he felt it begin to pound. He could barely breathe. "What on earth would make you say that?"

"Jesus, Ted! I heard her message. I asked Maria's daughter if she knew her from school, and she did. The girl is barely fourteen, Ted— a child. You've been sleeping with a child." She couldn't say it without having her mouth contort so her face became a mask of horror and despair. "There's a doctor, a psychiatrist, who specializes in this kind of thing. Diane Bidwell's cousin Burt was seeing him, and she thinks he saved his life. It was completely confidential."

"Until Diane found out."

"I remember the doctor's name, so we don't have to ask some other doctor for a referral or something. It can be completely—"

"Stop right there," he said. "Don't even finish. The answer is no."

"It's not that simple. This problem isn't going away. You can't have sex with children. If anyone finds out, you'll go to prison. And if this Kylie Miller is leaving messages like that on your voice mail, how long will it take? Her parents, her teachers, her friends, somebody, will find out."

Ted Forrest snorted. "This is actually pretty funny. You're completely wrong. She's just a kid who wants a summer job in the Forrest Enterprises office. She went in and talked to Denise, and Denise has been trying to set up an interview. That's all." He was aware that his voice was too flat, but he hoped she hadn't noticed.

"Denise gives out your personal phone number to job applicants?"

"Sometimes. Why not? This is a high school girl, not a stalker."

"Ted, this isn't a game. It isn't just the usual infidelity. I'm used to that. When you first stopped wanting me, I knew you had to be having sex with someone, and for a few years I tried to always know who. I found out about your friends' wives because I confronted one of them and she told me. I knew about the ones in your office because of the way they treated me. I knew there must be others because I saw receipts for hotel rooms in San Francisco and Sacramento that you had to have used in the daytime. I always blamed myself for not being attractive enough or fun enough or something, and kept quiet. Not this time. We've got to get you into therapy now."

"I know, inpatient therapy. Then, while I'm in some hospital so doped up I can't walk out the door, you can be out here spending my money, right?"

"I'm trying to save you."

"From what?"

"She's a child."

"She's a couple of years younger than you were when I met you."

"That whole period seems a lot different to me now than it did when I was seventeen and you were thirty. People talked, and now I know they were right to. You've got a problem, and you've got to admit it to yourself and see a doctor."

"You're a jealous woman who wants to lock me up. What sort of therapy do you recommend—chemical castration? This is the perfect revenge fantasy."

"My fantasies aren't that way, Ted. I dream about having a decent, normal life."

"Great! Have one. Go behave the way you would have if you had never met me. Have a decent, normal life. I'll pay you a salary. Find a nice guy. I'll pay *him* a salary, too."

"Are you so deluded you don't see? You're in trouble. If you're already in voluntary therapy before anyone knows, we might be able to keep you out of jail. We might even be able to settle the lawsuit her parents file when they find out. And make no mistake, they will. She has no sense of propriety."

He paced the foyer for a moment, then stopped in front of Caroline. "Listen carefully. You're wrong about Kylie, and you're wrong about me. You listened to a phone message in which a young local girl I don't even know called for an interview appointment. Your imagination and your bitterness toward me magnified it into a big story. It isn't."

"I didn't hear anything like that." Caroline looked amazed, then confused. "You don't seem to—" She stopped. "Didn't you hear it? Oh, my God. I guess you didn't. She called on the line in your office. I saved it after I heard it so I could hear the others." She stepped across the foyer to the small door beside the library, went inside, and returned with the wireless telephone from his desk, punching the buttons for the messages. She stopped a few feet from him and handed it to him.

He took the telephone and turned away from her. "You have no new messages, and four saved messages. To hear your—" He pressed the one key and heard "Hi, Ted." It was Kylie's voice. "I called your cell phone, but it must have been off, so I figured I'd try your private line. I missed you tonight. I was hoping that I would be in bed right now. Not alone. With you, silly. Instead, I ended up at a stupid party with Tina. I couldn't stand it, so I came home early and now I'm just lying here thinking about you." He had heard enough. He pressed the three key and heard, "Message erased."

He could think of nothing to say. Caroline knew who Kylie was and had found out how old she was. He was suddenly exhausted, his body stiff from sitting in the car, and his mind seemed to be racing, but nothing came to him. He walked to the staircase, set the phone on the step, picked up his suitcase, and prepared to climb.

"Ted?" She said it quietly at first, then, "Ted!"

"I don't want to talk about it now."

"You have no choice."

"I have nothing to say to you." He took the first step, and from the silence he knew she was following.

Her voice came from behind him. "You have one chance, Ted. One, and then it's over. You can help me try to fix this—break it off with the girl, pay her off if necessary, get into therapy—or I'll have to call the police."

He spun around to look down at her. He felt his neck and temples pulsing. Caroline looked as though she were wreathed in a red haze. He saw her step backward, and her expression of alarm seemed to tell him what to do. She pivoted and leaned forward as though she was going to run.

In a second, he was on her. His arm shot out and hooked around her waist and swung her off her feet, and then he was half-carrying, half-dragging her across the foyer.

She shrieked, "You're hurting me!"

He kept his arm around her waist and pulled her into the corridor that led toward the kitchen. He opened the door beside the pantry, held her at the top of the stairs to the basement, and turned on the light. She began to scream and struggle as though she thought he was going to throw her down the stairs, but he closed the door behind him, tightened his grip, and carried her down. She stopped screaming. Now she was just breathing hard from struggling against a bigger, stronger opponent.

Ted Forrest pulled her into the wine-tasting room with the theatrical-looking stone walls and false ceiling Caroline's decorators had added, past the long table surrounded by leather chairs and the glass-fronted cabinets of glassware to the end of the room. He opened the heavy oak door to the wine cellar and turned on the light. As he pulled her inside the long, narrow room lined with wine racks that reached the edge of the arched ceiling and shut the door behind them, she began to scream again. "Shut up!" he said. "Nobody can hear you."

She was wide-eyed and disheveled. "What are you doing? Are you crazy?"

"We've already had this conversation. No, I'm not crazy. I'm just giving you a chance to sit quietly for a while and think before you do something stupid that you can't undo when you cool off. I want you to step back and consider the fact that you're angry now because I've been seeing a younger woman."

"Not a woman. She's a *child*."

He ignored the comment. "Your jealousy is making you lose your sense of proportion. You're making terrible threats and wild demands, one after another. Isn't this really about 'who is the fairest one of all'? It's not as though you were still interested in me, and were fighting for my affection. You just don't want to lose, even if you don't want the prize."

"It's about a crime, Ted. A felony."

"Is that what you're afraid of? You could hardly be implicated. You know that in all the time you've lived in my house, we've been able to tolerate each other and you've been treated well. I'm willing to go on that way, if it suits you. If it doesn't, we can arrange a divorce with a fair settlement, and you can do something you like better." He paused. "However . . ."

"However?"

"Yes. You must know that I'm never going to let you get me committed into a mental institution or arrested. It just isn't going to happen."

"You're going to prevent it by imprisoning me?"

"Oh, please! You're in the wine cellar of our own house."

She glared at him but kept her distance, retreating a step until she backed into one of the floor-to-ceiling racks full of wine bottles. He could see that she was already beginning to feel the chill of the wine cellar. The two-ton temperature-control unit her decorators had insisted on kept the room at a constant fifty-five to fifty-seven degrees.

Forrest stepped out of the room, closed the door, and turned the key, but left it in the lock as usual. He heard her pounding on the door as he went to the long wooden table in the center of the tasting room and picked up the silver bucket Caroline had provided for people to spit their wine into at the ridiculous tasting she'd held down here last month. When she heard him turn the key to unlock the door, she stopped pounding.

He opened the door and saw her standing her customary six feet away, a smug expression on her face. He set the bucket inside. "I thought you might need this at some point."

"You son of a bitch."

He closed the door and locked her in. He walked upstairs and then along the hall to the suite where Maria, the chief housekeeper, lived. He knocked on her door, then knocked again. "Maria? It's Mr. Forrest." There was no answer, so he opened the door and looked inside. He walked through the small sitting room where she had her television set and the coffee table that held her sewing and a few magazines in Spanish. He went into her bedroom and looked at the perfectly made bed, the dresser with its top bereft of the usual cosmetics and hairbrushes, then stepped to the closet and opened the sliding door. The suitcase she always used when she took time off to visit her family in Ventura was gone. He looked at the clothes hanging along the pole, and saw that some of the outfits he was used to seeing on her were gone, too.

Caroline had told the truth.

27

Emily squinted in the morning sunshine outside the front door of the green stucco apartment building and rang the bell. It sounded terribly loud to her, and made her glance behind her to be sure nobody was close. The three-story buildings were identical, each with the same thick, heavy entrance door protected from above by a small curved overhang like half a barrel, and square windows beside it, two above it, and two above those. She knew she must have imagined that someone was watching her. How could he be watching? If he could see her, she could have seen him.

For most of her life, she thought of a stalker as a spectral presence, maybe a murderer who had been hiding in the back seat of her car when she had driven off, or sitting in the bushes near her house when she fumbled to get the key in the lock. She would feel a chill on the back of her neck, almost as if someone were breathing on it, and whirl quickly to protect herself. The stalker was never there, and so she had never given the enemy a specific shape. Until now.

It was not as though the man in the ski mask had accidentally stepped into place and merged with the stranger she had always feared. It felt as though he had always been there, and she had finally made the mistake of turning too fast, before he could vanish. Once she had opened her eyes that night and seen him standing over her bed, she had made him real.

There was a click from the speaker in the wall, and she heard April's voice: "Yes?"

Emily leaned close to the grating over the microphone. "April? It's me, Emily. I'm sorry to come so early, but it's important."

There was a moment of silence, as though April were trying to find a way not to have answered the ring. Then she said, "Emily, I'm sorry, but I really don't want this. I don't want to talk."

"Please, April, I'm in terrible danger. My house and the office were both burned down last night. I need your help." Emily waited for April to reply. Seconds passed, and then the loud buzz let her know that the electric lock on the door was being held open for her. She tugged the door open and hurried inside. She couldn't help looking behind her one more time, half-expecting to see the spectral figure in the act of reaching for her before the door swung to. She waited until she heard the click before she left the small lobby, turned the corner, and went up a couple of steps to the carpeted hallway.

The unwelcome thought came to her that she was walking in Phil's footsteps. He must have walked along this hallway often, stepped on this carpet. She kept down the mixture of hurt and anger and went on. When she found the apartment and reached up to knock, April opened the door. It made Emily remember apartments where she had lived, first alone and then with Phil. She could always hear someone coming toward the apartment door from the time they set foot in the lobby—something distinctive about the direction of their footsteps, and something audible in their intention, too.

Fidelity

April was wearing a pink sweatshirt and a pair of pink sweatpants, running her fingers through long blond hair tangled from sleep. "Come in." She turned away, and Emily saw that ACTRESS was spelled out across the rear of the sweatpants.

Emily stepped inside and closed the door. The living room was furnished sparsely with cheap furniture that was small enough for a woman to drag in alone and assemble, a few framed photographs of pink camellias and yellow daffodils vastly enlarged. There were magazines on the seats of each of the stuffed chairs arranged in homage to the television set, and Emily could see that April had not yet cleared the table from her breakfast. "I'm really sorry to bother you."

"You said there was a fire?"

"*Two* fires, both at the same time. My house and the office were both destroyed. I don't know if the person who did it was trying to make me run outside in the dark where he could kill me, or just trying to scare me. A man came to my house a couple of nights ago and wanted something that Phil had. He said it was information about a powerful man. When I said I didn't have it, he was going to kidnap me. Dewey came to my house and scared him off."

"I'm sorry," April said. "I heard that part of it, and I almost called you, but I wasn't sure you'd want to hear from me."

"Ever since Phil was murdered, I've been looking for something that would explain it—maybe a case that got out of hand, or some personal dispute. After that man came, I had Ray helping me tear the house apart looking for this evidence, and had Dewey and Billy doing the same at the office."

"I feel bad," April said. "Dewey asked me to help search the office, but I just couldn't. It was just too much for me." She was crying now. "I want to let this part of my life be over. I'm sorry for what I did to you—what I took from you. If I had it to do over, I wouldn't. I thought a detective agency would be exciting, and then I thought I loved Phil. Now I know I was stupid."

"April, I didn't come to browbeat you about Phil. You didn't do anything to me. You weren't the first. If there was a home wrecker, it was somebody twenty years ago. What I want isn't to—"

"I know."

"What?"

April shook her head. Her face began to crumple again. "I thought I was the only one ever, and that we had fallen in love. That was what he said."

"Oh. I'll bet. What made you change your mind?"

"Ray Hall."

Emily was shocked for a second, then realized she shouldn't be. "Ray talked to you about Phil? When?"

"After you and I talked. He made me see that it wasn't the way I thought it was. He told me there had been other women, that Phil had told them that same kind of story."

"I guess we all believed him. Look, April. I think you're right to want to put this in the past as soon as possible. I'm not happy about what happened between you and Phil. But now Phil is dead. He emptied our bank accounts, which means he was planning to drop me, and he didn't leave any money to pay the people who worked at the agency. I think that means he planned to leave town. I need to know some things, and I have to ask you."

"Okay."

"Was he planning to run off with you?"

April looked uncertain. "I've thought of that, but I don't know. I don't think so. He didn't ask me if I wanted to go away with him." She stared at the coffee table in front of her knees, as though she were trying to make out the small print in one of the magazines on it. "As I looked back on it since he died, I realized something. I don't think I would have gone. I thought I was in love with him, but I must have been wrong."

"I understand."

"Lately I've been growing my hair out and saving money for a great stylist—Adrian Nolfi. I made the appointment months ago for him to do me at the Beverly Hills shop, not the one in West L.A., where you get his assistants. Phil knew that. He didn't say, 'Don't make the appointment,' or anything." She paused and looked up at Emily. "I guess he was leaving me, too."

"I don't feel angry at you or blame you for what happened anymore," Emily said. "Phil had figured out all the ways of getting women to do what he wanted before you were born. I don't think he cared very much about whether he told us the truth."

"That's for sure," April agreed. "I just feel really bad about it."

"Right now I've got a terrible problem, and you might be able to help me."

"What can I do?"

"The man who broke into my house still thinks that Phil left me some information about a powerful man, and he wants it. There's no question in my mind that he'll kill me for it. I think the fires last night were either a first attempt to kill me, or a way of getting me outside into the open. I'm more terrified than before."

"I thought the information was burned up."

Emily's heart began to beat faster. She could sense April was lying. Did it mean she had the evidence? "I wish I could be sure one way or the other. Before the fires, I had already searched just about everywhere in both the house and the office. Ray, Billy, Dewey, and the police all searched. I keep thinking it has to be somewhere else, someplace Phil could have driven to that nobody knew about."

"It's not here."

Emily studied April's face. She seemed to be aware enough and guilty enough to want to help. Emily said, "Did he ever talk about having a special project in the works, or say he was about to come into money, or anything like that?"

"I don't think so. He was always the same. He never said much about what he was doing, even when we were in the office and it was the normal thing to do."

"Did he ever give you anything—a box or container of any kind—and ask you to keep it safe for him?"

"No," she said quickly, then looked uncomfortable. "Oh, wait. He did, I guess. It was a long time ago, though. Maybe six months. It was a box."

"What was in it?"

"I don't know, really. He told me not to look inside. It was one of those boxes like fancy stationery comes in. He put it . . . um . . . under my bed, and told me to just forget it was there."

"You looked, though, didn't you?"

"At first there was just a case file, and he had it hidden under the stationery. He added things once in a while. There was a manila envelope, a couple of cassette tapes. Then he would slide the box back under the bed, and we'd forget about it."

"Where is the box now?"

"I don't know. One time when he came over, he just picked it up and took it with him."

While April had been talking, Emily at first pictured him stopping here for a minute to take her out to a restaurant or something, but when she said "came over," the image changed. He was in the bedroom with her. It had to be early afternoon, when they could pretend to be out to lunch, so they had the blinds closed to keep the sunlight out. They were both naked because they had been here in the afternoon having sex. Phil must have looked at his watch, got up and put on his pants and then knelt down to pick up the socks he had tossed there, and pulled the box out from under the bed. When he drove back to work with April, he said nothing about the box, just took it with him. Emily wanted to cry, but she fought it. "Can you tell me what it looked like, exactly?"

"The box?"

"Yes."

"It was the size of regular paper. A ream. The bottom part was just plain white, but the top had a kind of maroon color, with gold letters that said something, some brand name of a stationery company."

"Do you remember the company?"

"I'm sorry. It was just words, no picture or anything. That much I remember. It just didn't seem to matter at the time."

"Was there still stationery in it?"

"There was some. Whenever he added stuff, he took out enough stationery so the box would still close. By then maybe it was only one-third stationery."

Emily recognized Phil's way of thinking. He had brought his papers to the apartment of his current mistress. And then he hid the papers in a box of papers. That was Phil. "He hid it here so it would be safe. Did he say from whom?"

"No."

"Did he say why he was taking it away?"

"I don't know."

Suddenly Emily knew. Just to be sure, she said, "April, did other people in the office know about you and Phil?"

"Ray Hall. I was sure he knew at the time, but he says now that he only suspected, but didn't know."

"Anybody else?"

"No. And Ray says nobody else knew. I would never tell anybody, and we weren't that obvious about it. Phil wasn't that trusting. He didn't like people to know things like that about him. If he could have had an affair with me without my knowing, he would have. I mean, he was married, and . . ." She paused, not sure how to end the sentence.

"I know. Tell me something else. Did you ever hear of anyone else he'd had an affair with?"

"No. Phil told me there had never been any others. Ray told me there had been, but he didn't say who. Nobody had ever said anything about it in front of me before."

"Not even Ray?"

"Not until after Phil was dead. I don't think anybody but Ray ever knew anything personal about Phil, and Ray was his friend. He would never gossip about him."

Emily stood up abruptly. "I've got to go now."

"What? Is something wrong?"

"I've just got to go," she said. "Thanks for telling me the truth. It may be the thing that keeps me alive."

28

Hobart watched Emily Kramer leave the apartment building. She looked as though she was in a hurry. He kept wondering why she would be out like this on the morning after the fires, going to see another woman. When she had left the house where she had spent the night in Van Nuys, he had expected her to be wearing the same pair of jeans and the same sweatshirt she had been wearing at the fire, but she had been dressed in black pants and a black jacket, with flat shoes. When he had seen her clothes, he had begun to scan the surrounding blocks for signs that an arson investigator had her under surveillance. If the cops had been watching, then the clothes would have been the clincher. A person who knows enough to pack up her best clothes the day before her house burns down is an arsonist.

Hobart was sitting in his third car now. He had given away Whitley's car, rented a car and kept it until he had driven to the fire, and now he had rented another. This one was a small SUV, a Lexus that was difficult to pin down as to color. It was a metallic shade and sometimes it looked gray to him and sometimes tan, so it almost seemed to fade into the road. He had chosen it because the windows were tinted, making a person inside into a dim silhouette.

Hobart had spent most of the early morning completing his preparations for Emily Kramer. He knew he should simply have killed her. It would have been so easy. He could have sat in the warm, dark corner of her back yard on a lawn chair and put a .308 bullet right through her head. She would have fallen in a heap like a marionette with cut strings. It would have been loud, but sleeping neighbors who heard a single shot seldom got up to investigate. Instead they lay still, barely breathing, waiting to hear the next pop: "Was that a shot? *Shhh*. Listen." And Hobart would have driven up to Theodore Forrest's place, collected his second two hundred thousand, and gone about his business.

No. He would *not* have gone about his business. He was so tired that each time the work got harder for him. That was probably why he couldn't resist killing Whitley. It was definitely what had made him decide he wanted the information about Theodore Forrest. When he added the money he could get from Forrest to the amount he had already managed to keep over the years, he would have enough.

Hobart supposed he had not lived as cheaply as some people, but he had saved. When a job was finished, he would put most of the money away. At first he'd had the misguided hope that Valerie would forgive him for going to jail. When that hope was revealed to be idiotic, he had still kept saving. Money became more symbolic than practical. He needed to pile it up to overcome the feeling of futility and emptiness he had felt since the day of his arrest. He tried to make himself feel as though he had succeeded and gotten the money, instead of prison.

Hobart watched Emily Kramer walk to her Volvo. She had parked it across the street from the apartment complex. At this time of day, that was a pretty smart thing to do. She had a very short walk to and from the apartment building, all in the open under the windows of a dozen tenants in the building, and in plain sight of two dozen in neighboring buildings. She had made it nearly impossible for him to approach her. She was thinking clearly now, as though she knew she was in danger.

She was smarter and more self-reliant than he had imagined, and the discovery made him more certain than before that she had been trying to deceive him about the evidence. She had set the fires to get rid of him, and that meant that she was now preparing a move against Theodore Forrest. She must have sent Ray Hall, the man she was staying with, up north to talk to Forrest in person while she scurried around here, probably hiding copies of the evidence, closing bank accounts, making travel arrangements.

She was dressed up today. Her dark hair looked as though she'd had it professionally styled, even though he knew that was not something she could have done without his knowing. He couldn't help thinking of the way she had looked naked, and it was a distraction that made him wish he had never done that to her. He was reluctant to harm that beautiful body, and he couldn't avoid feeling a sexual attraction to her that wasn't quite affection, but was appreciation. He couldn't let it make him hesitant. Today was the day when he would need to be hard on her. He had to persuade her to relinquish the evidence, withdraw, and leave Forrest to him.

He watched the Volvo pull away from the curb and move up the street. Hobart could tell from the way she accelerated that Emily was jumpy and anxious, but he was sure she had not spotted him yet. A few times he had noticed that people he had been hired to kill seemed to sense that he was around. It didn't matter if they had no rational reason to know that someone wanted them gone. It didn't matter if they had never seen Hobart before or had no suspicion that he was anyone to fear. He had even seen them get nervous and ignore him to look over their shoulders for someone else. They clearly felt something wasn't right, but they didn't know who or what was wrong. Sometimes they would change their plans: stay longer at a party or a bar because they didn't want to leave the light and the company, or come out of a movie theater and go back to the box office to buy a ticket for another film that was playing on a different screen.

Hobart waited until she had turned the first corner before he started the engine of the SUV and pulled out to follow her. At the corner, he let a few cars go past before he turned. He tailed her at a distance for a few minutes. It was easy to tell that she was not aware he might be the one. She was not making quick moves to force him to do anything noticeable. He stayed far behind her and followed her onto the Ventura Freeway.

After a couple of miles, she passed the interchange with the San Diego Freeway, but she didn't turn. It occurred to Hobart that she might be driving north past Ventura all the way to the Central Valley to meet Forrest. The thought put a little hitch in his breathing. She shouldn't try to go up there alone.

Theodore Forrest was rich, the most important member of a powerful family. If Emily Kramer went up there and tried to get Forrest to exchange his cash for her proof, Forrest was going to end up with the proof and the cash, and probably all that would be left of Emily was a couple of parts from her aging Volvo scrapped in a local junkyard. The Central Valley was his country, and she would never get near him. She would simply disappear at the hands of some hireling. It occurred to Hobart that *he* was the hireling. He had taken the job of killing Emily Kramer, but he hadn't done it yet.

He watched her take the Westlake exit, and he felt relieved. When he came to it, he followed, and as he was coasting down the ramp he saw her turning right onto Westlake Boulevard. After a few minutes and a couple of turns, he came up with her in time to see her going to the door of a small brick-fronted house. As he passed, the door opened and a tall black man wearing jeans and a red T-shirt admitted her.

Hobart was sure it was the other detective, the man who had interrupted him when he had been trying to take Emily Kramer out of her house. He began to search for a good spot to park and wait.

He couldn't let another night come and go before he had her.

29

Emily stepped in so quickly that Dewey Burns had to step backward to keep from being bumped. He closed the door.

"What's wrong?" he said.

"I don't know. Everything. I assume you know that the office and my house are gone?"

"Of course," Dewey said. "Ray called Billy and me around four in the morning. There's still the stuff we put in storage. It's possible that we missed what we were looking for and it's still hidden inside something."

"If it was there, we missed it, all right. And if we look again, we'll miss it again."

"I'm not so sure. We moved all the records that we went through. I think we know which ones we can eliminate, but there are some that are still possible. We haven't found anything yet, but it's too early to say we won't."

"No, it isn't. You and Ray are both professionals. You don't miss things like that. I was Phil's wife for twenty-two years, but that didn't help. He hid this really well, and the information looked like something else—*exactly* like something else. That's the way Phil hid things. But I think the reason we didn't find it in the house or in the office is that it wasn't there. I need your help."

"What kind?"

"I was just at April's house. She and I talked about things—about Phil, and about his plans. She knew some things I didn't. She didn't know all of them at the time, but she's figured them out since. I realized that was part of my problem. Phil was a secret-keeper. Each person who knew Phil knew a different Phil. It wasn't that he was lying to everybody. To be honest with you, the only one I'm sure he *actually* lied to is me."

"Don't do this to yourself."

"I'm not doing anything to myself. I have a problem. There's a man out there who is willing to murder me. He wants this evidence Phil had against a powerful man, and I still don't have it."

"I know. I've been trying to help."

"Phil almost certainly had multiple copies. He probably gave one—or at least a *taste* of one—to this powerful man. He would have needed to show the man he had something, right?"

"I suppose," Dewey said. "He would have to show a sample, at least, to get the man scared. And he would have to give him something tangible when he got paid. But he would have to let the man know he had retained something to keep the man from killing him."

"And somehow that went wrong."

"Apparently. He got killed. There doesn't seem to be anything that he left for us—for you, or for me, or for anyone else—to find after he was dead. There should have been something. If not the evidence, at least a letter."

"I think there was," said Emily.

"And we missed it, and it got burned up last night?"

"April had it at one time."

"What? Where?"

"Phil hid the box under her bed for some time while he was col-lecting the evidence."

"Why didn't she tell us she had it?" She could see that Dewey was angry.

"She wasn't about to tell me my husband hid anything under her bed. At first she didn't even know what it was. She didn't figure that out until after Phil was dead, and the man came to my house to get it. By then, she didn't have it anymore."

"Well, where is it now?"

"Phil came over to her apartment one day and picked it up. He took it away, and moved it to a place that he knew was safer."

"What was safer than that?"

Emily spoke quietly and carefully. "Dewey, you said Phil would have known he was doing something dangerous, and that he would have left the evidence for you, for me, or for April to find. But there's somebody important that you're leaving out of this. She might be the most important one of all."

"No," he said. He was irritated, uncomfortable.

"Yes. She would be the perfect person, the one of us no stranger would know was connected with Phil."

"She isn't involved in this. It's blackmail. It's dishonest. It's prob-ably the worst thing he ever did in his life, just a momentary lapse when he was having some midlife crisis—maybe financial trouble. She would never have gotten involved in that, or in anything he did."

Emily said, "I need to meet her."

"No."

"I have to talk to her, Dewey. Phil had the box at April's because that was safer than our house or the office. But there was somebody much safer than April. The only person who knew about her was his only living son."

"She doesn't have it."

"Let me talk to her. Please. I have a right to know her. And she has a right to know me. If I have to go through all the files in storage to find her name and address, I'll do it. If I have to, I'll hire a detective to investigate *you*."

Dewey turned away from her and walked to the kitchen. She heard him rustling around out there, putting dishes in the dishwasher, then standing silent for thirty seconds.

Finally he came back into the living room. "I'll call her."

30

Lee Anne Burns was beautiful, with smooth caramel skin and light brown eyes flecked with gold. She had to be Emily's age, but she looked thirty, with long, thin limbs and a graceful neck. Emily fought to keep the jealousy away. She had expected someone else, someone she could pity, but this woman was formidable.

Lee Anne said, "You look at me and you see the other woman, don't you?"

"I'm sorry. I didn't mean to look at you strangely," Emily said.

"I'm not the other woman, *you* are."

Emily drew in a breath. The words didn't seem to mean the same thing to the two women. "What do you mean?"

Lee Anne Burns held her eyes on Emily. She hesitated, as though she were deciding how much to say. "He wasn't married to you when I knew him. He hadn't met you yet." This time Emily understood. Lee Anne was revealing a secret that she had kept for a long time, a secret so familiar to her that she was sick of it. And getting sick of it had affected nothing, because she still had been required to live with it and think about it.

"Oh, my God," Emily said. "I didn't know. He never said anything, never mentioned . . ." She knew how much it must hurt Lee Anne to hear that. Lee Anne had known, as she'd known everything, so well that it was probably like being punched over and over on the same spot, so the bruise, and the hurt, never went away.

Lee Anne gave her a look of sympathy. "Don't feel bad for me. This isn't news to me, the way it is to you. Didn't you ever look at Dewey's personnel file?"

"No. I wasn't working in the office when Dewey was hired. I went to the office one day on an errand, and there was Dewey. Phil hired a lot of young men who wanted to work with him to get their licenses. I just didn't have any reason to look."

"He's twenty-four."

"Twenty-four?"

"Born two years before you were married."

"I didn't know that Phil was his father. I didn't suspect until a few days ago. Dewey was the one who came to see me, and saved me from that . . . the man who broke into my house. And while I was watching him check the doors and windows, it just hit me. He had some of the same mannerisms. I had the feeling I was looking at Phil. It was like a switch turning on. I couldn't see before, but all of a sudden I could." There was a silence that made both women uncomfortable. Emily spoke to fill it. "So you were with Phil at least two years before I met him."

"About three and a half years." Lee Anne Burns sat primly in her chair for a few breaths. "I should explain something. I know the things that you want me to tell you. And in a way, I think you have a right—or at least a legitimate wish—to know. But at the same time, you don't. And I'm sitting here thinking that I'm probably about to tell you some things that I've never even told Dewey. He has a better claim to a right to know than you do. But maybe he knows everything already, just from having lived with me, and from whatever Phil told him, and from the other ways of knowing that he had. He was always that kind of boy, even when he was little. He seemed to figure out everything by himself, as though he could look at one tiny detail and grow the rest of it in his mind. There have been lots of times when I found out that what I thought he was too young to know he had known for years, or what I thought had been hidden was plain to him."

"The others all say he has the gift for being a detective," Emily agreed. "But he also has a gift for secrets. I can't tell you what he knows because he never told me anything. And I didn't come here to claim some right to know things. Maybe I already know everything about Phil that I ought to."

"I loved him," Lee Anne said. "That's the main thing, I guess. It wasn't some kind of fling or something. I was living at home with my parents up in Oakland while I went to nursing school. My older brother Eldon was in the marines. He always had an orderly plan for his life. Even when he was young, he knew he was going to graduate from high school, go into the marines, then go to college. To me it always seemed like an invitation to fate, a sure way to have a disaster just to teach you that things aren't that simple. When he went in the marines, I was terrified because that seemed to me to be the time for it, but it didn't happen. Eldon served his enlistment, had a good tour, and made some good friends. One time he came home from a big navy base in the Philippines, and he brought a close friend home with him on leave."

"Phil?"

"Phil. It was an odd situation. I think about it a lot, even now. It was as though my brother Eldon brought something into the house that I would never have run into otherwise—some substance, like a drug—and it was something that I had no immunity against."

Fidelity

"You were attracted to Phil right away?"

"It caught me by surprise. I had a guy I was interested in at the time, and I was busy with nursing school, working long hours and studying. But I came home one evening, and there he was." Her eyes seemed to lose focus for a moment, as though she were seeing it again, and then they sharpened and returned to Emily. "I don't need to tell you. He had that sense of humor that made you start laughing when you knew you shouldn't, and then you would remember afterward and start laughing again, and people would look at you and wonder."

"I know," Emily said. "You would want to tell him, and wanting to tell him something was the same as missing him, and then you could hardly wait to see him."

"I wasn't on my guard because he started out being just some marine, one of Eldon's friends, not somebody who was there to see me at all, just a guy sleeping over on his way to spend the rest of his leave at his own home. But I started to like him. When they got their orders, he and Eldon were both transferred to Camp Pendleton next, and I found that as soon as I had a break in nursing school, I had an irresistible urge to fly down to San Diego and visit Eldon. I spent most of my time with Phil. One night after a couple of evenings out, we found ourselves in my hotel room in Oceanside, and the obvious happened."

"And you got pregnant?"

"Oh, no. Didn't I tell you that it wasn't that simple? This part of it was simple—that night. Neither of us planned it. I needed a ride, and he walked me to my hotel room. After that night, everything sped up and changed. I was in love with Phil."

"Was he in love with you?"

"I think he was, but you have to see that love was what I wanted it to be at the time, and later on, what it had to be to make my life a tragedy and not just a sad little story about a stupid girl who didn't know how to behave and got what you'd expect. He said he loved me, and he acted as though he did. But Phil was a man who kept a lot to himself."

Emily said, "What happened?"

"I kept going down to visit Eldon in Oceanside. Only I would come a couple of days early, then pretend to leave for home, and spend a few days in Escondido or Capistrano with Phil before I actually left for Oakland. My mother and Eldon would talk on the phone now and then, and she would say something like, 'Did you and Lee Anne have a nice visit?' It was never 'Did Lee Anne come to visit you?' because that would have meant she was checking up on me. I think that even if Eldon had suspected something, he would not have said anything to her. We were so close, and he knew what it was like to be living at home and trying never to disappoint our parents. Sometimes Phil would get time off and show up at my school in San Francisco. I would come out of class or out of the hospital, and he would be there waiting for me. It went on for a long time—about a year and a half—and then I missed a period. I didn't need a test, but I went out and got one."

"Did you tell Phil right away?"

"Not exactly. I had to have some time to think. Then I waited until the next week, when I was going to see him in person. I drove down to Oceanside."

"What did he say?"

"It was as though we both had been in a dream—a soft, beautiful one—and we woke up on the same day. I had been in college in San Francisco, maybe the most tolerant city in the country, and I was in medicine, where there are lots of people of every shade from every country—patients, nurses, doctors, technicians. When I went down to Oceanside, everybody we knew or saw was a marine or the family of a marine. One of the things about the military is that racism doesn't play. It's one of the reasons why there are so many black people. If you're a gunnery sergeant you're treated like every other gunnery sergeant—better than a corporal, but not as good as a lieutenant. Phil and I had both been in places where people were people, and nobody had much time or reason to think about color. But as I said, when I got pregnant, we woke up and everything looked different."

"How?"

"Race. I told my mother, and it nearly killed her. She begged me to break up with him. The thought of having a white man in the family and a half-white baby just made her sick. She cried so hard, rocking back and forth, with her arms wrapped around herself. From the morning when I told her until nearly five in the afternoon, she didn't stop. Then, at quarter to five, she stopped, took a bath, and pulled herself together so my father wouldn't know anything was wrong."

"Did it work?"

"It did. She was afraid my father would hurt somebody—maybe me, maybe Phil, maybe himself—and that would be the end of our family. That meant everything to her. When he went off to work again, she started in on me again. She wanted me to get an abortion, which I could have done practically that day at the hospital. Nobody would have asked any questions or anything."

"Did you consider it?"

"Not at first. I was a nurse, so I wasn't intimidated or anything. I just resented the idea that my own mother would think I wasn't strong enough to handle my own problems."

"Which ones?"

"Any of them. Being the wife of an active-duty marine stationed five hundred miles from my home. Taking care of my baby while I went through the hardest parts of the nursing program. Working to pay back my loans while my husband got shipped away somewhere. I was tough, and I told her so. I'd get through the hard time, and things would get better. But it was the story that bothered her."

"The story?"

"The story everybody has heard a million times. The smart, pretty black girl has a big future ahead. She gets through nursing school, and maybe after she works a few years she'll try to get through medical school, too. But something happens. She ends up with a baby—in this case, a white man's baby—and there's no way for her to have her future."

"Did you want to go to medical school?"

"I had thought about it. The main thing was that she and I saw what I was doing differently. I thought I was considering getting married and having a family. She thought I was setting myself up to be just another black girl with no money raising a child alone. I said it wasn't that way. She said I was living in a dreamworld. It wasn't that easy to be the black wife of a white man. I said I was strong enough. She said, 'But is he?'" Lee Anne stopped and held Emily with her eyes, and all at once, Emily knew.

"That's right. While my mother was talking to me, his family and friends were talking to him. He was trying to imagine the future, just as I was. And when he was through thinking, he had a different answer than I had. I remember so clearly the day when he told me. He had the foresight to have the conversation with me in Oakland, so I would be two miles from my family, at my apartment, near school. All I had to do was shut the door when he left, lie down on my own bed, and cry. If I had been nine or ten hours from home, among strangers in a cheap hotel in Oceanside, I don't know what I would have done. By then my brother Eldon had been promoted and shipped to Camp

Lejeune in North Carolina for some kind of special training, so I couldn't have gone to him."

"I'm so sorry," Emily said. "I'm ashamed for him. I want you to know I never knew any of this."

"Of course not. Oh, he wasn't so bad. Over the next twenty years or so, I came to understand him better, and maybe to see his point of view wasn't entirely selfish and cowardly. He contributed money to Dewey's support from that time until Dewey grew up and went in the marines. And even after that, he sent checks to me, in case I wanted to send money to Dewey. He sometimes made it here for Dewey's birthday, and he always made it on Christmas."

Emily was stunned. "It seemed as though he always was out on Christmas. He had me convinced that it was the best time to find out about the subjects of investigations. They all stopped looking over their shoulders."

"Well, now you know. Some of the time he was here."

"And the other times?"

"Honestly, Emily, I don't know. I was never his confidante. He may really have worked some or all of those times. After we broke up over twenty-four years ago, I wouldn't have that kind of relationship with him anymore. I was polite to him, but I didn't ask him for any-thing or try to be his friend. All we had in common was Dewey. That was for Dewey's sake, and not his."

Emily's head had sunk into her hands. The tension that had been keeping her erect and active had simply left her. She said, "I'm sorry I bothered you. I wasn't trying to pry into your personal life so I could live with mine. Believe me, nothing I've learned has made me happy." She raised her head. "I assume Dewey told you about the man in the ski mask?"

"Yes. It must have been horrible."

"Dewey saved my life. The man was in the process of dragging me off when Dewey got there. Today I had some faint hope that you might know the answer to the man's questions."

"That *I* would?"

"You were Phil's secret. Nobody knew that you and he had been . . . close. You would be the ideal person to keep something for him. It would have been a box, like stationery comes in."

Lee Anne stood up, suddenly agitated. She paced to the other side of the room, and back. "Oh, my God. I didn't know."

"What?"

"He left it with me."

"Where—here?"

"Yes."

"You didn't tell Dewey?"

"I didn't tell anyone. I didn't want anything to do with his secrets. But he said all he wanted me to do was take a big padded envelope and put it in the bottom of a drawer. He opened it to show me it wasn't drugs or money or anything that could get me in trouble. All that was in the box was a file—thick—an envelope with some snapshots, all people I had never seen before, and a couple of cassette audiotapes."

"Can I see it?"

"I don't have it anymore."

"What happened to it?"

Lee Anne didn't avoid her stare. "You think I should have given it to you. You think that because he married you, everything he left anywhere is for you. I don't blame you. It should have been for you. But he had postage stamps on it, and a mailing label. He said that if anyone asked about it, or anything happened to him, I should put it in the mail. When Dewey called me that day and told me that Phil was dead, I remembered the box. I thought about sending it to you, but I didn't want to. Maybe it was because all I could do for Phil was perform the favor exactly as he asked. His death naturally made me think about what had become of my own life, and maybe I was resenting you a little. So I took it to the post office and mailed it."

"Please, Lee Anne. The man with the mask—the one who was kidnapping me—is looking for it. I think that if I don't get it first, he'll eventually kill me. It's evidence against the man who had Phil murdered. Did you look at the address? Do you know where it was going?"

"Seattle. The address was in Seattle."

"Was the name Sam Bowen?"

"I think maybe that was the name. Who is he?"

Emily was up, clutching her purse. "He's an old detective who used to work with Phil years ago." She moved closer to Lee Anne. "I'm terribly sorry for the way Phil treated you."

Lee Anne said, "I'm sorry for what happened to all of us."

"You have a wonderful son," Emily said, then looked away. "I've got to go," she said. "Thanks for helping me."

31

Hobart could tell from the way Emily Kramer hurried from the black woman's house that she was more preoccupied than before. She wasn't looking over her shoulder for him, and she wasn't taking any precautions. As she walked to her car, he kept his eyes on her. He couldn't see anything in her hand or under her arm, so he couldn't be sure that she had the evidence with her, but something had happened. Maybe she had it in her purse. He had to do it now.

He drove after her. As he followed her car, he felt himself move into a familiar mental state. The world around him seemed unnaturally bright and clear. He felt he could hold in his consciousness all of the trajectories of the moving objects in the hundred eighty degrees he could see, and track in his mind the ones he had merely caught in an earlier glance. He felt it would be possible to predict the rest of the motion and intercept any one of them, but all he needed was to put himself where Emily Kramer was about to be.

He kept Emily Kramer's Volvo in his field of vision as he drove, but concentrated on keeping her from noticing him. After he had watched her drive for a few minutes, he was certain that she was driving to Ray Hall's house, where she had been staying. Maybe Hall was waiting there for her, but he could be up north setting up Theodore Forrest to pay for evidence. The thought made him more convinced than ever that he had to make his move now. Hobart turned at the next corner and drove hard toward the house. It was crucial that he be there before she was. He stopped his rented SUV one door from Hall's house.

Hobart got out, walked to Hall's driveway and around to the side of the garage, where he entered through the side door. There was no car in the garage, so Hall couldn't be at home. Hobart stood in the dim light, smelling the floating dust, a faint scent of wood stain, a whiff of motor oil. He moved to the side of the big garage door, so that if it opened he would be out of sight. In a minute, the sound of another car reached him. It was the distinctive high metallic hum of a Volvo's five-cylinder engine.

The car stopped outside. He heard a door slam. He listened and heard Emily Kramer walking on the concrete driveway toward the back door of the house. She must have a key. He moved to the side door of the garage, opened it a crack and risked a look. She wasn't carrying anything but her purse.

He waited with the door open an inch. When he saw her come close, Hobart began to move. He stepped quickly out of the garage right behind her, in step. With a single smooth motion, he slipped the purse strap off her shoulder and tugged the purse away. He could feel from the weight of it that he had guessed right about the gun. Even a novice like her would be too smart to meet Theodore Forrest without a gun.

Hobart kept her in motion, merely changing her direction and increasing her speed. His face was above her left shoulder, his lips almost to her ear. "Don't try to look back at me. You know who I am."

"Let me go," she said loudly.

He knew she was testing her courage, her ability to scream. He squeezed her arm more tightly with his right hand and jabbed the index finger of his left into her ribs. She gave a little cry of pain. "You've got to be very quiet right now, or I'll kill you. We'll talk later."

"I don't have what you want."

Hobart considered killing her. He could even reach into her purse and do it with her own gun. But her voice was quiet, its tone normal, so he didn't. It would look and sound to anyone as though they were walking along and having a cordial conversation. "We'll discuss all of it later. Right now, just get into the SUV."

He opened the door to the back seat of the rented vehicle and she climbed in. He tore a strip of duct tape off the back of the seat in front of her, pressed it across her eyes, and covered it with a pair of sunglasses. He reached behind her, dragged both of her wrists together and clicked a pair of handcuffs on her. He pulled the seat belt across her and belted her in. Then he got into the driver's seat and pulled out down the street. He turned left at the corner and went to Vanowen, then turned right. They were moving along at the speed limit.

Hobart could see her in the mirror as he drove. She was leaning her body forward a little, but the belt kept tightening. She tried to move both hands to the side to reach the belt buckle. There was no chance that she could reach the release with her hands cuffed behind her and the belt across her chest tightening every time she moved. He drove along the street trying to adjust his speed so he wouldn't have to stop at traffic signals. Whenever he couldn't make it through an intersection on green, he turned right so Emily Kramer wouldn't feel the vehicle stop and try to jump out. He was almost certain she couldn't free herself, and if she did, he didn't think she would jump. There were many people who might jump from a moving car, even in handcuffs. There were few who would do it blindfolded. He kept up the speed.

She said, "I don't have what you want. I've looked, but I haven't found it."

"Then you're a very unlucky woman."

EMILY WAS TRYING to fight off shock. She couldn't let fear make her sluggish and stupid. The man had simply materialized at her elbow while she was walking from her car to Ray's house, his big hand already tightening around her arm, his face beside her neck. She had nearly fainted, the pain making her unable to think or move.

She had been carrying the gun right in her purse, where she could reach it in a hurry. The thought had never occurred to her that putting the gun there wasn't smart, but of course it wasn't. She was wearing tight black pants and a short fitted jacket. There was nowhere else for a gun to be but her purse. This man had simply taken her purse, and then she was disarmed. She winced and felt the tape tighten across her cheekbones and her eyebrows. It hurt. She was furious with herself. For the first time, she forgot the discomfort and the surprise and realized she was almost certainly going to die.

Phil had warned her that if a man ever tried to drag her into a car, she should do everything she could to resist. She must instantly recognize that she was in a fight to the death. Whatever she was going to do to save herself had to happen before he got her into the car. Any chance she got after that would be a rare bit of luck, and probably would not be more than a second's inattention by her captor. Emily had not used her chance, not brought herself to fight to stay out of this car. And she had practically given him her gun.

Emily felt the car swing to the left again and tilt her against the door. The movement made her body push against the seat belt and then settle back, and when it did, the belt tightened another notch. She tried to move her hands again, but now she couldn't reach even as far as she had before.

Emily wanted to work her hands around behind her enough to release the seat belt. Then she would hold the belt in place with her fingers and rub the side of her face against the leather cording of the seat, looking as though she had collapsed in despair. That might push the tape off one eye and permit her to see well enough to open the door, lean out, and drop to the pavement of the street.

She was aware that she would roll and slide, but that she must try not to let her head hit the pavement or the curb squarely, or she would die. If she got out, the man might shoot her, but she believed he wouldn't. Shooting would add enormously to his risk, and shooting her would not get him the information he wanted.

The last thought caught her attention. She had meant to reassure herself, but when she considered it, she realized that it was not comforting. He certainly didn't want to kill her and lose the information. But now she really knew what he wanted—or knew where it was, anyway. Probably he was capable of making her tell. After that, what? What could he possibly do but kill her?

Strapped in the back seat with her eyes taped shut, she could only detect his presence by small sounds: the seat creaking or his breathing or his right foot slipping from the brake pedal and moving to the gas pedal. She still had not seen his face.

Emily realized she was crying. It might be that he would start killing her today, but stretch out the process for as long as he could. In Los Angeles, a woman who was driven away in a car might as well have been swallowed by the earth. There would be nobody even wondering about Emily until Ray came back at the end of the day and found her car parked in front of his house. That would be in—what? Six hours.

A lot could happen to a person in six hours. This man was a fear expert. It was as though he knew what scared her most. No, the word *scare* wasn't adequate. It was terrifying to imagine what he might do to her to get the information he wanted. No, she thought. She must push that thought out of her mind. The minute she gave in and told him, she was dead.

She knew that he could easily make the choice more ambiguous. What would he have to do to her before she was ready to tell him where the evidence was and die? Would she be so eager to live on after he popped out her eyes or burned her badly enough? Under the right circumstances, she would probably beg him for death.

She realized that she was doing his work for him. Her imagination had begun her torture as soon as she had felt his grip and heard that voice—so familiar, not because she had heard him speak that one night, but because she had heard it over and over every night since.

Emily felt the car was coasting, heard the difference in the engine, and prayed that they were just stopping at a signal, or maybe were in a traffic jam. She heard a truck. Were they in a construction zone? Could anybody hear her if she screamed? She could lean to the right and bang her head against the window. She tried to decide, but the car was moving again, much faster. She waited while the minutes passed, and the next time she felt the SUV slowing, she got ready. When the SUV stopped, she shrieked as loudly as she could and hit her head against the glass, but it didn't break. She rocked her body to the left and then tried again.

The door beside her opened quickly, and her head met nothing. She fell to the side, the belt holding her in. She felt a breeze that seemed to come in its full, steady current, not blocked by houses or even trees, and heard the call of a bird. It was far off, probably two or three hundred feet, but then another answered it with the same call. She could smell plants.

She felt fear come over her like nausea. Each second while she waited for him to kill her increased the sense of loss. She thought about her parents, Phil, her son Pete. They were all dead, and in a few minutes, she would be dead, too. She was the last one alive who knew what they had done for her and for each other, and then it was going to be as though none of them had ever lived. They would be no more real than the people in old photographs that nobody could identify anymore.

The man undid the seat belt, put something over her shoulders that felt like a big sweater, then half-lifted her out of the seat. He set her on her feet and she could still feel his hand on her shoulder. It felt the way a man walked with a woman he liked, maybe even loved. She knew he was doing it to hide the handcuffs that held her arms behind her, so she shrugged abruptly, turning, trying to pull away. He was prepared for each move, and simply tightened his arm around her shoulders and pulled her ahead. She did not stop resisting, but no amount of exertion seemed to have an effect on him.

He kept her moving up a slight incline, then stopped her. She heard him fiddling with keys, then heard a door. He said, "Step up."

Emily pulled back, away from the place where she had heard the door, but his arms came around her, swept her up off the ground and swung her. She was in the air for a second, trying to brace for a fall, but with her hands behind her back it was impossible. She hit the floor hard, shoulder and hip first, and then her head. She lay there dazed and in pain for a few seconds, trying to determine whether any of the bones that hurt were broken. She was having trouble breathing because the wind had been knocked out of her, but it didn't feel as though her ribs were broken.

She heard the jingling, the metallic clicks and snaps that she knew was the door being locked and deadbolted. His hand tightened around her arm again and jerked her to a sitting position. His face was close to hers. "You stupid woman. You can't beat me by dragging your feet. You have to kill me. Are you up to that?" She didn't reply. "Up!" he said. "Stand up."

Emily made an attempt, but succeeded only because he was lifting her. She said, "You kidnapped me for nothing."

He pulled her ahead by the arm. She heard another door opening. There was a peculiar smell. It seemed damp, musty, as though it had not been open in a long time. He led her across the room. She tripped, and realized that a curled-up edge of old linoleum had caught her shoe. He guided her through another doorway to what sounded like the center of an empty room. "Sit."

He pushed her onto a seat with arms, then unlocked the handcuff on her left wrist, dragged it around, and closed it on the wooden arm of the chair. He wrapped something around her right wrist to hold it to the other arm of the chair.

Her mind kept suggesting different kinds of pain: electric shock, heated iron, cutting. She sat very still, listening, knowing that whatever it was, he would administer the first dose without warning. She tried to decide whether talking to him would delay the start of it and give her more time, or if it would make him angry and make him hurt her worse.

"You're wrong."

"What?" she said.

"We're just going to talk for a minute."

She wanted to say something, but she knew he was probably tricking her. The last time, she had learned to speak only if he asked for a response.

He said, "You've been busy. I've seen it. You have the evidence I asked you for, don't you?"

"I probably would if you hadn't burned my house and my office."

"If *I* hadn't?"

"Yes. You. If you had given me time to find it, I probably would have." Talking helped Emily. It seemed to warm her, to make her blood circulate again. "Burning my house wasn't necessary. I was scared enough already. I was spending every minute searching for it."

He said, "Don't bullshit me. You burned your house and your husband's office yourself."

"What are you talking about? Is this some kind of joke? Why would I burn my own house?"

"Maybe to destroy the places where the proof could have been hidden, thinking if the evidence was gone, you would have seen the last of me."

"I didn't do that, and I didn't think of doing it."

"Then you did it because you had already found the evidence."

"I didn't do it. I'll tell you exactly what I did. I looked all over for what you described that night you broke into my house—papers, a case file, maybe tapes or photographs—that would embarrass a powerful man. You never said who the man was, and that didn't help. But I looked hard."

"And you're claiming you didn't find it?"

"I found hundreds of case files, hundreds of tapes, hundreds of disks that were labeled one thing and could have been another. But nothing seemed to prove anything mysterious about a powerful man. There were the usual divorce and child-custody things, the usual cases of workmen's-comp fraud, employees stealing from their bosses, missing persons who owed somebody money." She paused. "The last time you showed up, you demonstrated to both of us that I'm not the kind of person who would be able to use what Phil had to blackmail anybody. You must also know that I'm not a person who would risk going to jail for arson. We both know that. The only one around who might be up to that is you."

She could hear him walking around her, his footsteps heavy on the linoleum floor, making the wood beneath vibrate her chair. She braced herself, listening for a sudden movement that meant a blow was coming.

His voice came from right above her: "If you didn't want it, why were you looking for it?"

"A lot of reasons."

"What are they?"

"I still want to know who killed my husband, and what secret he was trying to protect."

"I thought your husband was screwing other women."

"He was. I *still* want to know."

"I got a long look at you without your clothes the other night. Your husband must have been really stupid." He paused. "Unless you cut him off. Is that what happened?"

Emily was beginning to sweat. She couldn't let him know how horrifying this topic was, or he would pursue it. "I loved him, and I thought I had a good marriage. After Phil died, I was surprised to learn it wasn't."

"What were the other reasons you wanted to find the proof?"

"You. I didn't want you to have it." She knew she was taking a risk to say that, but it was true, and she had to use what was true. "I hate you."

"I don't blame you. You should hate me for doing that to you. You should hate me because you're sitting here thinking I might do a lot worse."

She knew that if she didn't answer, he would feel he had to prove it. "Right."

269

"Hmmmm."

Emily waited. She would scream and hope that someone heard, even though he must have prepared for that. She would fight as hard as she was able, even though she knew it was futile and he would overpower her in a few seconds. And then she would die.

His voice came from farther away, not nearer. "What did the arson investigator say about your fires?"

"Just that the one in my house was intentional. He said there were lots of accelerants. That's why it went up all at once like that."

"And what did he ask you?"

"Why there was furniture piled up in the living room. It had looked to the firemen as though that was part of setting the fire. I told him about everything—my husband being murdered, you breaking into my house, and then about my friends and me trying to find out what you had come for."

"That doesn't say why furniture was piled up."

"I was planning on moving it into storage."

"Why?"

"I was searching each piece—every table, chair, or bed—so I could get it out of there, and go through the house itself. I wanted to look for hiding places that Phil knew about but I didn't. Maybe there were places in the walls or under the floors or something."

"You really wanted it bad, didn't you?"

"Yes."

"You couldn't live there without furniture."

"No."

"So you had a plan. What was it?"

"I was going to wait until this was over, and then sell the house and leave."

"When did you decide to burn it instead?"

"I didn't."

"It's a lot easier than selling it. And you knew that as long as the house was standing, I might be back. It wouldn't matter if there was a new owner. I might still think that the evidence would be hidden somewhere in the house. And you couldn't stand that. You didn't want to be responsible to them for me, and you didn't want me to find it. So you burned it."

"No. I didn't. I wouldn't."

"Why not?"

"Because it's wrong. It's illegal. The idea never occurred to me."

"But once you found the evidence, the house was a liability. If they can't prove you torched it, you get the money."

"I didn't."

She heard him take in a breath and let it out in a sigh. "All right. We'll talk about it again. I'm going to take you to the bathroom now. You can't get out through the window, and there's nothing left in that room you can use as a weapon. It's all been taken out. I'm warning you not to try anything. If you do anything that lets you see my face, I'll have to kill you. Do you understand?"

"Yes."

He led her in and attached her handcuff to a metal towel bar that was bolted to the wooden cabinet that held the sinks. "I'm locking the door. I'll be back when you least expect it."

She heard him walk to the door, heard the door close, and heard the key in the lock. She waited and listened, holding her breath. She didn't hear the other door close, didn't hear a car. She whispered, "Are you still here?" There was no answer, but she wasn't sure he had really left. She waited for minute after minute, listening for his breathing or some slight movement, but she heard nothing.

Emily was aware that people in situations like hers imagined much more time was passing than really was, so she began to count. She realized that she had never been good at counting seconds. She

271

tried thinking "one Mississippi, two Mississippi," but it was still too fast, because she was impatient and scared. She counted to one hundred instead of sixty and called it a minute. After ten of her minutes, she still had not heard anything, so she used her free hand to pull the tape from her left eye. She was alone. The room was old, with octagonal white tiles an inch across, and a bathtub with feet that had been painted pink, then gold, then white again.

She felt a sudden need to urinate. He was gone now, but he could return soon, and then she might never be left alone again. She managed to use her free hand to accomplish it, and to pull her slacks back up and refasten them, all the time watching the door and dreading his return.

Now she looked at the room. She could see that the one small window had been boarded up. The room would have been completely dark, if he had not turned on the light so he could see when he had brought her in here. She carefully examined the towel rack that held her handcuff. She found no screws on this side, and she couldn't stretch far enough to open the cabinet and reach in with her free hand. The handcuff was the kind that Phil had owned; he never used anything that wasn't police issue or better.

Emily had tried slipping the cuff off her wrist when her hands were behind her, and had no luck. She tried again, but the bracelet was too tight. She could almost stand up, bent over a bit, and half-turn to face the medicine cabinet, but the mirror was gone. Did the man think she would break it and use shards of glass as weapons against him? Or against herself? What was he planning to do that would make her want to kill herself?

She sat down again, listened, and waited, ready to push the tape across her eyes again. There should be a way out. She stood and examined the toilet, looking for something she could unscrew or tear off to use as a tool. The lid was off the toilet tank, and the parts in-side were the newer, plastic kind, not the old copper rods and bulb.

She tugged at the towel rack with both hands, but it held tight and strong. She grasped it and used her legs to lift, but it didn't move. It must be held with very strong bolts. She looked at it closely and re-alized it wasn't for towels at all. It had lines etched into it so the steel wasn't slippery. This was a handhold, so a weak or handicapped per-son could lower himself onto the toilet and get up again. It was made to hold a person's weight.

She kept searching. Maybe she could pry up an old tile and scrape her way through the wood of the cabinet. She tried, but they were all tight. Maybe she could undo the faucet, or at least one of the handles. She couldn't reach them. She wondered if she could pull the plywood off the window and call to some passerby. She got one knee up on the counter, but couldn't quite get to the window, either. Maybe this wasn't a freestanding building. Maybe it was an apartment building. If she hammered on the pipes or the floor, she could send a distress signal. She had nothing hard, so she took off her shoe and hit the heel on the faucet. It made a dull thump that she could barely hear.

She stamped her feet on the floor. She yelled. She rattled the handcuffs against the bar and rapped her knuckles on the wall. After a time, she knew that the house was freestanding and that the neigh-bors weren't a few feet away. Hours went by while she tried to attract attention.

Her fears grew as she became exhausted. When her mind drifted to the question of why he had insisted that she had set the fires, she couldn't stop thinking about them. He could easily have set some kind of delayed fire to burn her to death, and left. He could be hun-dreds of miles away by now. She could not see the light outside, but she was almost sure that it was evening. In a short time, she might be seeing smoke seep in under the bathroom door. He had burned her house and the office. Arsonists were all supposed to be crazy. They had some kind of sexual-power problem going on, and she could easily imagine this man getting a charge out of burning her to death. There was also some practical value to killing her that way. He would leave no fingerprints, hairs, or threads. He wouldn't have to carry a heavy, bloody corpse anywhere, either. She waited, but no fire appeared, even after a couple of hours.

She thought of Ray Hall. He must have found the Volvo at his house by now, searched all the easy places for her, and called the police. The man who had taken her had made no mistakes, had left nothing, had touched nothing. He had succeeded, and now there was nothing anyone could do for Emily. She was lost.

32

Ray Hall had been running, and he felt winded and sweaty. He had gone from one neighbor to another, knocking on doors and asking questions, but he had learned nothing. He had an idea that was unlikely to be worth anything, but he knew that he had to test it. He had to try every idea now because in a few hours it might be too late. As soon as he had thought of it, he had run up the street and around the block to the house that was opposite his house and one block north.

He rapped on the door. This was an old house, taller than the rest of the houses in the neighborhood, officially two stories, but with a dormer above that. An elderly woman lived here. He had seen her many afternoons, sitting in the back window of a second-floor room, gazing out across the yards at the mothers and children walking home from the school, or at the mail carrier, or the man who lived next to Hall walking his dog.

He knocked harder. The cops were moving from house to house along his block, canvassing the neighborhood in the usual way, asking a person in each house what they had seen, what they had heard, what time they came home, and whether the white Volvo had already been parked there. He knew they were doing precisely the right things. Thoroughness brought bonuses, and often investigators learned as much from things that weren't seen or heard as from things that were. Already the police knew that there were no shots, there was no noisy struggle, there were no signs that Emily had been hurt.

It was still possible that she was okay, that the man with the ski mask had not taken her. She could have seen him and be hiding somewhere, or even be doing some perfectly untroubled investigating without her car. Ray Hall looked across the street and saw that the long shadows were fading into the general shade already. The sun was down.

He rapped on the door, and heard a high voice from deep in the house. "Coming!"

He waited, and it seemed to take so long that he wondered if the woman had forgotten or looked through the peephole in the door, not seen him, and assumed he had gone away.

The door opened a crack, and he saw one faded blue eye. It moved down to his feet and back up to his face. "What?"

"Hello, Mrs. Kelly. I'm Ray Hall, your neighbor from one block over that way."

"I recognized you, or I wouldn't have opened the door. What are all the police doing over there?"

"They're searching for information about what happened to a friend of mine, somebody who was visiting me. I'm sorry to bother you, but I've noticed that from your upstairs window there's a clear view of the block where my house is."

"You have, have you?"

"Yes."

She looked irritated and moved back, as though she might close the door.

"Please, I think she's been kidnapped, and I wondered—"

"Kidnapped?" She looked skeptical, not shocked, as he had expected.

"Yes. It would have been after one o'clock or so. She parked her white Volvo in front of my house, and—"

"Oh, that one. I think you've got it wrong. I saw her leave."

"Was she with a man?"

Mrs. Kelly forgot her precautions and let the door swing open wide. Ray Hall saw a sadness come into the old eyes. She said, "Oh, I'm sorry, dear. She *was* with a man, but he didn't make her go. She was just going with him. They came down the driveway and walked over to the curb in front of the house next to yours and got into his car."

"Neither of them was acting strangely?"

She looked at him in deep sympathy. "I'm sorry. He had his arm around her all the way. When they got to his car, he opened the door, leaned in and helped her find the seat belt and clicked her in. He leaned in very close to her for what seemed like a long time. I can't be sure what that was about. When he came around to the driver's seat, she had sunglasses on. And he drove off."

"You didn't see anything in his hand?"

"No."

"He had his arm around her. Could you see both his hands?"

"Well, no."

"And the sunglasses. Did you see her take them out of her purse?"

She thought for a moment. "It's funny, but I don't remember her purse. I think she must have had one." She seemed puzzled, almost unsure of herself. "I'm sorry."

"No. You're doing great. You're resisting having your mind add things that should have been there, but weren't. Now, the one thing that would really help a lot is anything you can remember about his car."

"It wasn't a car, it was an SUV."

"What color?"

"It's indescribable, really. One of those new colors that sometimes looks kind of beige, and sometimes kind of gray."

"So you'd call it sort of a beige-gray. Could you tell what make or model it was?"

"Just an SUV. They all look pretty much the same to me. I'm sorry. I never did follow that kind of thing. It was too far away to read the words on it, and I had no reason to try."

"Was there anything else you saw around that time?"

"Well, yes. Your next-door neighbor, the man with the bald head. He came home just about that time. He drove up and stopped next to that SUV, I think because it was parked right in front of his house. He seemed to be taking a good long look at it, as though he wondered if it belonged to a burglar or something. Then he pulled into his driveway. He went inside for a while, came out, and drove away."

"Thank you, Mrs. Kelly. You've been an enormous help. I've got to go follow up on this. Thanks again." He turned and ran toward his house.

The man who lived in the house beside his was Ron Salvatore. He worked as a shop teacher in the high school. A couple of years ago, he and Ray had exchanged house keys and cell-phone numbers in case there was an emergency. Ray dashed into his house, flung open the door, then searched through the drawers of the sideboard by the dining-room wall until he found the number. He dialed, and in a moment he heard Ron's voice. "Hello?"

"Ron?"

"Yes."

"This is Ray Hall. I've got an emergency. Early this afternoon, you drove home. You saw an SUV parked in front of your house. Sort of beige-gray. You stopped to look at it. Can you possibly tell me anything about it?"

"Did my house get broken into or something? Or yours?"

"No. Did this happen?"

"Well, yeah. You want to know about the car?"

"Yes."

"It was a Lexus GX 470. It was brand new. I was looking at it because I'm in the market for an SUV, and I've just about decided on the model, but I was trying to decide about the color. That color is called 'silver sand.' I've got a brochure from the dealer."

"Great! Ron, do you mind if the police call you on this line? Can I give them your cell number?"

"I guess so."

"Thanks. I'll explain later."

Minutes later, Ray Hall was with Ed Gruenthal, the detective who had been in charge of Phil Kramer's murder case, and Emily's break-in. "I've got something. The car he used this time was a new Lexus GX 470 SUV, and the color is called silver sand."

"Who saw it?"

"The woman's name is Ruth Kelly. She lives one street over, but she sits in an upper rear window in the afternoons. The light is good at that time of day, and the window overlooks her garden. It also gives a great view of my street and the front of my house." He handed Gruenthal a sheet from his pocket notebook. "Here's her name and address. She couldn't tell what it was, but she noticed that my next-door neighbor stopped by right around then, and he saw it up close. I called him, and he knew all about it. That other name on the paper, Ron Salvatore, is my neighbor, and that number is his cell phone. He knows you'll want to talk to him."

Gruenthal glanced at the paper with little apparent interest. "I'll get somebody to see if this leads anywhere."

Ray Hall held his anger in and took a moment to disguise it. He reminded himself that this kind of anger was really something else. In this case, it was worry and fear for Emily. "I think the SUV may be a rental. He seems to be driving something different every time he turns up. If he was just going to drive by and shoot her, it might be stolen, but he'd never drive her around in a stolen car."

"You might be right."

Ray said carefully, "Mrs. Kelly didn't just see the car. She saw the guy putting Emily into it and driving it away. Ron Salvatore looked at the car practically with a microscope because he's shopping for one like it. It's not like there are eighty-five ways to go on this. Emily has been kidnapped, and there is exactly one lead to follow. One. Please. I'll do as much as I can to help, but I don't have any authority."

"Look, Ray. You got me cornered less than a minute ago. I haven't had a chance to get anybody to do anything, but I plan to. So don't climb on me just yet. Give me a chance to mess things up first."

"Sorry. I'll start trying to find rental agencies with Lexus SUVs."

"Good." Gruenthal handed Hall his card. "Use the cell-phone number if you get anything. If you get a *hint* of anything."

"I will."

Hall stepped toward his house to start looking through telephone books. The two cops who had been going from house to house approached. He said, "Did you find something?"

"Not yet," said the older one. "Do you have any pictures of her we might be able to use?"

Hall thought for a moment. "Yeah. I got one somebody took about two years ago, but she hasn't changed." He hurried inside, went to the big sideboard, and pulled open a drawer. He was a bit surprised to see it lying on top of the keys and coins and pens that he kept there. Sometimes things migrated to the surface, but more often they seemed to sink in the general disorder.

The picture was a shot that Billy Przwalski's girlfriend had taken at the party when Sam had retired. Emily was wearing the red dress, and looking at Ray Hall. She had half-turned when she had sensed the girl nearby, seen the camera, and almost smiled. He handed it to the police officer. "I'd like—" he stopped himself. He didn't need to have the picture back. "It's exactly the way she looks now. There may be other pictures, but they won't be any better."

The cop looked, and Hall could see he was thinking about how pretty Emily was. He said, "Is it possible this is an admirer or somebody she knows?"

"It can only be the guy who broke into her house before, the one who shot at a couple of men from our agency. She doesn't know him."

"Right. I'll try to get this back to you when they've copied it and got it into the system."

"Okay," said Hall. Before the two were out of his house he was dialing the first of the car-rental agencies. "Hello," he said. "I'm calling because I'd like to know which make and model SUVs you offer for rent."

He went down the page, writing the models on a list. Whenever there was a delay while a clerk went to his computer to see the selection of cars or had to handle a customer, Ray thought about Emily. She must be wondering right now whether anyone even knew she was missing, or if anyone had turned up a lead to follow. She would be afraid. Maybe she was in pain. Maybe she was already dead.

Hall kept talking and dialing, moving down the column in the telephone book. He kept the desperation out of his voice because he knew it had a bad effect on the person at the other end of a telephone call. Most of the time a desperate person was crazy or in some position of neediness. People felt uncomfortable and wanted to cut off contact as quickly as possible. He needed to have them spend extra time getting him the information he needed, so he was affable, friendly, calm. He made them like him. Behind the untroubled manner, his mind was in turmoil, trying to think of another path to Emily.

And then he dialed the right number. The voice on the other end was a young woman. "Everyday Car Rentals."

Hall asked her if Everyday rented any Lexus GX 470 SUVs.

"Yes," she said. "We have some Lexus SUVs. They're only about twelve dollars a day over the price of a full-size sedan."

"Can you tell me the colors available, please?"

"Colors?"

"Yes, if you don't mind."

"Well, okay. They come in black, brown, green, white. Another white. And beige."

"You have beige. Is it that kind of silvery-beige color? I think they call it 'silver sand'?"

"Well, yes. That's the color. I don't say it because nobody knows what I mean."

"But you have one?"

"Yes. We have one on the lot, but it's taken at the moment. I can't be sure when it will be back in, but if you wanted to rent another car, I could call you when it comes in, and you could trade."

"Could you tell me who rented that one?"

"I'm sorry, sir, but we can't give out information on customers. But would you like one of the other colors?" Her voice was cooler: He had gone too far.

"You know, I'm only interested in that color. Are there any other agencies that have the same model and color?"

"I can't be positive about the color. I did hear that Everyday is the only company that rents the same model. I would guess that Everyday probably got a deal by buying a fleet of them. Sometimes what happens is some company makes a special order and then cancels it, or the model doesn't sell, or something. These cars are perfectly good, though. I've driven one. There's another Everyday agency near the Marina, and one in Fountain Valley. You could ask them if they have the right color."

"If that one comes in, can you call me right away and hold it for me?"

"Sure. Let me have your name and number."

"I promise there will be a huge tip in it for you." He gave her the information, and then asked for her name.

"Carrie." The tone of her voice reminded him of a person who had taken a bet that she didn't expect to win.

Ray Hall dialed the cell-phone number on Detective Gruenthal's card. He said, "I think I've found where this guy rented his car. It's the Everyday Car Rental on Hollywood Way in Burbank. They claim they're the only company that has a Lexus GX 470 for rent, and their other shops are in Fountain Valley and Marina del Rey."

"Great, Ray!" Gruenthal said. "That's great news."

"They have only one that's silver-sand color, and it's rented out right now."

"Even better. I'll need a warrant to find out who the renter is, but I'll get it as fast as I can. Sit tight, and I'll call you as soon as I have it."

"It will be a stolen credit card or a fake name. Concentrate on getting permission to have the auto-theft guys trip the LoJack to find where the car is now. Please, this guy could be killing her."

33

Hobart had finished digging the grave. It was well over six feet deep, so the barrow of dirt on each side above his head was at least a yard high when he had hit rock. He liked working in the dark. He liked the feel of the night outside the city, the sounds and the smells. Hobart had done this kind of digging a few times before, and he had strong opinions about it. A deep grave was still the best way to hide a body because the police were never so overfunded or underworked that they could afford to dig to bedrock over a large area.

He would normally have used the shovel to dig a narrow incline to walk his way up out of the grave, but this time he didn't want to do that. It would ruin the squared-off, gravelike appearance. He stuck the shovel in the mound to his left, then placed both hands on the flat ground just beyond the edge, jumped, and pulled himself up at the head of the grave.

Hobart had spent a lot of time on Emily Kramer. He had stalked her, considered her in moments of absolute terror that would have reduced some women to hysteria or unconsciousness, but she seemed to maintain a shaky alertness. He respected people who clung to life that way, but he needed to finish this whole Emily Kramer business tonight. He was probably going to have to kill her and drive up to meet Theodore Forrest and collect his two hundred thousand.

Hobart left the shovel and walked through the field toward the house, feeling a kind of pride in his own workmanship. There was not a sliver of light coming from any window, although he had left the bathroom light on. There was a skill to being an outlaw. The only people who knew and respected it were the people who had it and the people who made a living chasing them down, but a man who did things right lasted a little longer.

He walked along, and suddenly felt the vibration of his cell phone against his thigh. He reached into his pocket, pulled it out and opened it. "Yes?"

The voice he heard was one he had not expected exactly, but dreaded. "Hi. Can you talk for a second?" Theodore Forrest.

Hobart said quietly, "I can, but I'd rather not."

"I mean are you alone?"

"For now."

"I've been afraid you had gotten into a mess of some kind. I had expected to hear from you."

"I told you about a day ago that I would call you after it's taken care of. I think I told you that I didn't want you calling me."

"I know, I know. But there were special circumstances. It was before I burned down the house and the office. And now I think I'm going to need you for something else."

Hobart's mind seemed to darken, and then flash wildly from one step to the next, changing each of the topics that had occupied him for the past few days. "*You* set those fires?"

"Yes, I did. Kramer had some things that I couldn't leave lying around much longer. They had to be in his house or the office."

"I told you I would handle everything here."

"It was a totally separate issue. You're handling Emily Kramer for me. I had to prepare for what happens next. After she's dead, the police would have searched her house and her husband's office completely. I couldn't have my name connected with the Kramers or the agency. So I took care of it."

Hobart could hear the pride in Forrest's voice. Forrest was enjoying telling him in this casual tone that he had taken care of his problem himself. Hobart stopped walking and stood in the dark field a hundred yards from the house. He turned to look at the road in the distance. He could see it, but only because a car came along, the bright cone in front of its headlights illuminating a stretch at a time. He said, "I'm surprised you would do something like that yourself. I hope you managed to accomplish it without getting noticed."

"I'm positive I did. That's not really why I called. I have another situation up here that I'd like to have you handle for me. When can you finish what you're doing down there?"

"As it happens, I'm sort of in the middle of it right now. I just finished digging the grave."

"Great! Wonderful. As soon as it's over, come up here."

"I was planning to, anyway. That was our deal. Have you got my pay ready?"

"Of course."

"All right, then. She'll be dead and buried in a half hour or so. This other thing you want me to do. What is it?"

"Just the same kind of job."

"Same pay."

"This one's much, much easier. I've already got her locked up. There's no hunting or stalking involved."

"The hard part isn't that stuff, it's keeping anyone from figuring out why. That's what the money buys you: never having to take the blame. I'll be up to get my pay for what I'm doing now. I'll probably be there tomorrow evening. If you want me to do anything else, fine. The pay will be the same. If you decide you don't, that will be fine, too. Are we set?"

"Yes. I'll have the money for both jobs here."

"As I said, the second one's up to you. From here on, let me be the one to call you. And after tomorrow, you'll want to throw away that cell phone."

"I will. See you tomorrow."

Hobart put his telephone away. The call from Forrest was not merely a shock, it was a contravention of the rules of the universe. He could accept the idea that Theodore Forrest would think burning the house and the office might be to his advantage. But he had not imagined that Forrest would drive all the way down here and set the fires himself, or that he could accomplish the job and drive back without getting caught.

Hobart had acted on the axiom that Theodore Forrest would never do anything risky himself, particularly when there was no guarantee that the evidence would be destroyed. Hobart had assumed that the ones who had set the fires had to be Emily Kramer and her boyfriend, the detective from the agency. Hobart had interpreted the fires as a sign that they had already found the evidence and wanted to throw him off.

Forrest's call changed everything.

It was entirely possible that Emily Kramer had never found anything, and that Theodore Forrest had succeeded in destroying the evidence himself, just by striking two matches. Hobart had spent all this time and effort to get his turn in line for the big money. He could have dropped the hammer on Emily Kramer on the first day, but he hadn't. He had taken risks, shown his face all over town, rented cars and hotel rooms. Now he was back at zero. While Hobart had been screwing around trying to find proof of whatever the hell Theodore Forrest had done, he had given Forrest time to burn it.

He hated Theodore Forrest. He had done something, all right. He had almost said it on the phone. He had done something so shameful that he would come all the way down here alone and take the chance of getting caught committing arson to hide it. What could he have done that rated this kind of risk? It had to involve killing somebody, at least. Knowing that made Hobart feel worse. He could have made Forrest pay millions to keep that hidden, but Forrest had beaten him.

Hobart thought about Emily Kramer and got angrier. He was going to have to put her in that grave and shovel the dirt on top of her tonight. He resumed his walk through the weeds toward the house. He had begun to like Emily Kramer. He knew that her looks affected him, but it wasn't her fault. She was not the sort of woman who was beautiful enough to have a lifetime of special treatment behind her. She had married a loser of a private detective instead of some billionaire. But she was appealing to him. He hated the fact that she was going to die so soon. He and Emily Kramer were both getting screwed by Theodore Forrest.

Hobart went to the SUV and took out the ski mask and the gun. He pulled the mask over his head and adjusted it so he could see through the eyeholes, slipped the gun into his belt, and walked back to the farmhouse. He stepped up on the porch, and when he was up there on the sloping boards, his head nearly brushed the overhanging roof. Most old farmhouses in places like this were small, like cottages. The farmer would build a little structure for his wife and himself, and if the marriage lasted and the crops came in, they would add rooms to the building for children. This farm must have been one where the marriage had soured. He walked across the bare parlor, hearing the boards creak under his weight, unlocked the bathroom door and opened it.

She was sitting where he had left her hours ago, her forearm resting on the sink so there was slack in the handcuff that held her to the bar. "Hello, Mrs. Kramer," he said.

"Hello." She held her head straight toward him. He could tell she had taken aside the tape over her eyes so she could see, and had pushed it back only when she had heard him step up on the porch. He reached to the corner she had pushed back. When he touched her, she pulled back and gave a startled cry.

"I'm taking your tape off."

"Please don't."

"Why not?"

"If I don't see your face, you can still let me go. And if you don't let me go, I don't need to see what's coming."

Hobart studied her for a moment. "I'm wearing the mask." He reached to her face and peeled back the part of the tape that was already stuck only lightly, then gave a quick tug to pull off the rest.

"Ow!" Her eyes remained shut for a couple of seconds, then squinted and blinked in the light.

Hobart reached into his pocket for the key, then unlocked the handcuffs from the steel bar. "Stand up."

She stood. He spun her around, took her free hand behind her back, and closed the handcuff on it. Then he stepped back, but the sight of him in the ski mask seemed to paralyze her.

"Come on." He took her arm and conducted her toward the door. She didn't resist, and it made him wonder. He expected her to ask where they were going, but as he pulled her through the house and opened the front door, she said nothing. She seemed to have realized that what she said would not dissuade him from whatever he intended to do, so she just walked. Later she would try to fight. She had her hands cuffed behind her, she was unarmed against a much bigger, stronger, armed opponent, but she would fight.

Hobart led her down the porch steps to the dry, dusty ground in front of the house, and then into the overgrown field. He heard the weeds whipping the fabric of their pants as they walked. He could smell the broken stems in the dark night air.

When they had gone a hundred yards, he could tell she saw the grave. Her breath caught, and she went rigid for a second. Then she walked a bit unsteadily for a couple of steps, but tried to hide it, until she began to cry.

EMILY WAS GOING to die. The earth, the calm, warm night air, the complex smell of the pollens and roots of the weeds and the juicy smell from the broken shafts all seemed vivid. She felt as though it was probably appropriate to cry, but she managed to stop. Crying was bleeding her of strength.

She said quietly, "I really didn't burn down my own house. I've been telling you the truth."

"I know you didn't."

"Doesn't it matter to you?"

"Matter? Sure it does. *I* didn't set those fires, and *you* didn't. *He* did—the man the evidence is about. He got there while I was wasting my time on you. Bad luck for both of us."

"So you're going to kill me and bury me in a hole in the middle of the night. My fam—my friends—will never know what happened to me."

"That's the plan."

"But that won't help you, it will just help *him*. If I'm gone, then there won't be anybody who knows he killed my husband to hide some crime. There won't be anybody left who knows he had any-thing to do with us."

"I gave it my best effort. If I had the evidence, then he wouldn't get away with any crimes. I searched for it, I held you up for it, I broke into your husband's office. I scared you into trying to find it. The time is up, and I still don't have it—my time and your time."

"It's *not* up. We can still keep trying."

"He's already destroyed it. He's in control now. All I can do is kill you and collect my money."

Emily considered telling him. She knew where the evidence was. She knew it had not been destroyed. She knew what the box looked like, and approximately what it contained. But she knew that the idea of trading the evidence for her life was an illusion. If she told this man, he would kill her. And then he would kill Sam Bowen to get the box. She had to get that idea out of her mind. There was no giving in, no surrender.

There was nothing left to do but try to fight him. She would try to butt her forehead into his face. She would take advantage of his momentary shock and pain and kick him, trying to push him into the grave. Then, whether she succeeded or not, she would run toward the highway. Immediately she noticed that having a plan, no matter how foolish, made her feel stronger.

As she walked, she worked out various details. She would have to make her move a surprise when she was at the grave. When she ran, she would have to sprint as fast as she could for a minute or two with her hands behind her. It would be difficult to keep from falling with her hands cuffed like that. She hoped that walking this way would be enough practice to help her do it. In any case, this was all the prepa-ration she would get. She concentrated on hating him, visualizing her head smashing into his face.

He said, "If you can tell me where the evidence is, then I'll leave you alive. I'll get in my car and drive off. It will take you an hour or so to walk to town and wake somebody up or flag down a car on the road. That's all the time I'll need. I'll leave you alone."

Emily made herself the perfect liar. She had no doubt that he intended to kill her, and that telling him about the box would only get other people killed. "If I had found it, I would have given it to you. I haven't found it. At this point, I'm wondering if this evidence even exists. Maybe if Phil said he had it, he was bluffing. I don't know. In a few minutes, it's not going to matter—at least to me. I'll be dead, won't I?"

The man in the mask kept her walking toward the grave, and Emily could make out its exact shape and contours. The hole looked deep and dark. There were two high piles of dirt—one on each of the long sides—but the head and foot were clear. She walked toward what she felt was the head, hoping he would come, too, and he did.

There were three more steps. Two. One. She whirled and used her legs to spring into him to butt his face, but he seemed to have become smoke. He wasn't there. He was already to the side of where he had been. He tripped her and pushed so she fell full length on her belly beside the grave. In an instant, he was straddling her. She felt the gun muzzle pressed against her cheek.

He said, "That wasn't a very effective move."

She was trembling a little, waiting. She wondered if she would hear the shot.

Then she felt the gun move away from her cheek. He seemed to be putting it out of her reach somewhere. So that was it. He was going to rape her before he killed her. She felt his weight shift downward so his body was above her thighs. She prepared herself for her clothes to come off.

He was fiddling with her handcuffs. There was a click, then another. The handcuffs came away from her wrists.

He said, "I can't let you walk a road like that with handcuffs on. If the wrong car comes along, you're liable to end up dead, anyway."

"You're letting me go?"

"You don't have what I want."

"But the grave. I thought—"

"I need to have a half hour or so before anybody comes after me. It'll take you that long to dig your way out. Get up."

Emily stood. He took her hand and lowered her into the grave. She looked up, and it disturbed her to see the sky as a dim rectangle of light with the man in the ski mask framed in it. All he had to do was pull out the gun, shoot her, and push the dirt in on top of her.

He said, "I'm sorry I put you through all that for nothing, especially making you strip that night and everything. I thought you had what I needed."

She said nothing.

He turned away, and for a moment she heard the sound of him walking through the weeds.

She stepped backward to the wall of dirt at the foot of the grave. She was not a tall woman, and the opening looked far above her head. She waited for the sound of the man's footsteps to come back, but she didn't hear any. The earth smelled wet and loamy, even though it hadn't rained for months. She imagined there were worms and bugs, but the grave felt like a refuge now.

After what seemed like a long time, she heard a car engine, and then the sound of tires on gravel, with the ticking of stones kicked up against the steel undercarriage. Then she heard the deeper sound of the engine accelerating. She couldn't tell which direction it was going from down here, and she knew she was going to regret not having better hearing. The sound faded.

Emily allowed herself to feel a tentative sense of relief, and then as though she had opened a window in a flood, the joy roared in to engulf her. She took a breath of air and it seemed to keep coming, her lungs filling to strain her rib cage. She let the air out in a long, low "*Oooooh—hooo.*" But her voice still sounded scared. "I'm alive," she said aloud. Then she put her head in her hands and allowed herself to cry. After a time, she seemed to run out of tears, and she took off her jacket and dried her tears on her sleeve.

Emily looked around her. She would have to dig her way out with her hands, just as he had said. She tried to jump up and pull some of the dirt down into the hole, but she couldn't reach high enough. She tried three more times, but with each jump she was farther from succeeding. She tried digging a set of footholds into the earth wall at the end of the grave, like the rungs of a ladder. It took a long time, and it hurt her fingers. She couldn't seem to make the holes deep enough to hold her weight, and each time she tried to climb, her foothold would break and she would fall back down. Finally she measured a spot on the wall that was as high as she could raise her foot, and concentrated on gouging one big hole in the wall at that spot.

When it was as deep as she could make it, she placed her right foot in it, raised her body up, and placed both her hands at the rim of the grave. She tangled her hands in the thick weeds, pushed off with her foot, and got her chest up to the surface. She used her hands to grasp other clumps of weeds as they came within her reach, dug her toes into the earth, and pulled herself out onto the ground. She lay there for a time, recovering her strength and her wind. Then she lifted her head to look around her slowly and carefully.

She could see the little house where she had spent the day and night handcuffed and in terror. It seemed harmless and empty now. She rose to her knees and took a long and careful look in every direction for some sign that the man had come back. She got to her feet and looked again, and then began to walk toward the distant road.

Fidelity

After a few minutes, Emily heard the sound of car engines in the distance, then saw a row of headlights coming up the dark road. She walked toward it, then began to trot, then broke into a run. As the lights approached, she could see that they were all too close together, too regularly spaced to be normal traffic. They were coming at a very high speed. When the cars reached the entrance to the long gravel road into the farm, they all pulled to the shoulder of the highway. Two men jumped out of the lead car in the glare of the headlights behind them, and she could see their car was a police car. The two men opened a metal gate, running with it to make it swing out of the way. The other cars all moved around the lead car. Four of them kept going, accelerating along the road past the farm, but the others all made the turn onto the gravel road.

Searchlights on the police cars swept across the weedy fields. When they crossed the gravel drive, they illuminated clouds of dust that their tires had kicked up. One of the beams swept across her, stopped, and came back to settle on her. Then the other beams joined it, and made it so bright that she couldn't keep her eyes open. She just stood still and held her arms over her head.

She heard a man's voice amplified electronically: "Are you Emily Kramer?"

"Yes," she shouted, and nodded her head dramatically so they could see it from a distance.

She heard the sounds of running feet now, heavy footsteps and the whipping of weeds against their legs. A closer voice said, "Where is the man who took you?"

"He left. I don't know how long it's been. I had to dig myself out of a hole. At least half an hour or forty minutes, maybe an hour." The lights seemed to dim a bit, so she opened her eyes. There were tall black silhouettes around her. One caught up with the others, and suddenly wrapped its arms around her.

"Emily," he said.

"Hi, Ray. I knew if anybody looked hard enough for me, it would be you."

"Are you okay?"

"I'm okay. He just kept me handcuffed and asked me questions. I'm just really tired."

"You'll be able to rest. They'll take you to the hospital and clean you up and make sure you're all right."

A big new silhouette appeared. "You're safe now, Mrs. Kramer." It was the voice of Detective Gruenthal. "Mr. Hall, I'd like you to ride with Officer Daniels here, and we'll take Mrs. Kramer with us. We need to talk."

Emily made a decision at that moment, and she was not even certain why. It was possible that it was simply the "You're safe now," which she had heard before and no longer believed. She would tell them all about the kidnapping and the man in the ski mask. But somehow the other part—the part she had figured out and kept from telling the man in the mask—didn't belong to the police; at least not yet. It belonged to her.

34

The police kept Emily talking until seven in the morning. Ray Hall was sitting in the hallway when they released her, waiting to take her home. They drove through the heavy morning traffic to his house, and when they were inside, she said, "Ray, do you have Sam Bowen's phone number?"

He looked at her for a moment, then went to the sideboard, opened a drawer, and pulled out an address book. He found the page and handed the open book to her.

"Thanks," she said. She dialed the number and waited. "Hello, Sam? This is Emily Kramer. Oh, things haven't been so hot around here since the funeral, but it's a long story, and I don't have the energy right now."

She listened for a few seconds, staring at the floor and nodding her head, then said, "Why haven't you opened it?" She listened for a few more seconds. "Well, open it now, and read it. I'll be up there as soon as I can get a flight. I don't know the schedule. I'll call you from the airport."

When she had hung up the phone, she said to Ray, "I know you won't agree with what I'm doing. You'll notice I haven't asked you."

"I assume what you were saying means Sam has the evidence. You haven't told the police?"

"He has a package. I'm going up there, and we'll see what's in it."

"That guy is still out there. He must have ditched the SUV within ten minutes after he left you, or they would have caught him. And he's nuts. He could be right outside waiting for you."

"If so, then the best way you can protect me is drive me to the airport and watch me leave." She picked up the telephone again.

THE HOUSE WAS a two-bedroom cottage with brown clapboards outside Seattle overlooking Puget Sound. There was a wooden deck lodged in the space between two pine trees, and a hot tub. On a cool day, Sam Bowen could step from the tub into the warmth of his house in two steps.

Sam wore a pair of blue jeans and a green flannel shirt with buttoned flaps over the breast pockets. He sat on an Adirondack chair staring out at the water. An empty glass was on the table, and beside it was the stationery box with a maroon top and gold print.

"I never opened it until you called, Emily," Sam said. "It arrived a couple of days ago, but the handwriting on the label was Phil's. I figured it had to be just another one of those housekeeping things that Phil did sometimes. He would have something he didn't want lying around the office, or maybe he even wanted to be able to tell somebody truthfully that he didn't have it. He would stash it somewhere, sometimes with someone like me."

Emily said, "Weren't you even curious?"

"Shit, Em. I'm seventy-three years old. I was a cop for twenty years, and then a private investigator for about as long. I'm cured of that. I'm not interested in getting hit in the face or staying up late anymore, and there aren't any secrets I haven't heard."

"But now you've read it, haven't you?"

"Yes. It's about a case we had."

"What kind of case?"

"A bad one. It was one of those jobs that you hesitate to take, and you probably wouldn't take at all, except that by the time you hear about it, the client is already sitting in your office. He's so distraught that you can barely stand to look at him, and he's there only because he's already tried everything that had a reasonable chance of success."

Emily said, "So it was a man who came to see you."

"Not me, Phil. I wouldn't have heard about it at all, except that Phil called me into his office to listen. He introduced me and said, 'I want my associate Mr. Bowen to hear this.' That was a bad omen. He never called anyone his associate unless that person was about to do something painful."

"What did you say?"

"I sat down and shut up and listened. The man was rich. I could see it by looking at his shoes. They were Mephisto walking shoes, handmade. That was a telling thing, to me. What it said was that he had enough money to buy whatever he wanted, but that he wasn't interested in impressing people. They don't look like anything. He had a good haircut, a watch that looked expensive, but with a French name I hadn't seen before. I could tell Phil had seen the same signs, and so I stopped thinking about what we were going to make, and listened to the story."

"What was it?"

"Nothing special—a story we've all heard about a thousand times. Sometimes I think a third of my working life was spent with daughters looking for their fathers, and another third with fathers looking for their daughters."

"That was the case?" Emily asked. "He was searching for his missing daughter?"

Sam nodded. "He had a lot of land in the San Joaquin Valley, and he lived in a big house on an enormous piece of land—the sort of place where if you want to gossip over the back fence, you have to drive there."

"What was his name?"

"Theodore Forrest, the Something. Maybe the fourth or fifth."

"And the daughter? What did he say about her?"

"Her name was Allison. He said that she had been a terrific kid at first, the sort of little girl who was always happy—maybe a little smart-ass, even—and who lit up a room as soon as she came into it. He brought a couple of old pictures of her at about age five and ten along with the others, and I could see what he meant. She was a really pretty kid, with a lot of intelligence behind the eyes."

"You said 'at first.' What was the problem later?"

"He said that around age thirteen or so, troubles started. She had a kind of personality change. All of a sudden she wasn't interested in the family anymore, just wanted to stay in her room. Her grades went all to hell. Her old friends seemed to move on, and they were replaced by a different kind of kid."

"That doesn't sound unusual. What kind of kid?"

"The kind that skips school, does drugs, and so on. This wasn't exactly a new story to me, but it was to him, so we listened. He said the girls were the worst in his eyes. They were the kind that gave a father a lot to think about, for sure. He said that he'd heard stories about a couple of them. They were promiscuous in that scary self-destructive way that girls are sometimes, kids who don't seem to give a damn whether what they're doing kills them or something else does. The more he tried to get rid of them, the more Allison liked them. She would sneak out to meet them. He moved her to a private school, and she would slip out at night to go out with them. Then she was gone."

"How old was she at that point?"

"Sixteen. By then she was looking very grown up. When her father came to see us, we saw the pictures, and I remember thinking she would be hard to find because she could pass for twenty-two or so in the right clothes."

Emily sensed something withheld. "Tell me more about the pictures."

"There are a few in here." Sam opened the box and pulled an envelope from a pharmacy's photo lab out of a file. He set the envelope on the table in front of her, and she began to shuffle through the photographs.

One showed an athletic-looking man in his early forties in a fancy cabin or ranch house—possibly some kind of resort—sitting at a table with his arm around the girl. They were both grinning at the camera with similar expressions, and Emily looked closely at the two faces, trying to detect a family resemblance. There was nothing obvious. The girl had long chestnut hair and big green eyes and a pretty face, but it was the sort of wide-cheeked, fair face with Cupid's-bow lips that she associated with Irish women she had known. The father had the long face with pointed, narrow nose that made her think of Englishmen. She found herself forming theories about Allison's mother.

She kept going, looking at each picture, and then noticed a similarity. There were lots of places—a houseboat on a lake in a treeless landscape that had to be Arizona, a white sand beach on the ocean, a redwood grove, a place that looked like a restaurant on a balcony above a lagoon, outside an apartment or condominium—but just the two of them. In some shots Allison was alone, and in others she was with her father, but there were never any friends, either her age or his. And there was never anyone who could be the mother. She said, "Was the mother the one who took the pictures?"

"I think she was out of the picture, literally. There was no mother I ever saw, and no shots of her, either, even in the pictures of the girl as a toddler. I think they were all taken by strangers, people he handed the camera to and asked to press the button."

Emily found one of Allison in a bathing suit, and understood what Sam had said earlier. The girl had an exceptional figure, like an hourglass, and it made her seem older than sixteen in spite of her smooth, untroubled face. "She was very pretty." Emily returned the photographs to the envelope and put them back on the table.

Sam said, "He gave us the pictures. He showed us the girl's birth certificate and a black-and-white photocopy of her driver's license. After the first meeting, we asked for things. Anything we asked for, he would send by overnight mail. Phil wasn't easy on him, either."

"What do you mean?"

"Well, a father from up north comes to you and says his sixteen-year-old daughter disappeared two months ago. He's already had the local cops on the case, and he's hired detectives up there. They've talked to all her friends and relatives, searched her room and her school locker, and every place she went regularly. Now he comes down to L.A. and hires a detective to find out if that's where she went. It's got to occur to you that most likely what you're looking for is a corpse. Phil went up and got fingerprints off some things she touched in a ranch the family owned that nobody had visited since she left."

"To identify her body?"

"Well, if the cops find a Jane Doe somewhere, they generally fingerprint her if they can. Our theory was that we might be able to end this guy's uncertainty just by a records check. It didn't pan out."

"What did you do after that?"

"We started to search for a live girl, thinking we probably would find a dead one. It was one of those stories you wish you hadn't heard. He grounded her because of her grades. She slipped out of the house on a school night in the middle of the week, and spent the night with a few friends of both sexes. There was drinking and, he suspected, some drugs. He got stricter. He said she couldn't go out for the rest of the year, and that she would have to earn his trust if she was even to go out during her senior year."

"Isn't that going a bit far?"

"He thought he might have laid it on a little thicker than he needed to. After we talked to him for an hour or two, he mentioned that maybe he called her a few names, used words he might not have used if he had it to do over again." Sam paused. "Only he didn't. They kind of coexisted for a week or so. They didn't talk much. His story fit one of the things I'd noticed a few times in this business. It's a lot easier to avoid people if you're rich. They lived in a big house with a lot of out-of-the-way rooms, and servants who would serve the girl a meal by herself so she didn't have to eat with her father. And just having servants around all the time makes the house too public to hold a big confrontation that will clear the air. Then she was gone."

"Gone? Just gone? No message?"

"That's what he said. He was out all day as usual, and he got home late at night and figured she was asleep. When he got up the next morning around ten, he figured she was at school. While he was at lunch, the phone rang, and it was the math teacher asking whether Allison was going to be sick another day and needed the homework assignment. He said it took him a day and night to realize that she wasn't just skipping school, and then to find out that she had probably been gone since at least the morning of the day before, or even at the end of school the day before that. She didn't take the car, didn't even take credit cards, so he wasn't ready to panic just yet. Then he discovered that she had taken out three thousand dollars from a savings account her grandmother had started for her. She was gone."

"He called the police?"

"That was the first step. They seemed to have covered all the friends, interviewed servants, teachers, relatives, and so on during the first week. At that point, he was crazy with worry. He's a rich man, so he offered a reward and hired a big detective agency that works out of San Francisco—you've probably heard of them—Federal Surety and Safety International. They had offices in Fresno, Modesto, and Sacramento, and they had people fanning out all over the place showing her picture and asking questions. Nothing. All this took time. At the end of a month, the cops were clearly preparing him for the probability that she was dead. His detectives, of course, were not about to give up, ever. They had a client who could keep paying until the end of time, and you know this business. There's always another door you can knock on, and when you run out, there's always another town where you can start the whole process over again. A customer who can pay can have as much time as he wants."

"What brought him to Phil?"

"I don't know. He said he'd had his attorneys check around with Southern California attorneys. Phil got mentioned."

"But why Southern California?"

Sam shrugged. "If he had really been thinking, he should have done it earlier. L.A. is one of the places where runaway kids are most likely to come."

"Did Phil take the case right away, or did he hold out?"

"He was pretty good about it. He said right off that he didn't want to keep the distraught father in suspense. He was willing to try to help. Then he said everything you would want an ethical investigator to say—that the cops were good at this, and that after a month, anything we found was probably not going to make him happy. But Mr. Forrest said he knew all that, and a few other things the cops had told him. He just wanted the girl found, and he wasn't ready to give up. Clear enough. We went to work."

"What did you do?"

"We got the pictures copied, and then we went out showing them to people and asking around. We went to nightspots and found kids who were willing to look in exchange for the reward. It was a hundred thousand, so we didn't hear 'No' a lot. Then we moved to street kids, who were always out there, always looking, always hungry. Next we found some upscale kids outside expensive stores, and got them interested, too. That was an idea of Phil's. If you think about Allison's background, you know that's who she would fit in with. And her looks were good enough to get her in anywhere. We talked to authorities, too—anybody who would run into somebody like her. We went to the volunteers who ran shelters and clinics, a few cops I knew in Hollywood, street vendors, hookers, cabdrivers, anybody who would talk to us. I used to find that I got a lot of good observation from the guys who drive around to fill the machines that sell newspapers. One of these guys will be out in the dead hours from three to six. He has to drive to each spot, get out of his truck, open the machine, empty a coin box, take out the old papers and put in the new ones. It takes a minute or two, and he's always looking closely at anybody nearby so he doesn't get robbed. He sees a lot."

"How long did that go on?"

"That phase of things kept Phil and me occupied for about a month. We went out with pictures day and night, on rotation. We tried to hit everybody's schedule who might have seen her—the night sleepers and the day sleepers. Then we started over again. Finally, after a couple of months, we got a breakthrough."

"What was it?"

"A pocket. When you're looking for people who have seen somebody, you get either none or some. If it's real, you usually get one, then a few more. If you do, then you've found the neighborhood where she hangs out. You chart the sightings—where, exactly, she was seen, and when—and you begin to get an idea of where she was at what time of day and what she was doing."

"So she was alive after all," Emily said.

"That's right. Allison's territory was a long, thin strip of pavement. She was seen in several clubs along Hollywood Boulevard near Highland. And during the day she was in stores and coffee shops along Melrose. She was seen as far west as Fairfax at Farmers Market. On the east she went as far as Crescent Heights. If she was on Wilshire, she'd go a little farther, at least as far as the art museum. It was like the territory of a cat, and for the same reasons. She was always on foot, and she wanted to skirt the dens of the scary animals. She went where she felt safe."

"Was she hiding?"

"She didn't want to be found, but she was just a kid. She thought all she had to do was travel to someplace new and call herself by another name. Once she was in Los Angeles, she forgot about laying low, and started to go places where other people would see her. She was on an adventure in the big city. I don't think she ever thought Forrest would hire anybody to find her."

"But you found her?"

"We did. Once we had mapped her territory, we picked some places for a blind."

"A blind?"

"A place to wait for her to come by. We got a plain white van with no windows in the back. We would put a different sign on the side of it every day, then park it and sit inside to wait. We figured the time to concentrate on was evening, from dark until maybe two in the morning. It was the best time to spot her because there weren't as many people out, and it was also the best time to do what we were planning."

"What was it?"

"We were going to jump out of the van, flash some badges, hand-cuff her like we were arresting her, and drive off."

"My God, Sam! What could you have done that was more illegal than that?"

"I know. If we were caught in the act, there wouldn't be much we could say about the badges and so on. But when the target is a minor, and you're carrying the father's written permission to use whatever force is necessary to bring his daughter back, you have a certain leeway."

"Did you get her that way?"

"We didn't have much luck at first. We sat and smoked cigarettes and stared at everybody on the street, then went home. The next night we would do it again. After she didn't turn up for seven nights in one spot, we would move to the next one. She had been gone a long time by then. We figured she must have a job or a boyfriend, a place to live, and fake ID, so it wasn't just looking for a lost person hanging on a corner. She had choices. But the thing was, we had plenty of time to do it right, because the money was behind us."

"What did Forrest say?"

"When we called him to tell him we were getting recent sightings from people—that his daughter wasn't dead, in other words—you should have heard him. We were all happy. Listening to him made us feel good. If we had asked him for a million dollars, he would have written the check. After he hung up, we replayed the recording, and I laughed so hard I thought I was going to have a stroke."

"Recording? Phil recorded the call? Why?"

"Well, think about it. We're about to do something that could get us arrested. He had written us a note giving us permission, but Phil wasn't going to take any chances. I mean, what if he said later that it was a forgery, or even that he'd never heard of us?"

"I guess your arrest would be a conviction."

"That was our guess, too. But at that point, the guy was ready to drive down here to be in the van when we grabbed her. As you can imagine, Phil didn't let him."

"Why not?"

"We knew where she had been a week ago and two nights ago, but not tonight. Also, he was an amateur, a first-timer. We were trying to grab a young girl off a public street, and the only way you want to do that is if you can do a convincing cop. I had been a cop, so I wasn't acting. Phil was a cop in the marines, so he wasn't really, either. Part of our credibility was that this Allison girl had never seen me or Phil. If she saw her father on a street, even four hundred miles from home, she would certainly recognize him and take off."

"So you were expecting her to resist?" asked Emily. "Wouldn't it be just as likely she would see him and want to come home?"

"If she did, she knew the phone number. And if she wanted to surprise him, she knew the way home."

"But to take her against her will—"

"You know better than that, Emily. In this state, a sixteen-year-old doesn't have a will, legally. She does what her parents tell her."

"I'm not talking about legal fictions."

"Neither am I. You know any success stories about runaway girls in L.A.? We weren't sure how she had gotten that far, but neither of us could think of any possible future for her that wasn't a disaster. I mean, she's got one thing to trade. We were convinced that we were saving her life."

Emily was silent.

"So we did it. One night we happened to be in the sweet spot. The van had a sign on it that night that said TWENTY-FOUR-HOUR PLUMBING. We parked it right off Hollywood, halfway up on the curb with orange safety cones behind it. We had the back door open so you could see one of those rooter machines Phil had rented that day, and the effect was great. I mean, what fake has one of those things?"

"And?"

"Along comes Allison. It's around midnight. She comes right along the sidewalk from the direction of those old apartments around Fountain. I don't know if she was crashing there with somebody she had met, or she just happened to like the route. I came from the building side and Phil came from the truck. We scooped her up and packed her into the back of the truck. Phil went in after her, and I drove off."

"Didn't she fight or scream or anything?"

"For a couple of seconds, I could hear her kicking and stuff. But then Phil handcuffed her and put a plastic restraint on her ankles. All the while he was reciting the Miranda warning. It's a great way to calm somebody down. It intimidates them, but persuades them in a deep way that nothing freaky is happening to them. They're still in a world where if everything goes wrong, they're going to court. It also tells them that you think what you say to them matters—that the truth matters. So she went limp and stayed quiet for a long time. We were on the freeway nearly to Camarillo before she figured out we weren't taking her to the station. She got really agitated, and we had to give her a little something to keep her quiet."

"You drugged her?" Emily was horrified. "With what?"

"Phil gave her a little shot of something. I think it was that stuff that the doctors give you to put you down before they anesthetize you. Thiopental sodium or something."

"Where in the world did he get it?"

"You know how Phil was. He had connections with everybody. People did things for him."

"I know he cheated on me, Sam. I think we can assume he talked some woman pharmacist or nurse he knew into giving him the drug."

Sam looked at her sadly. "He felt bad, Emily. He always felt like hell after. He really loved you."

"Just tell me the story."

Sam's eyes didn't move from her face. "It sometimes helps to forgive people for things like that. People have weaknesses."

"They sure do," she said. "Phil got some nurse to risk a prison term to give him a needle full of a sedative, and he risked killing the client's daughter by shooting it into her in the back of a van. Is that about it?"

"That's about it. For the rest of the trip she was okay and didn't fight or feel scared. He stayed in the back with her to keep an eye on her pulse and breathing. He had been trained to handle battlefield first aid, and I had been a cop for twenty years." He paused. "I can see that look on your face, and you're wrong, Em. If there had been a bad reaction or something, he would have told me, and we would have rushed her to the nearest hospital, even if it meant the next stop would be jail. We were doing a job, taking a young, misguided girl back to her family, which had the resources to help her. If it was drug rehab, or psychiatric help, or just sending her a check for a few thousand a month, she was going to be better off."

"How did it end?"

"We delivered her to her father at a ranch in the Central Valley. I recognized it from some of the pictures he had given us. There was a sign at the front gate that said ESPINOZA RANCH. There was a big living room he called the 'great room,' with beams made from tree trunks, and a stone fireplace and Tiffany chandeliers and oriental rugs."

"Odd," said Emily. "Why there? Why not the family home?"

"He had his reasons. He seemed to feel that it was likely she was going to make a scene about being snatched off the street like that, and that she would probably raise hell and fight. He didn't want the house staff and visitors to know all about it. He said he couldn't think of a way it would do anybody any good, and he didn't want her to become the staple of local gossip. I could agree with that."

"Were there other people there?"

"I didn't meet them, but there certainly were. This was a big place. When you got past the gate, there was a gravel road that wound a bit to get around a hill and past some old oak woods. The house was there. And beyond it there was a stream that looked as though it might have some trout in it. You need people to keep a house that size from turning musty and dusty. It was just private. He wanted to spend time with her and talk to her and see where he had messed up, and begin to fix it. He had always planned to have her go east to an Ivy League school. He said that running off in her junior year had probably blown that for good. But he said he had learned that it didn't really matter. She was home and she seemed to be all right, and that was all that mattered.

"We were still there when she started to come around. She was healthy, all right, and strong. She started to struggle right away, and make sounds. She was beginning to swear at him, but he said she would calm down as soon as she didn't have an audience. Phil and I offered to stay or fetch help, or whatever, but he said he was already in touch with a psychiatrist who'd had lots of success with runaways—he'd deprogrammed kids who had joined cults, and was part of some institute that helped kids get off drugs and so on. The doctor and three or four members of his staff would be there within a couple of hours. He said he didn't care what it cost or how long it took, he was going to save Allison. We drove home feeling pretty good about what we had done."

Emily waited. Sam seemed to leave her for a moment, his eyes staring out at the wall of mist that was moving into the sound from the open ocean. "It goes to show you," he said.

"To show you what?"

"Everything I just told you was a lie."

"A lie?"

"That's right."

"Everything?"

"All of it. Nothing was true."

"I don't understand."

Sam lifted the box with the maroon cover, pulled out a file folder, and set it on the table between them. Emily picked it up. It was a packet of plain sheets of paper, typed in single-space paragraphs with a line skipped between them. "Read that."

She began to read. "My name is Philip R. Kramer, and I am the owner and principal investigator of Kramer Investigations, Van Nuys Boulevard, Los Angeles, California. I swear on penalty of perjury that everything in this statement is true . . ."

35

As Emily read Phil's file, she recognized the pseudo-authoritative language he had often used in constructing statements for clients when she was still serving as typist for him.

In certain instances I have included photographs, copies of official documents, audiotapes, and newspaper accounts. I think they are sufficient to corroborate this assembly of facts. But these are not the only ones I have. If there are gaps or discrepancies between this account and other versions of the story, I can make available other documents, photographs, recordings, or independent narratives by others to verify what I say here.

I first met Theodore Forrest on October 23 eight years ago. He called my office at 9:15 A.M. and made an appointment to speak to me about a missing-person case. My colleague Samuel Bowen and I met with Mr. Forrest at 1:30 P.M. that day in my office. He told us he lived on a country estate outside Fresno, and that his sixteen-year-old daughter, Allison, had been missing since late July.

She recognized that what she was reading was the same story that Sam had just told her. But it wasn't, because it was Phil who was telling it. She pictured him as she read, and then she reached the end of the story Sam had told her. He and Sam delivered the girl to Theodore Forrest at the Espinoza Ranch, received their payment in the form of a cashier's check, and drove home.

> Our business was concluded, and that was the last time I saw or spoke with Theodore Forrest for eight years. I did not initiate any contact with him, nor did he with me or my employees.
>
> On the fourteenth of June this year, I was engaged in a project intended to increase the income of Kramer Investigations. Over the previous twenty years, the Kramer agency had served a great many satisfied clients. Some clients had been assisted in a once-in-a-lifetime matter: a divorce, a lawsuit, a search for hidden assets, a defense against criminal charges. But it seemed to me that it might be useful to compile a mailing list of former clients and remind them that the agency was still there to fulfill their needs.

Emily could hear Phil's voice saying the words, as though he were dictating them. She had been hearing him since she had begun to read, but now she could see him, too. It was June 14, only a few months ago. Phil was sitting in the office. He was behind his desk in the glassed-in room. She saw him through the clumsy, overly formal narrative he was typing on the computer, and then without at first expecting it or wanting to, she began to supply the other parts Phil had left out. Part of what she was seeing was memory, and where memory was not enough, her imagination supplied the rest, and he was alive again in her mind.

In her imagination, Phil was wearing the light gray super-100 wool pants that she had bought him around Easter. He had on a blue oxford shirt, and hanging on the spare chair at the side of the room was his navy summer-weight blazer. He wore a coat only when he was with a client or in court. It had been hot since the tenth of May, even though May and June were usually cool and overcast in Los Angeles. This year it had seemed to Phil that the climate had changed, and the little break that the June weather brought had been revoked.

Emily pictured him looking out through his glass wall toward the doorway. What was there to look at but April? She was so far away on the other side, and as he watched her, she must have seemed unreachable. Phil loved to touch, to put his hand on a small shoulder or around a thin waist, but he couldn't right now. She was probably talking on the telephone, reminding clients to pay on time. Emily had noticed she had a pretty voice, like a singer, and it seemed to disarm deadbeat clients and make them send in a check here and there—often it was just a token payment—as though they were giving her a little present.

Phil must have had a feeling of cynical amusement whenever he saw the smile appear on her face and knew that she had gotten one of them to agree. He would have said, "The stupid bastards." That would describe him, too, more than any of them. She knew now he was as susceptible to a pretty woman as any fourteen-year-old boy. He was a man who made resolutions, but these had probably all been broken when the first temptation presented herself. The resolutions undoubtedly never lasted long enough to include him actually turning a woman down and watching her walk away forever. She imagined that he had watched April through the glass for a few more seconds, and then forgave himself. He would have said it didn't really do any harm unless Emily found out, and he had always taken precautions to keep Emily from suspecting. He had kept her ignorant and resigned to a life she didn't really understand.

Emily stopped herself. That was a false note. Phil would never have called her ignorant in his thoughts. He would have fooled himself long ago into believing he was protecting his wife from being hurt. He would have said male promiscuity was an inevitable force of nature, but that there was no reason to hurt Emily's feelings.

But probably he wasn't thinking about Emily at that moment, only about April. She was sweet and loving, and when she looked at Phil, he must have felt young again, and attractive. It had been a long time since Emily had looked that way at him. Pete's death had been the major moment of her life. Since then she had looked at Phil as a partner in her hopes and disappointment, an old friend suffering with her.

Phil did a lot of brooding during the past year. Emily guessed that he had been getting ready to make a change in his life. He was coming up on his forty-fifth birthday, and for some reason, it was affecting him more than any earlier one had. Maybe for him it was Pete, just as it was for Emily. It was going to be five years since the crash, a big, round number.

Phil had always been intellectually and emotionally involved in his work, but not long ago, he had told her he could see the end of the detective business. He was being pinched. On one side there were huge security companies that provided an umbrella service against unpleasantness. They monitored alarm and surveillance systems for businesses, swept offices and phones for bugs, took care of paper shredding and burning, did background checks on employees, rivals, and customers. They supplied bodyguards for foreign travel, and forensic specialists for testifying in court.

On the other side, there were small, low-end operators. Those guys would tap telephones, do black-bag jobs to steal papers from offices and houses, threaten or beat up opposition witnesses. They seemed to spend every day with one foot in a jail cell. But the other foot was in the bank, on the way in to cash a fat check.

Phil wasn't sure what he wanted to do next, but he had said several times that he was in a game he was losing gradually, and all he could do was try to make his chips last as long as possible. Now maybe he had decided it was time to stand up and cash in.

According to Ray, for a couple of years, Phil hadn't been able to concentrate on the actual cases that came in. He seemed to have occupied his time looking for grand strategies and shortcuts. If he could have gotten to work again—really working—he might not have felt this way.

During one of these conversations Emily had wondered aloud if he was in a midlife crisis. He had been insulted. What the hell was a midlife crisis? Were troubles supposed to happen only when you were a child or a dying man? He supposed that if he made it to ninety, then forty-five was the exact definition of midlife. And he was sure as hell in a crisis. He had to do something that worked soon.

Phil's written narrative said: "For several years, Kramer Investigations had been running at a deficit. I had cut costs by not replacing personnel who left. I had been keeping the business going by using my family savings to keep the office open and the employees paid." Emily stopped. There it was: the explanation of where the money had gone, and the halfhearted way he had been running the office. He had been trying to keep it alive.

Phil continued: "I had begun a project of going through the company archives to find clients with open accounts." He was reading the files of his agency's old cases, looking for money. He assembled a list of deadbeats. He started a policy of reissuing bills to them, even if their cases were ten years old. Emily felt a sad closeness to him, because she had seen the letters in the files. As of May, the billings had not been a startling success, but April's wheedling had brought in a few dollars. Then, while he had been finding open accounts, he had noticed another kind of client: those he or his detectives had served especially well, and who had businesses that might require help again.

He started to build a mailing list of satisfied clients to remind them that Kramer Investigations was still around and still cared about them. A lot of companies did that and thrived. After a few weeks of work, he hit on the file of Theodore Forrest. It had been eight years.

Phil admitted he wasn't sure exactly what services a man like Forrest might need after eight years. But as Phil looked at the case file, he wrote, he "felt proud of how effective Kramer Investigations had been." He and Sam had found Forrest's daughter when several police forces and big security companies had failed. He and Sam had managed to snatch her off the street and deliver her to her father unharmed and without leaving a hint of how it had happened. The girl could go on with her life as though she had never had her little breakdown. It occurred to Phil that in the eight years that had passed, time had not stood still for Allison, either. She would be twenty-four or twenty-five. She had almost certainly gone to college, graduated, and done something with herself by now.

As Emily read the next portion, she could tell that Phil's mind was sparked, ideas blazing in his mind, each igniting others. Forrest had been obsessed with his daughter. He had wanted her back so badly that he had been willing to do just about anything, to pay just about anything. And Phil Kramer had delivered her. When it was over, he had not taken advantage, he had not padded the bill. He could have invented ten or fifteen imaginary operatives, or gotten thousands in cash to pay rewards to imaginary informants. He could have done almost anything, and Forrest would have paid and then thanked him. Maybe now, Forrest would consider paying a retainer for a permanent all-purpose security service, like the big companies offered.

Eight years was a long time. Maybe by now Allison Forrest had married. Maybe she had a husband Forrest wanted watched. She could even have a baby or two. Forrest would be the sort of grandfather who would pay for surveillance to be sure no harm ever came to his grandchildren. And whom could Forrest trust more than the detective agency that had saved his daughter from ending up as a teenaged prostitute or an unidentified body in the L.A. County Morgue?

The fact that Kramer Investigations had never tried to capitalize on the case would help a lot. In eight years, Phil had never even used Theodore Forrest as a reference. He had kept everything confidential to protect the family's privacy. Emily knew the truth was that he had kept it quiet because of the girl. Phil genuinely liked women, and the idea of compromising a young girl's reputation would have been unthinkable to him. But he was not in a position to turn down additional work if the Forrests happened to feel gratitude he had legitimately earned.

It was clear that he saw the Forrest family as a potential solution to a lot of his financial troubles. There were big, complicated family-business interests to protect. There were undoubtedly pieces of real estate to watch, employees to clear. There were probably deals all the time that would be safer if the parties on the other side were the subjects of quiet, discreet investigations.

He recorded his uncertainty about how to approach Theodore Forrest that day. He looked in the case file for the telephone numbers, picked the home number, and started to dial, then stopped. It had been eight years. What if something had happened in the past eight years that he ought to know about? If there had been some major event, Forrest might say, "Some detective," and hang up. Eight years was enough time for some fundamental change, and it was more than enough time for Forrest to forget how pleased he had been with Phil's work.

Phil turned to his computer and began to run searches. At first all he discovered was that Forrest Enterprises was mentioned a few times a year in regional newspapers in Fresno, Stockton, Sacramento, and even San Jose. But Theodore Forrest was almost never in the article. Phil tried typing in the girl's name—Allison Forrest, Fresno, California.

In Phil's narrative, he described the entire process. His computer screen had said: "Your search for Allison Forrest, Fresno, California returned no results." He deleted the request and typed "Allison + Missing." In seconds the search engines threw up dozens of references: "Allison Missing," "Still No Sign of Missing Girl." Of course there would have been local news reports from years ago. The fact that she had been missing was why he knew Theodore Forrest at all: Private detectives and cops met rich people only when disasters happened. He kept searching for something that sounded more recent. Finally he found a Web site titled "Allison's Story," and up it came.

Emily could imagine what it must have looked like: At first the opening page appeared in a small window in the center of his screen. He clicked on the Enlarge box and it blew up, the pale white face coming at him like a swimmer rising toward him from the bottom of a lake. The picture was a reproduction of a newspaper article. The caption: BODY OF MISSING GIRL FOUND.

There was a printout of the page in the file that Emily was reading. She could see that it was a picture of the same young girl that was in the snapshots. She could tell that seeing her face again must have been a shock to Phil.

Fidelity

She could almost hear Phil making that sound of surprise, just a quiet "*Uh*" as though he had tripped. He would have turned instinctively to exclaim to someone about what was on his screen, but there was nobody to tell. Sam Bowen had retired two years ago and moved to Seattle. Ray and Dewey and Bill were probably out of the office on jobs, and he had never told even Ray much about the case. The only one always in the agency office in the middle of the day was April, and she was beyond the glass wall, on the telephone. Even though he must have felt affection for her, the idea of telling her any of this would have seemed impossible to him.

Phil described the difficulty he had trying to understand the article. The name was Allison, and the picture was Allison Forrest, but it said she was dead. Could the paper have made some weird mistake at the time when Allison was missing?—maybe assumed some unidentified body was hers and printed her picture? He looked at the date at the top of the article. It was November eight years ago, a few months after he had brought Allison home alive and well. This made no sense. Maybe the mistake was that some other girl was missing and had been found dead, but the paper had accidentally used an old picture from the time when Allison Forrest had disappeared.

Phil said he looked at the screen and forced himself to scroll down and read the article—just as Emily read it now. The article said the girl's name was Allison Straight. She had been found in an abandoned irrigation ditch on a large farm ten miles outside Mendota. The ditch was just a trench about five feet wide and four deep that ran alongside a huge empty field about five hundred yards from a road. The trench was part of an old irrigation system that had been hand-dug around the early 1900s.

A hunter had come onto the land without permission, and was walking along the trenches looking for the game that hid in the ditches. He came across human remains. At first he thought it was a girl who had fallen into the ditch during a rainstorm and drowned. But the coroner was able to say the body was more recent than the rains, and a police officer and the coroner both thought they recognized the girl. Through photographs and dental records she was identified positively as Allison Straight, a sixteen-year-old Mendota girl who had been missing from her home for six months. Phil printed the article and searched for others.

Phil must have been sweating. This was unquestionably the girl he and Sam Bowen had taken off the street that night in Hollywood eight years ago. He kept his eyes on the screen and clicked on other articles. The story was repeated over and over. There was one that had been printed in the Stockton paper much earlier, when the girl had first disappeared. It quoted the girl's mother, Nancy Straight of Mendota. Emily could imagine Phil muttering to himself, "What the hell?" over and over, and dreaming up possible explanations.

Maybe the girl's mother had been Theodore Forrest's wife at one time. No, the girl's name would still have been Forrest. But in the paper it was Straight. Maybe the mother had been a girlfriend who had gotten pregnant. But Phil had seen a birth certificate that said Forrest.

Did Forrest even *have* a wife? Forrest had never involved his wife in the discussions with Phil and Sam. Phil thought he remembered some reference to her being "distraught," and after that he had thought little of her. Lots of his fancier clients didn't want to have their wives talking with anybody as rough and low-class as a private detective. He kept thinking of explanations that accounted for all of the seeming contradictions, then rejecting each one. Emily could tell Phil was trying to keep this from being what he thought it was. Anyone could see it was a horrible, sad story, but Phil wanted it to be a particular kind of sad story, an ordinary family tragedy.

Fidelity

Phil wanted Theodore Forrest to have been a doting father who had hired Phil Kramer to find his wayward daughter Allison and bring her back to her comfortable, safe home. He wanted the daughter to have been one of those girls who had a gift for getting into the worst kinds of trouble. Girls like that vanished all the time, and maybe two years later, or twenty years later, somebody found a small, delicate set of female bones in the woods.

That was a horrible story, but it was horrible in a banal, quotidian way. It was almost routine. In a lot of those cases, the killer was already in jail for some other girl before anybody found this one's bones. Phil couldn't keep the story from being horrible, but Emily knew he didn't want it to be horrible in the way he feared. He wanted Theodore Forrest to be what he seemed. Phil wanted to have given this sad, unlucky man a chance to see his beautiful young daughter again—if only for a month or two—and to have given the daughter a brief reprieve, a chance to pull herself together and live.

Phil worked the keyboard and mouse for an hour or two longer and then studied all of the contents of the old case file before he was certain. Then he wrote down the plain truth, not trying to spare himself. Theodore Forrest had not hired him to find his naïve, foolish daughter. He had hired Kramer to find a girl—*someone else's* daughter—who had escaped his influence, his abuse. Phil kept remembering that when he and Sam Bowen had found the girl, they had quickly gagged and later drugged her. She had never had a chance to give her side of the story, to tell them the truth about who she was. And a month or two later, Theodore Forrest had killed her and buried her body in a ditch at the edge of a remote field.

Emily imagined exactly how Phil must have felt. She also knew from years of observation that by now Phil must have been angry. His anger would be indignation and disgust at the horrible crime, but even stronger would be his hatred of Forrest for using Phil to help him commit it. Forrest had fooled Phil in a terrible way for a terrible purpose. He had manipulated Phil into finding and capturing the victim and delivering her to him bound and drugged, helpless and without hope.

Emily could feel the anger in the way he had written his account. He had constructed the first part of the story patiently and carefully, beginning with the parts that Sam Bowen had already told her, but now the sentences were short and terse: "I had the following facts: Theodore Forrest was not Allison's father. The documents he provided were forgeries. His victim's real name was Allison Yvonne Straight."

Phil went on to list the pieces of evidence inserted in the packet at this point:

I have included copies of the genuine birth certificate in the name Allison Straight I obtained by a search of the public record in Fresno County, the forged birth certificate in the name Allison Forrest given to me by Theodore Forrest, the letter signed by Theodore Forrest giving Kramer Investigations his permission to take charge of and physically transport his daughter Allison, photocopies of the cashier's checks he provided in payment for the agency's services, twelve photographs of Mr. Forrest and Allison Straight together in various locations, and copies of tape-recorded telephone calls from Theodore Forrest to Kramer Investigations.

Emily glanced at them, and they seemed to be what Phil said they were. The ones that still struck her as odd were the tape recordings. Even Emily knew it was illegal to tape-record anybody without his knowledge in California. Maybe Phil thought that if this file turned up, he would be beyond prosecution.

She read on. She noticed that Phil wrote the next part in a more measured way, moving away from what he had established to what he believed:

> I concluded that the reason Allison Straight was in Los Angeles was that she had fled Mendota to end a relationship with Theodore Forrest. The relationship was a secret one, and I believe it was sexual in nature. Theodore Forrest did not hire the Kramer agency out of concern for the girl, but out of extreme possessiveness and a refusal to let her end the connection. At some point after he had Allison Straight under his control, he caused her death and buried her body in an irrigation ditch on a piece of land he owned, called Espinoza Ranch.

Emily could feel the growing hatred as Phil laid out each phase of this. She knew he had been controlling himself with difficulty, trying to contain his anger. He wrote:

> Because of this day's discoveries, I began an investigation of what had happened eight years ago after I left Allison with Theodore Forrest. I collected evidence to help me understand the crime and the circumstances surrounding it.

Emily looked at the next packet of papers. Phil had a copy of the tax assessment for the Espinoza Ranch, showing its owner as Theodore Forrest. He had photographs of the place where the girl's body had been found and a map of the property showing precisely where that was. There were photographs of Espinoza Ranch, which looked to Emily like a pretty place.

Then she came upon a copy of the autopsy report for Allison Straight. Cause of death: Gunshot. Manner of death: Homicide. As Emily looked at the forms, she felt the way she had always felt years ago when papers of that sort came to the office—a squeamish sensation of alarm at each of the marks the pathologist had made on the simple outline drawing of a woman. But this time it was worse. She could imagine the torment the girl had gone through before she died, and she could also feel what Phil must have felt when he had learned about it and known he was partly responsible. There were marks around the wrists and ankles, signs of abuse that had partially healed. The thought of that made Emily feel physically sick, because she knew that meant it had gone on for a long time. She tried to calm herself by reading the paragraphs below, the results of the various tests that had been performed on the body—most of them only because they were always done. But then she read the sentence at the end of the third paragraph: "At the time of death the victim was pregnant."

Emily read on. The fetus was approximately three months old. Samples of its tissues had been retained as potential evidence in the homicide investigation. She imagined Phil's surprise and his grim excitement when he saw those words. If tissue from the fetus had been preserved, it would be possible to perform a DNA test.

Suddenly she understood the whole packet of evidence. She had been struck by the large quantity of it, the thoroughness of Phil's methodical collection. When she had seen the words "the victim was pregnant," she had wondered for a second why Phil had bothered with the rest of it. The police could compare the baby's DNA with Theodore Forrest's, establish that he had impregnated a sixteen-year-old girl whose body had been buried in a remote corner of a piece of land he owned. He had obviously killed her to prevent the revelation of the relationship.

But then Emily's mind began to supply the obstacles. Theodore Forrest was a rich, powerful man, apparently one who had at least a passable reputation. Phil would have to supply some very compelling facts before a judge would order a DNA test on Theodore Forrest for comparison with the fetus of a murder victim from eight years ago. So Phil had patiently gone about collecting just the sort of circumstantial evidence that would persuade a judge.

Then it occurred to Emily that there was another possibility. Phil was fairly sure that Forrest had killed Allison and, inevitably, her baby. But Phil could not know whether the baby had been Theodore Forrest's child. The girl had run off and been gone for a couple of months. It was entirely possible that the baby had been fathered by someone Allison met after she ran away. The DNA test could just as easily prove Forrest was not the father as prove that he was. Phil had no way to know in advance of the test. Phil didn't know the precise circumstances. Forrest might have killed Allison because he was the father of her child, or killed her because he was not. Phil had no evidence that would prove Theodore Forrest had even known eight years ago that Allison was pregnant. And Forrest had to know, if the baby was to be his motive for murder.

Phil had collected a great many exhibits showing that Theodore Forrest had a suspicious relationship with Allison Straight. If a jury believed Phil—and probably Sam Bowen, who would be called to testify—then they might agree with Phil's belief that Forrest had killed Allison. But they might not. Phil was a big-city private detective who would have to admit to having kidnapped a girl who was murdered a month or two later. And his credibility would also have to survive a thorough investigation by Forrest's own private detectives. Theodore Forrest could afford the best lawyers to make himself look like a victim.

So Phil had kept collecting and assembling evidence. He had left the box under April's bed while he had done it. He must have been afraid that his repeated visits to the Central Valley to collect more evidence might be noticed and reported to Theodore Forrest.

Phil had kept at his investigation for months. He had long before delegated all of the real work of the detective agency to Ray and Dewey. Billy Przwalski was still a trainee, but he was alert and energetic and smart. They could handle the cases, and April was appealing enough to keep buying them time when a client got impatient, and to keep at least some clients paying. Phil had spent all of his time on Theodore Forrest.

Emily sat on the wooden deck, holding the box of evidence in her lap and staring out at Puget Sound. The sun was getting lower now, and it looked like a pale red ball through the fog.

Sam said, "What do you think? Was he trying to blackmail Forrest? Is that what this is?"

"I don't know," she said. "I think that at first he was furious. I can feel it. He was trying to assemble all the evidence he could find to prove that Forrest murdered Allison. He was using his official-statement style to tell what happened. I don't think there would be any reason for him to do that for Forrest. He did a lot of work, and gathered things from up north that he didn't know before, just so he would have a complete package. I don't think he needed pictures of Forrest's ranch to prove anything to Forrest. I think he was genuinely trying to put Forrest away."

"Then what do you think happened?" Sam asked.

"I think he tried as hard as he could, and thought he'd failed."

"So do I. I think he collected it all, and put it in that box, and when he ran out of things to collect, he looked it all over. And I think that when he did, he realized that it wasn't enough."

"Was he right?"

"I think he probably was. It's hard to go into a strange town and get a local jury to convict one of their most prominent citizens of anything, and this is a capital offense. It's eight years old, and the evidence is all circumstantial. But Phil was damaged. He could never look at himself in the mirror again without seeing a man who had hunted down a young girl running from danger and dragged her back to be murdered. It's such a painful, debilitating piece of information that at first I don't think he even considered telling me. He didn't want me to have the same feelings he was having, unless and until it was unavoidable. I didn't hear from him during any of this. That's a sign of how much knowing this hurt him."

"But he left the box with someone, and he asked that it be mailed to you if he didn't come back for it."

Sam shrugged. "I'm the only one who was with him to see the first part of this story. I guess he figured that if he didn't come back for it he would be dead, and I'd be the only witness to swear it was true. He couldn't let Forrest off."

"When he was killed, he was out alone at one thirty at night, and it looked as though he was on his way back from meeting someone. He was getting into his car. And the man who kidnapped me said Phil had been trying to blackmail Forrest."

"I'm sure Phil set it up to look that way, but I don't think there's any chance Phil was really after money. There wouldn't have been enough money in the world to make Phil keep quiet about that girl. That's what it is, you know. When you blackmail somebody, you become their best friend. You're making sure that they'll never be punished. "

"Then what do you think he was doing? I want to know if you think what I think."

"And what's that?" Sam asked.

"I think that Phil realized he didn't have the perfect piece of evidence, the bit that makes a conviction a sure thing. I think knowing he didn't was eating away at him. He kept searching, but ran out of things to find. And then I think he called Theodore Forrest, and told him he wanted to meet with him. I think what he wanted to do was to manufacture the perfect piece of evidence."

"You think he was going to make a tape of Forrest paying him off?"

"Yes, and maybe admitting what he had done. But not that night. I think Phil went to meet Forrest and show him some of this file. Maybe he showed him copies of all of it. I think he probably showed him enough to make him pay blackmail. But this was a huge crime, and the payoff would have to be large, too, or Forrest would never believe it was blackmail—too much money for Forrest to have brought with him without even seeing the evidence. I think Phil was planning to meet Forrest again for the payoff—maybe with a microphone or a video camera, and maybe with a few police officers waiting to make the arrest."

Sam nodded and took another sip of his drink. "That's what I think, too. Phil knew Theodore Forrest was guilty—that he had used Phil and me to help him kill that poor girl—but that the only punishment he would ever get was what Phil Kramer brought to him. So he decided to trap him."

Emily found herself in tears. "Oh, Sam. You don't know how much I wish I were sure that was it. I feel as though it is, but I need to be sure."

Sam said, "I don't know everything. I do know that when I was a cop, the way we could figure out whether somebody was guilty of something was that he had come into some money he couldn't explain. I mean, Forrest wasn't the first person Phil knew bad things about. He could have blackmailed hundreds of people. Did Phil leave you a whole lot of money, Em?"

Emily laughed through her tears. "No. I'd declare bankruptcy if I could afford a lawyer."

"Good. Then we know he was an honest man."

"He was hardly that. He wasn't honest with me."

"He loved you, so you were the hardest, because the truth would chase you away. But if he didn't have any money, he wasn't blackmailing any millionaires."

"It doesn't seem likely, does it?"

"There's one thing that makes it certain he didn't. You read Phil's statement. He found out about Allison on June 14. He had enough to blackmail Forrest on the first day, but he didn't do it. He worked on the case for months, collecting all kinds of bits and pieces that didn't add anything to the prospects for blackmail, but would be helpful to the police. He kept at it until all he needed was that one last piece of evidence that made the case undeniable. He needed to have Forrest convict himself. He needed to have him on tape admitting he killed the girl. There's no doubt at all that Phil was trying to do the right thing. The only thing I'm disappointed in him for is trying to do it alone."

Emily could picture Phil going to meet Theodore Forrest. He had made sure nobody who would worry about him knew where he was going. He couldn't have anyone following him and making Forrest suspicious. Maybe he carried one of the tiny tape recorders from the office in his pocket, but probably he didn't, because he was afraid that Forrest would frisk him before speaking. He had already put together the copy of the evidence for Forrest, before he had brought the originals to Lee Anne's house for safekeeping.

She imagined that Phil made sure everything he brought to Forrest had been copied on a photocopier, even the photographs. It was all black and white and grainy. She knew that he had done that because he didn't want Theodore Forrest to think, even for a second, that he held the originals. Theodore Forrest was, after all, a murderer.

36

Ted Forrest sat in the kitchen of his house and tried to work out his next moves. The house seemed enormous tonight. Even the kitchen, which had always seemed crowded to him, now seemed cavernous and cold, with its long, empty granite counters with rows of identical cabinets and gleaming stainless-steel sinks and hoods. He sat at the butcher-block table at the end of the room because it was the only thing that seemed built to a human scale.

He felt he had to be where he could hear Caroline if she somehow managed to get out of the cellar, even though he had no definite notion of how she might accomplish that. Maybe she could break a wine bottle and use a razor-sharp shard as a blade to carve away some of the wood of the door and reach through, or use some part of a wine rack to jimmy the lock. The hardware was all heavy polished brass, but he supposed it hadn't been designed to withstand a serious attack.

He went to Caroline's desk in the sitting room off the library to look at her appointment book. He was relieved to see that she had written in nothing he would have to cancel. The day's page was just a list of things she had planned to initiate: making calls and sending notes.

Forrest couldn't recall a time when the house had seemed so empty. He would look out the front window occasionally, just to be sure none of the gardeners or groundskeepers had missed the word and come to work. But he saw no one. Caroline had made sure the servants wouldn't be around to hear what she had planned to say.

They were Caroline's servants, really. She had always been the one who cared about the house in the daily way. She inhabited it and used it as the setting of the social identity she had half-inherited and half-invented for herself. She had chosen the servants for their suitability, then trained and bribed them to exercise her will. Maria was the head housekeeper, Caroline's principal informant. People would assume she spied on the other servants, but the guests here didn't know that she also eavesdropped on them, and reported what she heard to Caroline.

It occurred to Forrest that he couldn't have them around anymore. After whatever happened next, he would have to get rid of them for good. It was possible he would have to commission a remodeling and leave the country while it was going on. That would give him an excuse to let all of them go the same day.

He could plan what he should do in a month, but his next step—the next thing he needed to accomplish—was still a mystery to him. One possibility was to turn her over to Jerry Hobart and leave immediately. Or—frantic with worry—he could report her disappearance to the local authorities and try to be sure his story conformed to the condition of the body. He could throw her body into the ocean. Bodies were found, but there must be thousands of others that never were. He could even dump her in the mountains and say she fell into the ocean.

But one other idea had occurred to him that had a certain appeal. It was to wait here for Jerry Hobart, get him to kill Caroline, and then kill Jerry Hobart. He had been thinking of Hobart as a way of sparing his nerves and his feelings because if he didn't have Hobart, he would have to get rid of the body and clean up any sign that it had happened. But if he killed Hobart, then all he would have to do was call 911 on the nearest telephone, and public servants would be dispatched to handle both bodies and clean everything up for him. Doing it that way would clear him of any possible suspicion in Caroline's death.

Hobart was the perfect sort of person to use. He would be armed. He had a criminal record of some sort. Hobart had told him it was for armed robbery. That was good enough, but Forrest had heard or read somewhere that people who had violent-felony convictions often had records with plenty of other serious matters on them that had not gone to trial, often sexual assaults. That would be ideal.

Ted Forrest could be the husband who came home and found his beloved wife killed by a sexual predator, and who, in turn, killed the intruder. Forrest would be simultaneously an innocent man, a bereaved widower, a hero, and—come to think of it—the beneficiary of a significant insurance policy. He had forgotten about that. It was as old as the marriage, purchased with the thought that there might be children. When Caroline was in her early twenties, the cost of insuring her was almost nothing. He had paid a single premium for a policy for each of them, and over the years he had almost forgotten.

Killing Caroline and then Hobart was such an appealing idea that his mind kept returning to it and refining it. One thing it would accomplish was to free him of the need to pay Hobart for Emily Kramer, or for Caroline. Forrest didn't think there was much risk of an unfriendly interpretation by the police. Hobart was a career criminal. Ted Forrest was now over fifty, and he had never done anything to arouse suspicion of any kind. And Caroline would make such a good victim. She had achieved the kind of reputation for goodness that only very rich women with a penchant for highly visible acts of philanthropy could hope for.

Forrest was highly attracted to the notion of having Hobart be the vicious intruder, the violent criminal who had burst in and attacked and killed the virtuous Caroline. It would enshrine her forever in exactly the role she had invented for herself: a secular saint. But could Forrest carry off the deception? Once Hobart had shot Caroline, it wouldn't much matter how crudely and inefficiently Ted Forrest managed to kill him. In any state—certainly the state of California—if a man came into your house and shot your wife to death, you wouldn't have a hard time getting the police to declare the shooting self-defense, no matter what the angles of the bullet holes were. All Ted Forrest would have to remember was to tell the truth about the positions of the three people at the time, and be consistent about the order of events. All he had to do was keep from contradicting what the cops would see.

Forrest got up from the kitchen table, opened the door to the basement stairs, and listened. He thought he should be hearing something—pounding or shouting—but he wasn't sure whether he did. He descended the stairs cautiously and walked quietly through the tasting room. He put his ear to the wine-cellar door and listened.

"I hear you, Ted," she called. "I know you think this is funny and you're really being clever, but you're not. Eventually you're going to have to face up to the way you've treated that girl. It's illegal."

He said nothing.

"I know you're there."

"Of course I'm here, Caroline."

"Don't you have anything to say?"

"I'm not arguing with you. I know it's illegal. Well, sit tight."

"Very funny!" she shouted. "You're just pissing me off and making it harder on yourself. If you'll let me out now, I may not show the cops the bruises you put on me last night."

He made a lot of noise walking up the steps, but stopped near the top, sat on a step and closed the door, and then listened. There were no scraping sounds, and there was no hammering. Maybe she had already given up on getting out by herself. He stood, opened the door, and went up into the hallway by the pantry.

Hobart had said he would be here this evening, so there was plenty of time for preparations. Forrest went about them thoughtfully. Since Hobart had to drive here, he would drive through the open gate, up the driveway, and park on the circle in front of the house. He would come to the front door.

Forrest went to the front door and studied it, and then went to the other door at the rear of the house that opened by the pantry. That door was the one where deliveries were made, the one a stranger would see first. He began to work on the door. He got a large jack-knife he had kept in the back of a desk drawer for years, went outside, and worked on the pantry door. He scraped away some paint and then dug more deeply into the woodwork beside the doorknob. He kept at it until he could slide the blade into the wood behind the metal plate and push the latch aside to open the door.

Forrest stepped back. He wasn't sure whether he had done a good job or a bad one, but it looked the way the latch on the door of Kramer Investigations looked the night he had burned the place, so he was sure it would do. He had no reason to believe that Hobart was a locksmith or a safecracker, so he was confident it would look to the police as though this was the way he had come in. Hobart would never see this door.

Forrest stopped and looked around the kitchen for a moment, and tried to evaluate his plan. Did he really need to do this to Caroline? Yes, he did. She knew about Kylie, and she intended to use the girl to force him into giving her control over his fortune and his freedom. When he had gone into a rage and grabbed her, he'd had no intention of killing her. He had simply been the victim of an immediate need to make her shut up. He had needed to be by himself and think. But having thought, he could not see any way of getting through this with Caroline alive. She really was ready to call the police. Right now she would probably be down there doing things to herself so she would have enough marks on her body to impress the authorities and make him look like an abuser.

He could hear the prosecutor now: "Surely she didn't make marks like these on herself. So who did?"

Nobody knew Caroline the way he did. They would never imagine that she was so opportunistic and calculating. At worst they would think she was a vengeful wife who was being replaced by a much younger woman. And the law's crude view of human life demanded that there be a victim and a criminal. Caroline was an expert at roles, and she would be all the victim that the law required. He was sure that if he opened the door right now, he would find her covered with bruises.

That was fine. His break-in story would account gracefully and smoothly for the bruises, too. They would all be fresh enough. He was sure doctors could tell how recent a bruise was, and she had never had any before. Those marks could have been caused only by the intruder. The more ways that Forrest found to think about his situation, the more certain he was that the intruder story was the best way to handle it.

There were several things he would have to prepare before Hobart got here. Forrest needed to put together the money to show

Hobart. That would be what Hobart demanded to see first. But Forrest had been assembling and keeping large sums of money in the house for weeks, ever since Philip Kramer had contacted him. He hurried upstairs and opened the safe, got the banded stacks of hundreds, and laid them out on the bed to count them. He put two hundred thousand in a large bag he used to take to the gym. That was the payment for taking care of the Emily Kramer problem. Then he counted out enough stacks of money to make the same payment for Caroline. He could probably fit those into the same bag, but he decided it was better to have two. That way, at some point Hobart's hands would both be encumbered.

Forrest found a bag of Caroline's in the closet. It was a piece of luggage—an overnight bag, really—but it was about the right size, and seemed to him to be a nice touch. If it got bloody or something, he could even leave the money in it and place it with the bodies, as though Hobart had forced her to open the safe before he killed her. If Forrest's fingerprints were on it, that didn't matter. After all, the money was his.

Everything fit together perfectly. It left nothing dangerous, nothing ugly, nothing messy or inconvenient. Thinking about his plan gave Ted Forrest a sample of the happiness that he was going to feel.

He needed a gun, of course. There were two in the house. One he retrieved from his nightstand, an M9 9mm Beretta. There was also another gun somewhere in the master suite. He had bought it for Caroline years ago, when things were still cordial between them. It might fit the story he was concocting if that turned up somewhere, too, but he didn't like the unnecessary complexity. He tested the story. Caroline hears noises downstairs, gets up to investigate, and brings her gun with her. She gets ambushed from behind, or shot—no, ambushed and beaten if there really are bruises on her—by the intruder.

She's killed. Ted hears the shots or something, goes downstairs and shoots the killer. No, too many guns. He decided to forget her.

He looked around to be sure there was nothing out of place. The bed had not been slept in last night. It was still made, the covers tight and the decorative pillows arranged at the head of the duvet as the chambermaid had left them. He moved the pillows to the couch where Caroline usually put them, and then pulled back the covers and punched the goosedown pillows to indent them as though someone had slept here. He turned off the light and hurried downstairs. This had taken too long. He should have been where he could watch the front of the house and listen for sounds from the wine cellar.

He stood with his ear to the door of the basement, heard nothing, and then opened the door. He went down the stairs into the tasting room, but still didn't hear her. He put his ear to the door of the wine cellar.

It occurred to him that he might have forgotten another problem. There was no real ventilation down here. The wine cellar wasn't a place where anyone had ever spent much time before. The new cooling unit worked by pumping water through a closed system, not blowing air. She could be suffocating. He reached for the door, then stopped. What if she *were* suffocating? His story would accommodate that comfortably. But if he opened the door, air would rush in again and revive her. She would be active and difficult.

He turned and walked toward the steps, and climbed. As he reached the third step from the top, his cell phone rang. It startled him because he had forgotten he had it, and then realized he had been below ground. It might have been ringing for a minute or more. He answered it quickly. "Hello?" he said. "Hello?"

He heard simultaneously Kylie's voice and a muffled shout from behind the door.

Kylie said, "Hi, baby," as Caroline shouted, "Let me out, you bastard!"

He stepped into the hallway and shut the door as he said, "Hi, honey. What's up?"

"What's up over there?"

"Nothing. I got back really late last night and I've been asleep."

"I heard somebody."

"It's just one of the maids yelling out the back door at the gardeners. This place can be really nuts sometimes. It's a big place, and there are always people running machines or yelling. Sometimes I wonder."

"Poor thing," she said. "So when are you going to pick me up so I can make you feel better?"

"Oh, how I would love to go get you right now. But I just can't. Caroline is home today and, well, you know."

"I know. Maybe when I'm older, things will be better."

"I promise. Now, I've got to go. I'll call you when I can. I love you."

"I love you," she said. "'Bye."

Forrest cut the connection, and then looked at his watch. He had been surprised to hear Kylie's voice, but it was three forty already. She was already out of school. He tried to calculate. He had called Hobart at around four A.M. Hobart had said he was nearly done with Emily Kramer. He would have needed to get rid of her body and probably take care of a few incidentals. Give him two hours for that. Then he would have to spend an hour showering and packing and checking out of wherever he had been staying. That would make it seven A.M. If Hobart drove up here it would take him at least six hours, and with stops, much longer. Make it four in the afternoon at the earliest. If Hobart arrived at four or five, he would want to check into a hotel, change his clothes, probably rent a different car, have dinner somewhere. He would not arrive here at the house until early evening, just as he had said on the phone.

And Forrest was all ready for him.

Forrest walked through the house examining doors and windows, then revisited the pantry door where the police would decide Hobart had broken in. He placed the two bags of money in two downstairs closets. That way he could produce the one for the already-completed job on Emily Kramer when Hobart arrived, and save the other to induce him to kill Caroline. The sight of so much money would blind Hobart to any little signs that something was out of place.

Forrest spent an hour rehearsing in front of the full-length mirror in the downstairs cloakroom off the foyer. He spoke to an imaginary Hobart, searching his own face for a furtive expression, listening to his voice for a false tone. Finally he devised and memorized a sentence he could say at the very moment when he was pulling out his gun: "I don't know how to thank you for taking care of this for me."

37

Ted Forrest saw the car coming up the dark highway when it was still a half mile away, even before it passed the riverbed that was the western boundary of the Forrest estate. There had been no water in the river for years, but it was still easy to see from a distance because ancient trees still ran in a line along the banks.

He wondered at first how he knew it was Hobart, but in this flat country, headlights could be seen for miles, and he had noticed the purposeful quality of the car's motion, then saw it slow slightly as the driver saw his house. The car nosed along the tall iron fence until it found the open gate, and then turned into the long driveway.

The car came up to the circle at the front door and stopped, and its lights went out. Hobart got out of the car and stepped to the front door quickly. He didn't have to knock because Ted Forrest was already holding the door open, standing back from the entrance so Hobart could step inside. Forrest had kept the light in the foyer dim, and it was the only one turned on in the front of the house. Hobart's arrival would be difficult to see from the road.

Fidelity

Things were going well. Hobart had brought a full-size black car of some American make, something that looked enough like one of Forrest's from a distance to be unremarkable to passersby. Forrest closed the door.

Hobart wore a short-sleeved shirt and carried a sport jacket that he had picked up from where it lay on the passenger seat while he was driving. Hobart was bigger, taller, and more formidable than Forrest had remembered. Forrest was athletic and had always kept himself in good physical condition, but the sight of Hobart's bare arms reminded him that there were people who weren't in his circle of golf-and-tennis friends. In prison men spent their time lifting weights and fighting. "Hi," he said. "Have any trouble?" He held out his hand to shake Hobart's.

Hobart chose that moment to put on his sport coat, and didn't seem to see the hand. "Not much," Hobart said. "Got my money?"

"She's dead?"

"Sure."

"The money is right here." Forrest went to a door that Hobart had not seen before, cut into the decorated wood that rose seven feet from the marble floor of the big open room. He opened it and Hobart saw it was a closet. Forrest came back with a satchel like a gym bag and handed it to Hobart.

Hobart took it with his left hand, squatted to set it on the floor, and unzipped it.

For Forrest, Hobart's movements were bad news. He was keeping Forrest in his line of sight, keeping his right hand free and unencumbered. Hobart was clearly aware that this was the perfect time for Forrest to alter the terms of their deal.

Of course, Forrest thought. Hobart did this routinely, for a living. He knew every aspect of his business, including the twinge of buyer's remorse a client might have after the person who had been threatening his happiness was dead and buried. From the moment when Hobart completed a job until he took the money and got out of sight and out of reach, he was in danger, and he knew it.

Hobart finished assuring himself that the whole bag was filled with stacks of hundreds. He zipped the bag and stood up with it in his left hand. "Good enough," he said.

Forrest held out his right hand again to shake Hobart's, but Hobart ignored it. Forrest felt uneasy. Hobart had already realized that if he shook, both of his hands would be full, but only one of Forrest's would. *Even that*, thought Forrest. Hobart was absolutely unblinking. There was no overconfidence, no forgetfulness.

Forrest said, "Was getting Emily Kramer hard?"

"You and I agreed on a price, and you just paid it. The time and trouble I had to put into it is my problem." Hobart started to move toward the front door. Forrest noticed that as he stepped in that direction, he didn't move his eyes from Forrest's.

"Don't go," Forrest said. "When we were on the phone, I mentioned I had another job."

"Oh, yeah. I'll put this in the car, and then we'll talk about it."

Forrest could tell there was no point in saying, "You can leave your money here in the foyer," or trying to dissuade or distract him from his intention. He was the expert at this. Hobart's money wasn't safe until it was in his trunk, and he had the only key. Car trunks could be popped or their locks hammered in, but not without Hobart's knowledge.

But Hobart was back already. He came in and shut the door. "All right. Tell me about it."

"It's my wife, Caroline."

"You want me to kill your wife? Why?"

"It's a long story. I offered to provide for her in a breakup, but she would rather destroy me."

"She could do that?"

"It doesn't matter, really. Leaving somebody around who wants to do that to me would be insane."

Hobart looked around him and up toward the vaulted ceiling and then his eyes followed the curving staircase to the second floor. "Are you planning to burn this place, too?"

"What? Why?"

Hobart shrugged. "I assume she has some kind of evidence on you, right?"

"No, just suspicions and resentments and an inexhaustible supply of anger. If I let her go, she'll spend all her time and my money paying people to dig up something or fake it. I can't let her do that. You can't let her do that. If people look hard enough at me, they'll probably find something that relates to my business with you. Neither of us wants that."

"Where is she now?"

"She's in the wine cellar. She was out of control—threatening to call the police, threatening me with everything she could think of, and refusing to listen to anything I said."

"Is she tied or restrained?"

"No. I just put her in there and locked the door. She's been in there for a long time."

"How long?"

"Let's see. I put her in there about four this morning, so I guess it would be about sixteen hours."

"All right. I'll take care of it. What you'll want to do later is tell the cops an intruder did it, stole something, and left. Figure out something you want stolen."

Forrest felt vindicated. It was so much like the idea he had thought of that nothing came to mind to say at first. Then he chuckled. "It won't be hard to find something expensive that only she ever liked. Just don't pawn it or something, okay?"

"I know better than that. Do I need a key?"

Forrest couldn't let him do it that way. He had to be around when Hobart did it. He had to shoot Hobart over Caroline's body. If he shot Hobart anywhere else, it wouldn't look as though he had been trying to save Caroline or that he had surprised Hobart in the act. If he did it up here in the foyer or outside, it might just look as though he had shot the man in the back. Revenge wasn't a legal reason to kill someone. "I'll come down and show you," he said.

"Okay." Hobart followed Forrest into the hallway toward the kitchen. Hearing Hobart's footsteps behind him made Forrest nervous and uneasy. He had to hide his feelings. Hobart would be good at detecting fear.

He went down the steps to the basement, hoping the gun under his sport coat wasn't making a lump that Hobart could see. He went to the door of the wine cellar.

Hobart put on a ski mask, then nodded at Forrest.

Forrest was disconcerted. He started thinking that there was no practical reason for a man to wear a disguise with a woman he was about to kill, but Hobart was a killer, and maybe that was how he liked it. A man like him must be crazy, must get something out of it besides money. Maybe the mask was part of it for him. Forrest unlocked the door and stepped back.

Hobart nodded at him again.

"Caroline?" he said through the door. "I'm back. You can come out."

There was a delay that seemed long to Forrest, and he began to hate her even more.

"Caroline," he called. "Caroline. I'm letting you out."

After about five more seconds, he reached for the door, but the doorknob turned. The door opened inward, and she stepped into the doorway. She looked profoundly tired. Her hair was tousled, and there were wispy strands that seemed not to have proper places in her hairdo. She squinted a bit in the light. "Who are you?" she asked Hobart.

"He's a friend of mine," Forrest said. "I invited him."

"To what?"

"He's here to prove to you that you shouldn't have behaved like my enemy."

"You hate me this much? You bring a man with a mask on? What is he going to do—kill me?"

Forrest turned to Hobart. "Same pay as before. Go ahead."

"Oh my God!" Caroline said. "You *did* bring him to kill me."

"What did you expect?"

"I wasn't trying to harm you. I was trying to keep you out of jail. This is crazy!"

"We've already had that argument. Go ahead. Kill her."

"Okay." With a smooth, relaxed motion, Hobart reached into his coat, pulled out a pistol, and raised his arm to aim it at Caroline's forehead.

Ted Forrest edged slightly away so he could be a bit behind Hobart. He just had to wait until Hobart pulled the trigger on Caroline, so the right man killed her with the right gun. He reminded himself that the report would be very loud, and he would have to be quick, to move through the shock of it, not taking time to blink or flinch.

Hobart pivoted and fired through Ted Forrest's brain. The sound was bright and sharp, and a blood spatter appeared on the stone wall beyond Forrest before he fell.

Caroline shrieked once and then stood frozen, staring down at the horrible sight of her husband's body on the floor. After a few seconds, she raised her confused, terrified eyes to Hobart. "Why did you do this?"

"None of your business. If you scream or follow me to the stairs, or do anything for the next fifteen minutes, I'll kill you, too. Do you understand?"

She nodded, her head barely moving.

He knelt and patted Ted Forrest's pockets. He took Forrest's gun and cell phone, then stood and moved to the stairs. "Remember what I said. This is the luckiest hour of your whole life. Make it last a long time."

And then he was up the stairs and gone.

38

Hobart began to divest. He drove to the San Jose airport to return the car he had rented, then went to another company and rented a different one with a credit card in a different name. He drove eastward into the mountains and began to get rid of things. First had to be the two cell phones: his and Theodore Forrest's. He took both of them apart to get to the SIM cards, drove the car over the two phones, and threw the pieces down a steep cliff. He cut the SIM cards into tiny pieces and fed them out the window into the slipstream.

Hobart's gun had to be next. He disassembled it—magazine, slide, spring, barrel, frame, grips, trigger, and sear. He hurled the springs, trigger, and sear into a lake in the Sierras, buried the frame, and pounded the barrel into the earth in the woods with a stone. He subjected Theodore Forrest's gun to the same treatment when he reached the east side of the Sierras and the land was drier and rockier.

One by one he tossed the items he had used in the past few weeks. His suitcase and the clothes inside it, the luggage that Theodore Forrest had used to hold the money, and the clothes he had worn to

Theodore Forrest's house, all ended up in Dumpsters behind businesses in towns that he passed along the way. He kept on driving through Nevada and on to Utah, ridding himself of things.

Hobart bought a car at a lot in Salt Lake City and turned in the one he had rented in San Jose. He bought new clothes, went to a fancy barbershop and had his hair cut much shorter than he had worn it before, and got a manicure. He drank only water and ate very little during these days. When he was ready, he drove back down from Utah into Nevada. He stayed on Interstate 15 until he was back in California, and then made his way to Interstate 10. At three A.M. the second night, he pulled into the trailer park outside Cabazon and parked. He walked across the blacktop to the side of Valerie's trailer, unlatched the door with his pocketknife, and stepped inside.

He said, "Valerie, it's me—Jerry."

He heard rustling noises coming from the bedroom. "Jerry?"

"I apologize if I scared you, but there didn't seem to be much sense in sitting alone out there waiting the rest of the night for you to wake up."

She appeared at the bedroom door, a blanket wrapped around her and her blond hair in complicated tangles. "How do you even know I'm in the bed alone?"

"I don't. I hope you are, but I don't have a right to expect it. If you want me to go away for an hour so you can settle that, I can drive down the road to the casino and have a cup of coffee or something, but then I'd like to come back and talk to you."

She pushed the bedroom door open all the way. "Oh, you might as well come on in. Nobody's here."

"I can still come back."

"You already woke me up and I can't sleep wondering what you want."

350

She sat on the bed and turned on the small bedside reading lamp, then moved it so she could see him. "You got dressed up." The light tilted higher. "Nice clothes. You got a haircut. Very handsome, especially for— What time is it? Three or so?"

"Yes."

She sniffed. "Expensive aftershave from a barbershop, too. You smell like a whore. And who would know better?"

"Not you."

She let the light stay on his face for a few more seconds, then turned it off. "What brings you here?"

"This is my last visit," he said. "Here's the way it is. I'm sorry I robbed that store twenty years ago. I apologize for doing it and going to prison. I did it because I wanted to have a nice life with you."

"It *would* have been a nice life."

"I thought the money would help us get away, and that away was better. I was young and stupid. I apologize."

"You were young. You apologized at the time, and you apologized after. But if somebody breaks something, it doesn't matter why or how. It's broken. Talking about it forever doesn't make it *un*broken. After the first day, it doesn't even matter whose fault it was."

"Yes, it does."

"No. You went to prison, and things happened there that changed you. I was out here. I changed in ways that I wouldn't have if you had been with me. We're not the same people we were. We can't have the kind of life we would have had."

"That's just bitterness."

She shook her head. "I think about it all the time—about you and me together then. I can still see us. It's like we were the first people. It's not the time that's gone, it's the innocence. We don't have it anymore, and we can't get it back."

351

"Okay. We can't."

"You said this was your last visit. I take it you've found somebody you like better."

"No. You're the one that I've always loved, and I'm going to love you until I'm dead. I want you to do what you should have done fifteen years ago and marry me."

"Oh, Jesus, Jerry." She sighed wearily.

He knelt in front of her, reached into his pocket, and grabbed her wrist. "I got you a ring."

"If this is a joke, I'm not laughing."

He put the ring in her hand, then leaned on the bed to turn on the reading light. He picked it up and held it above the ring. It was a three-carat solitaire, and in the intense white light it looked enormous.

She said, "Now I'm laughing." She looked terribly sad, and tears began to run down her cheeks. "Why did you do this?"

"We got off track, a long time ago. It was my fault. Now I'm grabbing us by the neck and wrenching us back on. We can't start over like we were eighteen, but we can take what's left at thirty-eight."

"I don't think so."

"Why not?"

She held out the ring in the palm of her hand. "I can see you have money. If I didn't notice before, I would now. Where did you get it?"

"Selling electrical supplies." He watched her face fall and her eyes harden. "All right, it's swag. I got it by being a criminal. But I'm done now. Regardless of whether you ever see me again, I'm done."

"Why?"

"Because it's not a life. It's just what you do when you don't have the heart to kill yourself and hope somebody will do it for you."

"So this is your last visit because now you have the heart. If I won't have you, then you'll go out in the desert and kill yourself."

"I didn't say that."

"You don't have to say things. I can hear you think." She paused. "You'll have to make me a promise."

"What?"

"If you do decide to kill yourself, you'll kill me first." She slipped the diamond ring on her finger. "I recognize this. It's the one I showed you in the magazine when we were kids. Same cut, same setting."

"Yes."

"When we go walking, the sun will light it up like fire."

39

Emily flew to San Jose and rented a car to drive the rest of the way. She didn't like the car because it was newer than her faithful Volvo, and it had a lot of mechanisms on the dashboard and the console that struck her as childish and self-indulgent. All the padding in odd places seemed to her to be designed to hide the sounds of an engine and transmission that were not to be trusted.

Emily drove the car anyway, in spite of the feeling she had that at every mile it was being used up like a pencil or a candle. She found her way on the 101 freeway to the Golden State Freeway, then down Route 152 to Route 33, which headed south and east into the Central Valley. Once she was on the right road, she tossed the map onto the seat beside her.

She sped across the open country, looking at the broad fields. They were lined with long, straight rows of low, leafy unidentifiable vegetable plants stretching to a vanishing point that seemed to move with her.

She drove fast, but it wasn't because she was in a hurry. It was because the roads were made for it. She got used to moving to the right shoulder to let over-height pickup trucks flash past, because it felt to her that it was their road and not hers.

Here and there near the towns—Los Banos, Dos Palos, Firebaugh—there were fruit and vegetable stands to sell produce to people like her driving down the highway between big cities. She had always loved stopping at those places, white-painted wooden-frame structures with homemade signs bigger than they were, where teenagers and grandparents handled the sales because everybody else was busy. Here the stands were tiny outposts at the edge of plots of land so big that from the road Emily couldn't see any farm buildings.

When she reached Mendota, it took her only a few minutes to find the police station and park. She got out of the car, walked to the trunk, and opened it. She took out her tote bag and walked to the front of the station, up the steps, and into the small lobby.

Behind the counter there were two police officers, one male on the telephone and one female busy at a computer. The woman noticed Emily first. She stood up and walked to the counter, then said, "Hello, ma'am. How can I help you?"

Emily said, "I wonder if you could direct me to the officer who was in charge of a murder case. It occurred here eight years ago."

The policewoman's shoulders seemed to hunch slightly. She leaned forward, and Emily could see a flat, guarded look in her eyes. "What murder case might that be?"

"The victim's name was Allison Straight. She was only sixteen when she was killed."

The policewoman turned to look behind her at the man who sat at the other desk. Emily could see that the policeman had sergeant's stripes on his biceps. He stood up and walked toward the open door behind the counter. As he passed the policewoman, he nodded.

The policewoman said, "The detective who handled that case is Lieutenant Zimmer. The sergeant just went to get him."

Two minutes later, the sergeant returned, accompanied by a tall, thin police officer in a sport coat. He said, "Come in, please," and lifted a hinged section of the counter so Emily could step inside the enclosure. She followed him into an office, and he pulled a chair to the front of his desk for her, then sat down. "I'm Lieutenant Zimmer. I understand you wanted to see me about the Allison Straight case?"

"Yes," said Emily. "My name is Emily Kramer. I brought you this." She reached into her tote bag, pulled out the maroon stationery box and set it on the desk.

"What is it?"

"My husband, Philip Kramer, was the owner of a private-detective agency in Los Angeles. Two and a half weeks ago, he was murdered—shot down on the street. Since then I discovered that the reason he was killed was that he knew what happened to Allison Straight. What's in that box is the evidence he collected to prove it."

She sat patiently while Detective Zimmer opened the box and examined the photographs, the written statements, glanced at the maps and charts and the autopsy report.

After a time, he looked up into her eyes, and she saw the sadness that had somehow been hidden in his face and brought back. He said, "Do you know that Theodore Forrest was shot to death two days ago while he was trying to kill his wife?"

"Yes. It's been in the papers, even in other cities. I read it in Seattle this morning."

"There's nothing anybody can do to him now. Why did you bring me this?"

"Because you—the police—have to know. Because trying to get more evidence for you was the last thing my husband ever did. This was the last thing I could do for him." She paused. "I'm afraid I have a long drive ahead of me and a plane to catch. I'd like to go now."

Lieutenant Zimmer said, almost apologetically, "I'll need to see your driver's license first. You understand."

She pulled her wallet out of her purse and handed the license to him. He examined it for a moment, then stood and set it on the copier a few feet away and made a copy of it. As he handed it back to her, he said, "When I've finished reading everything and cross-checking the facts, can I reach you at this phone number?"

"My phone isn't working," she said. "For the moment, the easiest way to reach me is to call Kramer Investigations at the number in the file."

"All right. Thank you for bringing this to me."

"I had to." Emily rose, walked out of the office, lifted the hinged section of the counter, and went through the lobby and out to her rental car. In a few minutes, she was driving fast across the green valley toward San Jose.